HUNTER KILLER

Also by Chris Ryan

CHRIS RYAN

HUNTER KILLER

CORONET

First published in Great Britain in 2014 by Coronet
An imprint of Hodder & Stoughton
An Hachette UK company

First published in paperback in 2015

1

A CIP catalogue record for this title is available from the British Library

ISBN 9781444753646
Ebook ISBN 9781444753615
A Format ISBN 9781473612976

Printed and bound by Clays Ltd, St Ives plc

Hodder & Stoughton policy is to use papers that are natural, renewable
and recyclable products and made from wood grown in sustainable forests.
The logging and manufacturing processes are expected to conform
to the environmental regulations of the country of origin.

Hodder & Stoughton Ltd
338 Euston Road
London NW1 3BH

www.hodder.co.uk

'If you have to kill a snake, kill it once and for all.'
— Japanese proverb

PROLOGUE

They drove a Mercedes.

Nothing flash: a 30-year-old W123 that had once served as a minicab and which still had marks on the roof where the sign had been. Nobody was likely to stop and search an old Merc, carefully driven through the pouring rain.

The driver's name was Jamal. He wore plain brown trousers and a neatly pressed checked shirt, open at the collar. He was cleanshaven, and his hair had been cut just two days ago. He had a pair of Ray-Bans aviator shades hooked over the top of his shirt. He kept glancing at himself in the rear-view mirror, as though he was still a curiosity to himself. There were beads of sweat on his forehead. They had the heating on full.

'Sarim,' Jamal said finally. 'Stop doing that. You making me nervous, innit?'

Sarim looked down. There was a paper wallet on his lap with the words 'National Rail' printed on the front. He had been slapping it against his left palm. Now he stopped. 'Turn left up here,' he said.

'I know, I know. Been here enough times before.' Jamal indicated left and checked his rear-view mirror, then swung the Mercedes into a street lined with terraced houses. The street sign said Heath Road. And, in smaller letters, London Borough of Sutton.

Heath Road was a dump. At least a quarter of the houses looked like they'd been condemned. Steel sheets boarded up their windows and doors in an attempt to deter squatters. But the squatters had moved in anyway. The signs were there — a door slightly ajar, smoke emerging from the occasional chimney.

The house they stopped outside, however, was not condemned or boarded up. Just messy. The bins were overflowing and the small, scrubby front garden hadn't been tended for months.

Jamal killed the engine and turned to Sarim. Rain hammered against the car, so heavy that they couldn't see out. 'You go get him,' he said. 'He likes you best. Make sure he's packed his bag, yeah?'

'What am I?' Sarim said as he opened the passenger door. 'Stupid?'

He didn't wait for the answer. As he stepped out of the car, he caught sight of himself in the side mirror. He wore an Abercrombie and Fitch hooded top — now he pulled it up to protect his head from the driving rain — and there were two nicks on his chin where he had cut himself shaving. He wasn't *used* to shaving. He stepped out into the road, ran to the pavement and up to the front door. He knew the bell didn't work, so he knocked.

The door opened almost immediately.

The face of the young man who appeared in the doorway was like sunshine. It glowed with an excitement that was apparent even though he had the characteristic features of Down's syndrome. Or maybe, Sarim thought to himself, it was *because* he had Down's syndrome that he looked so excited. A child's excitement, on the face of a man.

Sarim grinned. 'Alfie!' he said. '*Mate!*'

Alfie grinned back. A strand of greasy black hair fell across his face, which was podgy through lack of exercise. He blew it upwards, then giggled.

'You going to invite me in, buddy?' Sarim asked. 'I'm getting wet here!'

Alfie's grin grew broader as he stepped to one side. 'Come on in,' he said, his voice sounding slightly clumsy, as it always did.

Sarim squeezed past. He knew to expect the musty smell of unwashed clothes and neglected rubbish bins, and managed to stop his distaste registering on his face. He walked down the dark hallway and into the bedsit beyond. To his left-hand side, a small kitchenette. To his right, a bedroom area with an unmade double bed, a two-seater Ikea sofa and a TV in one corner. A suitcase was open on the bed, but it was empty. Piles of half-folded clothes littered the room.

'Packing,' Alfie said as he walked over to the bed. He bent down awkwardly, picked up a pile of clothes seemingly at random, and crammed them into the suitcase.

Sarim wandered over to the kitchen area. The floor tiles were stained with drops of tea, and one of the units was open, revealing the waste bin. Sarim glanced inside. It was brimful of empty crisp wrappers. Blue. Walkers cheese and onion. Sarim had the impression that Alfie seldom ate anything else.

'We need to hurry, mate,' he said. 'Train won't wait for us, you know.'

He looked over at Alfie. He had bent down again but this time, instead of picking up a pile of clothes, he retrieved a rolled-up poster from the floor and started cramming it into the suitcase.

'What's that, mate?' Sarim asked lightly.

Alfie looked up at him and gave Sarim one of his innocent, trusting grins. He unrolled the poster to reveal a picture of Miley Cyrus, not wearing much at all and with her hair draped coquettishly round her neck. 'I'm going to marry her,' Alfie said, quite sincerely.

Sarim nodded. 'Course you are, mate. Come on. I'll help you finish packing. We're going to be late.'

Two minutes later, the suitcase was full, the poster of Miley Cyrus neatly smoothed out on the top. Sarim did up the zips and lifted it off the bed.

'Wait!' Alfie said.

Sarim took a deep, calm breath.

'I need my cagoul.'

'Go get it then, mate.'

A minute later, Alfie had put on his navy blue waterproof and tied the hood tightly around his face. He and Alfie left the flat. It took the young man a full minute to lock the door, while Sarim stood patiently in the rain. Alfie turned to face the road, then stopped.

'Wait!' he said. A terrible frown creasing his forehead. He was a young man who couldn't help every emotion showing on his face. 'I can't go!' he shouted over the rain.

Sarim closed his eyes. 'Why not, Alfie?' he asked, his voice quiet but steady.

'My social worker's coming to see me on Monday.'

'You'll be back home by Monday, mate. We talked about it, remember? We agreed you weren't going to tell him anything about this, so he wouldn't stop you coming. You'll see him on Monday and it'll all be fine.'

'Oh. Okay.' Alfie shrugged and the frown fell away. He followed Sarim to the Mercedes. Sarim opened the boot. There were two smaller suitcases in here, both identical, each with a small padlock holding the zippers together. Alfie clumsily started to lift his own suitcase into the boot, but Sarim stopped him. 'I'll do that, mate. No problems.' He was rewarded with another trusting smile from Alfie. Sarim carefully lifted the larger suitcase and slotted it in next to the others. He shut the boot, then turned back to Alfie, who had rain dripping down his face but looked no less excited for that.

'Ready to go on holiday?' he asked.

Jamal was much chattier now that Alfie was in the car. As he weaved his way through the stop-start traffic of south London, he and Sarim kept the young man talking. 'You like the beach, mate?'

Yes, Alfie liked the beach.

'You like ice creams, mate?'

Alfie *loved* ice creams.

'We're going to get some buckets and spades, innit?'

Alfie was quite sure his sandcastles would be much bigger than those of his two friends. He drew a picture of them on his steamed-up window.

And so the journey to Paddington station passed in pleasant conversation. By 11.30 they were driving along the Westway, and at 11.40 Jamal drove the Mercedes into an NCP car park just off the Edgware Road. They parked up. Sarim opened the boot again, removed Alfie's suitcase, and handed it to him. He and Jamal took one of the remaining suitcases each, then locked the car.

Sarim checked his watch. 11.43. 'Train leaves in 25 minutes,' he said, casting a sidelong glance at Jamal, who nodded. 'Come on, Alfie, mate. Let's get moving.'

It took five minutes to reach the station. Sarim checked the departure board. 'Platform seven,' he told the others, and they walked towards it, trundling their suitcases behind them.

There were ticket barriers at the platform, but they were lodged permanently open so a friendly man in a British Rail uniform stopped them to check their tickets. 'Off somewhere nice, fellas?' he asked them.

'Haverfordwest,' Sarim said immediately. 'A short holiday.'

'Hope the weather improves.' The guard looked at Alfie and winked. 'You have a good time, sunshine.' Alfie was busy watching the pigeons high in the station roof, so the guard turned back to Sarim and Jamal. 'The wife's sister has a Down's syndrome boy. Lovely little lad. Very *trusting*, if you know what I mean. Shame really. But good on you for looking after him, fellas. Good on you.'

Sarim gave a sincere look as he took back the tickets. 'Community, mate. It's what it's all about, innit?'

'That's your train,' said the guard, pointing down the platform. 'Unreserved seating, Coach G. You want to book a seat next time, mate. Don't cost nothing.'

'Yeah,' Sarim said quietly. He pulled his hood up over his head. 'Next time.'

The platform was busy. A hundred people, maybe more. As they dragged their suitcases alongside the train, it felt as though Alfie was saying hello to every single one of them in turn. When they arrived at Coach G, however, he stopped and pointed at it. Sarim wondered if Alfie had ever actually been on a train. He seemed excited by the whole prospect.

They stopped five metres from the carriage door. 'Give me a minute, guys,' Jamal said. He looked meaningfully back towards the station concourse. 'I need to go take a slash.'

Alfie looked confused. 'What's a slash?'

'Need the toilet, mate. Can't stand going on the train. All stinky. Won't be long, innit?'

'We'll wait here,' Sarim said.

Alfie looked alarmed. 'What if the train goes?'

'Plenty of time, mate,' he said. And when Alfie continued to look worried, he added: 'We *have* to wait for Jamal, Alfie. That's what friends do for each other.'

Alfie nodded. He looked disappointed in himself. 'We'll wait here,' he agreed.

Jamal walked away. Sarim checked his watch. 11.55. He turned to Alfie.

'Why don't I go and get some snacks for the journey?' he said.

Alfie looked alarmed again. He glanced at the train, then back at Sarim. 'It's getting full,' he said.

'You hungry?' Sarim persisted.

Alfie shook his head.

'Long journey though, mate. What's your favourite?' His eyes narrowed slightly. 'Cheese and onion crisps? The blue ones? I'll get a big bag, shall I?'

Alfie's face was a picture of indecision, but after a few seconds he nodded. Sarim put a reassuring hand on his shoulder. 'I'll only be a couple of minutes,' he said. He stepped away from Alfie and the little cluster of suitcases. 'Don't go wandering off, will you?' he added. 'We'll be in trouble if we leave our bags unattended. They'll tell us off.'

The thought of being told off made Alfie look even more anxious. He stepped closer to the suitcases and clutched the handles of two of them.

Sarim winked at him, just as the platform guard had done, then strode quickly back towards the concourse. As he left the platform, he looked back over his shoulder. He only just caught a glimpse of Alfie through the crowds, his face still tightly framed by the hood of his cagoul.

It was enough to tell him that the young man was guarding the suitcases diligently.

Sarim and Jamal met at their prearranged spot outside WHSmith at 11.59. Only when they were out on the street and walking swiftly through the torrential rain away from Paddington did Jamal speak. 'Fucking hate that geezer,' he spat. 'Looks all weird. Gives me the creeps, innit?'

They turned into a little cobbled mews where there were no pedestrians, but a couple of flash cars – an Aston Martin and a BMW – parked up.

'Have you got it?' Sarim asked. He had to speak loudly over the rain.

Jamal put one wet hand in his pocket and pulled out a mobile phone.

'Speed dial one!' Sarim shouted. 'That's what he told us. It'll do them both.'

Jamal licked his lips nervously. 'You trust him?'

Sarim nodded. 'With my life,' he said. 'Not that I'm afraid to lose it.'

'How can he be so sure we won't be caught?' Jamal asked. 'There were cameras everywhere in that station. I know we look different to usual, but . . .'

A pause.

'You scared to do it, Jamal?' Sarim asked. There was an edge to his voice. 'You not what we thought you were?'

Jamal looked uncertain. He didn't reply.

Sarim grabbed his upper arm. With his free hand, he pointed up into the sky. 'Look,' he shouted. 'Look up there. Tell me what you see.'

With a perplexed expression, Jamal looked up. He blinked as the rain fell directly on to his face.

'What do you see?' Sarim insisted.

'I . . . I don't know,' Jamal said. 'Nothing . . . rain . . . and clouds.'

Sarim nodded fiercely. 'Clouds,' he said. 'That's right. Do you like clouds? You like it when it's cloudy?'

Jamal shook his head.

'You prefer the sun, yes?'

'Of course.'

Sarim made a soft hissing sound. 'In your country – in Pakistan, *your* country – they pray for clouds. They *pray* for them. Do you know why?'

Once more, Jamal shook his head.

'Because when there are clouds, the drones do not come.'

A moment of silence.

'They think they are our judge, our jury and our executioner, these British and Americans.' Sarim was loud now, but his voice was almost drowned out by the downpour. 'They think they can kill our innocent women and children, and that we will be too weak to fight back. Well, *are* you, Jamal? *Are* you too weak to fight back?'

Jamal drew a deep breath. 'I'm not weak,' he said. 'Innit?' His sopping wet face frowned, and the hand that held the phone trembled.

'Then *do* it!' Sarim shouted. '*Now*. The idiot won't wait forever, and if the bags are unattended someone will raise the alarm.'

Jamal gritted his teeth. His finger hovered above the '1' button on the phone.

'*Do it!*'

Jamal pressed his thumb on to the button, and held it down.

Alfie knew nothing of the explosion.

He didn't hear the noise, like thunder, that echoed in the vaults of Paddington station, and which was audible in the West End, and Shepherd's Bush, and at the top of Primose Hill, and anywhere else within a two-mile radius.

He didn't hear the shattering of the train windows, or the metallic drilling of shrapnel peppering its chassis.

Or the sound of Coach G crunching in on itself from the violent shock wave, turning into a hot, twisted coffin that crushed everybody inside.

Or the buckling of a second train that was pulling into the opposite platform at the moment of the explosion.

He didn't hear the strange, ghostly silence that lasted for only a few seconds.

Or the screams that followed.

Some were screams of pain. Some were screams of horror. The horror that only someone who has witnessed such atrocities can know. The horror of men and women forced to look upon those parts of the human body that nobody should ever see. The horror of mothers cradling their dead children.

And Alfie, of course, didn't see these atrocities. He didn't see the body parts, grotesquely separated and mutilated, that flew to the concourse, and as high as the roof, and up the stairs at the far end of one platform that led to the tube station. He didn't see the blood that coagulated with hot dust and sprayed like thick paint over concrete and iron and mangled human bodies. He didn't see the corpses, some of them a full hundred metres away, that had been killed by shock waves if not by debris. He didn't see the faces, their skin burned away to reveal damaged networks of capillaries. Or the shower of dead birds that rained down from their roosting places in the ceiling and spattered as they hit solid ground. Or the rain that leaked in from the devastated ceiling, creating pools of watery, pink-red blood all over the platforms.

Alfie saw none of this. At the moment of the explosion, he had been waiting patiently for his friends, who had promised him such a lovely weekend away, and whom he had trusted implicitly, just as he trusted anybody who showed him the slightest kindness. Like good friends should, he had been clutching their suitcases, quite unaware that each one contained twenty-five kilos of military-grade explosive, and plastic bags filled to bursting with hard, anodised five-inch nails.

And as he was at the very centre of the explosion, he had of course been the first to die.

PART ONE

Hammerstone

ONE

'What the fuck do they think we are?' Spud Glover muttered. 'Twenty-four-hour locksmiths?'

Danny Black grunted, then looked left and right up Horseferry Mews. The name made this little side street – a hundred metres end to end and lined with railway arches – sound a lot posher than it actually was. Some of the arches were cavernous, full of litter, plastered with fat, colourful graffiti, and stinking of piss. Others had been turned into lock-ups and mechanics' workshops. Danny and Spud were standing alongside the central arch. The frontage was painted grey, with a red roll-top grate for vehicles to get in and out, and a steel door to one side. Both locked. The adjacent arches were empty, with no frontage. Over the sound of the hammering rain, Danny could hear larger drops echoing as they fell from the top of the arch on the right to the concrete floor. Between the two arches was a corroded metal downpipe reaching all the way to the ground from the railway above. The torrential rain was too much for it. Water sluiced down its sides, and belched up from the grate at its mouth.

Danny was as soaked as the drainpipe, and pissed off. Ordinarily, theirs was a life of aircraft carriers, forward operating bases and active missions behind enemy lines. But this? This was donkey work. He and Spud had been entrusted with nothing else since they got back from Syria six months previously.

Their two Regiment mates, Ripley and Barker, were at either

end of the street. Danny could just make out the glowing end of Ripley's cigarette as his mate leaned against the ten-foot-high wall, topped with razor wire, that faced the railway arches. If you saw Ripley round Hereford, he'd probably be wearing a leather biker's jacket. Motorbikes were his obsession. He owned, what, six or seven of them? But his biker's jacket would be no good for tonight. It couldn't conceal a rifle. Neither Ripley nor Barker showed any sign of the HK416s secreted under their Barbours and attached to their shoulders by means of a short length of bungee rope. But they only needed to open up their coats and extend their right arms to be as heavily armed as anyone in London – and in the wake of the Paddington bomb that was saying something.

Spud and Danny were less heavily armed. Their jeans and North Face jackets covered the Sigs holstered at their waist. Spud wore night-vision goggles propped up on his forehead. No body armour for either of them, though. They'd discussed it back in Hereford, and agreed that it wasn't necessary. This was Lewisham, not Lagos. Nobody expected a job like this to go noisy, and there wasn't a single self-respecting member of the Regiment who actively *chose* to strap on plate hangers if they didn't have to.

'I said, who do they think we *are*?' Spud repeated. 'Twenty-four . . .'

'They're just a bunch of geeks,' Danny interrupted. 'Open the frickin' door and we can get out of here.'

Between Danny and Ripley, about thirty-five metres from Danny's own position, was an old grey Bedford van with a dent on the nearside wing. It was parked up on the other side of the road opposite the arches. All lights off, nobody behind the wheel. But in the back, hidden from view, was a police tech unit. As soon as Spud had broken into the lock-up and given them the all-clear, the tech unit would swarm in and take detailed photos of everything inside. Then they'd go away and make a replica of something – a lamp, an old oil can, whatever they could find

– doctored with surveillance equipment. Which meant it was odds on they'd all be doing this again in a couple of nights' time, when the police could replace the chosen object with their specially altered one.

'I don't care if they've got Stephen fucking Hawking hiding back there,' Spud said. 'I'm missing a piss-up at Karen Macshane's place thanks to a bunch of plods scared of their own shadows.'

'Shame,' Danny said distractedly.

Spud turned to look at him. 'Shame?' he asked. '*Shame?* She sent me a selfie the other day. *With her tits out!* She's *gagging* for it . . .'

Danny looked meaningfully at the implement in Spud's right hand – a snap gun, about the size of an old-fashioned kids' potato gun, with a narrow, pointed blade protruding. Fit a tension wrench in the lock, then insert the snap gun and squeeze the handle – one of those should get a lock like this open in about thirty seconds, if you knew how to use it, which Spud did. 'You going to get started, mate? Get this done quickly, you'll be back in time to give Karen Macshane a night to remember.'

Spud gave him a dark look, but turned his attention back to the lock.

There was a voice in Danny's covert earpiece – one of the armed police guys keeping a 200-metre cordon. 'We've got a blue Passat heading towards the north end of Horseferry Mews. Two drivers, one male, one female.'

Ripley's voice: 'Roger that.'

And five seconds later, the glare of headlamps shining through rain as the vehicle passed the end of the street, then disappeared.

Danny looked back at Spud. The lock should have been open by now, but the snap gun was still inside it, and Spud was swearing under his breath. Danny raised an eyebrow. Spud scowled back. 'It's fucking *wet*, okay?'

Danny smiled. 'You'd have got it open by now if it had hair on it,' he said.

Spud grinned. 'True that,' he said. No false modesty there. Spud Glover was short, squat and broad-shouldered, with a face like a young Phil Collins. But he still pulled more regularly than anyone Danny had ever met. He started pumping the snap gun again. Ten seconds later, the lock clicked. Spud removed the snap gun, handed it to Danny, and pulled down his NV goggles.

Danny pressed a button on the radio fixed to his belt and spoke into the mike fitted to his collar. 'We're in,' he said.

'Roger that.' The same voice that had announced the arrival of the Passat. 'Red Mini Cooper heading south.'

Danny looked at Spud and nodded. Spud drew his Sig, opened the door just enough to step inside, and entered the lock-up.

For thirty seconds there was no sound except the hammering of rain on to the cobblestones and the drip-dripping inside the empty arches. Danny kept alert, looking up and down the street, acutely aware of Barker and Ripley's positions and of the old Bedford holding the tech team. Those lads were nervous. Fired up, too. There had been reports of suspicious activity in this lock-up over the past few days, and in the wake of the Paddington bomb, Danny could tell the techies were getting a hard-on at the thought of uncovering something – *anything* – that might give the security services a lead. And more power to them, Danny couldn't help feeling. Whoever had orchestrated that strike was a sick bastard and deserved everything that was coming to him.

'Okay, lads.' Spud's voice over the comms. 'I'll give you the good news first. No infrared sensors, no pressure pads – as far as surveillance devices go, the joint looks clean. Now the bad news – there's fuck-all for you to photograph. There's a pallet of some kind against the far wall but you'll never make a replica. I'm going to check it out, but if this is a bomb-making stash, you can butter my arse and call me a biscuit.'

A second voice over the radio. 'Black cab heading north.'

Danny frowned. It was typical – you get dragged all the way

from Hereford to London and the whole op's a dud. He wiped some rain off his forehead with his sleeve, and started walking towards the tech unit's van. They'd still want to see the inside of the lock-up for themselves, and they'd need Danny accompanying them. But the job was a washout in more ways than one.

He had only walked ten metres when he stopped. Spud's voice had burst over the radio. 'Well, fuck me sideways . . .'

'What is it?' Danny demanded, suddenly tense.

'That crate I mentioned? As high as my knee in packets of powder. I'm guessing it's not Persil.'

Almost immediately, Danny heard the second voice again. 'Another black cab, heading south.'

He froze, then looked up and down the street.

Black cabs?

What the hell were two black cabs doing headed for a line of deserted lock-ups and empty railway arches where there were no fares to drop off or pick up?

The penny dropped. It wasn't just the security services who used black cabs to get around London unobserved.

He ran back to the lock-up Spud was investigating and called in through the crack in the door. 'Mate, you sure you haven't triggered any surveillance devices?'

'Clean as a whistle,' Spud's voice called back, echoing slightly from inside the lock-up. 'We're going to be out of here quicker than you can . . .'

'*Spud*,' Danny interrupted. 'Tell me you checked the door seals when you entered.'

Silence.

And then Spud muttered, almost under his breath: '*Shit.*'

Danny didn't hesitate. He pulled a pencil-thin Maglite from inside his jacket pocket and strode into the lock-up. He directed the fierce white beam at the crack where the door was hinged. He saw it instantly: a silver strip – tin foil, maybe – reflecting the light of the torch, with a fine wire leading from the foil up towards the dark ceiling of the lock-up.

'You can forget about Karen Macshane,' Danny said, his voice unnaturally calm. 'Whoever owns that stash is on their way.' He loosened his Sig from its holster and cocked it, then activated his radio. 'Barker, Ripley, we're about to have company. Two black cabs. Expect them to be armed. Everyone else, stay out of it. Repeat, stay . . .'

Before he had even finished, he heard the screeching of tyres.

'*Spud!*' he shouted. But Spud was just a couple of metres away, running towards him from the back of the lock-up, NV goggles raised, Sig cocked. They pressed their backs against the wall, nodded at each other, then swung round into the cobbled street.

The rain was as bad as ever. It badly hindered Danny's visibility. From his position by the door he looked north, while Spud covered the southerly direction. He could only just make out the shaky outline of a black cab, its headlamps dazzlingly bright through the rain. Distance: 50 metres. He searched for Ripley. No sign of him, but that was probably because the mixture of headlamps and rain was blinding him. Danny swung his head to one side, forcing himself to use his peripheral vision, more effective in the dark. Now he could just make out Ripley's silhouette. He had moved in front of the Bedford van – Danny's end of it – which put him 35 metres from Danny's position, out of sight of the black cab. Now he was opening his Barbour jacket. Raising his HK416.

From the corner of his vision, Danny saw a second cab pull up at the south end of Horseferry Mews, 50 metres in the opposite direction. The Regiment guys and the police tech unit were blocked off at either end. Danny saw figures emerging from the first cab to the north.

Four guys. Drug dealers, he figured, aware that someone had just uncovered their stash. From Spud's description, that stash would be worth millions. These fuckers would be armed. No question.

The cabs headlamps shone across the 50 metres of open ground towards him. They were compromising his visibility. He needed to blow them out. In any case, maybe a couple of shots would put the shits up them. If Danny and his mates could get them on the ground and disarm them, the police could take them in. A good night's work all round.

He was too exposed here in front of the lock-up. He quickly ran to the cavernous open arch to the left and sensed Spud moving to the one on the right. He stepped three metres in, where he would be shadowed inside the arch but would have full view of the cab, which was now between 40 and 45 metres away. He crouched down in the firing position, raised his Sig, aimed carefully and fired two shots in quick succession. The suppressed weapon made two dull knocks, camouflaged by the noise of the rain. Result. The newcomers would be unable to work out his exact location.

The headlamps shattered and went dark.

From the arch on the other side of the lock-up, he heard two more shots. Spud had used his Sig to do exactly the same thing to disable the headlamps of the cab to the south.

Danny could see the sillhouettes of the four guys to the north. They had opened the doors of their cab and were standing behind them, two on either side, for protection.

'*Get on the ground!*' he shouted aggressively above the rain. '*Hands on the back of your heads! NOW!*' He sounded fierce, but his breathing was shallow. His pulse slow. He was calm.

One of the newcomers shouted something in a language Danny didn't recognise.

Then, suddenly, there was a sharp burst of gunfire: the rough bark of an AK-47 switched to automatic, and maybe a couple of shots from a MAC-10. He heard the distinctive sound of rounds drilling against metal.

Shit.

Rounds had punctured the side of the Bedford van where the tech unit were hiding out. There were perhaps eight entry holes in a neat horizontal line just a couple of inches from the roof. Narrow beams of interior light streamed out from each of the holes. It would be clear to anyone with half a brain that the back of the van was occupied.

Danny made radio contact: '*Tech unit, are you hit?*'

A horrible silence. Then a panicked, breathless voice over Danny's earpiece. '*No...*' it whispered. '*No ... we're okay ... Oh my God, what are we ...*'

'*Crouch on the floor of the van, as low as you can, now! Spud, options?*'

'*They know the tech unit are there,*' said Spud firmly. '*They're armed and they've fired on us. I say we give it to them.*'

Danny gave it a fraction of a second's thought. Spud was right. There were five guys in that tech unit and their lives were in danger.

'I've got eyes on four guys to the north,' Danny said. 'Spud, what have you got?'

'Three guys to the south.'

'Barker, Ripley, have they seen you?'

'Negative,' from both men.

Suddenly a voice shouted from the direction of the cab to the north. In English this time, but accented. 'Put the guns down, or we fire on your friends in the van!'

Silence. Movement by the cab. Three figures stepped forward. A fourth remained behind the open passenger door. He had a rifle, and it was trained on the Bedford van.

Danny raised his Sig. He aimed it, his hand perfectly steady, on the head of the guy behind the passenger door. The other three stepped forward. They had that swagger common to every amateur carrying a gun. Like their weapons could protect them from anything. But they couldn't see Ripley, crouching in front of the Bedford van.

The figures were five metres from the cab now, ten from the Bedford van. They walked abreast, though one of them, broader than the others, was perhaps a couple of paces ahead. He let loose a random burst of automatic fire, but it was just a warning shot: the rounds sparked against the cobbles.

'Show yourselves!' the leader shouted.

No response from the Regiment.

The men swaggered forward again.

They were alongside the tech unit's vehicle now. Danny still had his Sig aimed at the shooter behind the cab, ready to fire.

'What's happening with your guys, Spud?' Danny breathed into the radio.

'Still behind their vehicle. We can't get a shot.'

The three figures were still moving forward. They were alongside the Bedford van. The beams of light from the bullet holes dotted their faces and bodies. Danny could tell from the bulky frames that they were wearing body armour.

A terrified voice in his earpiece. The tech unit. *'What's happening?'*

Danny didn't answer. He just kept all his attention on the shooter behind the cab. It would be a difficult shot. Fifty metres through the dark and the rain. He had to keep sharp.

The three men had passed the Bedford. They were five metres beyond Ripley, who had silently turned and had his weapon pointing at the back of their heads. Danny double-checked that his own weapon was properly on target, before issuing the instruction.

'Take the shots.'

There was no hesitation. Like Danny and Spud's handguns, Ripley's HK416 was suppressed, so with the noise of the rain it was barely audible. Danny could only just hear the three head shots, like someone rapping sharply on a wooden door. The three figures crumpled to the ground, one after the other, like a line of dominoes.

A millisecond later, Danny fired. A single shot. It hit his target square in the head. He crumpled to the ground behind the open passenger door.

'*What's happening?*' A voice from the tech unit.

'*Stay down!*' Danny hissed.

Four targets down to the north, but it wasn't over yet. There were still three guys hiding behind the cab to the south, almost certainly armed.

Aware, from the corner of his eye, that Ripley had thrown himself to the ground in order to present less of a target to the remaining three shooters, Danny spun round in the opposite direction, semi-protected by the corner of the arch. Now all four soldiers were facing south. They had a few seconds before the three remaining guys realised their mates were down. When that happened, they'd do one of two things: shoot, or run.

They decided to shoot.

It was a sudden, intense burst of fire which lasted about five seconds. Rounds sparked on the cobbles. A couple smashed into the front window of the Bedford van – far too close to the tech unit for Danny's liking but even closer to Ripley, who was pinned down on the ground.

'Open up,' he ordered.

The barrage of fire from the unit's weapons was much quieter than the shooters'. These were not noisy rounds fired at random to assert anyone's authority. They were precisely aimed shots from four suppressed weapons. They shattered the windows of the parked-up cab fifty metres from Danny's position, and flew through the chassis. Danny clearly saw one body slump back from the car, but Barker's voice in his earpiece clearly told him that he hadn't seen it all. 'I've got two targets down. No sign of the third.'

'Hold your fire,' Danny instructed.

The gunshots fell silent.

No movement from the cab to the south.

Rain.

Then, suddenly, like a frightened animal scampering away from a predator, a third figure broke from behind the black cab. He started sprinting away, firing a handgun randomly backwards from above his head towards Danny and the others.

Barker's voice: 'I've got him.'

Danny couldn't see Barker – he had to be taking cover in one of the arches to the south of the mews – but he heard the single round popping from his rifle and he could tell from the way the target fell that the round had entered the gunman's right shoulder. The force of its impact gave him a little extra momentum: it looked like he was diving as he fell forward and collapsed on the cobblestones.

Silence.

Then Spud, over the radio: 'Goons.'

'Ripley,' Danny ordered, 'see that the tech unit's okay. Spud, check Ripley's three are dead.'

'He shot them in the head, mucker. Normally does the trick.'

'Just do it, Spud.' Danny was already running south, towards Barker's position. Barker was standing easy, his HK416 lowered. Distance between them, 20 metres. Close enough for Danny to see the adrenaline-fuelled grin on his face.

It didn't last long.

'*GET DOWN!*' Danny barked.

The final shooter – the one Barker had downed with a single shot of his rifle – had moved. He was on his back, 15 metres from Barker's position, and the shot that he fired from his handgun was unaimed. But it found its mark. Danny saw a flash of blood spark from Barker's right arm, and his SAS mate hit the floor.

It was like the flick of a switch. Until that moment, Danny had been calm. Collected. His breathing had been easy, his pulse slow. But suddenly something changed. The red mist. Anger burned through him. He ran up to the bastard, to see that he was bleeding from the groin and torso. But he still had his gun in one hand, and the fingers were clenched round the pistol. He waved it aimlessly. Danny sensed that his target's vision was going.

It was as if something else was controlling Danny. Some other force. He bent down and forced the gunman's hand, gun and all, until the barrel was pointing between his lips and into his throat. He squeezed the trigger. Once. Twice. Three times. The body thudded with each shot. Blood spread immediately from the back of the man's head, and foamed between his lips. Spatter covered Danny's hand.

And then, like the switch had been flicked once more, Danny was himself again. Leaving the bleeding, brutalised corpse at his feet, he stood up and spun round. Barker was still on the ground, but moving. Danny sprinted over to him to find his mate writhing on the wet cobblestones.

'The *cunt*!' he shouted. 'The fucking *cunt* got me in the arm!'

He was clutching his upper right arm with his left hand. He'd be fine, though Danny could see that the rain was washing significant amounts of blood away from the wound and over the cobblestones.

'Stay there,' he told Barker. 'We'll get you to a hospital.'

'Did you put the dickhead down?' Barker demanded through gritted teeth.

Danny looked back at the recumbent body, then at the stubborn bloodstains on his right hand. For an unpleasant moment it was as though he saw himself from above, forcing his victim's gun into his mouth, taking the shots. He looked like some sort of animal, crouching in the rain.

Danny put a reassuring hand on the shoulder of his wounded mate.

'Yeah,' he said quietly. 'Yeah, I put him down.'

TWO

Tessa Gorman, Her Majesty's Principal Secretary of State for the Home Department, stood at the open door of Number 10 and looked out on to Downing Street to see that it was *still* raining.

Not that it made much difference to her. As Home Secretary, she had the benefit of a chauffeur who even now was trotting up the steps with a black umbrella. He ushered her to the ministerial car. She was still quite dry when she slipped into the back. Her driver had turned the seat-heaters on, so the soft leather was rather comforting.

If only the same could be said for the meeting she'd just left. They'd all been there: the PM; Michael Mears, her opposite number at the Foreign Office; Tim Atkins, the PM's head of communications, whose bald head and hairy eyebrows made him look more like a clown than the power behind the throne. Three men, each of them greasily shifting responsibility for the decision they had all just made on to the one woman in the room. She had a reputation for taking a hard line in matters of national security, and those three bastards had just hoist her with her own petard. Mears especially. He'd been feeling the heat ever since the Syrian situation had escalated. The Russians seemed to have one over him in every negotiation. He was clearly glad for the spotlight to fall on someone else for once.

'Home, Secretary of State?' her driver asked as he settled behind the wheel.

She shook her head. 'Thames House, please, Robert. I'm afraid it's going to be a late one.'

The drenched officers at the entrance to Downing Street – her husband *would* insist on calling them 'the plebs', like it was the funniest joke in the world – nodded respectfully to the Home Secretary as they let her out. Their numbers had been bolstered by four soldiers who carried their weapons overtly and stood with grim, expressionless faces in the rain. Bloody good job you could rely on your armed forces at a time like this, she thought to herself. She was on the verge of rolling down her window to offer them a few words of encouragement, but she shivered at the thought of the rain sluicing in and decided not to.

As the car crawled through Whitehall, Gorman flicked through the front pages of the following day's first editions that were piled next to her. The usual fodder. More photos of the devastation at Paddington on the broadsheets, while the tabloids had run with pictures of the nation's current favourite hate figure, the radical cleric Abu Ra'id, one finger raised as he preached outside the Holy Shrine mosque in north-west London. She shared the PM's frustration that every time they tried to deport this awful man, the courts got in their way. And all the while his dreadful wife – the papers liked to call her the White Witch – was living on benefits in a large three-bedroom house in Ealing ...

Ten minutes later, they were pulling up outside the archway that formed the entrance to Thames House. Robert parked the car and opened her door. The Home Secretary stepped out to find an efficient-looking young woman in a well-cut trouser suit waiting for her.

'This way, Home Secretary,' she said. The young woman ushered her into the building and towards an open lift. Once inside, she pressed a button for the third floor and they silently ascended. As the doors hissed open, the greeter stepped into the corridor. 'May I fetch you a coffee, Home Secretary?'

Gorman shook her head briskly. 'No thank you. I need to see Victoria Atkinson right away.'

The young woman inclined her head and led her down the corridors of the third floor without another word. She stopped outside a door and knocked.

'Do come in,' said a male voice.

'I'll take it from here,' said the Home Secretary. She opened the door and stepped inside.

The room was very ordinary. As a student of history, she had always imagined that important decisions were taken in important rooms, with chandeliers and frescoes. Now she lived in the real world, she knew the opposite was true. Life-and-death decisions got made in bland, corporate rooms like this one in MI5 headquarters. A man was sitting behind a desk. He was extremely handsome – the spitting image of Hugh Grant, Gorman couldn't help thinking – and he had a friendly, open smile.

'Where's Victoria Atkinson?' she asked.

'Unavoidably called away,' the man said. 'A family crisis. Something to do with her youngest ...' He smiled. 'I'm afraid kids are no respecters of national security. I'm Buckingham. Hugo Buckingham, on secondment from MI6.'

'You're one of the Hammerstone team?'

Buckingham nodded gently. 'I am, Home Secretary.'

Gorman nodded, then took a seat opposite him. 'Buckingham?' she said, as though trying to place the name. 'Sounds familiar. Weren't you our man in Syria for a while?'

'In a manner of speaking, Home Secretary, yes. A lively place.'

'So I hear.' She looked around. 'The room is secure?'

'It is.'

'Right then. I've just come straight from Number 10. The PM's been informed you have a lead on the perpetrators of the Paddington bombing. We made the decision not to convene a meeting of COBRA. Too many loose tongues, if you understand my meaning.'

'I understand entirely, Home Secretary.'

Gorman found herself warming to this young man. He seemed sincere. A safe pair of hands.

'The PM feels that the public no longer have the stomach for more terrorists abusing the legal process. We're a laughing stock as it is. The Hammerstone team gave the PM a second option . . .'

'The *pre-emptive* option, Home Secretary?'

'Call it what you will. Obviously there is no way he can officially condone such action, and we don't need to know the identity of the individuals involved. But I'm here to tell you that if the pre-emptive option were taken, Her Majesty's Government would not investigate the matter too closely. Do I make myself clear?'

'Perfectly clear,' said Buckingham. 'I shall inform my three Hammerstone colleagues of the gist of this conversation immediately.'

'Obviously . . .' Gorman started to say.

'. . . this conversation never happened.'

The politician and the spook locked gazes. A silent acknowledgement passed between them. Tessa Gorman stood up and outstretched her hand. Buckingham did the same.

'Family crisis, you say?' The Home Secretary was unimpressed.

'So I understand. Something to do with . . . chickenpox?'

'Hard to do this job well if you're running off to mop little Johnny's fevered brow every five minutes, I'd have thought.'

'Not for me to comment, Home Secretary.'

The door suddenly opened. Gorman and Buckingham looked across the office to see a short, slightly plump woman bustle in. She wore a flowery blouse and sensible trousers that didn't flatter her figure. Her mousy hair was wet and bedraggled. She carried a sopping raincoat over the crook of her arm. Her cheeks were red and she was out of breath.

'Sorry . . . late . . .' she gasped, then tapped her chest several times in quick suggestion. 'Something going on in Lewisham . . . police everywhere . . .' She blinked at the other two. 'Have you started?'

'Actually, Victoria,' said the Home Secretary, 'we've just finished. I'm sure Mr Buckingham will fill you in. '

Victoria flushed, and she drew herself up to her full height, which wasn't very high at all. 'He certainly *will* fill me in,' she said, her voice suddenly more prickly and authoritative. 'My son . . .'

'Plenty of brownie points,' Gorman interrupted her, 'if you bring this business to a successful conclusion.' She directed her words towards Buckingham rather than Victoria. 'I can promise you that. *Plenty* of brownie points.' She scraped back her chair and walked towards the door. Then she stopped and looked back at Buckingham. 'I'm obliged to leave the details up to you,' she said. 'I trust you have somebody in mind capable of carrying out an operation like this?'

'Yes,' Buckingham replied coolly. 'As a matter of fact, a couple of names do spring to mind. If Victoria approves, of course.'

'Hereford Regiment?'

'Yes, Home Secretary. Hereford Regiment. But as you say, probably best to leave the details down to us.'

00.02hrs

There was flashing blue neon at either end of the street. Two members of the police armed response unit had arrived to get Barker on his feet and away to the nearest hospital. He hadn't let them help him, and insisted on walking unaided to the unmarked squad car parked just outside the lock-up. The five guys in the tech unit were a gibbering mess after their ordeal in the Bedford van, but they were alive and unharmed.

Danny's earpiece was a torrent of voices. The Met's command room had been patched in, and so had Hereford. The instructions were clear. The Regiment boys were to make themselves scarce. SCO19 would mop all this up, and no doubt claim the credit for seven dead dealers, a sizeable seizure of cocaine, and none of their guys down. And that was fine by Danny and the boys. For them, anonymity was the name of the game.

They stood together by the cab at the south end of the street.

'He going to be all right?' Ripley asked, pointing at Barker's receding silhouette.

'Flesh wound,' Danny told him. 'Might have to use his left hand to spank the monkey for a while, that's all.'

Spud looked meaningfully over at the corpse of the man Danny had wasted. 'You gave that fella's mouth a good rinse out with his nine-milli,' he said. 'What was all that about?'

For an uncomfortable moment, Danny remembered the rage that had taken him over.

'Bad breath,' he muttered. 'Got a thing about it.'

Spud raised an eyebrow at the insufficient response, then nodded towards the arm of Danny's North Face jacket. 'You've still got a piece of the bastard's brains on your sleeve,' he said, as if he were pointing out a ketchup stain to a kid.

Danny shrugged. 'Come on,' he said. 'The headshed want us out of here. Let's go.'

They put their heads down, and walked silently away from the flashing lights and the scene of devastation they'd created. Their own vehicle was an unmarked white Transit van parked up two blocks away. Three minutes later they were climbing into the back, their coats dripping rainwater over the metal floor. They each had a holdall with a change of clothes, so they stripped out of their wet gear and pulled on dry jeans and T-shirts, leaving the wet, bloody garments sprawled over the vehicle's floor.

Ripley took the wheel. Spud sat next to him in the middle seat, with Danny by the passenger window. They eased slowly away. After a couple of minutes they came to the police cordon, but the armed officer recognised their vehicle and waved them through. A minute later, they were driving down Lewisham High Street. Danny wiped the condensation away from the inside of his window and stared out.

The pavements were empty, but it wasn't just because of the driving rain. There was unease on the streets. He'd been in London after 7/7, and there'd been a similar feeling then. If anything, it was worse in the wake of the Paddington bomb. The death count had been higher – last thing Danny heard, the number of fatalities had exceeded a hundred – and people were scared. Everyone knew someone who knew somone who'd been affected. Barker had a good mate in A Squadron, young bloke called Hancock, whose brother had been on the train and hadn't made it. Hancock had been offered compassionate leave but had turned it down. Wanted to be around to do his bit as and when the time came. As they passed Lewisham station, Danny saw a group of four armed police guarding the entrance. The sight was supposed to put the public at their ease. Danny wondered if it didn't have the opposite effect.

Spud switched the radio on. 'Bat out of Hell' by Meatloaf blasted out of the speakers. Spud turned it up even louder. 'I fucking love this one!' he shouted over the music, and he started singing along tunelessly. If there was tension on the streets, the inside of the Transit was a little cocoon of released adrenaline. It didn't matter how many times you found yourself in a firefight, the heady mixture of relief and exhilaration when it was over never got old.

Meatloaf's final chords died away. There was a chirpy Radio 2 jingle that grated on Danny's ears, then a news bulletin. 'The number of fatalities from the bombing at Paddington station last Friday has reached 107. Buckingham Palace have today confirmed that Orlando Whitby, fiancé of Princess Katrina, is among the dead ...'

Spud switched the radio off again. 'Fucking sick of hearing about it,' he said.

Ripley indicated right. 'Still,' he said. 'That's one for the Princess Di nutjobs to get their teeth into.'

'Hey,' Spud said. 'Enough of the nutjob.'

Danny smiled. It sometimes seemed to him that there wasn't a single member of the British public who *didn't* think the SAS had killed Diana using some fiendishly elaborate plot cooked up by the establishment and sanctioned by the royal family. And there were even some guys in the Regiment itself who thought that way. Spud included. Where there was a conspiracy theory to believe in, Spud was always first on the bandwagon. Not Danny though. Those Diana rumours were entertaining, but in his opinion the world didn't work that way. If somebody had wanted Diana dead, they'd have made the hit in a far more practical or covert way. Car chases under the Seine? Packs of paparazzi? Blinding flashes of light? No. There were too many variables. Too many things that could go wrong. Diana's death was an accident, nothing more. And the same went for Orlando Whitby, whoever the hell he was: just one of the unlucky sods who found themselves in the wrong place at the wrong time.

'Put your foot down, mucker,' Spud said to Ripley. 'Too late for the headshed to call a debrief tonight. Floor it down the M4, I might get to Karen Macshane's gaff before she opens up her muff for some other little turd.'

'Thought you were seeing that bird from Warham.'

'Nah, she dumped me. Said I was always exaggerating.'

'What, *you*?' Ripley said with a grin.

'I know – I was so surprised I nearly tripped over my dick.' Spud started whistling 'Bat out of Hell' again, then stopped suddenly and turned to Danny. 'Want to come, mucker? Reckon you could use a few jars – you know, chillax. You went a bit OTT with that dumb-ass back there.'

Danny stared out of the window again. 'Don't want to cramp your style, mate.' He glanced sideways at Spud, who was giving him a piercing look. 'Clara's staying,' he said. 'Day off. I'd better . . .'

'. . . get your rocks off with your posh bird. Yeah, yeah, 'nuff said, fella.'

Danny had two phones. One for work, one personal, and at the moment he was only carrying the work one. It rang. He looked at the screen: number withheld. This was an encrypted phone, and nobody had the number – so far as Danny knew – except the ops room back at base. 'This could be interesting,' he said. He accepted the call and put the handset to his ear.

Danny didn't have the chance to say hello. The Regiment's ops officer Ray Hammond was already barking down the phone at him. 'Nice one, fellas. I send you down to the smoke to pick a lock, I end up with seven dead Cypriots, the worst case of suicide I've ever seen and half the fucking journalists in London trying to get past the police cordon.'

'It went noisy,' Danny said calmly.

'*You're fucking telling me it went noisy!*' Hammond screamed so loudly that Danny had to move the handset a few inches from his ear. 'The CO wants you and Spud in his office the second you get back.'

Spud, who had clearly heard the conversation as he was sitting so close to Danny's phone, started mouthing swear words silently next to Danny, who tried to block it out and keep his concentration.

'What does the boss want?'

'Oh, I don't know,' the ops officer said. 'Perhaps he wants to know how one of your targets managed to accidentally shoot himself three times in the mouth. Get a fucking move on. You're expected here in three hours.'

The phone line went dead. Danny stared at the handset, then turned to Spud. 'Sorry mate,' he said. 'Looks like I'm your date for the night. CO's called us in.'

Spud gave him a sick look. 'You know what?' he asked. 'I've got millions of nerves in my body. How come that fucker Hammond manages to get on every single one of them?'

THREE

The unit arrived back at RAF Credenhill at 03.30hrs. The car park was unusually full, the lights were on in all the squadron hangars and even the HQ building was lit up. Busy times. Danny was dog-tired. Even Spud had been nodding off on the motorway. As they pulled up in front of the main regimental HQ building, Danny elbowed him in the ribs. He pointed through the windscreen. The wipers were still flapping furiously, so they could make out the sight of Ray Hammond waiting for them just inside the main entrance.

'Let's get this over with,' Danny said. Spud and Ripley grunted in agreement. They debussed, and ran across the courtyard up the steps to the HQ building.

Hammond had dark rings round his eyes and an even darker frown on his forehead. 'Not you, Ripley,' he said. 'You can get the hardware back to the armoury. You and you' – he pointed at Danny and Spud in turn – 'follow me.'

They marched through the building. Company clerks were scurrying around in uniform, or sitting at computers taking phone calls. But they hardly saw any of the lads. There was barely a UK-based member of the Regiment that wasn't out on the streets, fully tooled up and ready to assist the police in the event of a hard arrest being necessary. Half of B Squadron had been deployed to major shopping centres round the country. Only a few weeks previously, a bunch of Al-Shabaab militants had taken out a number of civilian targets in a Kenyan shopping mall.

Word was that the security services were bricking themselves that there might be a repeat performance.

They walked in silence towards the area at its centre known as the Kremlin. The warning signs were on Hammond's face, and even Spud didn't venture any sarky comments. The Kremlin was where Johnny Cartwright, CO of 22SAS, had his office, opposite the briefing rooms and just down the corridor from the main ops room. Hammond raised his fist to knock on the door, but at that moment the door opened and a clerk walked out carrying an empty coffee cup. Hammond stepped inside. 'They're here, sir,' he said.

'Send them in, Ray. You can go home now.'

The ops officer looked a bit put out that he wasn't invited into the meet. But he stood to one side and let Spud and Danny pass without a word. Seconds later, they were alone with the CO.

Danny liked Cartwright. As ruperts went, he was one of the better ones. True, Danny suspected that his past few months of humdrum, UK-based ops was a hundred per cent down to his CO keeping him out of the firing line since everything that had happened on his last major overseas op, but he had his reasons. Cartwright seemed to have a genuine concern for his men's welfare. Not that he was touchy-feely – far from it – but he was always prepared to stand up for the guys. When Danny and Spud had returned from Syria with their mate Greg Murray, he'd insisted on being present at every debrief the authorities could throw at him. Whenever questions came up that Danny didn't feel like answering – and there were plenty of those – the CO pulled rank and stonewalled the fuckers. And when it was clear that Greg's injuries at the hands of the Syrian *mukhabarat* spelled an end to his time in active service, Cartwright had made sure he kept a desk job in Hereford on full pay. Danny would always be grateful for that.

Not that he'd ever say it to Cartwright. Nor would Cartwright want to hear it. Especially now. The CO had a face like thunder.

'So what are we supposed to tell them?' he demanded without any pleasantries.

Danny kept a poker face. 'It was very weird, boss,' he said. 'The guy obviously didn't want to be captured alive. Took his own life before we could nail him.'

'Three times in the back of the throat?'

'Like I say, boss. It was weird.'

Cartwright stared at each of them in turn, then shook his head as if he was dealing with a couple of particularly exhausting children. 'Leave it to me,' he said under his breath. 'I'll sort it out.' He stood up from behind his desk. 'You're not here for a bollocking, anyway. Take a seat.'

They did as they were told.

'You're both being assigned to E Squadron,' Cartwright said. 'Effective immediately.'

Danny blinked, then glanced at Spud.

The existence of E Squadron was an open secret. You'd never find an SIS or Regiment representative acknowledging its existence. But it existed all right – a special, hand-picked cadre of operatives individually selected to carry out the more sensitive operations that the intelligence services deemed necessary. Back in the day they'd called it the Increment, or the RWW. Now, this covert unit took its pick from the cream of 22SAS, the SBS and the Special Reconnaissance Regiment. Danny knew they'd been active in Libya and North Africa, but even he had no firm knowledge of what they'd been up to. E Squadron was for the most experienced, the most comprehensibly vetted. The best.

'For what it's worth,' Cartwright said, 'I think it's a fucking terrible idea. But you two were specifically requested by London about two and a half hours ago. Looks like your old mate Hugo Buckingham's taken a shine to you.'

Danny couldn't stop the contempt showing on his face. He'd neither seen nor heard from Buckingham ever since they'd got back from Syria, and he was glad to keep it that way. He was loathsome. Cowardly. Danny couldn't trust him one bit, which made this sudden summons all the more suspicious. E Squadron operations generally took the guys to the hottest spots in the world, often to protect MI6 personnel. Danny wasn't sure he could stomach another op babysitting that piece of shit.

Cartwright was talking again. 'I don't have a lot of details, but Buckingham's part of a joint MI5/MI6/CIA task force following up the Paddington bomb. They need a covert team on the ground to help them. You're it. You head to London tomorrow, meet with your police liaison. We've got a safe house being prepared for you as we speak. You stay in the capital for as long as they need you there. I don't expect you'll be back in Hereford for some time.'

'Boss,' Danny started to say, 'this Buckingham guy, if he'd had his way Spud would be rotting at the bottom of a mass grave in Syria . . .'

'Get over it, Black. I know your feelings about him, but the decision's made. You can take it as read by me that there's a ton of downward pressure from Whitehall at the moment. The security services will be feeling the heat and I guess you two must have impressed that little shit out in the Middle East. Take it as a compliment if it makes you feel better. Or not, as the mood takes you. A chopper will give you a quick lift to London at 08.00. You'll have a vehicle waiting for you and you're expected at Paddington Green Police station at twelve hundred. You'll receive a further briefing then. Any questions?'

Yeah, Danny thought. Like, a million. But none that his CO was likely to answer. And even Spud seemed lost for a clever remark.

'In that case,' Cartwright said, 'go home and get some sleep. My feeling is you're going to need it.' He opened one of his desk drawers and produced a sealed brown envelope, which he handed to Danny. A London address was written on the front, and the envelope was heavy with what felt like keys.

Danny was experienced enough to realise there was no use arguing with the headshed. He was a soldier, and he'd just been given his orders. The briefing was over.

Like the CO had said: get over it.

Home, for Danny, was little more than a place to store his personal possessions. The life he'd chosen didn't lend itself to comforts, and if Clara hadn't been waiting for him, he would probably have kipped down at base where he had a bunk and a change of clothes on hand. But Clara *was* waiting for him, despite the lateness of the hour. As he parked his motorbike on the kerb outside his small, ground-floor flat in the western part of Hereford, just south of Whitecross Road, he could see the front-room light burning. She'd obviously ignored his instruction not to wait up.

He let himself in and stripped himself of his wet-weather gear in the narrow hallway. He could hear the TV, and as he stepped into the front room he saw Clara curled up on the sofa, fast asleep in front of some late-night discussion programme. An audience member with a neck thicker than a bulldog was getting very hot under his sizeable collar. 'If this Abu Ra'id can't live by our rules, he shouldn't be allowed in our country.' The audience clapped and the man folded his arms with obvious satisfaction. On a screen behind them was the familiar face of a bearded Islamic cleric – or 'hate' cleric as everyone liked to call him – whom the government had supposedly been trying to deport for more than a year now. Danny wasn't the only one who couldn't quite work out what the problem was with getting rid of the bastard, or quite why his wife was allowed a large, comfortable house in the suburbs that so far as he could tell they didn't pay for. Ra'id's face had been all over the place since the bombing, though whether he was involved or not nobody really seemed to know.

Danny stepped across the room and switched the TV off. Clara was roused by the sudden silence. She sat up quickly, her blonde hair mussed and her tired face confused, as though she didn't know where she was. But then she saw Danny, and her features softened.

'You're back,' she said.

'I told you not to wait up.'

She gave a winsome little shrug. 'Bed's too big without you,' she said.

Danny sat next to her, a wave of tiredness crashing over him again.

'Hard day at the office?'

'Just the usual,' Danny said evasively.

'You can tell me, you know.'

Clara had a habit of saying things like that. Of trying to find out what Danny had been up to. The nitty-gritty of his job. Deep down, he understood why. Clara had been through the mill out in Syria, where he'd found her deep in the rebel heartland. Most couples got together over a few pints down the local. Danny and Clara's relationship had kicked off among the ordnance and flying rounds of a devastating civil war. She'd seen him at his work and she'd gone through things at the hands of the Syrians that nobody should have to experience. It had changed her, forever. The bed might be too big without Danny, but barely anything ever happened when they were in it. Again, Danny knew why. Intimacy was difficult for her after the abuse the *mukhabarat* had inflicted on her.

But Syria had changed Danny, too. More than changed him – turned his life on its head. Maybe that was the reason he had these moments when he felt he hardly knew himself. Maybe that was the reason some piece-of-shit drug dealer had wound up with three 9mm rounds at the back of his throat that evening. And would Clara understand *that*? Of course she wouldn't. Danny didn't even understand it himself.

'Just the usual,' he repeated, in a tone that indicated that the conversation was over.

They sat in silence for a moment. 'Can I get you anything?' Clara said finally.

'I'm being moved to London,' Danny said. 'Starting tomorrow. I don't know how long for. Could be a while.'

'But . . . that's *great*!' A pause. 'Isn't it?'

Danny shrugged. 'It is what it is.' He'd already decided he wasn't going to mention Buckingham. If anything, Clara hated him more than Danny did. And he sure as hell wasn't going to speculate with her about the nature of the op. Clara was a sweet girl. She wouldn't even begin to understand or accept the kind of things he might be called upon to do.

'Maybe you could stay with me?'

'No, Clara,' he said in an unintentionally withering voice. 'I won't be staying with you. It doesn't work like that.'

Her eyes widened, and Danny instantly regretted being so short with her. 'We can see more of each other, though,' he added.

She smiled, relief obvious in her face. 'What will you be doing?' she asked. 'In London, I mean.'

'Just . . . general security,' Danny said. 'After the bombings and everything. All hands on deck.' He knew it was an explanation Clara would understand. As a medic working out of St Mary's Hospital, she and her colleagues had been inundated with casualties. She'd been at work at the time of the explosion and had by all accounts been one of the few doctors that had managed to keep their heads as the injured started arriving in their droves. Which kind of figured: Clara was used to explosions, after all. But Danny didn't feel like reminding her that the Regiment were only ever called in when a violent outcome could be expected.

She started snuggling up to him. 'You're all tense,' she said.

'Long day,' Danny replied. The image of the dealer he'd shot in the throat jumped back into his head. The thudding of his skull against the cobblestones. The liquid mixture of blood and rain spreading from his body.

There was a sharp knock at the door.

'What the ...' he muttered.

'It's four in the morning,' Clara said.

More knocking. Louder this time, as though someone was using the flat of their fist.

Danny stood up. 'Don't move,' he said quietly. And to himself, he said: *When someone comes knocking at this hour, it's never good news.* He instantly thought of his dad, who was stuck in a wheelchair in a ground-floor flat not far from here. And then he thought once more of his recent briefing back at base: of Five and Buckingham, who would think nothing of sending someone round in the middle of the night if they needed to. He stepped down the corridor, noiselessly approaching the solid wooden front door. When he reached it, he peered through the spyhole.

'Fuck's sake,' he muttered when he saw who was on his doorstep.

Danny's brother Kyle looked worse every time he saw him – which was, admittedly, as infrequently as Danny could make it. He was a waster – a jailbird and an alcoholic. Danny seemed to have spent half his life digging him out of bad situations of his brother's own making. Even through the spyhole Danny could see Kyle was in a bad way tonight. Dishevelled, several day's growth on his face, dark rings under his eyes. Sunken cheeks, the left one badly swollen, several shades of purple and red and bisected by a thin line of steristrip. A professional job – Danny could tell his brother was fresh from A&E. He opened the door.

'What do you want?'

'Mate!' Kyle said with a forced smile. A sour waft of stale booze punched Danny in the face. Kyle was wearing jeans and a T-shirt. The T-shirt was soaking wet, and clung to his thin, bony body.

'It's late, Kyle, I was just going to bed.'

Kyle's grin fell away. 'You've got to help me, mate,' he breathed. He looked over his shoulder – a dramatic gesture, but there was something in his eyes that Kyle wasn't faking. A look of genuine fear. 'Can I come in?'

For a moment Danny didn't move. Then, after a few seconds, he reluctantly stepped aside. 'If you have to,' he said.

Kyle entered the flat and walked unsteadily up the hallway and into the front room. He stood in the doorway for a moment, then looked back at Danny. 'Didn't know you had a fuck buddy,' he said.

'Call her that again, Kyle, and you'll need someone to fix the other side of your face.' Danny pushed past him and answered Clara's questioning look with a single word: 'Brother.' He'd warned Clara about Kyle.

'Pleased to meet you,' Clara said in a small voice from her place on the sofa. Kyle didn't reply. He and Danny stood opposite each other, a couple of metres apart.

'Tried calling,' Kyle said. 'But you didn't pick up, as usual.'

Danny's personal mobile phone was lying powered off on the floor by the sofa.

'Some of us have jobs to go to,' Danny said.

'What was it today, running up hills with rocks on your back? Laser Quest with your knucklehead friends?'

'Something like that. Better than staying home with a bottle of Scotch. You're rat-arsed, Kyle. What the hell do you want?'

'Got a bit of a s. . . s. . . situation,' his brother said. He had suddenly affected a casual air, but still had to have three goes at saying the word 'situation'. 'You know, business-wise.'

Danny almost laughed. The only business Kyle ever had was with the guy behind the counter at the discount booze store.

'Got a bit of a hitch in the supply chain,' Kyle continued. 'Nothing serious. Just need a bit of muscle to sort it out. Thought I'd give you first refusal on the job, seeing as that's your game. You know, muscle . . .'

'Seriously, Kyle, what the *fuck* are you talking about? Who did that to your face?'

'Well, are you interested, or *not?*' Kyle had suddenly turned aggressive, but Danny could hear the hint of panic in his voice. He caught his brother's glance again, and only then did he notice it: it was bright in the room, but Kyle's pupils were large. Dilated. Danny felt his contempt for his brother double. Not only drunk, but high.

'What is it?' he asked quietly. 'Ketamine? MDMA? You've got a nice little cocktail going, by the look and smell of you. I thought you were clean of that shit.'

Kyle was in the corner of the room now, diagonal to the door. A trapped animal. His dilated eyes darted around. In an instant, his demeanour had changed yet again. Defensive. 'I'm not here for a lecture,' he breathed. 'Specially not from *you.*'

'Then what *are* you here for?' He paused. 'Money?'

The word 'money' caught Kyle's attention, but only for a moment. He screwed up his face, as though he were suppressing some violent emotion. 'It's not my fault, okay?' he muttered, almost as though he was talking to himself. 'It's not my fucking *fault.*'

'Danny,' Clara said quietly. 'He needs help. He's been using.'

'Of *course* he's been using.' Danny fronted up to his brother. 'Spit it out,' he whispered.

Kyle's face was a picture of conflict. 'They should know this kind of thing happens all the time.'

'*Who* should know?'

'The Poles.'

'Which Poles, Kyle?'

'What do you mean, *which* Poles? The ones who run Hereford.'

Danny nodded. He understood what Kyle was talking about. Every town had its drug problems, and Hereford was worse than most. He'd heard the rumours that a Polish crew was flooding the street with everything from cannabis to heroin. The needle-exchange programmes had never been so busy. Hardly surprising that Kyle had fallen in – or should that be fallen out – with them.

'So what exactly *has* happened?'

'They lost some product.'

'*They* lost some product. Or *you* lost it for them?'

Kyle's face twisted again. 'Some bastard junkie stole it from me!' he exploded. 'I told the Poles. I *told* them it wasn't my fault, but they still want their money. But I'm not paying them. You can go and put the shits up them, get them off my back. It's what you're good at, isn't it?'

Silence in the room. Danny stared at his brother. He was family, sure, but Danny felt nothing but contempt for him. If he was in a mess, it was of his own making. Danny had stopped taking responsibility for Kyle a long time ago.

'Get out,' he said.

A pause.

'I'm not going anywhere,' Kyle breathed. His hands were shaking slightly. He looked pathetic.

'I said, get out.'

'What are you going to do about it, little brother?' Kyle's voice had gone a little higher. 'Play your hard-man macho bullshit? Beat up your own brother? Shoot me with one of your big fucking guns? What would Daddy say? Or Uncle Taff? He's been off the scene for a while. Maybe he doesn't love you any more?' Kyle laughed at his own joke, but the laughter descended into a wheezing cough.

Danny turned to Clara. 'Make sure he doesn't steal anything,' he said.

'Shouldn't you call the police?' she whispered.

But calling the police would mean a barrage of questions. Their dad might even be dragged into it, and Danny didn't want that.

'Just watch him,' he said.

Danny left the front room and walked along the hallway to the one double bedroom at the back of the flat. It was bare – almost spartan. Plain white walls and a built-in cupboard along one side. 'Like a cell in a psychiatric ward,' Clara had joked first time she saw it. Danny opened the cupboard and shifted some shoe boxes off the floor before peeling up a rectangle of old carpet and removing the loose floorboard that it covered.

A chilly draught wafted up from underneath the floor, and a smell of damp. Danny buried his hand into the cavity and his fingers made contact with a dusty old shoe box. He grabbed it, and pulled it up to floor level. His fingers smeared the dust as he opened the box.

There were bank notes inside. A mixture of sterling and American dollars. Out in Afghanistan, there had been money swilling around. Some of it, the guys had been given float money for when they were out on ops. A lot had been confiscated from militants out in the field. The guys had handed a proportion of it back to the ruperts, but they'd kept a far greater chunk and smuggled it back to the UK, where they'd distributed it among the rest of the squadron. A nice little backhander that everyone at Credenhill knew about and which nobody would admit to. The lads in the Regiment risked their lives for a pittance. Nobody begrudged them a little private income on the side.

There was about two and a half grand in here. In a corner of Danny's mind he'd been setting it aside against the day when he and Clara moved in together. Not that he'd ever mentioned it to her. Until that time, it was just fine where it was. Untouched, except for now. He removed a crumpled fifty-pound note, replaced the box in its hiding place and strode back to the front room. Kyle was still in the far corner. He'd grown paler, and there was a thin mist of sweat on his forehead. Danny held up the note like a guy trying to catch the attention of a barmaid. Kyle took what looked like an involuntary step forward. His bruised face actively twitched.

'Danny,' Clara breathed. 'He needs *help*.'

'He needs to get out of here,' Danny replied. He turned, walked to the front door and opened it. Seconds later, Kyle was there. He stepped over the threshold, then eagerly took the note Danny brandished under his nose.

'If I hear you've been touching Dad up for money,' he said, his voice dangerously quiet, 'I *will* call the police. And when they've finished, *I'll* get to work on you. Understood?'

Kyle pocketed the money, then wiped a drop of mucus from his nose with the back of his hand. 'Twat,' he said.

Danny didn't react. He just watched Kyle disappear into the rain before slamming the door closed. He stalked back to the front room where Clara hadn't moved. 'Don't say it,' he scowled at his girlfriend.

There was an uncomfortable silence while Danny peered through the curtains to check that Kyle wasn't still lurking somewhere outside.

'Will they really hurt him?' Clara asked in a small voice. 'The Poles, I mean?'

Danny let the curtains fall shut. 'Probably,' he muttered.

'And you're okay with that?' she said. 'He's your brother, after all.'

'Yeah,' Danny said. 'I'm okay with that.'

And that might have been the end of the conversation, had Clara not given him a look that made Danny feel as if he was the most heartless bastard she'd ever met. 'I've done everything I can for him, Clara. I've dug him out of more holes than I can count. If I can't stop him screwing his life up, maybe these Poles will knock some sense into him.'

And that really was the end of the conversation. 'I'm hitting the sack,' Danny said. 'I've got an early start tomorrow, and a lot to do.'

He turned his back on Clara and marched back to the bedroom. He kicked off his clothes and noticed a smear of blood just above his left wrist, from shooting the guy in the mouth. He didn't even bother to wipe it off before collapsing into bed. He closed his eyes, then heard Clara stepping into the room.

'Why are you really moving to London?' she asked quietly.

'I told you,' Danny replied. 'General security.'

'Is it dangerous, this "general security"?'

Danny sighed. 'The extremists have had their fun, Clara. Atrocities like this come in ones. Look at 9/11. 7/7. They've stuck their heads above the parapets. Now they'll be scurrying back down the holes they came from. Trust me.'

He rolled over and closed his eyes again. Seconds later, he was asleep.

FOUR

Sarim had never felt so nervous. Even before he and Jamal had detonated the Paddington bomb, he hadn't been suffering palpitations like this. He hadn't had this sensation of cold dread flowing through his lungs. Abu Ra'id could do that to you.

He coughed politely. Anxiously. 'Ex. . . excuse me, *ustath*. He is ready.'

Abu Ra'id had his back turned. He was broad-shouldered and seemed too big for this room, even though the room itself was spacious. The furnishings were ultra-modern: gleaming white sofas, an enormous plasma screen against the far wall, colourful abstract art on the walls. In the corner there was a bar area, with a line of spirits on a glass shelf along the wall – untouched, of course, by the current occupant of this extravagantly luxurious apartment. On a glass table was a collection of framed pictures. They showed a Middle Eastern family in traditional dress – a man with a very crooked nose, a woman and three children. Sarim wondered who they were – the owners of the apartment, perhaps – but didn't dare ask.

Two sides of the room were taken up by floor-to-ceiling windows, but these were covered up by internal electric blinds. Sarim understood why. From this penthouse apartment, more than two hundred metres high and in the heart of the Docklands, you could see for miles across the London skyline. But a gleaming glass tower like this required constant cleaning, and should the window cleaner in his ascending cradle happen to see inside, there was no chance he wouldn't recognise Abu Ra'id, whose face had peered out of every newspaper in the past few days.

Abu Ra'id was not using any of the expensive lamps dotted around the room to light up the early morning darkness. Instead, a single candle burned on a low cabinet. It made the cleric's shadow flicker against the wall as he walked over to a small sink behind the bar area. He washed his hands very carefully, and dried them on a white towel hung on a chrome bar to his left. Only then did he turn round.

He was, Sarim had always thought, a good-looking man. The pictures of him in the papers never did him justice. True, he wore the line of a permanent frown, but he looked much better than he ever did in print or on TV. The newspapers always tried to make him look as crazy as possible. In fact he looked anything but. Calm. Collected. Beneath the black beard that reached down to his chest, Abu Ra'id's cheekbones were pronounced and his nose in perfect proportion. And when he smiled, he had a way of making you think that nobody else in the world mattered to him at that moment.

Abu Ra'id smiled now. 'I don't know what I'd do without you, Sarim. You are like a son to me.'

'I owe everything to *you*, *ustath*.'

Abu Ra'id stepped over to the centre of the room where his prayer mat was unfurled on the floor. He had obviously just finished praying and had washed his hands, because to desecrate a prayer mat was a sin. He rolled it up carefully, then placed it on the cabinet next to the candle.

Sarim had no idea who paid for this apartment. He was sure it had to be just about the most expensive place to live in London, and a far cry from his own shoddy ground-floor flat in Hammersmith, or even Abu Ra'id's large home in North Ealing where he had lived up until the day before the Paddington bomb, and where his wife still did. And he had no idea why the cleric was so convinced that this Docklands penthouse was safe, although he *had* noticed that the concierge was of Middle Eastern origin, so perhaps he was one of them. But Sarim trusted Abu Ra'id without question. He was more than simply his imam. He was, as Sarim had called him, his *ustath* – his teacher. And so he just accepted what he was told. He accepted that Abu Ra'id must live in these luxurious surroundings, while he must live in near poverty on the other side of London. And he accepted that nobody would find them here. They were perfectly secure.

The cleric turned towards Sarim again. He wore a plain white *dishdash*, spotlessly clean. 'He has prayed?' he asked. Although Abu Ra'id's features were Middle Eastern, his accent was English.

'Yes, Abu Ra'id.'

'And washed his hands and feet?'

Sarim nodded.

'And how does he seem? In himself?'

'Scared, Abu Ra'id, if I'm honest.'

'Ah,' the cleric said sadly. 'That's to be expected. But it is us, Sarim, us who live in the lands of the infidel and wage our war against them, who have more reason to be fearful. Shall we join him?'

Sarim nodded. He opened the door and held it open for the cleric, blinking as his eyes grew accustomed to the bright light in the corridor outside. As he passed Abu Ra'id stopped, tenderly put one hand behind Sarim's head, and gently stroked his hair. Then Sarim followed him along the corridor and into the dining room of this extravagant flat.

They had chosen this room because it was the largest and because the floors were tiled. The floor-to-ceiling windows took up only one side of this room. These too were covered with their blackout blinds, but they also had black sheets draped over them. Against one end, Sarim had personally hung a white drape, about five metres by five, with the Arabic symbol for God painted on it in black. In front of the drape was a large piece of plastic sheeting, folded double, as wide as the room and three metres deep. On the sheeting was a stool. Facing this little stage, at a distance of six metres and next to the dining table which they had moved away from the centre of the room, was a video camera fitted to a tripod. It was angled upwards so that it could get the drape and the stool fully in frame. And behind the camera, lighting up the scene, was a bright spotlight, illuminating everything. Jamal stood behind the camera, fiddling with the controls, ensuring everything was working. He looked as anxious as Sarim felt, and couldn't take his eyes from Abu Ra'id now he had entered the room.

'Fetch him,' Abu Ra'id told Jamal.

Jamal nodded. He left the room. Sarim stood awkwardly by the stool, not knowing what, if anything, he should say to Abu Ra'id. The cleric broke the silence first. 'You have done well, Sarim,' he said.

Sarim felt himself almost shiver with pride. That was the thing about Abu Ra'id. Everybody was scared of him when he wasn't around, but a simple word of encouragement like that would make you feel ten feet tall.

'Jamal is nervous,' the cleric continued. 'More nervous than you. I sense it.'

'Because of the bombing, *ustath*,' Sarim explained. 'He doesn't want to be caught, and thrown into a British jail.'

'He does not believe me when I tell him he is safe?'

'I think he *believes* you, Abu Ra'id. It's just . . .'

'Faith is difficult sometimes,' the cleric observed. 'But without it, we are nothing. And you and Jamal must know that I would not risk your safety for anything.'

The door opened. Jamal re-entered, and behind him a young man whom Sarim knew to be only 16 years old. He was gangly, with a hooked nose, a protruding Adam's apple and thin arms. His cheeks were covered in soft, downy facial hair that he had clearly never shaved. He wore a black *dishdash*, and an expression of hopeless terror. His eyes looked sore from crying and lack of sleep.

'Karim,' Abu Ra'id said quietly. 'You are ready?'

Karim didn't answer. His eyes darted around the room. Jamal stepped behind him, closed the door, and then locked it with a key that he dropped back into his pocket.

'Are you ready?' Abu Ra'id insisted.

'I . . . I have a question,' Karim said. His voice shook.

'Then please ask it.' There was a dangerous edge to his voice. Sarim wondered if the kid had picked up on it.

Karim licked his dry lips. 'You said . . . You said that this was the greatest of all honours.'

'And so it is,' Abu Ra'id nodded.

'Then why . . .'

The kid stumbled over his words. He looked like he *wanted* to speak but his tongue was frozen.

Abu Ra'id didn't take his eyes off him. They were suddenly cold and cruel.

'Why *what*, my son?' His voice was level.

Karim was shaking uncontrollably, clearly torn between his need to ask the question and his fear of Abu Ra'id.

'Why . . .'

He closed his eyes, bowed his head and took a deep breath.

'Forgive me, Abu Ra'id, but why don't you want to do it yourself?'

There was a sudden silence in the room. Sarim was shocked that Karim had even dared to ask this question, but Abu Ra'id's face showed no expression. For a moment, the cleric didn't even move. But then he stepped towards the teenager, extended both arms and placed his hands on the kid's shoulders. Sarim saw his fingers massaging Karim's muscles. 'Believe me, my young friend,' he whispered in a scarcely audible voice, 'I would do it in an instant. But God has told me that it is not my time.'

Abu Ra'id lowered his arms and nodded at Sarim, who

approached the young boy and took him gently by the arm. 'Come and sit,' he said.

The kid was shaking now. Gulping short gasps of breath. 'I ... I don't think it's *my* time either,' he said. His voice wavered. 'I've changed my mind ... I don't want to do it ...'

'Karim!' Abu Ra'id said sharply. 'Do not forget yourself. When you came to me you had nothing. No family. No God. I have been like your father. Sarim and Jamal have been your brothers. Together we have shown you the path. Will you cast all that back in our faces now?'

The teenager appeared unable to speak. Jamal had to force him towards the plastic sheeting. His eyes were drawn to the Arabic symbol draped behind the stool.

'Sit,' Sarim repeated, a bit firmer this time.

The kid's knees buckled as he walked up to the stool and sat down. His eyes were closed now, and he was muttering to himself. Tears stained his cheeks. Sarim sensed his tension. He knew that the kid would try to bolt, if fear hadn't drained all the energy from his limbs.

'Let us prepare ourselves,' Abu Ra'id said. From the table, he removed a plastic bag and a long wooden box. He handed the plastic bag to Sarim, who removed from it two black balaclavas, one for him, one for Jamal. They donned their masks. The scratchy wool irritated Sarim's skin and he bizarrely remembered that he had not yet moisturised, as he did every day. He rubbed his palms against his face to relieve the itching, then took his place to Karim's right. Jamal stood on his left.

Abu Ra'id was behind the camera, holding the wooden box. He opened it with a certain ceremony to reveal a long, bone-handled knife. The blade was seven inches long and Sarim knew it to be viciously sharp. Abu Ra'id stepped towards Karim and offered him the box. With trembling fingers Karim removed the knife, grasping the ornate bone handle lightly. He stared at the blade as Abu Ra'id retreated behind the camera again.

'You know what to say?' Abu Ra'id asked. His voice was calm and kind again.

Karim nodded. He couldn't take his eyes off the blade. Abu Ra'id looked meaningfully at Sarim. A look that said: *Be careful, my son.*

'I shall start the camera now,' said the cleric. 'You understand, Karim, that you must be the only one to speak?' He bent down, pressed a button, and then nodded.

Karim licked his lips again. His voice cracked slightly as he started talking, but now the camera was rolling, Sarim had the impression he did not want to appear cowardly. But his words were quiet and stilted. A child, reciting his lines by rote.

'My name is Karim Dahlamal. I was born in Hatfield. My parents are Raniyah and Yussuf Dahlamal. They will not understand what I am about to do. They do not understand the world.'

He wavered slightly on the stool. For a moment Sarim thought he was going to fall, but he kept his balance, raised his head again and continued to speak.

'Four days ago, my friends struck a glorious blow in the holy Jihad.' He looked left and right to the masked figures of Sarim and Jamal. 'It is the first of many. We will not stop until the sins of the infidel are washed clean by their own blood.'

He paused again and breathed deeply.

'The bombs will continue until all your sons and daughters have died. You think you can stop us, but I tell you that you cannot. Because unlike you, we are willing to die. We welcome death. We embrace it.'

Another pause. And then, in scarcely a whisper: '*I* embrace it.'

Karim's eyes were wide, now, and more than a little wild. He raised the knife to his throat. It wavered in his trembling hand. Abu Ra'id said nothing, but gave a slow, encouraging nod from behind the camera.

The blade touched Karim's Adam's apple. As soon as it made

contact, a trickle of blood seeped down his throat and collected at the hem of the *dishdash*. But then he moved his trembling hand away again. Sarim saw a dab of blood on the knife. He looked over at Abu Ra'id whose face was, for a moment, expressionless. But then the cleric's eyes narrowed. He looked directly at Sarim and nodded sharply.

Sarim understood what he meant.

If the teenager couldn't do it by himself, he would need some help.

Sarim grabbed the hand with which Karim held the knife. The teenager panicked. He tried to throw himself off the stool, but Jamal had already gripped his left arm and held him fast. Sarim forced the blade towards the kid's throat. Karim leaned back and tried to push Sarim's arm away. But Sarim was the stronger of the two, and the blade eased inexorably towards the already bleeding throat.

The scream, when it finally came, was ear-piercing. Karim roared for his mother. 'Mum! *Mum! Help me! I don't mean it! I don't want to do it! I DON'T WANT TO DO IT!'* At the same time, a foul smell wafted towards Sarim's nose, and he heard urine dripping on to the plastic sheeting. Sarim felt himself sneer under his balaclava and found that, all of a sudden, his fear had turned to anger. He wanted to dispatch this cowardly, so-called jihadi – as much for pissing near him as for anything else. He strained harder to get the knife to Karim's throat, but as he did so, the kid fell backwards off the stool.

Sarim fell heavily to the floor with him, as did Jamal. The stool toppled. To Sarim's revulsion, he felt moisture on his skin as the kid's urine ran along the sheet and soaked his trouser leg. The camera was still filming, but he couldn't help that. With his free hand he grabbed Karim's hair and yanked the head back. His other hand was still wrapped around Karim's. He gripped it tighter and, with one final effort, forced the blade back down onto the fleshy part at the side of the kid's throat.

The blade was sharp enough that he didn't have to swipe. It slid easily into the skin and didn't stop until it was a good inch into the flesh. Karim eyes widened with shock, and he opened his mouth to scream. But no sound came.

Only blood.

Sarim realised he must have cut an artery. The blood didn't merely seep out of Karim's throat. It pumped out, with the sturdy regularity of a heartbeat. There was so much of it. Sarim hadn't expected such a quantity. It washed over his hand and gushed on to the plastic sheeting, which became slippery with the mixture of fluids. Karim's body writhed, his limbs flailed. Sarim kept the pressure on, pushing even harder so that the knife remained embedded in the throat. Karim's body slid over the sheeting. His hands flapped against puddles of blood, which spattered over Sarim's balaclava. Sarim was reminded of a fish flapping on the side of a river bank.

It seemed to take a long time for Karim to die, though in reality it was probably less than a minute. A grotesque gurgling came from his throat, like the noise a child makes when he's sucking up the last drops of lemonade through a straw. The flailing limbs fell still. Sarim realised he was out of breath from his exertions. He let go of the knife, leaving the blade embedded in his victim's throat, then stood up.

Jamal was standing on the other side of the sheeting, staring at Sarim. Only his eyes were visible through the balaclava, but they were full of fear. Abu Ra'id was still behind the camera. His arms were folded and he was quite expressionless, as though he were watching something boring on TV. 'Please,' he said. 'Move him in front of the stool.'

Sarim nodded at Jamal, who walked over towards him. Silently, they bent over and each of them took one of the dead boy's legs. They dragged him across the sheeting, leaving a line of blood in his wake, until he was centre stage. Jamal picked up the stool and placed it back in its upright position. Instinctively, the two masked men stood on either side of the corpse, their arms folded like Abu Ra'id's.

They remained like that for about 30 seconds. Then the cleric leaned over the camera and switched it off.

'*Allahu Akbar*,' he announced.

'*Allahu Akbar*,' Sarim and Jamal replied in response.

'I did not expect him to be so weak when the moment came,' Abu Ra'id said.

Sarim swallowed hard. Now it was over, he found that he was shaking. He was aware that blood was still seeping from the dead body, but he couldn't bring himself to look at it. He felt nauseous – not that he would ever admit this to Jamal or the cleric. He told himself that it was the smell of Karim's piss that was making him feel sick, but he knew deep down that this wasn't true. Sacrificing someone with a bomb was easy. You didn't have to *be* there. You didn't have to witness the grisly reality of what you were doing. Sacrificing someone with a knife was different.

But then he looked back at Abu Ra'id, whose peaceful expression calmed him. Abu Ra'id, who had first set him on this path. Abu Ra'id, who promised him glory that members of Al-Qaeda or Al-Shabaab could only dream of. Abu Ra'id, who had first explained to him, as they sat together in the mosque after evening prayers, the pleasures awaiting him in paradise if he waged the holy Jihad in *this* world.

Those thoughts consoled him. Sustained him.

'Jamal,' said Abu Ra'id. 'Will you please prepare the footage?'

Jamal nodded. He stepped over to the camera and removed it from the tripod. Jamal was good with computers. Soon he would have cut their little home movie together. Abu Ra'id had made it clear that he wanted it distributed that very day.

'And Sarim. It will be your job to dispose of the body of this excellent martyr, who at this moment is looking down on us with gratitude. There is acid in the bathroom. Please make sure you clean up after you.'

'Yes, Abu Ra'id.'

And as Jamal and the cleric left the room he started about his next task, rolling up the surprisingly heavy body of young Karim in the plastic sheeting, then folding up the ends of the resulting tube like gift wrap. Breathless, he stood up.

He was still wearing the balaclava, and his skin was sweating and itchy underneath it. He walked over to the cabinet from which Abu Ra'id had taken the knife. There was an old mirror above it, misty with age. Sarim stood in front of the mirror and slowly peeled off the balaclava. He stared at himself. *I look different*, he thought to himself. *I have grown up in the last ten minutes. I have become closer to God.*

God.

He looked over at the sheet draped at the end of the room, with its Arabic symbol. Then he looked at his right hand. Karim's blood was still wet on his fingertips. He moved his right forefinger up to his forehead, where he smeared the same symbol, clumsily, on his skin.

He stared at himself. Bloodied. Blooded. And in a little corner of his mind, he imagined seeing his face on computer screens and newspapers around the world. *The face of terror*, they would call it. Western soldiers would hunt the world for him. But away from the lands of the infidel, he would be a hero. Admired and loved by all.

But every hero has to start somewhere. Sarim tore his attention away from the mirror, stepped back to the rolled-up sheeting, and continued his transition from killer to undertaker. It was clever of Abu Rai'd to think of putting down the plastic, he thought. It made it much easier to clear up the mess.

FIVE

Tuesday, 08.00hrs

The rotor blades of the Regiment's Augusta Westland were already turning on the Regiment helipad as Danny and Spud ran towards it through the early morning drizzle, wearing civvies but with their heavy Bergens slung over their shoulder. The headsetted pilot gave them a thumbs-up as they secured themselves in the aircraft. Seconds later, they were airborne. Time to target, 45 minutes plus.

There was something disorientating about heading back in to London just hours after they'd left it. Danny stared down at the green patchwork of fields below them. His usual view from a helicopter was the gold and browns of desert terrain, which seemed somehow better suited to the business of war. Neither he nor Spud spoke. The events of the previous night kept spinning through Danny's mind, but there was something else too. Danny was on edge about the prospect of seeing Hugo Buckingham again. It wasn't just that he hated the bastard. Somewhere deep down, Danny realised, he associated the MI6 man with his last major op in Syria and all the terrible things that had happened there. Images of that time flashed into his head. Burning buildings. Dead-eyed mercenaries. An old friend, bleeding to death . . .

What was it Clara kept saying to him? *Danny, you have to stop remembering the things you want to forget.*

Danny and Spud almost never talked about that operation,

but Syria had also been a very dark time for Spud. Maybe he was thinking back to those devastating few days too. Or maybe he was just too tired for his usual flow of wisecracks. Whatever the truth, the journey passed silently.

It took 40 minutes for the outskirts of London to come into view. The chopper followed the line of the Thames, winding into the city past the sights that looked familiar even from the air: Battersea power station, Parliament Square, the MI6 building. Between the Millennium and Southwark bridges, the chopper veered to the left, heading north-east over St Paul's and the Barbican. Moments later, the wide green open space of the Artillery Garden behind the Honourable Artillery Company came into view. Even from a height, Danny could tell how neatly manicured it was, laid out with the perfect lines of a cricket pitch, even though nobody would be playing cricket in this constant autumnal rain. The pitch had been turned into a landing zone surrounded by the high buildings of the city. It had clearly been given over to the security services: Danny's eyes picked out five police cars and a number of other unmarked vehicles, as well as police officers and military guys in camouflage gear. A small, open-air operations base in the beating heart of London.

The chopper had barely touched down before Danny and Spud disembarked with their gear and ran from the downdraft towards a soldier with a red beret standing by a black Land Rover Discovery.

'Hereford?' he asked as they approached.

Danny and Spud nodded.

'Heads down,' he said. 'We've got some cunt from the press sniffing around. MoD gave him access, fuck knows why . . .'

Instantly, Danny and Spud turned their backs on the northern end of the LZ where everyone else was milling around. The soldier handed each of them a set of keys, and they climbed behind the camouflage of the Discovery's tinted windows. Spud took the wheel, and followed the gesture of the soldier who pointed them across the LZ towards the exit, which was manned by two more soldiers. Moments later they were heading down City Road towards the river.

Danny punched a postcode into the vehicle's satnav that would take them to their safe house, then quickly checked through the glove box of the Discovery. Here he found the vehicle's radio, hardwired in, and a magnetic siren that could be thrown on to the top of the vehicle if Danny and Spud needed to cut though the traffic. These were the only modifications that distinguished the vehicle from an ordinary civilian Land Rover. With those exceptions it was anonymous from the inside and out.

At 09.55 they arrived at what was to be their digs for however long this operation lasted. The house itself was on the south side of Battersea Park, a two-storey, redbrick, Victorian end-of-terrace that to the untrained eye looked no different from any others along this street. As they stepped out of the car, however, black rucksacks slung over their shoulders, Danny immediately saw the security cameras pointing down towards the front door. He wondered who was monitoring them. Five? The Firm? GCHQ? Hereford? Could be any of them. Or all of them. He made a point of looking up into the camera and winking.

He opened up the envelope Cartwright had given him the night before. Among the contents were two house keys – one for each of them – and a six-digit alarm code. Danny gave Spud his key and unlocked the door. A high-pitched beeping sound came from the alarm just inside. Danny punched in the code and it stopped. They quietly closed the door behind them.

Danny and Spud checked over the flat wordlessly. Spud examined the windows on the ground floor – all locked from inside – while Danny moved through to the kitchen and checked the back door. It led out on to a decked area about six metres by five, on the far side of which was a locked gate. The kitchen itself was unmodernised, with plain white units and an old oven. There was a brew kit on the side but no milk, and the fridge wasn't even on. Danny opened up a tall broom cupboard. Inside was a steel strongbox bolted to the floor. He fished inside the envelope for a third key, which opened up the safe. Inside, he found two Glock 9mm pistols – standard issue for the security services, even though the MoD had spent millions on the Regiment's preferred Sig P266 in recent years. But the composite, hammerless Glock was light, easy to conceal, and reliable enough. There was a silencer for each handgun, two covert holsters and several boxes of ammunition, which he unloaded on to the kitchen table before returning to the strongbox. There was more stuff in here: two radios, which looked like chunky mobile phones, a couple of spare batteries, and a well-thumbed spiral-bound notebook containing lists of numbers, call signs, frequencies and codes. Tucked at the back was a snap gun, almost exactly the same as the one Spud had used the night before, along with a collection of bits and a small handbook of lock makes and sizes. Also, a small method-of-entry kit, comprising a two-ounce strip of military-grade explosive, about the same size as a packet of chewing gum, a two-inch-long, pencil-thin detonator, a battery pack and a roll of coated wire. A couple of vacuum-packed SOCO kits, no bigger than a paperback book. And, weirdly, some foil-wrapped ration packs, as if they were going to need *those* in the middle of London.

Danny chucked all the gear back in the safe, locked it up again and returned to the kitchen table. He loaded each weapon, then wandered back up the hallway to find Spud. Danny's mate was standing at the bottom of the stairs. He accepted the weapon from Danny, and together they moved up to check out the top floor.

There were three bedrooms here. In two of them, the beds and furniture were covered in dust sheets. The third bedroom contained two single beds. 'Hope you don't snore,' Spud muttered. He plonked himself down on one of the beds. The springs squeaked. 'When I pull,' he said ungraciously, 'you get the couch.' But they both knew there wouldn't be much time for pulling.

Danny checked the time: 11.03hrs. They were expected at Paddington Green police station at midday. He stowed his Glock under his jacket and walked out of the room. 'Let's get moving,' he said over his shoulder.

The traffic around Paddington was a disaster. Half the streets had been cordoned off, and the police presence was higher than Danny had ever seen it in the UK. Even though it was four days since the bomb, an unpleasant burning smell lingered in the air. The railway station itself was closed, of course – as it would be for months – but having dumped the car and continued towards the police station on foot, they were given a sharp reminder of the sheer magnitude of the device when they saw shop windows more than 200 metres from the station boarded up: the shock waves had shattered them.

'Bet it was like a fucking butcher's shop in there,' Spud muttered as they caught a glimpse of the station through a side street 100 metres to the south. He sounded as sombre as Danny felt. Sure, he'd witnessed destruction like this in other parts of the world, but there was something about seeing it on your home turf.

As they passed a junction, a BMW X5 waiting at a red light caught Danny's eye. Something about it looked different, and Danny instantly realised that it was the slightly darker-than-usual tint of the windows. Bullet resistant. He found himself checking out the occupants. Four guys, all in their twenties or thirties. Two of them in black T-shirts, one in a leather jacket, one in dark Gore-Tex. Armed police conducting covert surveillance. No question. To confirm his suspicions, Danny zoned in on the grate at the front of the car. He could just make out the police lights hiding out of view.

Spud gave Danny a look that suggested he'd clocked the unit too, but the X5 went totally unnoticed by the other members of the public who hurried past them. Amazing what you don't see, Danny thought, when you don't look.

There were uglier buildings in London than Paddington Green police station, but not many. It was a bleak concrete block on the north side of the Westway flyover, with a raised upper level surrounded by security bars that looked more like a World War Two observation tower than a modern police building. Danny was no stranger to this place. In one sense it was just an ordinary police station serving this area of north-west London. But the sixteen secure underground cells meant it was the first port of call for any high-profile criminal or terrorist suspect. Only a few weeks ago, Danny had been called on to escort a police unit moving a Chechen bomb-maker from here to the Old Bailey.

They didn't enter the building. Not yet. Instead, they loitered by a post box on the other side of the road while Danny pulled his encrypted mobile phone and dialled a number that he'd already pre-programmed. A voice answered immediately. 'Paddington police station.'

'Do us a favour, mate,' Danny said. 'Tell DI Fletcher that his special package is ready for collection.' He hung up immediately.

They didn't have to wait more than a couple of minutes. A fresh-faced duty sergeant who looked like he was barely out of school appeared at the main entrance of the police station. He stood for a moment, looked round, and finally clocked them. Once he'd nodded in their direction, Danny and Spud crossed the road and wordlessly followed him into the station. The officer led them down into the basement, through two sets of locked doors and into a small office at the end of an antiseptic corridor. A middle-aged man with a greying moustache sat behind a desk. He had a friendly, open face, but a tired one. It occurred to Danny that there was no more thankless task than being a copper in London right now. The officer wore civvies – a slightly crumpled suit and tie, top button of his shirt undone – and had a pile of papers in front of him a good 30 centimetres high, which he was signing with a ballpoint pen. Along the side wall was a bank of 16 screens, each of them showing the inside of a cell. All but two were occupied. Without exception, the prisoners were stretched out on their single beds, staring at their TVs.

'I've been in Holiday Inn rooms worse than that,' Spud said as the office door closed behind them.

The police officer looked up as if he'd only just noticed the new arrivals. He stood up, walked over to them and tapped on one of the screens. 'See this one?' The officer had a soft West Country accent. 'Picked up at the Port of Dover trying to cross over to France. Seems he's the one behind that beheading video that went viral on Facebook.'

'Trouble with blokes like that,' Spud cut in, 'is they've always got an axe to grind.'

'They'll have him extradited by the end of the week, shouldn't wonder,' the officer continued. 'Don't suppose he'll find it quite so comfy in one of them American prisons. We've got it all wrong, if you ask me. Have a bit of fisticuffs with your mates after a couple of pints, we'll have you cooling down in a bare cell quick as lightning. Try to blow up a plane, we have to give you a telly to watch while you're in custody in case your lawyers accuse us of being inhumane. Lack of stimulation breaches their human rights, least that's what they say.'

'Just give me the word,' Danny said with a twinkle in his eye, 'I'll go keep him company.'

'Now *that*,' said the officer, 'I would like to see.' He chuckled and held out his hand. 'Frank Fletcher,' he said. 'I'll be your police liaison. Anything you need – always a pleasure to work with gentlemen from the Regiment.'

They shook hands, then Fletcher returned to his desk. He

shifted some papers around as if looking for something, then grimaced. 'Paperwork,' he said. 'Bane of my life. Especially now. They cut our numbers after the bankers ripped us all off, now they're complaining we don't have enough of us to police the streets. We've cancelled all leave and put every single man and woman we have on the pavement. Not just the Met, of course. Every other major city's on high alert – Birmingham, Bristol, Cardiff, Manchester, Glasgow . . . Bad week to be a copper. Don't make a blind bit of difference, of course. I mean, if someone's going to blow up a train station, they're going to blow up a train station, right?'

'Right,' said Danny and Spud in unison. They were well used to police officers having a moan about the job. Best thing was to let them get it off their chest early, otherwise they'd be whingeing all day long.

'And in the meantime,' Fletcher continued, rummaging through his in-tray, 'all the everyday stuff goes uninvestigated. There's a young lady up off Praed Street, had an intruder on Saturday night, and we don't even have the manpower to send round a fingerprint team.' He picked up the report on his desk that he'd been signing as Danny and Spud had entered. 'And this poor fella, a Professor Gengerov, lectures at one of them universities up Bloomsbury way, cycling to work last Friday just as he has done every day for the last twenty years, some idiot knocks him off his bike and kills him stone dead. We haven't even collected the witness statements yet.'

Danny looked at his watch, and Fletcher took the hint. 'Sorry, gentlemen. Listen to me banging on, no wonder this stuff is piling up.' He did a little more rummaging. 'Ah, here we are!'

He held up two laminated documents, each the size of a credit card. Danny and Spud stepped forward to accept them. Danny looked at his card. It had a year-old passport photo of him in civvies, a nine-digit identity number and a barcode. The card was made out in the false name of Mike Banfield. 'SIS identification cards,' Fletcher said. 'Should get you past most of my lads, if the situation requires it.' He located a couple of brown A4 envelopes and handed them over. Danny looked inside his: a wad of £20 notes. 'A thousand each,' Fletcher said, 'as a float. They're sorting out company credit cards in the right names, but it always takes a few days.' He looked a bit embarrassed. 'They'll want receipts, gentlemen. Bloody ridiculous if you ask me, but you know the drill.' He picked up a set of keys from his desk. 'Shall I drive? Probably best, we'll get out of the area quicker in a police car.'

Danny and Spud exchanged a glance as they tucked their brown envelopes into their jackets. 'Drive where?' Danny asked. 'I thought the RV was supposed to be here.'

Fletcher looked surprised. 'No,' he said. 'Too high-risk for the great and the good in our little police station just at the moment. My instructions are to drive you out of town.'

'Where to?' Spud asked.

It looked almost as if Fletcher was trying to avoid eye contact. He moved from behind his desk.

'Hammerstone,' he said. 'Shall we go?'

Fletcher's police vehicle sliced through the chaos around Paddington just as he'd said it would, the windscreen wipers flapping furiously against the rain. Within minutes they were heading down the Westway.

'Ever been to Hammerstone?' Fletcher asked as he pulled on to the M25.

'Never heard of it, pal,' Spud said from the front passenger seat.

'Lovely place. Georgian, I think. Kings and queens stayed in it, back in the day. I suppose that's why these government types like it. Makes them feel at home.' Fletcher's moustache twitched with laughter at his own joke, then he glanced in the rear-view mirror to see if Danny was joining in. He smiled briefly, then stared at his nails. There was, he noticed, a stubborn smear of blood underneath his left thumbnail despite the hot shower he'd had in Hereford that morning. He picked it away then looked out of the window to watch the traffic passing. He counted three military vehicles in ten minutes. Just before junction 11 there were two mobile police camera units. Ostensibly they were checking the traffic with speed guns, but it looked more like surveillance to Danny. Fletcher didn't comment.

At 13.30 they exited the M25. Fifteen minutes later they were in the heart of the Kent countryside, driving down winding lanes with thick hedgerows on either side. The car slowed down and Fletcher indicated right. They turned off the road and found themselves in front of a set of large iron gates. A brass plaque read 'Hammerstone', and on the opposite side stood an armed soldier in camouflage gear. Danny watched as he checked the registration number of the vehicle against something he'd written in a pocket-sized notebook. He gave a satisfied nod, then opened the gates and flagged the vehicle through. They drove up a long, winding, tree-lined driveway. Up ahead, they saw the house.

It was a large, austere stately home. It comprised one main house, three storeys high, flanked by two smaller wings on either side. All three buildings had an array of decorative chimney pots, and they were surrounded by substantial but somewhat over-grown formal gardens. A grey mist hung around them that wasn't just to do with the rain, and which made the scene look like an old sepia photograph. Even from a distance Danny could tell that parts of it were falling into disrepair. There was a scaffold over part of the roof, and three of the top-floor windows were boarded up. This had been an impressive building in its day, but now it was just a shadow of what it had once been.

The police car pulled up on the weed-strewn gravel outside the main entrance. There were four other cars parked here. Two of them – both black Mercedes, one with diplomatic plates

– had chauffeurs sitting behind the wheel. The third was a grey Audi TT, the fourth a BMW 5 Series. As they climbed out of the police car, Spud eyed up each of the vehicles in turn, the same way Danny had seen him eye up girls in the pubs of Hereford. 'If I had those lot,' he said, 'I'd flog 'em and retire.'

Danny grunted his agreement, but his attention was on the net curtain of a ground-floor window. He saw it twitch, then fall still.

'This way, gentlemen,' Fletcher said. They followed him up the stone stairs that led to the front door, and entered the house. They found themselves in a large, chilly entrance hall, where their footsteps echoed. There were paintings hanging crookedly on the oak-panelled walls on either side, and a frayed, discoloured rug covered the scuffed floorboards that were riddled with the markings of woodworm. It smelled of neglect. Danny felt uncomfortable in here. He was used to barrack rooms and army bases. This stuffy, decaying, fading splendour was for other people, not him.

A door on the right-hand side opened, its hinges creaking. A figure appeared in the doorway. Danny recognised those absurdly handsome, maddeningly smug features immediately.

Hugo Buckingham strode forwards, hand outstretched. All his focus was on Danny, and for the moment he didn't seem to notice Spud or Fletcher. He smiled broadly, a flash of white teeth, and held out his hand. 'Danny, old sport,' he said. 'Bloody good of you to come along. Long time no see, eh?'

Danny didn't allow any expression to cross his face. He looked down at Buckingham's outstretched hand. The spook didn't seem remotely perturbed as he allowed the hand to fall. 'You're looking bloody good, I must say.' He turned to Danny's colleague. '*Spud!*' He sounded like he was greeting his best drinking buddy. 'Recovered from your *sejour* with the old *mukhabarat*?'

Spud kept up the poker-face routine, but rolled up his sleeve. There was an angry, jagged red scar from just above his wrist to his elbow. 'Still hurts a bit in wet weather, pal,' he said in a contemptuous voice. 'You know how it is with these old war wounds. Or maybe you don't.'

Buckingham smiled blandly. 'Not really, old sport. Managed to keep everything pretty much in order. Please forgive the Downton Abbey routine. Best to be safe from prying eyes in matters like this.' There was something about the way he pretended to be an old hand that particularly grated with Danny. Buckingham looked over at their police liaison officer. 'Thank you, Fletcher,' he said, as if he was talking to the butler. 'You can wait in the car.'

Fletcher's moustache twitched with irritation, but he nodded obediently and headed back out of the house.

'Bit of a reception party next door,' Buckingham said. 'All bloody eager to meet you. Just give us a couple of minutes, would you?'

Danny shrugged, but Buckingham had already turned his back. He walked into the room and closed the door behind him. Instantly, Danny walked up to the door and put his ear to the crack. He heard voices – muffled, but just clear enough to understand.

An American man was speaking. 'Considering we're offering you the full backup of US intelligence,' he was saying, 'I would hardly say my presence here is controversial.'

'Not controversial at all, Harrison,' said a woman's voice with a slight northern accent. She sounded rather prissy, as though she was offended by something but was pretending not to be. 'Simply not strictly necessary. But that doesn't mean we aren't delighted to have you on board. I daresay the NSA will be sending you transcripts of our every conversation in any case.'

'As it happens, the NSA were unaware of Hammerstone until you first invited me here. I guess none of you ever had a game of Angry Birds in here?'

Nobody laughed at the badly judged joke. 'Well, it's good to know we have *some* secrets. Yes, Hugo? Are they here?'

'Waiting outside,' Buckingham said.

'Well, for goodness' sake show them in, will you? We haven't got all day, we do all have desks to get back to, you know.'

Danny stepped back from the door. Buckingham appeared. 'This way, lads.' He smiled at them. Danny and Spud followed him into the room.

It was large, oak-panelled like the hallway, and similarly depressing. There was an old grand piano in one corner, and a collection of sofas and chaises longues dotted round the room. A large inglenook fireplace, but no fire. Just to its left, six empty dining-room chairs set in a circle. Two chandeliers hung from the ceiling, but the scant light they gave out was barely enough to burn away the gloom that pervaded the whole room.

'Danny Black, Spud Glover, bloody good soldiers, just the men for the job,' Buckingham announced as he walked into the room. Three figures stood around the fireplace. Danny's practised eye immediately started to record their details as Buckingham made the introductions.

They were a mismatched trio: one woman, two men. The woman was short – no taller than five foot six – and in her forties. There were hints in her tired face that she was once a beauty, but those days were long gone. 'Victoria Atkinson,' Buckingham announced. 'MI5. We all –' he indicated everyone in the room, then made a show of pointing to Danny and Spud in turn '– report to Victoria.'

'Thank you very much for joining us, gentlemen,' she said in her strangely nasal, northern accent. Then she removed a tissue from up her sleeve and blew her nose. Danny could almost feel Spud's repressed sarcastic comment. This was no Stella Rimmington, for sure. She was carrying a bit of weight, and wore a strangely unfashionable floral blouse. Her hair was dyed black, but the roots were grey. She smiled at them, but couldn't hide the flustered frown on her forehead.

The suited man standing next to her had a square, craggy face with a nose that looked like it had been broken several times. His right eye bore a slight squint. He was a little older than the woman, and prematurely balding, though he had combed a lot of hair over from one side of his head to disguise it. He had a distinctly military bearing. Danny thought he recognised him. From the papers, maybe? Or perhaps he'd seen him around Hereford?

'Piers Chamberlain,' Buckingham said, and something clicked. Of *course* he knew the name. Chamberlain had been an SAS rupert back in the day. He had a bit of a reputation around Hereford for his work in Northern Ireland. Now he was in thick with Five. He was close to certain members of the royal family too, and his features were often to be seen lurking at the back of a royal photo. Danny was pretty sure he had some letters after his name, just to show how important he really was. Chamberlain winked at the two SAS lads, a strange gesture for an officer to give a soldier, and if he thought a bit of forced friendliness would bridge the gap across the ranks, he was wrong. 'Aye, aye,' Spud muttered. Bang on cue, Chamberlain's squint grew a bit worse, and for a moment there was an uncomfortable silence in the room.

The second man was younger. Late thirties, Danny reckoned. A full head of thick, blond hair, an open collar and stylish brown blazer. 'Preppy', as Clara would say. Danny would put money on him being the Yank. 'Harrison Maddox,' Buckingham said. 'CIA liaison. There were several American casualties last Friday, as you know. Harrison has been most helpful in providing us with relevant intelligence from Langley's sources.'

'It's a pleasure, gentlemen,' Maddox said in his soft American accent, very urbane. 'I know a number of boys in Delta Force who speak highly of your regiment. Met a couple of them who joined up with a few of yours to undermine a Spetznaz operation in the Middle East. Nothing but praise.'

Danny and Spud nodded a brief greeting, but said nothing.

'Right,' Victoria said briskly, 'well, I'm sure we're all very pleased to meet each other. We're also all very busy, so shall we get down to work? Please take a seat, everyone. Hugo, now we're all here, I think we should see the footage.'

Buckingham nodded. As everyone took a seat at the dining chairs to the left of the fireplace, he withdrew a laptop from a leather case and placed it on an occasional table so everyone could see it. He fired it up, then double-clicked on a desktop icon. A Quicktime video filled the screen, but it didn't play immediately.

'Not for the fainthearted, I'm afraid,' Buckingham said with a grimace. The screen showed three figures. One of them was sitting on a stool. He looked to be of Middle Eastern extraction, and young. He held a long, ornate knife in one hand. On either side of him were two other figures, wearing black balaclavas. Behind them, a drape with a black Arabic symbol.

'Why do I have a feeling I know how this movie ends?' Spud asked, and before anyone could reply: 'What does the writing say?' It looked like a 'w' followed by an 'l', with various other squiggles above them.

'It's the Arabic for "Allah",' Buckingham said. 'A very sacred symbol to the Muslim community.'

'Looks like a bird's arse,' Spud breathed.

'Of course, the Muslims have 99 names for God,' Victoria said, covering up her obvious embarrassment at Spud's comment. '*As-Salam*, the Source of Peace; *Al-Gaffar*, the Forgiver . . .'

'Who's the fourth person in the room?' Danny interrupted quietly.

Everyone looked at him sharply, then back at the screen.

'Only three people in the room, old sport,' said Buckingham. He had a sudden edge to his voice, as though Danny was embarrassing him.

Danny shook his head. 'Count the shadows,' he told them.

He was right. Each of the three figures in front of the camera cast a small, distinct shadow. But there was a larger one too, very faint and fuzzy around the edges, that seemed to encompass the other three. Danny stepped forward and traced the outlines with his forefinger.

'Ah, yes,' said Buckingham, flushing slightly. 'Well I suppose there must have been a camera operator.'

'For *goodness'* sake!' Victoria snapped. 'Why haven't our people flagged this up already?' Her irritation was clearly directed at Buckingham, who looked momentarily flustered.

'I'll have them follow it up.' He tapped the laptop screen. 'Shall I?'

'I think you'd better.'

Buckingham clicked the 'play' button.

The young man in the middle of the picture started to speak. *'My name is Karim Dahlamal. I was born in Hatfield. My parents are Raniyah and Yussuf Dahlamal. They will not understand what I am about to do. They do not understand the world.'* A pause as the kid looked nervously at the floor. *'Three days ago, my friends struck a glorious blow in the holy Jihad. It is the first of many. We will not stop until the sins of the infidel are washed clean by their own blood. The bombs will continue until all your sons and daughters have died. You think you can stop us, but I tell you that you cannot. Because unlike you we are willing to die. We welcome death. We embrace it . . . I embrace it . . .'*

With a trembling hand the kid raised his knife and put it to his throat. A trickle of blood dribbled down his Adam's apple.

'Jesus,' Danny breathed.

But then the image flickered. Suddenly the kid was stretched out on the floor. The knife was embedded in his throat and although blood was still oozing from the wound, it was clear that Karim Dahlamal had already done most of his bleeding. The plastic sheeting on the floor was covered in blood, and there was a trail leading up to the body which suggested someone had dragged the corpse to its current position. The two men in balaclavas stood on either side of the body. Danny could see that their hands were bloody. Patches of dark stickiness glistened on their clothes.

The footage stopped, frozen on that final image. Danny looked round the room. Victoria had removed her handkerchief again and had it pressed to her mouth. The CIA man Maddox had his head bowed respectfully. Chamberlain was staring straight at the screen, his squint somehow more pronounced, his jaw set. Buckingham still stood by the laptop. He hadn't looked at the images at all.

'Am I the only one who thinks that kid had a bit of help?' Danny asked.

'That's what our analysts seem to think,' Victoria said. 'Not that they've had much time to examine it. This video found its way to Al-Jazeera about three hours ago. So far we've managed to lean on them to keep it under wraps, but they're a law unto themselves and we don't know how long they'll keep mum.' She looked at Buckingham. 'I think we've seen enough.'

Buckingham obediently closed up the laptop and sat down.

'We have good reason to believe that the two men in balaclavas are the same individuals involved in the Paddington bomb. I think we can take this as fair warning that they intend to repeat the atrocity. Hugo, the pictures, please.'

From his leather case, Buckingham removed a sheaf of A4 black and white photographs, which he handed to Danny. They were enlarged CCTV images, the first four of which showed a group of three individuals walking across the concourse of, Danny assumed, Paddington station. One of them was wearing an Abercrombie and Fitch hoodie. The second wore a neatly pressed shirt, and his head was bowed. The face of the third – who was shorter than the other two – was very visible. He looked different from normal people – his eyes were a little closer together for a start – but he had a wide grin on his face.

'Who's the patsy?' Spud asked.

'A young Down's syndrome man by the name of Alfie Thorne. People with Down's syndrome have a very trusting nature, as you probably know. Our working theory is that his two companions spent some time grooming him so that he would agree to take a trip with them. You'll see that each man has a suitcase.' Sure enough, all three were pulling a case with wheels behind them. 'In later pictures, you'll observe the two companions walking separately back across the concourse, *without* their luggage. We think that their plan – successful as it turned out – was to . . .'

'. . . leave Alfie Thorne minding the cases so that nobody raised the alarm when they saw them unattended.' Danny filled in the gap for her. 'I'm guessing all three cases were stuffed full of, what, C5?'

Victoria nodded.

'And the kid?' Spud asked.

'They haven't even found any remains.' Victoria blew her nose on her tissue again.

Even Spud looked disgusted. Of course, Alfie Thorne was just one of more than a hundred fatalities, but to fit up a young Down's syndrome man like that was about as low as it got.

'I'm guessing,' Danny asked, 'that you want these two bombers taken out?' None of the spooks had said it explicitly, but the bottom line was this: the Regiment was only ever called in for the hard stuff. Danny didn't have the patience to listen to them euphemistically talking round the subject.

'One of life's enthusiasts!' Chamberlain announced with a grin. 'Not like us old farts, chained to our desks night and day. Still, not too onerous a task, I wouldn't have thought. Wouldn't mind having a crack at them myself instead of pen pushing all day.'

Danny didn't take a shine to Chamberlain, but on one level he couldn't help agreeing with him. Sometimes, in their line of work, you were called upon to do something that felt morally dubious. Nailing the two bastards involved in this atrocity wasn't going to be one of them.

'So what do we know about them?' he asked. Because identifying a target was one thing. *Finding* them, when they didn't want to be found, was quite another.

'We have their names and their addresses,' Victoria said immediately. 'In fact, unusually for such situations, we know a fair amount about them. I shouldn't expect it will take you very long to deal with them. Hugo *does* speak extremely highly of you.'

Buckingham gave them what was clearly meant to be a friendly smile. Neither Danny nor Spud reciprocated.

'Your first target is Sarim Galaid. Second generation Somali immigrant.' As Victoria spoke, Buckingham passed round another photo of a thin, dark-skinned man with sunken eyes and high cheekbones. 'His parents are peaceful, well-integrated Muslims.'

'If there *is* such a thing,' Chamberlain interrupted. 'Eh, lads?' That wink again. Danny and Spud turned their attention back to Victoria.

'*Please*, Piers,' she said under her breath. 'The parents disowned him several years ago when he started showing extremist tendencies. I mean, *really*, it must have been a *terribly* difficult thing for them to do. He was on the MI5 watch list a couple of years ago, but slipped through the net in recent months, I'm afraid. Very low profile, not considered high-risk. He lives in a one-bedroom flat in Hammersmith. We've been staying clear of the place so as not to spook him, but I wouldn't be surprised if you found a substantial amount of bomb-making equipment there.'

'Look forward to making his acquaintance,' Spud muttered.

'Target number two,' Victoria continued, as Buckingham handed round a second picture of a slightly plumper, more fresh-faced young man. 'Jamal Faroole. Born in the Quetta region of Pakistan. Previously unknown to the security services. Lives in a council block in Perivale. We've had surveillance on the block for the past twenty-four hours, however, and there's been no sign of him.'

'He's been busy,' Danny said.

'Well, quite.'

There was an uncomfortable pause. Victoria and Maddox exchanged an awkward look. 'Go ahead, Victoria,' Maddox said quietly, like he was pushing her into doing something she didn't want to do.

'Your third target,' she announced, 'might be familiar.' She clicked her fingers at Buckingham, who obediently handed her a third photograph. She held it up for everyone to see.

Spud gave a low whistle.

'Amar Al-Zain,' Victoria said. 'Otherwise known as Abu Ra'id. You probably know something of his history. But not everything. Born and brought up in the UK, attended Thames Valley University where he studied political science. Up until the age of twenty-one he lived quite the high life. A keen drinker. His flat mate chalked up a warning for cannabis possession, and we have a copy of an official warning from the university reprimanding him for bringing pornographic material into lectures.'

'*Naughty* hate cleric,' Spud muttered.

'Youthful high jinks,' Victoria said with a dismissive wave of the hand.

'But still,' Harrison Maddox cut in, 'not your standard resumé for a Bin Laden wannabe.'

'Not at all,' said Victoria. 'To the best of our knowledge he was radicalised about halfway through his university career, after which time we see a spike in extremist rhetoric around Thames Valley. He's a very persuasive speaker and attracted quite a crowd of young Muslims around him during the rest of his time at university. And has continued to do so, of course, at the Holy Shrine mosque in north-west London, among other places. All our intelligence suggests that his sympathies lie with the militant group Al-Shabaab, which as I'm sure you know recently became aligned with Al-Qaeda, though it's unclear whether he's most strongly linked with the Somali or the Yemeni branch. What does seem certain is that he's committed to the reintroduction of Sharia law and to the use of terrorism. We think his recent activities are intended as a means of getting himself further up the Al-Shabaab hierarchy.'

'Like a job application?' Danny said, incredulous.

'If you like. He's no fool, though. We can't pin a single actual *crime* on him, at least not on UK soil. He *is* wanted in Jordan on terror charges, and the British government have been trying to extradite him there for some time, only to be blocked in the courts.' She glanced at the CIA liaison officer. '*Much* to the dismay of the prime minister.'

Harrison Maddox gave a mirthless little snort. 'That's what I love about you Brits,' he said. 'You don't get even, you get mad.'

Victoria gave him a frosty look. 'Personally, Harrison, I'm extremely pleased my children can grow up in a country where the rule of law can be relied upon, and extended to all our citizens, regardless of . . .'

'Regardless of how many people they're planning to kill, Victoria? Please, spare me the passive aggression. The US has been offering to take Abu Ra'id off your hands for years now. We've all known that he has a group of disciples hanging on his every damn word. He doesn't *need* to get his hands dirty because he's got untold numbers of young extremists willing to do the work for him. Hell, we've just seen that he even wants his people to commit suicide at his command.'

'That's the problem with these bloody ragheads,' Chamberlain interrupted. 'They all think they're going to get their seventy-two virgins if their sordid little plans go tits-up.'

Both Maddox and Victoria threw Chamberlain an irritated glance. Maddox drew a deep breath. 'If you'd accepted our offer,' he told Victoria a little more mildly, 'we wouldn't *be* in this situation in the first place.'

'We are not in the habit, Harrison,' Victoria said crisply, 'of throwing people into black camps on the basis of a hunch. In this country, the legal process still *means* something.'

'Ah,' Maddox said lightly, 'the legal process.' He slowly folded his arms. 'Remind me again what it is we're here to discuss? The summary execution of three terror suspects, was it?'

Another silence. Victoria visibly bristled and Danny had the sense that she was forcing herself to calm down. She drew a deep breath, then carried on as if the interruption hadn't happened.

'Both Sarim Galaid and Jamal Faroole were students – if you want to use that word – of Abu Ra'id's at the Holy Shrine mosque. Our analysts are almost certain that he was the driving force behind the attack. We simply can't risk a repeat performance, so approval has come down from Number 10 to act pre-emptively. Unfortunately, we have been unable to locate him.'

'Why don't you ask the missus?' Spud said. 'What do they call her? The White Witch?'

'Oh, we intend to, just as soon as we get through the layers of legal protection with which she has surrounded herself.' Maddox rolled his eyes at this comment, but Victoria continued briskly. 'I think it rather unlikely, however, that she will know of his location. We've directed all our resources into looking for him, but until he puts his head above the parapet, you'll have to concentrate on the foot soldiers.' She looked from Spud to Danny. 'Are you under any doubt about what we're asking you to do?'

Danny gave her a flat look. 'You want us to hunt them down,' he said, 'and kill them.'

A pause. Victoria nodded uncertainly. 'I trust you don't have a problem with . . .' – she struggled for a word – '. . . ethics?'

Danny almost allowed himself a smile. 'Far as I'm concerned,' he said, 'that's a county near London.'

Nobody laughed. Victoria took a moment to collect her thoughts. 'One final thing,' she said. 'It's most important that these . . . these . . .' She struggled for the word.

'Hits?' Spud suggested helpfully.

'That they look like accidents,' she continued. 'There can be no sign of a struggle. No sign of interrogation, violent or otherwise.'

'You're crazy,' Danny said. 'These foot soldiers are your best lead to Abu Ra'id.'

'We have our own avenues of inquiry,' Buckingham replied sharply. 'Your job is quite simply to eliminate the targets. When we give you Abu Ra'id's location, we'll give you the go-ahead for the hit.'

Danny shrugged.

'We won't be able to stop the conspiracy theories flying around,' Victoria added, 'and we're quite happy for any of the terrorists' associates to infer what is happening. But there can be no link between the security services and these . . .'

'Hits,' Spud said again.

'Quite,' said Victoria. 'That, of course, is the reason for all this secrecy.' She waved one arm to indicate the room in which they sat. 'From now on, we communicate by dead-letter drop. That's how you will receive the details of your targets and any other instructions. And it hardly needs to be said, I hope, that if either of you are exposed in the course of your duties, we will be obliged to deny all knowledge of your activities.'

'How does the drop work?' Danny asked.

'Hugo will give you the details. Any day-to-day requirements, speak to your police liaison. Otherwise, unless you have any other questions, I think we're done.'

She stood up abruptly. The remaining three spooks did the same. They clearly wanted to leave as quickly as possible.

'Actually,' Danny said, 'I *do* have a question.'

Silence. The spooks sat down again.

'Go ahead,' Victoria said reluctantly.

'How come it doesn't add up?' Danny said quietly.

All eyes were on him. 'What do you mean?' Victoria asked.

'The bomb was, what, three days ago? Already you've got the names and addresses of two suspects. They're still in the UK, not even lying low. From what I can tell, they might as well be walking round with targets on their chests. If I was one of the most wanted men in the UK, I'd be a bit harder to find than that.'

There was no response. And no eye contact. From any of them.

'I'm just saying,' Danny added, 'are you sure you've got the right guys?'

A pause.

'Yes,' Victoria said quietly. 'We're *quite* sure we've got the right guys.'

'Good,' Danny said. 'Because I'd hate to kill the wrong ones.'

'What you've got to remember,' Chamberlain butted in, 'is that these bloody terrorists aren't quite the master criminals they'd like to believe they are. Not a match for England's finest, eh, lads?'

'If it's all the same to you, I won't underestimate the enemy.'

An irritated frown crossed Chamberlain's forehead.

'What I think Piers is trying to say,' Buckingham interrupted smoothly, 'is don't over-*think* the whole thing, old sport. We're on top of the intelligence. All we require of you is to act on it.'

Or to put it another way: shut up and follow your orders. It was the second time in twelve hours that somebody had said something similar to Danny. He could take his orders as well as the next man, and he was quite used to knowing only half the story. Why, then, did he feel so uneasy?

The spooks filed out of the room. Victoria first, dowdy and flustered. Then Chamberlain, with his strange squint and soldier's gait. And finally Maddox, calm, relaxed, as though he was a vacationing tourist wandering through this tawdry country house for pleasure.

Which left Hugo Buckingham, standing by the fire, waiting for the door to shut, with a small flicker of something approaching satisfaction showing in the corner of his handsome mouth.

SIX

Danny, Spud and Buckingham stood alone in the murky room. Buckingham had walked over to the window, where he watched the others climb into their chauffeured cars and, one by one, drive away. There was a thunderclap overhead. A few seconds later the rain started again, suddenly as heavy as it had been the previous day. Buckingham turned his back on the window and looked at them.

'Is everything clear?'

Spud turned to Danny. 'Do you get the feeling the grown-ups have fucked off and left us with the office boy?'

Buckingham's eyes narrowed momentarily, but he quickly recovered himself. 'We're all office boys,' he said. 'And girls, of course. That's what intelligence work is these days. Not often that you don't find us behind a desk. MI6 for me, Thames House for Victoria. Chamberlain has an office at the MoD building in Whitehall and Maddox works out of the American embassy. Seven days a week, twenty hours a day. Hammerstone's good neutral ground, and out of the way, of course.'

He removed a slip of paper from the top pocket of his jacket, stepped forward and handed it to Danny. It contained a Gmail address and a string of fifteen random digits: a password.

'Your instructions will be left on that account as a draft message. Once you've read the message, delete the draft. Don't save it, print it out or forward it to anyone. Not foolproof, of course, but as Victoria said, the less contact you have with the security services the better. Only myself and the other three will be monitoring that account, and GCHQ tell me it's as close as we'll get to being secure.'

And as close as you'll get, Danny thought, to keeping your distance from the whole op. Because an anonymous e-mail could come from anyone.

The guys said nothing. They just stared at Buckingham. A flinty look entered his eyes. 'You don't like me,' he said tersely. 'That's fine. You don't have to. But a word to the wise lads.' He looked over his shoulder at the window through which he had just watched the departing cars. 'Right now, I'm your best friend.' He walked over to the door and held it open. 'Spud, you'll return to London with your police liaison. Danny, you're coming with me.'

Spud opened his mouth, clearly about to tell Buckingham where to get off, but Danny put a restraining hand on his arm. 'It's all right,' he said. 'We'll RV back at the digs.' He gave Spud the piece of paper with the e-mail address and password.

Spud wasn't pleased, but he took the details without comment, shoved them in his pocket and left the room, giving Buckingham a baleful look as he passed. They heard the main door of the house slam shut, then Buckingham held up the keys to his BMW. 'I'll drive, shall I?' he said.

Spud was sitting in the back seat of Fletcher's police vehicle as they stepped out into the rain. It crunched along the driveway and out of sight. Buckingham put up an umbrella and offered Danny some cover, but Danny simply strode ahead to the waiting Beamer and stood by the passenger door with the rain hammering down on him. By the time Buckingham had let him in, he was soaked.

'Perk of the job,' Buckingham said, indicating the leather seats and walnut dashboard of the car. 'Got to be a few sweeteners, hey? You're soaking, old sport. Let's put the heat on, shall we? They say the seat-heaters give you piles, but I think we can risk it.'

They slid away from Hammerstone with the air-con on full blast. Danny watched the receding building in the rear-view mirror. The old country house looked grey and decrepit in the rain.

'So, old sport,' Buckingham said. 'It's been a while.'

'There's a reason for that.'

'Still seeing . . . what's her name? . . . Clara?'

'Not that it's anything to do with you.'

'Let us know when you've had enough. Quite a filly, that girl. Wouldn't mind a crack at her myself. May have mentioned that before, of course.'

Danny breathed deeply, but managed to keep his cool. He said nothing. They drove in silence for a couple of minutes. If Buckingham had a reason for getting Danny on his own, he'd no doubt get to it eventually.

'Bit of a rogue's gallery back there,' Buckingham said finally. He gave a studied laugh. 'What is it they say about an organisation being like a tree full of monkeys? The ones at the top look down and see a lot of smiling faces, the ones at the bottom look up and see a bunch of arseholes?'

'What are you?' Danny asked. 'A smiling face or an arsehole?'

'I might ask you the same question, Danny Black,' Buckingham said quietly.

Silence.

'And anyway,' Buckingham continued, brighter now. 'Aren't we all a bit of both?' He indicated right and checked his blind spot. 'What's your take on Victoria?' he asked.

'I don't have a take on her.' Which wasn't quite true. She seemed far too mumsy for a high-level MI5 operative. Like she should be working behind the reception desk of a dental surgery, not running a covert killer group.

'I report directly to her, of course,' Buckingham said, breezily continuing the conversation as though Danny hadn't cut him dead with each comment. 'Rumour is, she was a bit of a shagger in her day. Can't see it myself. Still, wouldn't do for me to speak ill of my boss, eh?'

'Then don't.'

'Wouldn't dream of it, old sport. Not quite what she seems, anyway. Bloody good intelligence officer, as far as I can tell. Five years in Moscow in the bad old days and almost a decade in Saudi. Ever been to Riyadh? Lovely place, but a tough intelligence station to run, or so I'm told.' He paused for a moment. From the corner of his eye, Danny could see Buckingham glance at him, as if judging his reaction. 'She met her husband out there. Saudi national. Caused a bit of gossip behind her back over at Thames House. Nasty. Not as if having a Muslim husband is a handicap, eh? Sure he's been thoroughly vetted. Clean as a whistle.'

He paused.

'Can't say it hasn't caused a *bit* of a glass ceiling for her, but that's the way of the world, I suppose.'

Another pause.

'Doesn't help that she went AWOL for six months during her Saudi stint, of course.'

'What do you mean, AWOL?' Danny asked, suddenly interested in spite of himself.

'Exactly that. Off the radar. Claimed a period of depression, said she went of to "find herself". Nobody ever did discover where. It's all in her file.'

'Which you've read, of course.'

'Forewarned is forearmed, old sport. Forewarned is forearmed. And I think we can rest assured that our friend Harrison Maddox is up to speed on all of us. You and me included. Whether he knows exactly what went on in Syria is doubtful, but we all have to have some secrets, don't we?'

Danny stared at the windscreen wipers flapping against the rain.

'Don't think there's much doubt,' Buckingham continued,

'that he takes a rather dim view of Victoria being in charge of the Hammerstone operation.'

'You think he'd prefer you?' Danny sneered.

'Certainly not. Charming fellow, Harrison Maddox, but his contempt for the UK is difficult for him to hide, wouldn't you say. Not the only one of our American cousins who takes a dim view of our government's sudden change of heart with respect to supporting the Americans' interventionist foreign policy.'

'He should spend some time in a war zone,' Danny muttered. 'See what he thinks then.'

'Ah, you're preaching to the converted,' Buckingham sighed theatrically. He seemed suddenly delighted that the two of them had a bit of common ground. 'Always the way, hey? The men in suits make the pronouncements and the soldiers do the bleeding.' The barrack-room comment sounded ridiculous on Buckingham's lips, but he showed no awareness of it. 'Still, not sure how comfortable I feel about having a Yank calling the shots in what is, after all, a very *British* affair. Plenty of rumours circulating in the Firm. Not beyond the CIA's capacity to get into bed with the right sort of terrorists, you know, if it suits their purpose. Keep everyone on their toes, and if the occasional atrocity reminds their allies why they're fighting a war on terror, well, who's counting?'

'You telling me the Yanks blew up Paddington?' Danny said with a sneer.

'Of course not. I'm just saying he's one to watch, that's all.'

'I watch everyone,' Danny said flatly.

'Bloody good policy, old sport.' Was Buckingham deliberately misinterpreting Danny's meaning? Danny couldn't tell.

They continued to sit in silence. The miles passed, and so did the minutes, but Danny could sense that Buckingham was working up to continue his character assassination of his Hammerstone colleagues. 'I suppose Piers Chamberlain's a bit of a legend in your neck of the woods,' he said finally.

'You suppose that, do you?'

'Well . . . rubbing shoulders with the great and the good as he does. He's a regular visitor at Clarence House, or so I'm told.'

'And you think an ordinary SAS trooper has wet dreams about becoming a royal flunky?'

Buckingham smiled indulgently at Danny's sharpness. 'Seems a bit odd to me that he's so close to the royal bosom,' he continued. 'Keeps the company of some peculiar types.'

Danny didn't ask what he meant. He knew the explanation was coming at any moment.

'Not saying they're right-wing,' Buckingham said, 'but they do rather make our friends in UKIP look like card-carrying Marxists. Retired military, mostly. Look up to Chamberlain like he's some sort of guru. I think they like the fact that he was the scourge of the Mick in Northern Ireland back in the seventies. Loonies, the lot of them. Trouble is, of course, that it's the loonies you have to watch out for. Chamberlain's chums have formed a sort of cabal. They've been lobbying government to set up a transfer of power to the army in the event of Islamic extremism getting out of control. Not too many people take them very seriously, naturally, but they're a vocal minority and recent events haven't exactly harmed their argument.'

'Get to the point, Buckingham.'

'No point, old sport. Just chewing the fat. Up to you whether you think Chamberlain's the kind of fellow you want to be taking orders from, that's all.'

'Stop the car,' Danny told him.

Buckingham blinked. 'Not really a good time, old sp—'

'*Stop the fucking car.*'

Buckingham looked at him: a cold, calculating expression that Danny recognised well. Then he pulled over and turned off the ignition. Rain drummed on the roof of the car, and now that the engine was off, the windscreen was opaque with running water.

'Why me?' Danny said.

'I don't know what you mean.'

'There's a whole regiment full of guys just as well qualified to pull off this job as me and Spud. *Better* qualified, some of them. So why the hell have you been pulling strings to get *us* involved?'

The windows were misting up inside. Buckingham stared directly ahead.

'You should be thanking me for giving you a chance, Black,' he said. 'The lads who eliminate these bombers will be showered in glory. And as for Abu Ra'id . . .'

'Bullshit,' Danny said. 'At best, the lads who eliminate these bombers will go back to Hereford until the next time they're needed to carry out someone else's dirty work. At worst, you'll shit on us from a great height like those Military Reaction Force guys who did your dirty work in Northern Ireland. The only people who'll get showered with glory are you and your Hammerstone chums, and as far as I can tell, you're sticking the knife into them already. Which is hardly surprising, because that's what you do.'

Buckingham's nostrils flared. As he turned to look Danny full in the face, all pretence of friendliness had fallen away. 'If I were you, Black,' he breathed, 'I'd do exactly as I was told. I'd make very, *very* sure that I carried out this operation to the letter.'

'Because Hugo Buckingham's on his way up the slippery pole. And he's very keen for that glory to be showered all over *him*. Most people see an atrocity. You see a fucking opportunity.'

'How dare you speak to me like that?' Buckingham hissed.

'Go to hell.'

'Can you carry out this operation? Quietly, effectively and without any hitches?' And when Danny didn't immediately reply: 'Well, *can* you?'

Danny did it swiftly, slipping his hand into his jacket, pulling out his handgun and thrusting the barrel against Buckingham's temple in one swift movement. Camouflaged from the gaze of any passing pedestrians by the rain-sluiced windows, neither man moved for a full thirty seconds. Buckingham's jugular pulsed. His breathing became shallow.

'Of course I can,' Danny whispered. 'Killing people is easy. It's keeping them alive that's the hard bit.'

He nudged his weapon. It made Buckingham visibly start, and close his eyes. 'Put the bloody gun down,' he breathed. 'You're not such a damn fool that you're going to shoot me.'

'Maybe I was a "damn fool" to save your fucking life – several times over.'

Danny lowered the weapon.

Buckingham drew a tremulous breath. 'I told you earlier on that I was your best friend in all of this, Black. But believe me, I've enough dirt on you to make life very, *very* difficult. You'd better bloody well stay in line, soldier, and remember just who is calling the shots.'

'The only one calling the shots,' Danny breathed, 'is the guy with the gun.' He sneered as he stowed his weapon. 'I report to Hammerstone,' he said. 'Not to you.'

Buckingham was clutching the steering wheel with one hand, the gear stick with the other. His knuckles were white. He was scared, and that pleased Danny. He opened the door and stepped out into the rain. A busy street. A red London bus passed in the opposite direction, its large wheels trundling through puddles and spraying the almost deserted pavement. To his left, a Middle Eastern food store, 'The Star of Damascus', rain sluicing off the canopy protecting its crates of vegetables. Arabic writing on the window, behind which the pale pink and white carcass of a sheep hung from a hook. Above the Star of Damascus was a window. A face looked out. Its features were strange – the eyes slightly too close together, the face itself podgy. Danny remembered what Victoria had said, about the bombers using a Down's syndrome kid. He felt a pang of sympathy, and an equally strong surge of revulsion. There were no rules for these terrorists. No strategy too low. In that sense, at least, they and Buckingham weren't so different.

The face above the Star of Damascus disappeared. Danny slammed the car door behind him and hurried off through the rain. He was cold and wet, and didn't know exactly where he was, but anything was better than being stuck in a moving vehicle, being fed poison by Hugo Buckingham, the most venomous creature he knew.

17.50hrs

Clara stood by a child's bedside.

She knew he wouldn't make it. The wounds he had sustained were too severe, the septicaemia too advanced. It was frankly a miracle he had lived this long. He had lost both legs above the knee, and a piece of shrapnel had robbed him of the sight in one eye as well as splintering his right cheekbone. He'd been unconscious since the blast, thank goodness, unaware that he was already an orphan. Here in St Mary's Hospital, Clara had seen more than a dozen victims die of their injuries. But there was something about this little lad that was too sad. Normally, when children were unconscious, they looked peaceful. But this kid looked like he felt every ounce of the torment he was suffering.

She sat by his bed, holding the thin hand from which a cannula emerged, attached to a saline drip. Not long now, she thought. His breathing had changed. There was fluid on his lungs. The end was close. She could do nothing for him, except be there.

It seemed to Clara that her life had been turned on its head. She had become a doctor to help people. To save lives. But now, wherever she went, innocent people seemed to be dying in their multitudes. Was it something to do with her, she sometimes wondered in the illogical panic of the darkest nights.

He died at three minutes past six. The breathing suddenly stopped, the heart rate monitor flatlined. Clara didn't do anything at first. She simply sat there holding his hand. Tears welled up in her eyes and trickled down her cheeks. Her friend Emily found her like that ten minutes later. She put one arm around her shoulders and gently disentangled Clara's fingers from the child. Then she took her to have a cup of hot, sweet tea in the crowded hospital canteen. And then, seeing the dark rings of tiredness around her eyes, she sent Clara home.

Clara *was* tired. She had left Hereford at sunrise, just as Danny was heading in to base. He was able to function on a couple of hours' sleep, but that wasn't enough for Clara. Her lids were heavy and her limbs ached. She walked along the Edgware Road and out towards Maida Vale, huddled under her umbrella, the shins of her trousers soaked. When she arrived at the small ground-floor flat in a mansion block just by the canal which her parents had bought her on the promise that she would never – *never* – work for Médecins Sans Frontières again, she was bone-cold. She ran herself a hot bath, then slipped into her tracksuit. She'd only just finished getting dressed when the doorbell rang. She padded to the front door and looked through the spyhole. She saw Danny's dark features, distorted by the lens and bedraggled by the weather. She didn't know whether to feel glad to see him, or apprehensive about the severe look on his face.

She opened the door and forced a smile. 'Hi,' she said.

Danny didn't reply.

'Come on in.'

'Let's take a walk,' he said.

The rain had stopped, but the sky was still heavy. 'Right,' she said, discouraged by the tone of his voice. 'I'll get my coat.'

They trod the streets in silence. As they left the flat, Clara felt for Danny's hand. But he didn't reciprocate like he normally did. They walked side by side without touching.

She wanted to tell him about her day, but for some reason couldn't find the words. Or maybe she was scared to start a conversation, because she didn't know where it would end.

'I was at the hospital today,' she said finally. 'That kid – you know, the one I told you about? – finally died.' They walked a little further. 'Oh, God, I hope they *find* the people who did this. And I hope they put them in a *British* jail, not send them home where they'll be treated like heroes.'

'Don't hold your breath,' Danny muttered.

Clara stopped walking. 'Why?' she asked.

Danny gave her a look she'd seen before. A look that said: *Don't ask questions you know I can't answer.* She felt her hackles rising. 'For God's sake, Danny. You *can* trust me, you know.'

Danny suppressed a sneer. Clara thought she'd seen it all in Syria, that she was safe back here in London, but Danny knew that wasn't true. London wasn't all Beefeaters and bars. It was a place where bad things happened. The Iranian Embassy. God's Banker. Litvinenko. Guys from both sides killed each other on the streets of London just as surely as they did in the shit-holes that ended up on Channel 4 news. And now Danny was one of their number. He was being sucked in.

'The list of people I can trust,' Danny said, 'is getting shorter.'

Clara shook her head, confused. 'What do you *mean*?' She looked around. They'd been walking blindly, and she couldn't remember what route they had taken. Somewhere in the distance she heard the traffic of the Edgware Road, but she saw they were standing outside a dilapidated United Reform church. Its red bricks were crumbling, its windows were boarded up and covered in graffiti – as was the road sign on it that said 'Station Way'. An old metal padlock clamped the main doors shut.

Danny wouldn't look at her. She put herself in his line of vision, but he just moved his head.

'I can't see you any more,' he said quietly.

She'd been expecting it, but it was still like an ice-cold corkscrew in her heart. 'Why?' she whispered.

'Does it matter why?' Danny snapped. His brow was furrowed and he still refused to look at her.

'It matters to me.'

Danny took a deep breath. He sounded like he was controlling his anger. 'Go home, Clara,' he breathed. 'Go home and stay home. That's my advice.'

Her eyes widened. 'Stay home? What do you ... oh my God, there's going to be more, isn't there? These awful bombings, there's going to be more of them? Danny, I understand you're worried about me, but you don't have to do this ...'

'You're not going to see me again, Clara. Get used to the idea.'

Clara tried to stop herself from crying, but she couldn't. 'Danny, you're not thinking straight. It's Syria, isn't it? It's affected you. I've told you before ... you have to stop remembering the things you want to forget.' She grabbed the hem of Danny's jacket but he pulled it away. A loud sob escaped her lips.

She turned and ran away, her wellington boots splashing in the puddles as she went. She only looked back once, to see a dark figure standing in the lamplight by the church, casting a long shadow on the pavement, its head bowed, its hands deep in the pocket of its jacket.

Danny watched her go. Just before she reached the end of the side street and turned left into Edgware Road, he followed her. Once he was on the Edgware Road, he kept a distance of 30 metres, closely following the line of shops so he could disappear if she turned to look back. But she didn't. She reached her flat five minutes later, let herself in, and was gone.

He felt sick. Sick with himself, and sick with everyone. He tried not to think of the distressed look in Clara's eyes as he had rejected her. But that was impossible. Not only did he *see* her despair, he felt it in his gut.

But he knew one thing for sure. Right now, the best way for a person to be safe – no, the best way for *Clara* to be safe – was to stay away from him.

Because when death gets its claws in you, it never lets go.

He heard her voice ringing in his ears. *You have to stop remembering the things you're supposed to forget.*

Sure, he thought to himself. But you also have to stop forgetting the things you're supposed to remember. Like how death stuck to men like Danny and Spud like shit to a stick.

There's going to be more, isn't there? These awful bombings, there's going to be more of them?

Yeah, he thought as he cast one final look at Clara's mansion block. It's not over yet.

It's hardly even begun.

The Star of Damascus sold vegetables, rice and halal meat at bargain prices. There would be no point doing anything else, because this part of New Cross was not well-to-do. Unemployment was high, rents were cheap – and none so cheap as the small studio flat above the supermarket. The one room had thin, shiny carpets and smelled overwhelmingly of the rubbish rotting in the kitchen bin. There was a single, unmade bed at one end of the room, and a small table, at which a young man sat, his eyes staring wide at his computer screen.

He was exceedingly pleased with his computer. It was an old PC, very slow, but he didn't mind that. He'd never had one before, and when his social worker had arranged an internet connection for him three months ago, it was as if that little flat had become a gateway to a world he never knew existed. She'd shown him how to send e-mails, how to read the BBC news website to stay up to date, and even how to access his bank account. But of course, he'd barely done any of this. He spent his days and nights staring at pornographic videos that even now made his hands tremble with excitement and gave him a thrill in the pit of his stomach. He liked it best when the girls looked directly into the camera. It was as if they were looking straight at him. Inviting him to join in. Sometimes he clicked on the banners at the right-hand side of the screen – the ones that offered to put him in touch with 'fuck-buddies' in his area. They always filled his screen with banner ads, but that didn't stop him from trying again each day, sometimes more than once. He just couldn't resist.

And in those moments when he wasn't staring at porn, he was browsing Twitter. It hadn't taken long for him to discover that there were ladies out there who took pictures of themselves naked and tweeted the images. He followed them all, and sometimes sent them badly worded messages. They didn't answer back, so he removed the photo from his profile. He knew that he looked different to most people. That his Down's syndrome features sometimes made strangers cross the street to avoid him. They *still* didn't answer back. His social worker told him he should put the photo back up. The way he looked was nothing to be ashamed of, she said.

And then, of course, there was Facebook. He didn't have many friends, even though he had sent out lots of requests. And of the 'friends' he had, only a handful were people he knew in the real world. That didn't worry him. He liked having friends of any description.

But as he logged on to his Facebook account that afternoon, when the air outside was thick with rain, he saw a 'friend' request that made his heart pound.

Her name was Nicki, and he could not stop staring at her profile picture. Her eyes were dark, her skin a dusky brown. The lips were full and pouting. The curly hair was shiny. There was a tempting cleavage that made him feel weak. In some ways, she reminded him of the girls from the websites he liked. But she was different in one very important way. He had met Nicki before. In real life.

It happened just a couple of days ago. He'd gone to the corner shop to buy some milk. On the way, he'd seen her walking alongside him. She was very pretty, and when he smiled at her, she smiled back. That never normally happened. Inside the shop, he found that he didn't have enough money for the milk he wanted to buy. As he stood, confused and embarrassed, at the counter, there she was. She gave him the ten pence he needed, and he was sure she had fluttered her eyelashes at him. He'd gone to bed that night smitten. He'd even avoided looking at the internet. He felt that it would have been somehow unfaithful.

But now, here she was again, wanting to be friends.

And maybe she wanted something more.

He clicked the mouse to accept the 'friend' request.

Ten minutes later, she sent him her first message.

PART TWO

Hunter Killer

SEVEN

21.30hrs

The safe house was dark when Danny arrived back. As he put his key in the lock, he wondered for a moment if Spud had sodded off to the pub. But the alarm didn't beep, and there was a black jacket hanging over the banister as he stepped into the house. Looking along the hallway, he saw a faint greenish glow at the kitchen table. Spud was there, sitting in the darkness at his laptop. As Danny entered the kitchen he saw a carton of milk on the side and three used tea bags next to it. Spud raised his cup of tea in greeting. 'Thought maybe you'd fucked off and joined the French Foreign Legion,' he said sarcastically.

'A few loose ends to tie up,' Danny said evasively.

'Oh aye? And what did that little turd Buckingham want?'

'Catch up on old times.' And when Spud raised an eyebrow, Danny said: 'Forget about it. I told him where to get off.' He looked at the laptop. 'Anything?'

Spud nodded. 'There was a draft message sitting on the account, just like twat-features said. We've got an ID and address for the first target.'

'Just like that,' Danny murmured. He pulled up a chair and sat down next to Spud at the laptop. An e-mail window was open. A single line of text gave an address:

GROUND FLOOR FLAT, 27 DALEWOOD MEWS, HAMMERSMITH, W14 6PS

And beneath that, embedded into the e-mail, a picture Danny recognised from the briefing back at Hammerstone: the gaunt, Somali features of Sarim Galaid.

'Why didn't they just give us the intel earlier on?' Spud said. 'Save all this fannying around.'

'Obvious, isn't it?'

'Not to me, mucker.'

'A dodgy draft e-mail on some random account? Could have been sent *by* anyone, *to* anyone. We're doing something illegal and they want to make sure we take the fall if there's a screw-up.'

Spud nodded darkly. 'Perhaps,' he said. He held up a couple of Yale keys. 'Fletcher gave me these. The first-floor flat opposite number 27 is up for rent. But if you're right, I'm guessing SIS didn't sign the deposit cheque.'

Danny's eyes narrowed. 'I don't like it. Too convenient. If our target's got any kind of brains, he'd have checked that already.'

Spud shrugged, and stuffed the keys back into his pocket. 'We don't *have* to use it,' he said, a bit huffily.

'Have you checked out the location?' Danny asked.

Spud closed down the e-mail and opened up a browser window, before navigating to Google maps. He typed in the address. In an instant, a glowing pin was floating above Dalewood Mews. With a single click, Spud changed the image to satellite view, then zoomed out slightly so they could get a decent scope on both the mews itself, and the surrounding area.

Dalewood Mews ran from north to south in the heart of a little network of residential streets on the west side of Hammersmith Grove. It was a cul-de-sac, with vehicular access at the south end only. No trees, and only three parked cars in this particular satellite snapshot. An enclosed space with almost no cover: from a surveillance point of view, a nightmare. At least, that was how it looked from here.

'We need to get down there,' Danny said. 'Get eyes on, work out this Galaid's routine.'

'Then what?' Spud asked.

'He's a bomber, isn't he?' said Danny. 'If we cause an explosion at his flat and the place is full of bomb-making gear, no one will bat an eyelid. So we set things up so he meets with an accident.'

Spud grinned. The idea obviously appealed. 'When do we start?'

Danny shrugged. 'How does now suit you? This gaff isn't so cushty I want to stick around any longer than I have to.' And what he didn't say was that a period of surveillance would keep his mind from other thoughts. He picked up his black rucksack from the floor where he'd dumped it that morning, then started unpacking it of crumpled clothes which he dumped on the kitchen table.

Spud watched him steadily. 'You're bushed, mate. Why don't we catch some shut-eye, get started in the morning?'

Danny shook his head and walked over to the broom cupboard that contained the strong box. 'I'm fine. And if he's a night owl, we'll lose twenty-four hours if we wait till morning.'

Spud inclined his head. He put one hand into his pocket and pulled out a small packet of tablets which he rattled to get Danny's attention. There was no dispensing sticker on them.

'What's that?' Danny asked.

'Ephedrine,' Spud said. 'Breakfast of champions. Pop a couple now, keep you sharp for a few hours.' And when Danny started to protest: 'Just take them, mucker. You're running on empty.'

Danny relented. He took the box of pills and swallowed two of the little caplets. Then he returned his attention to the strong box. He opened it up and started stowing the contents into his black rucksack: snap gun and bits, MOE kits, even the ration packs. He fitted one radio to his belt and inserted the covert earpiece, then handed the other to Spud.

'Let me see the picture again,' he said as he tightened the straps on his rucksack. Spud brought up a new browser window and redirected it back to the Gmail home page. He keyed in the username and password that Buckingham had given them. The mailbox appeared on the screen and Spud hovered the cursor over the drafts folder.

It was empty.

So, Danny thought. Our every move is being monitored. They know we've read the e-mail, so they've deleted it from the system.

Spud shut the computer down with an expression of disgust. 'Good to know they trust us,' he said.

Danny slung his rucksack over his shoulder. 'Sooner this job's finished, the better,' he said. 'Let's go.'

It took half an hour for the ephedrine to kick in, by which time Danny was as alert as he'd ever been. They headed over Albert Bridge, then west along the north side of the river, before coming to a crawl as they crossed the King's Road, where the ever-present Met were stopping and searching cars at random. Danny got his ID ready, but in the event a uniformed police-woman waved them on. Ten minutes later they were heading down Talgarth Road and on to Hammersmith Broadway.

They left the car two blocks from Dalewood Mews, and debussed separately. Spud went first; Danny followed two minutes later, carrying his heavy rucksack and taking the oppo-site side of the street to Spud. He walked past a lap-dancing club, its windows blacked out and music throbbing inside. Twenty metres further on, a drunk couple were having an argument outside a gastropub, where the chairs were upside down on the tables. Danny sidestepped the arguing couple and continued on his way. The roads were lined with parked cars. Some enter-prising person from an Indian takeaway had gone round sticking a flyer behind all the windscreen wipers, but the flyers hadn't fared well in the drizzle – they were sticking to the windscreens and in some instances the wind had torn the paper, leaving only a portion of the flyer behind. Three minutes later, Danny was on the pavement opposite the entrance to Dalewood Mews. Spud had already entered the side street and was lurking at the far end, bent down on one knee as he pretended to do up his shoelace.

Danny spoke quietly into the mike clipped to his lapel. 'What we got?'

'Bugger-all,' came the reply in his earpiece. 'The ground-floor flat has a separate entrance, but if we're going to put in surveillance, we'll need access to one of the houses opposite. We can't use a vehicle – it'll stick out like a turd in a fruit salad.'

'Maybe we can get into the first floor.'

'Maybe.' Spud didn't sound keen, and with good reason. Moving into the flat above would involve drilling spyholes into the floor and all manner of noisy – and obvious – work.

'Any sign of activity in the flat?'

'Negative.' Spud swore under his breath. 'I reckon we've got days of surveillance. I fucking *hate* surveillance. And I bet the bastard's not even at home anyway.'

'Maybe we can get him to poke his nose round the door,' Danny breathed.

'What do you mean?'

'Get back here, mate. You've been doing your shoelaces up for two minutes now.'

From a distance, he saw Spud stand up and saunter back up Dalewood Mews. Thirty seconds later he had rejoined Danny, who pulled his mobile from his pocket and was pulling a flyer from the windscreen of one of the cars.

'Let's order our friend some dinner,' he said. He dialled the number on the flyer, but instantly Spud stopped him. 'Think about it, mucker. If he gets suspicious, we'll just be putting the delivery kid at risk. Galaid *is* dangerous.'

Danny stared at the flyer, then scrunched it up and threw it to the ground. Spud was right. But they couldn't simply hang around on the corner of the street for hours on end. They'd be too obvious if anyone was watching.

And recently, Danny had the impression that somebody was *always* watching.

Spud pulled Fletcher's key from his back pocket. 'It's our best bet,' he said firmly. And when Danny started to protest, he interrupted. 'Mate, I know that Chamberlain bloke was a twat, but he's right – these aren't master criminals. We'll case the joint when we get in, keep our weapons cocked and locked. As soon as we confirm our target's hiding out in number twenty-seven, we'll wait for him to go out, then check out his flat, see if there's any bomb-making gear there. Then we'll work out his routine, and when we know he's going to be out of the house for more than an hour or so, we'll go back and booby-trap it.'

For a moment Danny didn't react. He had paranoia twisting through his mind. If he was honest with himself, he was less worried about the enemy targets knowing their location than he was about Buckingham and his colleagues leading them around by the nose. Something wasn't right, and he couldn't put his finger on what it was.

But there was no space for paranoia in the middle of an op. Spud was right. The flat was their best option. Put in an OP and wait for their quarry to show himself. He nodded. 'I'll go first,' he said.

Danny didn't enter Dalewood Mews immediately. First he walked along the pavement, removing more takeaway flyers from the car windscreens. Only when he had a thick wodge of them did he enter Dalewood Mews. Starting at the end nearest the main road, he approached each door in turn and put a flyer through the letterbox. As he approached number 27, he removed his phone from his pocket and surreptitiously switched it to camera mode. When the moment came, he opened the creaking iron gate of number 27, walked up the short, weed-strewn path, and delivered a pizza flyer. At the same time, he took a photograph of the lock, before dropping the phone immediately back into his pocket. He continued delivering flyers till he'd reached the end of the street, then turned and started along the opposite side. He kept on high alert, every sense keenly searching for the sign of someone watching him. But as far as he could tell, there was nobody.

Flat 24a. It had its own entrance – a wooden door with two frosted-glass panels that immediately jumped out at Danny as a security risk. Checking once more that he wasn't under observation, he slid the key into the lock, turned it and slowly opened the door. He could tell before he even stepped inside that the flat had been unoccupied for some time. It had that smell, damp and musty. He clicked the door behind him, then put the key into the lock without turning it. Spud would lock them in again when he arrived. Danny stood for a moment in the hallway, allowing his eyes to adjust to the dark. Five metres ahead of him was a narrow staircase. He unholstered his weapon, cocked it, and started to edge forward.

The stairs creaked as he climbed them, even though he put pressure only on the edge of the treads to reduce the noise. He paused at the top. Up ahead was a kitchen, beyond which he thought he could make out the open door of a bathroom. The landing wound round to his right. There were two closed doors off it, and one at the end – that would be the room overlooking the street.

He heard Spud's voice in his ear. 'Entering the flat in ten.'

Danny stepped forward, his weapon primed, moving into the kitchen. An empty table. Bare units. The tap was dripping, and the splash of water against the steel basin sounded louder than it should. He edged through the room and stopped at the door of the bathroom. Toilet, basin, large bath with a fabric shower curtain wrapped round it. Danny held up his gun and with his free hand ripped back the curtain.

Nothing.

Back to the door. He could see Spud silhouetted at the top of the stairs. Stepping forward, he pointed along the hallway to indicate that his mate should check along that way, then raised his gun again to cover him.

Bedroom one: empty.

Bedroom two: empty.

Spud approached the door of the room overlooking the street. Danny stood three metres back as he slowly unlatched the door, then kicked it gently open with one foot. The hinges creaked. Spud stepped inside.

His voice again, both over the radio and directly from the room.

'Clear.'

Danny exhaled slowly. He'd been more nervous than he cared to confess. Quite why, he didn't know.

There was no furniture in the front room, and only a single, bare lightbulb hanging from the centre of the ceiling. They didn't switch it on, and they avoided standing directly in front of the windows, which were covered with old net curtains. Instead, they walked round the edge of the room, each man approaching the window from one side, Danny on the right, Spud on the left. They didn't touch the nets, but simply peered through them at an angle out on to the street.

The front door of number 27 was to Danny's ten o'clock, and it was flooded in the yellow light of a street lamp, the beam of which lit up a light mist of rain. There were no pedestrians. No moving vehicles. All was still.

'If we're going to set up an IED in his flat, we'll need to make sure we don't take out the whole fucking street,' Spud said.

Danny nodded, but didn't reply. He felt Spud's eyes on him.

Spud sniffed. 'Could be a long night,' he said.

He hadn't slept. How could he, when Nicki, his new friend, kept sending him those messages? He stared back over the time-line, reading each message in turn. *I saw u in the shop two days ago. Do u remember?*

Of course he remembered.

I was the 1 that gave u some £££ to buy milk.

He blushed when he read that, embarrassed that he hadn't had enough money. A man should always have enough money to take his girlfriend out. He knew that, even though he'd never *had* a girlfriend.

I think u maybe smiled at me????

He felt his limbs go weak when he read that. He could only think of a one-word answer: 'Yes.'

Then she started sending him photos. The first one showed her sitting on her bed. It was a single bed, he noticed. Did that mean she didn't have a boyfriend? She was wearing pyjama bottoms and a strappy vest top. The left-hand strap had slipped down, revealing her shoulder. He could make out the curve of her breasts underneath the vest. And he was absolutely sure that she was pouting at him.

Do u think I'm pretty? she asked.

Yes, he had replied, his fingers shaking as he typed. He thought she was *very* pretty.

Would u like to see me without my top?

He had swallowed hard when she asked him that question. It crossed his mind that it might not be polite to accept her offer. But then, he asked himself, why would she *suggest* it if she didn't want to *do* it.

He wrote back: yes please.

For a few minutes, he thought he'd gone too far. There was no reply. He wondered if the delay was because she was taking her clothes off. But then another message appeared on his screen.

U first.

He looked down at the clothes he was wearing: a grubby white T-shirt and a pair of jeans that were too big for him around his already chunky waist. He felt shy. But then he looked at the picture of Nicki again. At the lovely soft skin of her shoulders.

At her curves. Suddenly scrambling, he took off his T-shirt and used the computer's webcam to take a picture of himself, just as his social worker had showed him. The resulting picture wasn't nearly so nice as Nicki's. He knew that. His skin was pasty, flabby. His eyes somehow looked even closer together than they normally did. But he reminded himself that it was Nicki who'd got in touch with him, and although he felt self-conscious, he sent the picture anyway.

He waited for two excruciating minutes. He was cold without his T-shirt, but he didn't want to put it back on, so he hugged himself to keep warm as he listened to the rain hissing outside.

Then the next photo arrived.

Nicki had removed her vest. Beneath it, she was wearing a strapless bra. It pushed her cleavage together, and he couldn't take his eyes off that. He stared at the photograph, mouth agape. It was so much better than all the pictures he normally looked at on the internet. They were more explicit, sure: but this one was for him, and him alone. He touched the screen, allowing his trembling fingers to trace the shape of her body. There was no doubt, of course, that he was in love with her. Madly in love. He imagined meeting her, and how he would treat her like a princess. He knew that other boys treated beautiful women very badly. He would *never* be like that. He would do anything she wanted. He would buy her flowers and chocolates. And in return . . . *in return* . . .

His fingers were still tracing the shapely frame of her body when another message appeared on the screen.

It said: *Would u like to meet me for breakfast?*

The first thing Danny did was check the photograph he had taken of the lock on the front door of number 27, cupping his hands over the screen of his phone to stop the light spill. It was a Union deadlock. He unbuckled his rucksack and removed his booklet of lock sizes and details. Still carefully using the light from his phone, he established which bit he needed on his snap gun and carefully fitted it. If and when the time came to force an entry into the opposite flat, he'd be ready.

Spud fetched a couple of stools from the kitchen and they sat at either side of the window. There they watched, and waited, concealed by the net curtains but able to see everything that was happening by the light of the street lamp. They sat in silence as the time ticked past, and saw nothing except a red fox that scampered along the street at thirteen minutes past midnight, and then again at twelve minutes to two. Danny felt the ephedrine wearing off. His eyes grew heavy.

'Get some kip, mucker,' Spud said quietly. 'I'll keep stag.'

Danny started to protest, but Spud cut him short. 'I'll need to sleep soon too,' he said. 'I'll wake you in two hours.'

Danny relented. He lay down on the hard floor and shut his eyes. Seconds later, he was asleep.

He loved McDonald's. If he had his way, he'd eat there every day. But because he hadn't much money, he seldom did. Now, however, he had scraped together every last piece of change he could find from around his flat and carefully counted it out. Five pounds, ninety-three pence. That meant he could buy a cup of tea for himself, and a McDonald's breakfast for Nicki. He'd never taken a girl out for a meal before, but this much he knew: the boy had to pay.

The tea was very hot, and he was very anxious as he sat in McDonald's on Lower Regent Street. This was where she had suggested they meet, at 7.30 exactly. He'd been surprised that she wanted to hook up so early. Wouldn't it be more romantic to meet in the evening? But she had insisted. *I can't wait that long*, she had said, and he'd felt that strange churning in his stomach once more.

So there he was, at a table of his own, ignoring all the early-morning punters as they walked in and out with their Egg

McMuffins and paper cups of coffee. He took a sip of tea. It scalded his tongue and he spilt a bit on the table. He tried to wipe it with his sleeve and spilt a bit more. He started to panic – this sort of thing *always* happened to him – but then he became aware of somebody standing over him.

He looked up. It was her.

He blinked.

She was even more beautiful than in her picture. Her full lips were glossy with red lipstick. Her curly dark hair tumbled over one shoulder. She wore a black jumper, but it was tight enough to reveal the curves that had captured his interest in the night. And she pouted at him, in a way no girl ever had done, except on a screen, or in his head.

'Hello,' he said. His voice croaked unattractively as he spoke, so he tried again. 'Hello!'

'Hi,' she said in a throaty, husky voice that made him feel weak with desire. 'Can I sit down?'

He nodded and watched as she took a seat next to him. It was only then that he realised she had something with her. A small suitcase on wheels, the handle extended so she could pull it behind her. The zip was fastened with a tiny padlock.

It crossed his mind that you only ever pack a suitcase if you're planning to stay the night somewhere. He felt goosebumps emerging on his skin in anticipation.

He smiled at her.

She smiled back.

'Would you like an Egg McMuffin?' he asked.

'Wake up. *Wake up!*'

Danny started and sat up immediately. Daylight. It took him two seconds to remember where he was, by which time he was back at his stool and looking through the net curtains. Time check: 07.38. Spud must have let him sleep for a good five hours. The door to number 27 was open and a figure had his back to them, closing it. Danny narrowed his eyes and watched carefully. The figure turned. Like a snapshot being taken in his brain, Danny recognised the face.

Sarim Galaid. They had a positive ID.

EIGHT

Danny turned to Spud. 'Follow him,' he said.

Spud looked unsure. 'What you got in mind, mucker?' he said. It was clear that he didn't fully trust Danny to do the right thing.

'I'll recce the flat. But you need to keep on him, so I know when he's coming back.'

Spud looked through the net curtain again. The kid was walking up to the iron gate at the end of the short front path. 'Roger that,' he breathed. Without another word he jogged from the room and down the stairs. Danny heard the door open and shut, and a moment later saw Spud following the target down Dalewood Mews, walking on the other side of the street with his head down.

A strange calm descended on Danny as he picked up his pre-pared snap gun and shouldered his heavy rucksack. Spud's voice crackled in his ear: 'Heading up towards Hammersmith Broadway.'

Danny tapped the pressel switch on his radio twice: universal code for 'Roger that'.

He headed downstairs and out into the street. He could hear traffic nearby, much louder than it had been during the night. The rain had stopped, but the morning sky was threatening. He reckoned a storm was coming. As he closed the door behind him, he saw a woman emerge from a separate entrance to the first-floor flat above number 27. Her hair was tied back in an Alice band and she was eating a muesli bar. Late for work. She didn't give Danny a second glance. He waited for her to hurry down the road, then headed across the street right up to the door of number 27.

With a single, swift movement, he inserted the snap gun into the lock. A few squeezes of the trigger and a tweak from the tension rod, and the door was open. Danny stepped inside and closed the door quietly behind him. The latch clicked shut.

The front door had opened directly on to the front room of the flat. A smallish room, eight metres by eight. Thick floral curtains, closed. A sofa bed against one wall, opened up but without any bedclothes. A strange smell: dirt, with a tinge of cordite. Danny instinctively knew he was going to find something here.

He didn't step any further into the room. Not yet. His presence here needed to be totally deniable. That meant no fingerprints and no DNA traces. He fished in his rucksack for one of the two vacuum-packed SOCO suits he had stowed inside, and bit into the stiff plastic wrapping. The pack expanded like an inflating lung. He carefully tore it open and removed a pair of latex gloves, which he pulled on to each hand, covering his cuffs with the latex to make a tight seal. Next up, he donned a polythene hairnet and a paper mask that gave him the air of a surgeon. All that was left in the kit now was the paper suit, which he pulled over his clothes and shoes to avoid contaminating the scene with any stray fibres that might contain his DNA. Once he was properly suited up, the only weak point was his rucksack, but he'd just have to take a risk with that. He shouldered it again and, holding his cocked weapon in his right hand, stepped forward.

The front room led directly to a second reception, exactly the same size and just as scantly furnished. A window on the right-hand side of the far wall was covered with an almost opaque blind, but he could see through it into a badly kept garden. Next to the window was an opening into a small galley kitchen. Just like in the flat across the road that they'd been using as an OP, there was another door at the far end of the kitchen that Danny assumed led to the bathroom.

But of much more interest was another door in the corner of the room to his left. The geography of the place meant it could only lead down to a basement. Danny stepped towards the door and opened it up.

Sure enough, he found a flight of stone steps leading downwards.

He spoke into his radio. 'Do you copy?'

'Roger that.'

'Where are you?'

'Tesco Metro, two blocks away. So far he's bought a carton of soya milk and a four-pack of Andrex. Looks like he's in for a great morning.'

Danny looked down the stone steps. 'How long have I got?'

A pause.

'What you doing, mucker? I thought this was just a recce. If there's any bomb-making gear, we'll go back later.'

'Just a recce,' Danny agreed. 'But can you distract him?'

More silence.

'What do you mean, distract him?'

'I don't know, ask him directions or something. Just keep him out of here as long as you can while I search for explosives.'

'Okay,' Spud said with obvious suspicion. 'But it's not going to be long. He's queueing up with his bog roll right now. Get the hell out of there as quick as you can.'

'Keep radio contact,' Danny said.

He pulled a thin, bright Maglite from his bag and shone it down the stairs. He heard interference over his earpiece. The signal was bad down here. There was a large room, the size of both ground-floor receptions put together, with a long trestle table set up in the middle.

Weapon primed, Danny descended. His breath was hot behind the paper mask and he could feel his own pulse: not fast, but pumping hard . . .

He shone the torch towards the four corners of the cellar.

Nobody there. He directed the beam at the trestle table. It illuminated what Danny immediately recognised as two old artillery shells. They looked like bullets, rounded at one end, pointed at the other. But larger: a good couple of feet in length. He wondered where they originated from. Eastern Europe, maybe? These things were two a penny after the Bosnia conflict. Either that or the Middle East. Not that it mattered much. What was important was that someone had carefully cut away the base of each shell and started to scoop out the contents – military-grade high explosive. It was accumulated in three small piles between the shells. It didn't look like a lot, but no doubt the process of evacuating the shells wasn't yet complete. And even that small amount of explosive could do a lot of damage in the wrong hands.

Danny paused for a moment, and gave serious thought to hiding out in the flat, waiting for the target to come home and simply killing him. But that wouldn't do. Hammerstone had been very clear: it had to look like an accident.

Danny touched nothing. He moved back out of the cellar and up the stairs, extinguishing his torch but keeping his weapon at the ready. Back up on the ground floor he pushed the cellar door closed with one latexed hand, then headed towards the gloomy, unlit kitchen. There were dirty plates in the sink and crumbs on the worktops. The tiles on the floor were scuffed and sticky. A door to his right looking out on to the scruffy garden. There was a key on the side – presumably to open the back door. And there was a second door at the far end, which he thought led to the bathroom. It was slightly ajar.

Danny stepped up to the door and slowly pushed it open. It creaked. He stepped inside.

He needed his torch again. There was only one window in here, overlooking the unkempt garden. But it was covered with a blackout blind that completely blocked the daylight. It didn't take Danny long to work out why. Galaid needed privacy. The bath was stained with rings of limescale. It contained three plastic bottles filled with a clear liquid. He undid each one of them in turn and smelled the contents. They each gave off the unmistakable aroma of nail varnish. Acetone. Danny felt sure that if he nosed around the flat a bit more, he'd find bottles of hydrogen peroxide. Acetone peroxide wasn't as explosive as the military-grade gear in the basement, but it was a hell of a sight easier to make, with a couple of easily bought chemicals and some instructions from the internet.

The Hammerstone quartet were right. There didn't seem much doubt that this bastard was planning another spectacular.

A crackle in his ear. Spud. 'We've left Tesco. I think he's heading back.'

'Keep on him.'

'Fuck's sake, Danny, what are you doing? Did you find any bomb-making gear?'

'You could say that.'

'Then get out. We'll wait until he leaves the house again, then set something up.'

'*Keep on him!*'

Danny turned his attention back to the contents of the bath-room.

There were enough explosives in this place to kill a hundred extremists. But Danny knew better than to use any of Sarim Galaid's gear. If he came back and noticed anything out of place, he'd be gone. Hammerstone had lucked out knowing this kid's exact location. If Danny gave him any sense that the authorities were on to him, he'd go immediately underground.

Maybe he *should* leave now.

Or maybe he should grab this opportunity while he had it. Galaid might not leave the house again for another two days, or longer. Spud would be pissed off, but he'd get over it.

Whatever Danny did, it had to be subtle. Covert. Something the terrorist would never expect until it was too late.

He turned his attention to the toilet.

If Galaid was buying bog roll, that was likely to be his first port of call when he got back.

He spoke into the radio. 'What's your status?'

'We're three minutes away.'

'I need five minutes minimum. Keep the radio open. I need to know what's happening.'

A pause.

Under his breath, Spud whispered: 'Jesus Christ.' But then, over the open radio, Danny heard him call, 'Hey, you, mate! You got a ciggie?'

Danny's paper SOCO suit whispered as he bent over and removed the heavy ceramic lid from the top of the cistern. He laid it gently on the tiled floor, then shone his torch into the cistern and examined the flush mechanism. It was caked with limescale, but looked to be in working order. He lowered his rucksack on to the toilet seat and felt inside. The constituent parts of his MOE kit were exactly where he'd stowed them. He withdrew the shaped charge, the silver detonator, the roll of coated wire and the battery pack.

Spud's voice: 'What's your fucking problem, mate? I just asked for a ciggie!'

A faint reply: 'I ain't got no ciggies. Leave me alone.'

Spud: 'Touchy bastard. I was only asking. What are you anyway, a fucking Paki?'

Danny gave a grim smile. If the best way to delay a target was often to pick a fight with them, Spud was extremely good at it.

Quickly, he went to work.

He looked at her half-eaten Egg McMuffin, sitting unappetisingly in its wrapper. She obviously didn't want to finish it, and now he'd spent most of his money so he couldn't offer her anything else. Even worse, he was panicking that he didn't have enough cash to buy her a tube ticket back to his house. He'd forgotten all about that. This wasn't going anything like as well as he'd hoped.

But then she put her hand on his and smiled at him again.

'Shall we go for a walk?' she asked.

He nodded.

They stood up and headed to the exit. Lots of people stared at them. He knew why: such a beautiful woman with such a strange-looking man. But he was used to people staring, and she had, after all, gone out of her way to find *him*. That made him feel very special.

Outside McDonald's he noticed that the sky had turned black. He half wished it would rain, because that would be more romantic. He looked at her suitcase. 'Allow me,' he said very politely, and he took the handle.

'Thank you,' she said. She took hold of his free hand. Her skin was so soft. His own hand was sweaty and clammy. He hoped she didn't mind. He wanted to squeeze her hand affectionately, but felt shy of doing it. So he kept it limp as they sauntered up Lower Regent Street, the suitcase trundling along behind them.

The charge itself was a block of plastic explosive backed with a strong adhesive: he had to peel back a strip of waxed paper to reveal it. You could stick one of these to the hull of a boat in high seas and be confident that it wouldn't shift, so there would be no problem fitting it to the inside wall of the cistern. He inserted the detonator into the charge. He cut two pieces of wire, each about ten inches in length, then stripped an inch of plastic coating from each of the four ends. He attached the end of one piece of wire to the detonator, the end of another to the battery pack. When the two free ends touched, the charge would explode.

Voices in his earphone: muffled curses. Danny zoned it out. Spud was giving Galaid some proper aggro. That was all he needed to know.

He turned his attention back to the cistern. With a single finger he flushed the chain. The water was noisily sucked down into the pan, but he lifted the dark blue float ball to stop it refilling. With his free hand, he picked up the charge and stuck it to the wall of the cistern. The front wall – not the back. The presence of water behind the charge would encourage it to blast forwards. The ceramic of the cistern would explode violently. He was, in effect, creating an enormous, static Claymore mine.

A mine that he hoped the victim would detonate with his own hand.

The charge held fast to the front wall of the cistern, even though it was damp. Danny carefully coiled the free end of the wire round the flushing mechanism. Still holding the float ball to stop the cistern from refilling, he picked up the battery pack. It was waterproof, so he knew there was no problem getting it wet. He tied the adjoining wire round the flush mechanism, making sure that – for now, at least – there was no risk of the two bare ends touching.

'He's running away,' Spud said in his ear. 'You've got two minutes, no longer. I've got some have-a-go hero eyeing me from the other side of the road. If I go at him again, I'll cause more of a distraction than I want.'

'Roger that.'

'What are you doing in there, mucker?'

Danny didn't reply. He released the float ball and the cistern started to refill.

It was painfully slow. The water pressure was bad. A full minute passed before the cistern was full again.

Danny felt a prickle of urgency down his spine. But he couldn't rush. Carefully, gingerly, concentrating on keeping his hands steady, he bent the two bare ends of the wires so that they were above the water line, but just millimetres apart. He gently let go. They shook somewhat, but didn't touch. But as soon as someone pressed the flush . . .

121

'Are you still in there? Fuck's sake, buddy, he's thirty seconds away . . .'

The most dangerous part: Danny lifted the cistern lid and replaced it *incredibly* gently. He was, he realised, holding his breath, and when ceramic met ceramic he winced, knowing that too much force would shake the wires into contact. But they remained separate. Danny carefully lifted his gear from the toilet seat and stuffed it into the rucksack.

Time to get out. IEDs had a habit of going wrong. Danny didn't want to be in the vicinity when it exploded. He stepped out of the bathroom and hurried to the kitchen door, grabbing the key that he'd noticed on the side. He needed to get out into the garden.

He put the key in the lock. It didn't fit. He looked round for another one. Nothing.

'He's turning into Dalewood Mews,' Spud reported.

Danny suppressed a moment of panic. He edged out of the kitchen . . . into the reception . . . the front room . . .

Shit! He realised he'd left the bathroom door open, wider than it had been. But he couldn't go back, because there was a scuffling sound at the front door. Galaid was back. He had his key in the lock.

Danny's pulse was racing. There was no place to hide, other than under the extended sofa bed. He quickly chucked his rucksack underneath it.

The door started to open.

He fell to the ground and, his paper suit rustling against the grimy carpet, rolled under the bed. He held his breath. Any movement would make a noise, and if this bastard found him here it would be a clusterfuck of epic proportions.

And even if he didn't, Danny was about to find himself trapped in a flat he'd just booby-trapped.

Footsteps. A slamming door.

'Fucking . . . *fucker!*' Sarim Galaid's feet appeared to Danny's left. They were heading into the second reception room, but he suddenly turned round to face the door again. 'Fucking *FUCKER!*' he screamed. Danny realised he was yelling at an imaginary Spud. 'You're the worst of them! I hope *you* get fucking done over next time. I'll put a bomb in your mother's house! *I'll put a bomb in your fucking mama's crib!*'

Galaid switched from English to Arabic and continued spewing a stream of obscenities at the front door. Danny breathed out very slowly, feeling his breath hot and wet under the paper mask. *Stay still. Stay calm. Trust that you've set the charge correctly. The blast won't reach you in here . . .*

After thirty seconds, his target fell silent. The feet changed direction again. Danny saw the bottom of a plastic supermarket bag swinging as Galaid finally walked out of the room.

Danny's body grew even tenser. From the kitchen, he heard the sound of units being opened and slammed shut. Galaid barked another word, again in Arabic.

Silence.

What was he doing? Pouring himself a glass of *fucking* soya milk? Or was he moving into the bathroom? Danny pictured the bare wires of the device in the cistern. There was a chance that he'd detonate the whole thing simply by sitting down.

Or perhaps he was staring at the bathroom door, wondering why it was now open when he had left it closed.

He gripped his weapon a little harder. If it came down to it, and Galaid twigged that something was up, Danny would have to deal with this the old-fashioned way.

Hammerstone wouldn't like it, but Hammerstone weren't on the ground . . .

A noise. Liquid. Gushing. It took a couple of seconds for Danny to understand what he was hearing. It was the sound of Sarim Galaid pissing thunderously against the porcelain.

Danny silently cursed. From the sound of it he was taking a piss, not a shit as he'd expected. There was always a chance that the filthy fucker wouldn't flush.

A burst in Danny's ear. Spud. Pissed off. 'Mucker, what the *hell's* going down?'

Danny didn't reply.

The gushing stopped.

Five seconds passed.

'Mucker, you need to respond or I'm coming in.'

Ten.

What was happening?

Danny felt his breath trembling. He tried to picture the scene in the bathroom. Was Galaid still in there? Maybe Danny should just burst through and throw him against the toilet, let the impact do its work . . .

It would put him in the line of the blast, but Galaid would surely absorb the shrapnel . . .

He started to move.

The paper suit rustled again.

He emerged from under the bed, and for a moment saw a silhouette pass in front of the floral curtains.

Spud?

'Stay away,' Danny hissed. 'It's under control . . .'

No reply.

'*Stay away!*'

And then, without warning, it happened.

The explosion was a short sharp crack. Loud, certainly, but there was no boom or echo. Danny felt the floorboards beneath him vibrate with the detonation. He heard a shower of shrapnel pelting the walls of the bathroom. A shock wave almost topped him and a lump of plaster fell from the ceiling a metre to his right.

Then silence.

Danny felt for his rucksack. If everything had gone according to plan, he didn't want to trail bloody footprints back across the flat. He pushed himself to his feet, shouldered the rucksack and held his gun firmly with two hands. Just because the device had exploded, it didn't mean Galaid was there when it happened. There was a thick cloud of dust in the second reception, and Danny could hear a high-pitched hissing sound. He could still see the door frame of the kitchen, but inside was dark and obscured. He edged forward. The hissing sound grew louder. In the kitchen, the floor was damp. The paper shoes of his SOCO suit crunched over shards of porcelain. The glass pane in the kitchen door had shattered outwards. The bathroom door was open. Danny lit his torch again and looked inside.

His makeshift Claymore had worked like a dream. Through the darkness and the smoke, Danny saw that the cistern itself was completely destroyed. The hissing noise came from the twisted inlet pipe that was spurting a tight jet of water up on to the ceiling. But the real devastation was on the floor.

Sarim Galaid had clearly been facing the cistern when it blew. Now he was on his back, feet at the toilet end, head at the door end. At least, what was left of him was.

The exploding cistern had ripped out the core of the bomber's groin and abdomen. Where there was once a stomach, there was now just a bleeding cavity. A thick, jagged shard of ceramic jutted out of where the corpse's bollocks once were, and although the heart had clearly already stopped, a thick slurry of blood, gastric juices and semi-digested food oozed from the catastrophic wound. Water from the spraying inlet pipe caused rivulets of pink to smear over the tiled floor.

Galaid's face was unrecognisable. Shrapnel had peppered it, and proximity to the explosive charge had burned away the skin. The eye sockets were weeping blood. His hair had been burned away. He was nothing more than a smouldering, bleeding piece of meat.

Danny stared at him for a moment. For some reason he found himself thinking about Clara. About finishing with her because he knew that in the days that followed, death would be his constant companion. Looked like he'd been right.

He'd seen enough. He trod carefully back into the kitchen where he started to remove his SOCO suit, though for the moment he kept the gloves, mask and hairnet on. As he shoved the paper suit back into the bag, he heard a thumping noise from the front door – neighbours, probably, wanting to find out what had happened. He spoke into the radio. 'Spud, is that you?'

'Negative,' Spud replied tersely. 'I'm at the end of the street. You've got two coppers and a neighbour banging on the door. You need to get out of there, mucker.'

The thumping on the front door grew louder.

'RV at the car,' Danny said.

He trod over to the kitchen door, checking over his shoulder that he hadn't left footprints. All clear. He clambered through the shattered pane of the kitchen door and jumped outside into the garden. Only then did he remove the remainder of his SOCO gear. He stuffed it in his rucksack, then ran down the overgrown garden.

There was a rickety, two-metre-high wooden fence at the end of the garden. Several panels damaged. Danny scaled it with ease and landed with a thump in a weed-strewn, litter-strewn alleyway. He looked both ways. Deserted. He ran north. Thirty-five metres to the end of the alleyway. Thunder cracked overhead. Heavy droplets of rain started to fall.

He reached the end of the alleyway and found himself in the road where, several hours previously, he'd collected pizza flyers from the parked cars. He caught sight of Spud, standing on the opposite side of the street, his expression darker than the sky. Danny nodded. From the direction they needed to go came the sound of sirens. Instinctively, Danny and Spud walked the opposite way. After thirty seconds, Danny crossed the road and fell in beside his mate.

'Been busy?' Spud asked from between gritted teeth.

'Spotted an opportunity,' Danny said. 'Grabbed it.'

'Feel like telling me what happened?'

Danny sniffed. 'Put it this way,' he said. 'If that Abu Ra'id cunt wants to blow up London again, he'll need to find another bomber.'

Her name wasn't really Nicki, of course. The lustrous curly hair was false and she would never normally wear so much lipstick or eyeliner that it made her look like a Western whore. And it went without saying that she did not find her gullible victim remotely attractive. Quite the opposite. He made her flesh creep with his strange features and lecherous glances. But as Abu Ra'id had said: in war, sacrifices have to be made. In Pakistan and Afghanistan, and across the Muslim world, the British and American monsters had targeted the weak and the helpless. So why shouldn't *they* use the weak and helpless in their retaliations?

She looked up ahead. Police officers at the corner of Lower Regent Street and Piccadilly Circus. Four of them, in high-visibility jackets. After Paddington, the sight of an Arabic woman, a Down's syndrome man and a suitcase would surely arouse suspicion.

'Let's cross here,' she suggested.

He looked a bit confused, but of course he agreed.

Hand in hand, they crossed the road and stepped into Norris Street, a quieter back street just south of Piccadilly Circus.

'I like the arcade machines,' she said once they were away from the busy main streets. 'Shall we go and play them?' And then, when he looked suddenly worried: 'My treat!'

He grinned at her. They turned a corner. Another main road was up ahead and she saw two more police officers, a man and a woman, walking towards them. Her pulse raced. She had hoped she wouldn't have to do this, but now there was no choice. She stopped, pinned him against the wall and pressed her lips to his. She felt his tongue, wet and warm, twitching in her mouth. An unpleasant bulge in his trousers.

The police officers passed. She pulled away and saw his foolishly grinning face.

'That was nice,' she said.

Two minutes later, still hand in hand, they entered the Trocadero. It was very crowded, even at this hour. They walked past outlets selling brightly coloured sweeties, royal-family plates and tacky models of red London buses. They stood close to each other on the escalator as it carried them down into the basement. Here, the air was filled with the pinging and beeping and roaring of the arcades. Kids stood shooting light guns at imaginary foes. Others sat in arcade cars, speeding round imaginary racetracks. She pointed at an empty car and tugged at his sleeve. 'Let's go on that,' she said.

Dragging the suitcase behind him, he followed her to the car.

'You go first,' she said.

Obediently, he propped the suitcase up next to the car and climbed inside. She fed a pound coin into the machine and watched his pitifully malcoordinated attempt at playing the game, which was over in 45 seconds.

Dude, you caused a pile-up, said the machine in a robotic voice.

'You're really good,' she cooed, and she inserted another pound coin. She was aware of a couple of kids loitering nearby, coiled up with suppressed laughter at his strange looks and ineptitude on the arcade.

'Thank you,' he said. And then, after a moment's thought, he blurted out the word: 'Darling.'

She cringed, and smiled.

When his second go was over, she whispered in his ear, allowing her lips to brush lightly against him. 'I need to get some more change.' That look of panic again. She whispered in his ear: 'We'll spend a bit more time here, then go back to your place.'

And, of course, he nodded.

'Will you look after my overnight bag?' she asked.

He nodded again. Disgusted, she wondered if he might actually start drooling.

'I'll be back in a minute,' she said. 'Darling.'

She walked towards the escalator. Only when she was at the top did she look back down. The lairy kids had surrounded his car. They were pointing at him and laughing, no doubt as much at his strange looks as at his hopelessness on the arcade. More fool them. She turned her back on them and hurried out of the Trocadero, past the buses and tea towels and sweets, and out into the street. The sky was very dark. Thunder was in the air. She crossed the road and pulled a mobile phone from her coat. She walked briskly as she pressed speed dial number one.

There was no point listening for the ringtone, because she knew there wouldn't be one. There would just be the explosion, and she braced herself for that.

She was at least thirty metres from the Trocadero's entrance when it came, but it nearly knocked her from her feet nonetheless. The ground seemed to shake, and the boom seemed to reverberate against the high walls of Shaftesbury Avenue. She fell against another pedestrian – a woman in a blue raincoat, whose expression changed in an instant from annoyance to terror.

As the boom subsided, there was a moment of almost-silence. As though London was holding its breath.

And then a thunderclap cracked overhead. Like an echo of the explosion. Huge droplets of rain spattered on to the pavement. She hurried south, a faceless figure in the faceless crowds, as the desperate screams from the direction of the Trocadero reached her ears.

NINE

'You should have told me what you were doing, mucker. That's all I'm saying.'

Spud wasn't the type to lose his rag, but he was close to it now. For some reason, Danny didn't care. He was tense. Maybe an argument would do him good.

'I was thinking on my feet. That's all *I'm* saying.'

Spud glared at him from the passenger seat and Danny suddenly felt bad about himself. His mate was right. It was one of the first things they'd learned – never do something by yourself, if you don't have to.

Chastened, he said: 'Okay. Point taken.' And to cover the uncomfortable pause that followed: 'Fucking traffic. What the hell's going on?' They were nose to tail down Fulham Palace Road. It was pissing down and the other drivers were getting lairy. Danny switched on the car radio, wondering if it was too early for there to be any news of his morning's work.

There was news all right. Just not what they expected. They listened in horror as fragments of information filtered through the breathless reports of harried journalists. *Massive explosion . . . scenes of devastation in the West End . . . scores feared dead . . .*

The two SAS men sat in sickened silence. If Danny had felt any satisfaction at nailing Sarim Galaid, it was fast disappearing.

'The Hammerstone lot will be feeling the heat,' Danny said. 'We need to get back to the safe house, see if they've tried to contact us.'

It took an hour. They were tempted to use their siren, but in the end made the call not to. They'd just have been one of many, and in any case Danny didn't much feel like drawing attention to himself. By the time they reached Battersea Park, he was ready to explode with tension, and he sensed Spud felt the same. As they pulled up outside the safe house, his mate retrieved his Glock from the glove department. 'Come on,' he said. 'Let's check the dead-letter box.'

'Wait.' Danny pointed through the windscreen.

At the end of the street was a main road running at right angles. Rammed with traffic, just like everywhere else. On the opposite side, no more than thirty metres from the safe house, was a large billboard advertising *The Lion King*, which sure as hell wouldn't be running tonight. And standing underneath the billboard, looking quite out of place in this shitty part of town, with his heavy black overcoat and patrician features, was a man they both knew.

'Piers Chamberlain,' Spud muttered suspiciously. 'I thought those fuckers didn't want anything to do with us.'

'They don't,' Danny breathed. Not as a foursome. But individually, perhaps?

The two men debussed. Danny clicked the key fob and the vehicle beeped itself shut. He didn't think Chamberlain had seen them yet, but he knew that putting himself in their line of vision was an invitation for them to make contact. Chamberlain might be a rupert, but he was a Regiment rupert who knew damn well he couldn't expect to go unnoticed by two active SAS operatives. Danny and Spud walked side by side to the end of the street. He clocked them in a few seconds, nodded, and then started walking along the opposite side of the main road. Fifty metres further along, he stepped into a greasy spoon. A good place for a covert RV. Cheap cafes like that never had CCTV, and it was usual to have different clientele of all types each day. They wouldn't look out of place.

Danny and Spud stopped.

'Do we join him?' Spud asked.

Danny nodded. 'We join him.'

'Then he's buying the fucking sarnies.'

They crossed the road. The front window of the greasy spoon was misted up from the inside, but Danny could make out the dark shadow of a big man sitting by the window and instinctively knew it was Chamberlain. With the sound of three different police sirens fading in the background, the two SAS men stepped inside.

It was warm in here, the atmosphere a fug of tea and fried food. Tatty posters of exotic beaches on the wall, torn at the edges. About half the tables were occupied. In one corner, above the serving bar, there was a TV tuned in to BBC News 24. Shaky camera work rolled on the developing scenes in Piccadilly. Danny saw a flash of red as a wounded body was stretchered from the remains of the Trocadero. All the punters inside the cafe – perhaps fifteen of them – were transfixed. One guy had a copy of the *Sun* in front of him. He absentmindedly licked a forefinger and turned the page of his newspaper. But he was staring at the screen, not the paper. A constant babble of reportage filled the air: *Many feared dead . . . extent of the damage not known . . . police appealing to the public to avoid all non-urgent travel to central London . . .*

At a table by himself, along the left-hand wall, sat an elderly guy, a workman by the look of his paint-spattered overalls. He had dark skin and Arabic features: his beard was white, his face deeply lined and his bald head covered in liver spots. He looked kindly, but also distinctly uncomfortable as he waited for his breakfast. Some of the other punters cast him the occasional hostile glance.

Danny's eyes picked out Chamberlain. He was sitting in the corner to the right of the door, his back against the wall and a mug of tea in front of him, the tea bag still floating in the cup.

He looked up, but because of his squint it wasn't immediately obvious if he was looking directly at them or not.

'Sit down, lads,' he said quietly, so his voice was drowned by the TV for everyone except Danny and Spud. 'I've ordered the full English for you both. Sounds like you've had a busy night.'

Wordlessly, they sat opposite him, Danny by the window.

'You know what I can't abide?' Chamberlain said. 'Go to Glasgow, they'll place a portion of haggis on the plate and call it the full Scottish. Dublin, you'll have a slice of white pudding and it's a full Irish. Load of bloody nonsense if you ask me.' Only now did he glance up at the TV. 'You've heard the latest?'

They nodded.

'Mark my words, lads. If this carries on, we'll have an extremist with a bomb on every street corner. The royal protection boys have already moved the senior royals from the palace and Clarence House. Her Majesty is spitting blood – this is far worse than the glory days of the Provos. Medals all round for the person who stops these little shits, I shouldn't wonder.' He gave them both a meaningful look.

'I'd have thought Her Majesty would be pissing rainbows,' Spud said coolly.

A flicker of irritation crossed Chamberlain's face, but he quickly mastered it. 'Don't quite follow you, old man,' he said.

'Didn't that pretty boy who was banging her granddaughter get a lump of shrapnel in his skull at Paddington? Nice neat solution to a nasty messy problem.'

Typical Spud. Zero tact. But it didn't seem to bother Chamberlain. He looked up at the approaching waitress – a sour-faced woman in her sixties with an egg-spattered apron, carrying two immense plates of food. He indicated that she should set them down in front of Danny and Spud. Only when the food was in front of him did Danny realise how hungry he was. Sarim Galaid's butchered body was just a memory. It hadn't affected Danny's appetite.

Chamberlain watched them eat for a couple of minutes before speaking again. 'I suppose you're wondering why I'm here,' he said finally. Danny didn't feel inclined to give him the satisfaction of admitting that was true. Clearly Spud felt the same. They continued to wolf down their food. Chamberlain looked round the cafe, obviously checking that nobody was paying them any attention. When he spoke again, it was in a quieter voice.

'That Hammerstone lot,' he said. 'All very well for them to give out edicts from on high. Don't think they quite realise how difficult it is to make these little ... *events* ... look like accidents. Can't have all your targets blowing themselves up while they're taking a leak, eh? Thought you might appreciate a bit of input. Three heads better than two, and all that.'

Danny scraped the remnants of food from round his plate, finished it off, then pushed the plate forward.

'I'm all ears,' he said.

'The Province was my hunting ground, back in the day,' Chamberlain said. 'Had to be bloody careful, of course. The Micks were all hot under the collar about internment at the time. Not sure they'd have been quite so vocal if they'd seen some of the animals in Long Kesh, but there you have it.'

Spud belched and pushed his empty plate away. Danny kept quiet. Northern Ireland was a sensitive subject for him. He certainly didn't want to discuss his own family's involvement in the Province with the arsehole across the table.

'Handful of Provos we couldn't bang up, of course.' He traced two imaginary speech marks in the air. '"Lack of evidence". Or they'd have caused more trouble inside than out. Not unlike this bloody ridiculous situation with Abu Ra'id. Had to see to it that they "met with an accident".' Speech marks again. 'Happy to share the fruits of my labours.'

'Like I say,' Danny answered, 'I'm all ears.'

Chamberlain put his cup of tea to his mouth and drained it in one gulp. 'Shark's eye,' he said. 'Worked every time.'

Danny inclined his head. What Chamberlain said made sense. The shark's eye was very simple, but very effective: a black tube, not much more than a foot in length. Fire it at night-time and it would give a directional burst of dazzling light that would blind anyone. Fire it towards the driver of a moving vehicle and, nine times out of ten, it would cause the driver to lose control. Net result: road kill, and very little in the way of evidence.

'I've done a bit of homework on your second target,' Chamberlain continued. 'They'll have sent you his details already, I shouldn't wonder, but the DVLC have a motorbike registered to his name. Shark's eye would be ideal, I'd have thought.'

'Sounds familiar,' said Spud. 'All we need now is a tunnel under the Seine and a pack of paparazzi chasing after him, we can do the full Diana.'

A poker face from Chamberlain. 'I rather thought,' he said, 'that the gentlemen of Twenty-two were immune to that sort of gossip.'

'The gentlemen maybe,' Spud drawled. 'But not me. What about that Regiment fella who said he saw one of your lot in Paris the night before the hit?'

By 'your lot', Spud meant the Firm, and Danny was well aware of the rumour. It was no secret that a small team from the RWW – the Regiment's precursor to E squadron – had investigated the possibility of conducting a hit on Milosevic back in the early nineties. The method was to be exactly what Chamberlain was suggesting to them now: a shark's-eye attack on the war criminal's convoy as it negotiated a particularly treacherous mountain pass. The RWW team had rejected it as a possibility for exactly the reasons that Danny knew the Diana conspiracy was a load of hokum: too many variables. A shark's-eye hit was fine for a Provo shithead who was heading for an early grave anyway, but for a high-profile target like Milosevic, against whom you'd only get one chance, it was just too blunt a tool.

But the rumour was that the night before Diana's death, an MI6 agent had been spotted in Paris with one of the RWW guys on the Milosevic 'hit team'. Enough of a coincidence to get tongues wagging, and wild theories spreading.

'I can absolutely assure you,' Chamberlain told Spud mildly, his lips barely moving and his voice little more than a whisper, 'that an attempt on the life of a prominent public figure such as Princess Diana would require a far greater level of premeditation than was evident during the events of the Place de l'Alma.'

'Sounds like you've given it a lot of thought,' said Spud.

Chamberlain's lips went thin. 'Practically none,' he said. 'Although I'm sure I'm not alone in feeling queasy at the thought of a rag ...' He checked himself. '... a Middle Eastern playboy becoming stepfather to our future monarch.'

'Doesn't bother me, pal. They're all German anyway, far as I can tell.'

For the first time, Chamberlain looked as though he was on the point of losing his cool. He drew a deep breath, and scratched the eyebrow above the eye that had a squint. Danny found himself recalling Buckingham's words of the day before. *Keeps the company of some peculiar types ... Not saying they're right-wing, but they do rather make our friends in UKIP look like card-carrying Marxists ... they've been lobbying government to set up a transfer of power to the army in the event of Islamic extremism getting out of control ...*

Behind him, Danny heard a sudden scraping of chairs. He looked round. A couple of burly punters had stood up and were moving towards the old Middle Eastern guy sitting by himself. The TV continued to babble in the background, but suddenly nobody was watching it. The atmospherics in the cafe had changed. The workman looked up. His friendly, lined face instantly acquired a hunted expression.

'S'pose it's one of your mates done this?' said one of the two burly men. The accusation in his voice was ugly.

The old Middle Eastern man shook his head nervously. His eyes darted around, looking for an exit. But the way out was barred by these two menacing white guys, who were clearly looking for trouble. One of them bent over and lifted the edge of the Middle Eastern man's table. His cup of tea toppled and spilled all over his lap. The man looked confused, then angry – it was an emotion that didn't suit his face. But then he calmed himself. 'Please, my friends,' he said mildly. 'I'm very sorry for your loss. This is a terrible thing, but it is not done in my name. Please, I don't want any trouble.'

'Bit late for that, sunshine . . .'

Danny turned back to Spud and Chamberlain. On his mate's face he saw an ill-concealed look of disgust. On Chamberlain's, quite the opposite. Not approval, exactly, nor even enjoyment. Just a kind of bleak satisfaction.

Spud stood up. He walked across the cafe and tapped the two burly blokes on the shoulder. They were both half a head height taller than Spud, and didn't look like they appreciated the interruption.

'Sit down, fellas,' said Spud. 'You're blocking the telly.'

The men sneered at him. 'We'll sit down when we've dealt with the Paki.'

'You'll sit down now,' Spud said, his voice dangerously quiet now, 'or you'll fuck off out of it.'

The two men looked at each other with malicious grins.

Neither of them expected Spud's pre-emptive strike.

He whacked his solid fist against the head of the man on his right. It cracked sharply against the second man's head and they both staggered, dazed, across the cafe floor. The Middle Eastern man jumped up to his feet. His old bones couldn't move very fast, but he shuffled up to the door and left the cafe as quickly as he could.

'He hasn't paid!' shouted the waitress. 'He hasn't bleedin' *paid*!'

Spud pulled a ten-pound note from his pocket and chucked

it on the Middle Eastern man's table. He cast a dangerous glance at the still-staggering men. They looked a lot less certain of themselves now, as if they wanted to hit back but were afraid to muscle up to the tough, broad-shouldered Spud. Typical bullies, crumbling when things didn't go their way. Spud took a step towards them. 'Word of advice, fellas,' he said. 'Keep yourselves to yourselves. Any more of that shit and if *I* don't put you down, my mate over there will.' He pointed in Danny's direction, who gave the thugs a dark look as Spud returned to Chamberlain.

'Breakfast's on you,' Spud told the MI6 man. 'Let's go, mucker.'

Danny stood up. He nodded at Chamberlain.

'You'll find the details of the second target waiting for you,' Chamberlain said.

As Danny and Spud walked towards the door he found himself zoning in to the commentary from the TV again. *At least fifty people are feared dead in what some are calling the worst terrorist strike since 9/11. The prime minister has called it 'a sickening, cowardly act' and vowed to bring those responsible to justice.*

Out on the street, nothing had changed. The traffic was still backed up. A cyclist was shouting at a driver who'd just opened his door without looking. Exhaust fumes filled the air, and there was no sign of the Middle Eastern man Spud had just saved from a pummelling. Suddenly, Danny heard a familiar sound: the crescendo of helicopter rotors. A khaki RAF Merlin flew low overhead. Not your average, everyday sight in London. They crossed the road and strode back in the direction of their safe house. Danny only looked back once. Chamberlain was at the door of the cafe. He had lit a cigarette and was watching them go.

'What the fuck was all that about?' Spud asked. 'Shark's eyes – what does he think it is, 1975?'

Danny had no answer. But plenty of questions. Why was Chamberlain so keen to help them? Why had he sought them out, away from his Hammerstone colleagues? *What the hell was going on?*

'Is it just me,' Danny said, 'or did he not look like he gave a flying fuck about this latest bomb?'

Spud shrugged. 'He's a spook and a rupert, mucker. What d'you expect?'

Two minutes later they reached the safe house. There was something on the doorstep.

It was a black flight case, two foot wide, a foot high and a foot deep. They eyed it suspiciously for a moment from a distance of a couple of metres. Then Spud said, 'Fuck it.' He stepped forward, picked up the flight case, opened the door and stepped inside.

In the kitchen they opened it up, carefully but with interest. The flight case contained a black tube, about a foot in length, with a built-in battery pack and a trigger.

'Shark's eye,' Danny said, and Spud nodded his agreement.

Looked like Chamberlain had left them a present.

Jamal Faroole did not like this place.

He knew it was secure – that Abu Ra'id was too clever to allow the authorities anywhere near this penthouse flat in the heart of the Docklands, right under their very noses. And he knew he hadn't been followed. His usual strategy to avoid a trail was to travel to the end of the central line and walk half a mile up a country lane so that anybody following him would be forced to show themselves. But in the wake of the Trocadero bomb that morning the underground was completely shut down. He gave some thought to using his motorbike, but soon discounted that idea. It was parked at his flat in Perivale for a start, and he hadn't returned there since the day of the Paddington bomb, choosing instead to bunk down at a B&B in Ruislip. More importantly, where a motorbike went, a car could go, and he knew he wouldn't be able to spot skilled vehicle surveillance. Instead, he had used his pushbike to traverse London, and had squeezed through walkways that no car could possibly cross.

He had avoided the centre. He knew the West End would be

locked down, and that police would be everywhere. He'd seen the helicopters flying overhead and heard the sirens screaming past the B&B all morning. From the window he'd seen military trucks, no doubt filled with soldiers, passing on their way into London.

He'd watched the footage on TV, of course, and seen the devastation on Shaftesbury Avenue. The emergency services coming out of the building into the sheeting rain with body bags. The wounded, their faces and clothes bloody, staggering shell-shocked across the debris-strewn pavement. He'd seen the screaming family members weeping into the camera, as increasingly dramatic statistics rolled underneath them. *Fifty feared dead ... a hundred feared dead ... a hundred and fifty feared dead ...* Part of him exalted at the success of this latest strike. Another, admittedly smaller, part of him hoped that this would not be as spectacular as his own bombing. There was pride at stake, after all.

A little after ten o'clock, however, he'd seen the other major news item. It twisted him up inside as if someone had put a hand round his heart and squeezed it. A second bomb had exploded almost simultaneously in a ground-floor flat in Hammersmith.

One fatality.

A twenty-three-year-old man believed to be of interest to the security services in the wake of last Friday's explosion in Paddington Station ... explosives found in the flat ... thought to be an accidental detonation ...

Jamal's lip had curled. He had thumped the arm of his chair in anger and indignation. *Thought to be an accidental detonation?* He spat on the carpet. He shouted at the TV, loudly at first, though he quickly checked his voice so as not to alert his landlady. He had paced the room, wondering what he should do. Finally he decided that he had no choice. He *had* to speak to Abu Ra'id. And since there was no way to contact him by phone or e-mail, he would have to go and see him in person.

And so here he was. Pacing the tiles of the posh dining room that made him feel so uneasy. He had bad memories of it.

Memories of making the video in which their young jihadi colleague had tried – and failed – to sacrifice himself. Of the strange sound the knife had made when Sarim had forced it into his throat. Of the blood. Detonating a bomb was easy. There was no need to see anything, or to witness the brutal reality of what you were doing. Killing someone with a knife was different. Like slaughtering a chicken, instead of buying it ready-fried from KFC. He had relived the moment in his sleep, countless times, and always woken up sweating.

He continued to pace the room. There was no remnant of that moment of martyrdom. The blackout blinds still covered the floor-to-ceiling windows, but there was no bloodied tarpaulin. No backdrop. No camera. Did the room smell a little different to usual? Jamal thought perhaps it did. He tried not to think of that as he sat rigidly on a high-backed dining chair.

The door opened. Jamal felt his heart pound as he expected Abu Ra'id to enter. But it wasn't the cleric who walked in. It was a young woman, about Jamal's own age. She had dark skin and curly hair, and wore no make-up, but was beautiful nonetheless. There was a wariness in her dark eyes. A hardness. But she also seemed anxious. She looked around the room, as though checking it for threats. Only after a few seconds did her eyes fall on Jamal. She nodded in an unfriendly way.

'I'm Jamal.' He introduced himself uncomfortably. 'I've seen you down the mosque, innit?'

The girl shrugged.

'Posh crib, this,' Jamal persisted. 'Don't know who pays for it.'

No reply.

'What's your name?'

'I keep it to myself,' she said quietly. 'Maybe you should do the same.'

Jamal bristled. 'Yeah?' he said. 'Well I'm here to see Abu Ra'id.' He said it with a certain pride, because to be granted an audience with Abu Ra'id was to be favoured.

'Me too,' said the girl.

'Yeah, well …' Jamal started to say. But he suddenly stopped speaking. A figure filled the doorway. Broad shoulders. Beard flecked with grey.

Abu Ra'id.

'Welcome, both of you,' he said. 'You're sure you were not followed?'

'*I* am,' Jamal said boastfully.

Abu Ra'id gave the girl an enquiring glance. She shook her head and that seemed to satisfy him. He stepped further into the room. For a moment he stood a couple of metres from where Jamal was sitting, his face quite calm. Suddenly Jamal realised he had taken the only seat in the room. He jumped up as if it had suddenly turned burning hot and looked nervously at the cleric.

'Thank you, Jamal,' Abu Ra'id said. 'I'm not as young as I was.'

He sat down. The chair seemed far too small for him. It creaked as it took his weight.

He paused. Then he looked at each of them in turn.

'You have done very well,' he said. 'I am pleased with you.'

Jamal looked at the girl. 'Is she …?'

'The Trocadero,' Abu Ra'id said calmly. 'She used her charms to lure a young man to his destiny.'

Jamal found himself exchanging a glance with the girl. He clenched his jaw. 'Sarim is dead, Abu Ra'id.'

The cleric inclined his head sadly and outstretched his palms. 'We mourn his passing,' he said, 'and rejoice that he has achieved paradise.'

Jamal blinked. 'But … but Abu Ra'id, surely you understand what this means.'

Abu Ra'id gazed calmly at him. 'What does it mean, Jamal?'

'Well, that he was killed … that the security services executed him. *That they know who we are, Abu Ra'id.*'

There was a dead silence in the room. Abu Ra'id looked again from one to the other. 'You do not need to worry,' he said.

'But Abu Ra'id, they killed him!'

'No,' the cleric said. His voice was suddenly sharp, and it made Jamal jump. 'Listen carefully to me. They did *not* kill him. Sarim was meddling with explosives. He should have known better. His death was an accident. A terrible accident, but an accident.'

Jamal stared at the cleric. He barely knew what to say. 'Abu Ra'id . . . that's what they say on the news, but surely you don't *believe* that?'

Abu Ra'id nodded. 'Yes,' he said. 'I believe it.'

Jamal glanced at the girl. She also looked uncertain at Abu Ra'id's statement. To contradict the cleric took a braver man that Jamal, however, and he bowed his head in a gesture of respect.

He raised it again as the girl spoke.

'Abu Ra'id,' she said. 'Forgive me, but if you are so certain that the authorities do not know who we are, why are *you* in hiding *here*? Why aren't you at the mosque, where your children are eager to see you and hear your voice? Why aren't you with your family?'

Jamal held his breath. He had never heard *anyone* talk to Abu Ra'id like that. The cleric's face was expressionless as he sat in silence for a moment. Then he stood up and walked over towards the floor-to-ceiling windows. He pressed a button on the wall. Almost noiselessly, the electric blackout blinds rose, to reveal the pristine glass of the windows and the vast sprawl of London spread out beyond.

'Abu Ra'id,' Jamal said urgently. 'Do not stand so close to the window . . .'

But his warning was ignored as the city presented itself before them.

It was an impressive sight. Jamal could see everything: the Shard, the London Eye, the dome of St Paul's Cathedral, Big Ben, the bridges over the snaking Thames. He saw the Millennium Dome, and the unused landing strip of City Airport, framed by an inlet of the river. It crossed his mind how many targets there were in London, each one more iconic than the last.

All three of them continued to stare for a moment. There was something strange about the sight. It took a moment for Jamal to realise that there was barely any traffic on the river, and with a flash of intuition he realised that there were probably only police boats and those run by the security services allowed on the water. Jamal picked out two helicopters hovering lower than them over the north bank of the river. He realised they were flying over Piccadilly, over the site of the latest bomb.

London, he could see from this snapshot, was running scared.

'Two weeks ago,' Abu Ra'id said quietly, 'a drone strike in eastern Pakistan killed one hundred and thirty-six people. It was not even reported in the British press. And yet, when their own people start to die . . .'

His voice trailed off.

He didn't sound angry. Sad, if anything. That gave Jamal a bit of courage. 'Abu Ra'id,' he said. 'They are mentioning your name on the television and in the newspapers. They are wondering why you have disappeared from the streets. I am worried for you, that they will . . .'

'*QUIET!*' Abu Ra'id roared with such sudden violence that Jamal physically started. He exchanged a glance with the girl, who looked similarly shocked and was edging away from him.

Silence.

Abu Ra'id breathed on the window and, in the mist that formed, he drew the Arabic symbol for God. Jamal felt a chill. He was reminded of the last time he saw that symbol, in this very room, hanging on a backdrop in front of a bloodied tarpaulin.

Abu Ra'id pressed the button again. As the blinds silently descended, he turned. There was a hard glint in his eyes. 'If you do not wish to continue this important work, please just say the word. Your allegiance will not be in doubt, but there is room in our organisation for many different people' – he looked over to the wall where the young man had been sacrificed – 'who we may use for all sorts of different purposes.'

The girl's eyes fell to the floor. She looked chastened. And scared. There was no doubt in Jamal's mind that she understood just what Abu Ra'id was threatening her with. As did he.

Abu Ra'id stepped away from the window. 'You will return to your homes,' he said. 'Your *home*, Jamal. You will not hide like a coward. And you will stay there. Wait for your instructions. And remember: God looks after the faithful, and so do I. But the unfaithful?' He looked at each of them in turn. 'The unfaithful are punished.'

He turned his back on them again. The audience, Jamal understood, was over.

He walked backwards to the door. Neither he, nor the girl, he sensed, could get out of there quickly enough.

The corridor that led to the exit was brightly lit. Jamal and the girl hurried down it, shoulder to shoulder. They passed a bathroom on the right-hand side. The door was slightly ajar, and as he hurried by it, Jamal saw inside. It was all marble and mirrors, with crisp white towels piled by the sink and a bath twice the size of any he had ever seen before. Two white towelling dressing gowns hung by a hook on the wall, but in the split second that he passed the door, he noticed something else: black robes of some description, hanging alongside them. A burka. He didn't know why, but the sight made him feel very uneasy.

Outside the main entrance to the apartment sat the two men who had been in attendance both times Jamal had visited. Dark skin, broad shoulders, no hint of a smile. Jamal didn't doubt that they were armed, and he felt their aggressive stares burn into his back as he and the woman waited for the elevator to arrive. It seemed to take an age, but even when the doors had closed around them and they had started the long, silent journey to the ground floor, he felt far from safe.

Claustrophobic. Hunted.

Stepping out on to the glamorous marble atrium of the ground floor, with its tinkling fountain and barely audible piped music, Jamal immediately felt the hot glare of the concierge, smartly uniformed behind his desk. He and the girl hurried past him without a word, then out into the early evening.

The plaza in front of the building was crowded. An outdoor fountain glowed thirty metres ahead of them, but none of the pedestrians paid it any attention. They seemed only intent on getting home. It struck Jamal as ironic: they no doubt thought that here, in the business centre of the capital, they were most at risk. And yet their enemy was hiding out right in their midst.

He pulled up his hood and turned to the girl. She still hadn't told him her name. He thought about asking her again. She was very beautiful, and for a crazy moment he wondered what would happen if he tried to kiss her, even though he knew he was far too shy to do it.

'What are you going to do?' he asked her, keeping his voice low.

The girl was less haughty now. A little unsure of herself. 'Go home, I suppose. Like he told us.' She frowned. 'Do *you* think we're going to be all right?'

'Yeah,' Jamal said. 'Course.' He peered upwards. The enormous glass tower loomed threateningly above them. Then he looked across the plaza to the other side of the fountain. There was a row of Boris bikes neatly lined up, and next to them his own bike, chained to a cycle rail. 'Better make a move,' he said.

He nodded, then hurried across the plaza and unchained his bike. He looked back at the tower block again. A window-cleaning cradle was descending to the ground floor. The guys inside were wolf-whistling the girl. Jamal felt a surge of anger. He wanted to go over and defend her honour. To tell the men that he was the Paddington bomber, and see how arrogant they felt then. But the girl was in charge of the situation. She gave the window cleaners an evil look before turning her back on them. Jamal calmed himself, then suddenly felt uneasy again. He realised that those window cleaners could easily have observed them when Abu Ra'id had opened the blinds in the penthouse, and he wondered again how the cleric could be so sure that he was safe.

As he pedalled back across London, Jamal's mind was ablaze. Abu Ra'id seemed so *certain* that they were beyond the reach of the authorities. So *certain* that Sarim's death had been an accident. But did Jamal believe him? Did he *dare* to believe him? Sarim had trusted Abu Ra'id implicitly, and look where that had got him. The cleric had insisted on Jamal returning home, but surely to do that would be madness.

Then again, did he really dare to disobey Abu Ra'id? He knew, better than most, just what he was capable of.

It took a long time to cross London. The traffic was bad, the police presence high. But as he cycled through Bayswater and past Shepherd's Bush, he realised that he was not heading back to the B&B in Ruislip, but to his own flat in Perivale. And in a flash, he realised he had made his decision.

To run. To go into hiding from both the authorities and from Abu Ra'id. Tonight.

TEN

Clara went about her work in a kind of daze. The dead were everywhere. The hospital mortuary was overflowing. Injured men women and children were dying, one an hour, at the very least. It had become necessary to set up an overflow mortuary in a ward deep in the bowels of the hospital, where rented air-conditioning machines sucked the warmth from the air to stop the corpses decaying before they could be released back to the families. A poor substitute for the hospital cold room. Clara had already seen a fly crawling on the face of a dead woman.

When she was at school, she saw her history lessons not as an endless succession of facts, but a succession of pictures: injured men laid out in field hospitals in the wake of the Crimea, in the trenches of the Great War, on the outskirts of Saigon. Those grainy black and white images didn't look so different from the sights that surrounded her now. London was at war. The enemy was unseen, the casualties were civilian. But it was a war nevertheless.

It wasn't just the endless procession of injury and death that seemed to suck everything out of Clara. After Paddington, she had been able to talk about what she had seen with Danny. He wasn't the type to try to comfort her, but he *did* listen. And she knew that beneath it all, he cared. She missed him more than she knew how to express. It was a constant dull ache somewhere deep inside her. She had told herself that morning that she would deal with it by throwing herself into her work, and the influx of casualties from the shock bombing in the Trocadero meant she didn't have much choice. But in a corner of her mind, she felt his absence more than she would ever have admitted to anyone.

She worked long past her shift time. They all did. It was gone nine o'clock when she scrubbed down, disinfected her hands for one last time, put on her ordinary clothes and clocked out. She walked alone through the foyer of the hospital and flashed her ID at one of the crowd of policeman guarding the front entrance. Police guarding a *hospital*? Had it really come to this? She shuffled out in the cold night air with her head down. She was exhausted, but dreaded going home. Now was not a time to be alone.

She could walk to Maida Vale from here, and a good thing too – there was no public transport running, and every cab in the city seemed to be taken. She set off. She could get home in half an hour if she kept her pace up. There was a short cut round the back of the hospital that very few people knew about. It was a narrow, dark alleyway, uninviting at the best of times and especially this evening. Clara stumbled along it, her head down, barely aware of her surroundings, her mind lost in unpleasant thoughts.

She didn't realise that she was being followed until she felt someone grab her by the arm.

On another occasion, she might have screamed. But not tonight. Whoever had grabbed her had done so from behind, and in an instant 24 hours of frustration seemed to come steaming out of her. She spun round. 'What the *hell* . . .'

It was so dark. She couldn't see clearly at first. She blinked and tried to clear her head.

Then she stopped.

Danny?

She started at him. He was in a terrible state. His right eye was purple, bulging and bruised. There was a cut on his upper lip, sealed together with a length of steristrip. She caught a whiff of stale booze from his body.

And only then did she realise that it wasn't Danny at all.

'Kyle?' she whispered. 'Oh my God, what's *happened* to you?'

'S nothing,' Kyle said. His speech was slurred.

'Then let go of me.'

Kyle let his hand fall.

'Who *did* this?' Clara asked. And then, almost immediately, she answered her own question. 'The Poles? The ones you were talking about?'

Kyle nodded, and averted his gaze. He looked humiliated. He was also shivering.

The doctor in her decided that what Kyle needed most was a hot drink. 'Come with me,' she said, and she started striding along the alleyway. A moment later they were in the main street. Kyle trotted to keep up with her, and as they passed a pub he looked longingly towards it. But Clara knew that more booze would be a disaster, and five minutes later they were sitting opposite each other in Starbucks. There was a copy of the *Evening Standard* on the table. The front page showed the devastated frontage of the Trocadero, and the baristas, when they weren't looking at Kyle's beaten face, were talking feverishly about the latest explosion. Kyle had his shivering hands wrapped round a hot drink. The smell of booze was more obvious in here. It turned her stomach.

'Tell me what happened.'

'Told you already. 'S nothing.'

'It's not nothing. How much do you owe them, Kyle?'

Danny's brother shrugged. 'Five Gs. It's not a problem. I'll get my hands on the money somehow.' He took a sip of coffee and winced as the hot liquid scalded his damaged lips.

Clara stared at him. 'Where are *you* going to get five thousand pounds from?'

Another shrug. 'There's always Danny. Been trying to call him. Fucker's not answering.'

'How long have you been waiting for me outside the hospital?' She vaguely remembered telling him where she worked when he'd turned up in Hereford and Danny had left them alone for a few minutes. But the thought of him stalking her like this creeped her out.

'Couple of hours. Thought Danny might pick you up. He's not around Hereford, least not as far as I can tell.' He took another painful sip of coffee. 'So where *is* the cunt?'

'*Don't* . . .' Clara felt her pulse rising at his language, but she managed to hold her tongue. 'I don't know where he is,' she said.

Kyle clearly couldn't hide it – the flicker of panic that shadowed his face, the frown that creased his forehead. He was even less successful at keeping the emotion from his voice. 'Don't matter,' he said. 'I know people. I'll get it sorted.'

Clara couldn't help a pang of sympathy. Kyle was like a bolshie kid, unable to confess that he was in trouble. If she'd had five grand in her pocket, she reckoned she'd probably have given it to him. But she didn't have that sort of money, either in her pocket or in her bank account.

'These Poles,' she said. 'You *can* go to the police about them, you know.'

Kyle gave a harsh, mirthless bark of laughter. 'Right,' he said.

Silence. There was something unspoken between them. Clara tackled it first. 'If you give them *something*, will they lay off you for a while?'

He looked at her sharply. 'Maybe,' he said. There was a sudden eagerness in his eyes, and a wiliness too. 'Depends what I give them.'

'Well, it won't be much,' Clara said. 'I don't *have* much.'

It was as if Kyle couldn't stop himself from being offensive. 'Yeah, right. You sound like a right daddy's girl.' He looked like he was going to say something else, but perhaps he noticed the steel in Clara's eyes.

'Come with me,' she said.

The nearest cashpoint was three doors down. There was no queue. Clara had the impression that nobody wanted to stay in the same place for long, and the passers-by did just that: pass by. She had two credit cards. The maximum withdrawal on each was £250. She maxed each of them out. Kyle couldn't keep his eyes off the money, and Clara was honest enough with herself to admit that this was probably a very bad idea. But Kyle was Danny's brother, and he was in trouble. And she never had been able to refuse help to a person in trouble.

She handed over the money. Kyle snatched it from her and stuffed the wad into his pocket. His eyes darted around again. He didn't have the grace to utter a word of thanks. He just turned on his heel and walked back down the street. After ten metres or so, he looked over his shoulder to see if Clara was still watching him. When he saw that she was, he continued on his way.

Quickly, Clara crossed the busy road. There was a doorway set back from the pavement, where she hid in the shadows. She only had to wait a couple of minutes before she saw Kyle again, walking back the way he'd come. He looked around furtively, then shuffled into the pub they'd walked past.

Clara shivered with the cold. She felt so stupid. She wondered if she should follow him into the pub and demand the money back, but she quickly discounted that idea. She'd half known he'd drink it away. At least she'd confirmed one thing: that Danny had been right about his brother all along. He was past anyone's help.

The thought of Danny made her shiver again. She wondered where he was now. And then she felt the familiar twist of anguish when she remembered that it wasn't her business any more.

But that didn't stop her thinking about him. About the abrupt way he'd finished with her. About what was going on in his head.

About where he was now, and what he was doing.

About whether the man she still loved was safe.

Jamal had already decided that if he wanted to get far away from London, the pushbike would be no good. He needed to fetch his motorbike. And he needed to do it tonight. It was a risk returning home to Perivale, he knew that. But as he kept his bike in a lock-up a good 50 metres from the flat itself, he could collect it without even showing his face at home.

It was ten o'clock exactly when he stopped cycling. He left his bike against the railings of the local primary school, and didn't even bother to lock it up. He knew perfectly well that it would be stolen, but that was okay – it wasn't like he was going to need it again, after all. He covered the last half mile to the lock-up on foot, his hands shoved deep into his pockets to keep them warm. His skin tingled. He felt like everyone he passed – small groups of youths, couples hand in hand – were staring at him. But that was ridiculous, he told himself. Nobody knew he was here. On the corner of one main road, a squat man in a black leather jacket who looked uncannily like Phil Collins *did* make eye contact. But then he pulled out his phone and started having an argument with his girlfriend, and Jamal carried on his way.

He stopped about 20 metres from the lock-up – it was a line of three sectional concrete garages in a quiet side street, with a patch of cracked tarmac in front of them. He looked up and down the street, checking that nobody was watching him. The place was deserted, so he crossed to his lock-up – the middle of the three – and opened it up with the key he had in his back pocket.

It was dark in the lock-up, and entirely empty apart from the bike, and the helmet which he kept slung over the handlebars. Jamal hurried in and, moments later, was sitting on the vehicle. There was half a tank of petrol – enough to get him out of

London. He had already decided that when he needed to refuel, he would fill up a plastic jerry can, so he didn't have to expose his bike to the security cameras at any petrol stations. He pulled on his helmet, started the ignition, revved the bike a couple of times and slowly moved out of the lock-up. He was so eager to get away that he didn't even bother to close the garage door. He wouldn't be returning, anyway.

The air temperature had dropped. It was a cold night. But Jamal couldn't risk returning to the flat for warmer clothes. He would just have to man it out. He peered to the end of the side street. No sign of anyone. He drove on, to the corner of the side street and the main road. Here he stopped again and checked around him. There were a handful of pedestrians on the street, but none of them seemed to be paying him any attention. A bus trundled past, its windows misted up, followed by some regular cars. On the other side of the road, exactly opposite the side street, was a black Land Rover Discovery. A broad-shouldered man was behind the wheel reading a newspaper. Probably just a cab driver from the cab firm up the road, waiting for a fare, Jamal told himself. He turned left and followed the bus, which was now 50 metres ahead of him.

He kept one eye on his side mirrors. For 30 seconds or so there was nobody behind him. Then he saw a single pair of headlamps. But there was nothing suspicious about that. It wasn't like he could expect the streets to himself. He concentrated on driving: safely and not too fast. He *certainly* didn't want to be pulled over.

From Perivale, he headed on to the A40 out of London. There was more traffic here, almost all of it leaving the capital. He found it strangely comforting, as if the camouflage of other vehicles made him more difficult to pick out. The road headed west, past Heathrow. The Terminal Five building glowed in the distance, lighting up the sky, but there were no planes arriving or leaving. London, tonight, was still a no-fly zone for civilian aircraft. He remembered how Sarim used to talk about one day organising a terrorist hit on an aircraft – he had elaborate plans Jamal didn't fully understand that involved stealing passports in Thailand – and how pleased Abu Ra'id would be with them if they pulled off another 9/11. Up until today, pleasing Abu Ra'id had been all Jamal wanted to do. Now, however, he just wanted to get away from him. He was acting, he realised, out of fear.

Jamal didn't really know where he was going. He had no friends, to speak of. No relations who hadn't disowned him. All he really knew was that he wanted to get someplace quiet. He could get a cheap room in a Travelodge somewhere while he worked out his next move. Maybe he could skip the country. Get over to Pakistan. As one of the Paddington bombers, surely there would be people who would give him sanctuary.

He was thinking these thoughts as he checked his fuel gauge. It was almost empty. He cursed himself for having passed a petrol station a few moments before. Now he would have to get off the A40 and hunt for another petrol station nearby. He pulled off at the next exit, took a left at the roundabout and continued along an almost empty B road for a mile or so until he came across a Texaco garage on his right. He pulled into a lay-by, killed the bike's engine, and quickly crossed the road to the petrol station. A red Ford Focus was filling up, but otherwise the forecourt was deserted.

As he approached the shop to buy a jerry can, however, another vehicle that had come from the same direction as Jamal turned into the petrol station. Its headlamps were very bright, so at first glance he couldn't tell what kind of vehicle it was. Something about it, though, made him uneasy. Inside the shop he took another glance. It was parked up by the air and water station. A black Land Rover Discovery.

Jamal froze.

He was standing by the sweets. The guy behind the counter was staring at him. He looked round. Green jerry cans were on sale on the far side of the shop. He walked over and picked one up. 'Going to fill this up, mate,' he said to the attendant, who nodded back at him.

He exited the shop and walked up to one of the pumps, watching the Land Rover from the corner of his eye. The driver stepped outside. He had dark hair and black stubble, and was very broad-shouldered. He didn't even seem to notice Jamal as he filled up his jerry can. He just walked into the shop and stood at the sweet counter, browsing.

It couldn't be the same man Jamal had seen reading the newspaper back in Perivale, could it?

A minute later, the can was overflowing. Jamal swore as the petrol spilled over his hand. He replaced the nozzle in the pump, tightened the can, and returned to the shop. The dark-haired man was at the counter with three Snickers bars and a can of Red Bull. He accepted some change from the attendant, then turned to leave. As he passed Jamal they made eye contact. The man nodded. 'All right, mate?' he muttered.

Jamal put his head down and walked to the counter. As he stood there paying in cash for his petrol, he watched the man return to the Land Rover. Relief crashed over him when he saw the vehicle move. It turned left, back towards the A40.

His hands were trembling as he accepted his change. He pocketed it, then carried his jerry can out of the shop, across the forecourt and over the road to where his bike was waiting. He could almost feel the attendant's eyes burning into him, watching him for his strange behaviour. He didn't care. He'd be away from here soon enough.

He poured the fuel into the tank, then carelessly chucked the jerry can away into the verge. The sight of the Discovery had churned him up and he struggled to become calm again. Although it had driven away and was therefore clearly not following him, he decided he wasn't going to head back towards the A40, just in case. He kicked the motorbike into action again and continued in the opposite direction along the B road at a steady thirty, the beam from his headlamp lighting up the road and the high thick bushes on either side.

A vehicle shot past from the opposite direction. Jamal watched its tail lights disappear in his side mirror. He was relieved to see that there was nobody behind him. He focused on the road ahead. A minute later, another car zoomed past from the same direction. Jamal swore again – it had its headlamps on full beam, which dazzled him. He checked his side mirrors again. With reduced, blotchy vision he saw the red tail lights disappearing. He screwed his eyes shut momentarily to try and get his full vision back again.

He opened them.

He almost shouted out in shock.

A vehicle had suddenly appeared no more than 30 metres behind him. Its headlamps were switched off, which was why he hadn't seen it approach. It was closing in fast. Jamal couldn't make out the outline, but he knew, beyond question, that it was the Discovery.

Panic surged through him. He opened the throttle on his bike. The speedometer crept up past thirty.

Forty.

Fifty.

The road had grown narrow. It twisted and turned. Jamal tried to hug the edge, praying that his skills on the bike were up to the task. He checked in the mirror. The Discovery was obscured by a bend in the road. But five seconds later the road straightened out. It was closer now.

Twenty metres.

Ten.

Another vehicle sped by from the opposite direction. Its horn sounded angrily, but faded quickly. Jamal increased his speed even more. The speedo flickered past sixty. Seventy. It was too fast. He could feel himself losing control of the bike. There was a great roaring in his ears. One glance in the side mirror told him that the Discovery was on his tail.

Now it was overtaking.

He looked to his right. The man from the garage was behind the wheel. But in the back seat he could just make out another face that he recognised – the Phil Collins lookalike he had walked past in Perivale.

His stomach churned. He didn't know what to do. Speed up? Slow down? He was panicking. The Discovery eased passed him, and as it did, he saw the rear window sliding down. The vehicle was five metres ahead of him when the passenger leaned out slightly. He was carrying something: a black metal tube. A gun, maybe? Jamal found himself shouting in fear under his helmet. *They were about to shoot him* . . .

It happened so suddenly. There was a blinding white flash, like electricity behind his eyes.

He couldn't see anything. He was totally blind.

Time seemed to slow down.

In a fraction of a second, he heard the Discovery's engine pitch up a notch and he knew the vehicle was accelerating away. At the same time, he felt his tyres losing their grip on the road surface.

He was screaming again. Still blind.

A dreadful, high-pitched whine escaped the motorbike's engine and he felt himself falling sideways to the right. But before his body hit the road, the vehicle came to an abrupt, jarring stop. He knew he must have crashed into the side of the road. The dreadful force of the impact jolted through him. At the same time, he felt the bones in his right arm and leg crush as they became sandwiched between the bike and the road.

And then time sped up again. Agony coursed through him. He was still blind, but he had a picture of himself in his mind's eye, the twisted skeleton of the bike wrapped around his own damaged frame.

The pain was unspeakable. He tried to scream again, realised he didn't have the strength to do it.

There was liquid in his helmet, warm and thick. He recognised the taste of blood. He knew he had to get his helmet off, and he tried to do it. But his limbs weren't working. He couldn't move. He panicked even more, and inhaled a lungful of his own blood, as a hoarse choking sound came from the back of his throat.

He couldn't breathe.

Seconds passed. The vision was clearing. Through the bloodied, misted visor, he saw the outline of two men standing over him. He tried to speak, but only gurgled before inhaling more blood.

'Is he dead?' said a voice. It sounded deep and slow, like a voice in a dream.

'Not yet,' came the reply.

'Told you it wouldn't fucking work. I'll finish him off.'

'No weapons.'

'Won't need them, mucker.'

He was a hunted animal. Dread almost overcame his agony. He tried again to shout out for mercy, but again there was just a bubbling of blood and a burning in his lungs.

One of the figures was bending over him. 'You've planted your last bomb, sunshine,' it said.

Moments later, he felt a boot on his neck, grinding down into his jugular. His broken body started to shake. His lungs burned worse than ever. His vision clouded again and went black.

The boot on his jugular ground down harder, constricting whatever airflow had been going through his system.

For a moment there was no pain. Just a strange, floating sensation, like he was bobbing under water.

Ten seconds later he was dead.

ELEVEN

Spud had blood on his boot where he'd used his heel to finish off the bomber. He wiped it on the soft grass of the verge. Danny examined the corpse. The limbs were twisted, jutting out in different directions. Blood was seeping through the bottom of the helmet. There was a burning smell in the air, and Danny knew there was a risk of the bike's fuel tank igniting. More crucially, a car could pass at any moment. They needed to be off the scene.

'Let's get out of here,' he said. Spud nodded his agreement.

The Discovery was 20 metres away. They jogged up to it. Danny took the wheel. Seconds later they were driving away, and a few seconds after that a saloon car thundered past in the opposite direction. They were leaving just in time.

'Muppet,' Spud said as they drove. 'I tell you what, mucker, these lot are like shooting fish in a barrel.'

'Yeah,' Danny murmured. 'That's what worries me.'

'What?'

'Nothing,' Danny said quickly. And the conversation was rescued by his phone ringing over the Discovery's hands-free system. Number withheld, naturally. Danny pressed a button on the steering wheel to answer. 'Who's this?'

'Buckingham, old sport,' came the voice over the loudspeaker.

Neither of the SAS men answered.

'I'm going to work on the assumption that you've recovered from your little temper tantrum,' the MI6 man said. 'Glad to see it hasn't interfered with your work, in any case. That was a nice

little hors d'oeuvre in west London, gentlemen. Very tasty.'
Danny and Spud exchanged a withering look at Buckingham's
covert language. 'Much appreciated by everyone, but they don't
like to be kept waiting. Any progress on the *fish* course?'

'Yeah,' Danny said. 'Battered.'

A pause.

'Right,' said Buckingham. He sounded a little wrong-footed.
'Sooner than we expected. But good. *Good*. You'll need to check
your letterbox. You'll find details of your next course waiting.
Lots of pressure from above after this business in Piccadilly. All
hands on deck, and we've come up trumps.' Another pause.
'Don't let her get away, lads. Lot riding on this. Sure you understand.'

A click, and the line went dead.

'Wanker,' Spud said.

'He said "her",' Danny noted.

'Got a problem with that?'

'Guess not.'

Danny looked over his shoulder to the back seat. 'We've got
the laptop,' he said. 'Let's find somewhere to get online.'

The somewhere they found was a service station on the A40.
As they pulled in, they saw an ambulance and two police cars,
sirens raging, heading the other way. Spud headed into the
service station to get food, while Danny hooked up their laptop
to the flaky 3G connection on his work phone. Spud returned
with a paper Burger King bag. They wolfed down their food,
then logged on to the Gmail account. Sure enough, there was a
draft message waiting for them. Danny clicked to open it. Twenty
seconds later, a picture appeared of a young woman.

She was good looking. Dark hair and skin, pretty face. As
usual, her details were clearly printed underneath the picture.
Name: Tasmin Khan. Address: Flat 38, Manfred Tower, Alperton.
'Fuck's sake, we're going to nail half of west London at this rate.'
Unusually, beneath the picture was a link. Danny clicked it, and

the browser directed him to a Facebook page, or at least a copy of one. 'GCHQ to the rescue,' Danny muttered.

The page displayed a conversation between the girl – she was using the pseudonym Nicki – and a young man whose profile picture clearly showed the recognisable features of Down's syndrome. The two SAS men read the conversation – a crass and obvious honeypot trap, but one the target was too trusting and unsophisticated to see.

'I'm almost looking forward to doing her,' Spud said.

'They're going to keep on coming,' Danny replied.

'What d'you mean?'

'Her. The kid on the motorbike. Galaid. They're just the foot soldiers, like that Victoria woman said. You can bet anything there are more waiting in the wings.'

'Which means more bombs,' Spud observed.

'Yeah. Unless . . .'

'Unless what?'

'These kids are just puppets,' said Danny. 'We want the guy pulling the strings.'

'Abu Ra'id?'

'Abu Ra'id.'

'Hammerstone don't have a handle on him.'

'Hammerstone aren't asking the right people. For Christ's sake, they're going after his *wife*. I'd bet my left bollock she doesn't know where he is.'

'You think we should speak to the girl?' Spud tapped the screen to indicate Tasmin Khan.

Danny nodded.

'Hammerstone won't like it. She won't talk without a bit of persuasion. It'll leave marks. We're supposed to make these hits look accidental, remember?'

Danny clicked on the inbox. He wasn't surprised to see that the draft message had already been deleted. He shut down the laptop, then gave Spud a bleak smile.

'We're clever lads,' he said. 'I'm sure we'll come up with something.'

Manfred Tower, Alperton, was a shit hole: a squat council block with rain stains down the concrete and a background stench of piss in the foyer, which looked on to a dark stairwell. It was pissing down again outside, but even colder inside. A single strip light flickered with a noisy electric sound. There was nobody about, not at this time in the morning. They'd recced the exterior of the building and seen that only three flats had their lights on. One of them was on the third floor. Flat 38? They were about to find out.

Danny led the way up the concrete staircase, his rucksack slung over his back. Behind him was Spud, carrying a Domino's box full of hot pizza that they'd bought just round the corner, the cardboard damp from the rain and steaming slightly. 'Vegetarian,' Danny had reminded him before he made the order. 'Or at least, no pork.' Spud had scribbled the address of their target on top of the box.

'What if she doesn't open up?' Spud said.

'Then we'll try it another way. But if she's there, I think she will.' There were a hundred ways to force an entry into a flat. Danny and Spud were adept at all of them. But the best way, by far, was to get the occupier to open up of their own free will. Danny's calculation was that if their target was at home and in hiding, she'd be feeling pretty hungry about now.

The front door of flat 38 was one of two along a stark corridor, each door set about 15 metres apart. There was a light on a push-button timer, but Danny left it for now and headed along the corridor in the darkness, leaving Spud at the top of the stairs with the pizza. He walked past flat 37, and as he passed the door to flat 38, he saw that there was a spyhole at head height, just below the scratched painted number. He cleared it by about two metres, then picked out the latex gloves, face mask and hairnet that he'd stowed carefully inside his rucksack. He put them on, stood with his back against the wall and gave Spud a thumbs-up sign. Spud hit the push button with his elbow to avoid prints. The corridor lit up. Still carrying the pizza, he walked up to the door and knocked twice.

Silence.

Spud and Danny looked at each other. Spud knocked again.

A voice on the other side of the door. Female.

'Who's that?'

'Pizza,' Spud said. He affected a bored expression, looking round the corridor like a kid daydreaming in class.

'I didn't order no pizza.'

Spud read the address off the top of the pizza box. 'Flat 38?'

'Yeah.'

'Margherita, extra olives.'

'I didn't order no bloody pizza, go away.'

'No need to get mouthy, love. Someone's paid for this. You got anyone else in there? Boyfriend or something?'

'*No! Go away!*'

'Right.' A pause. 'Well, look love, you might as well have it.'

Another silence. Danny found himself holding his breath, ready to pounce the moment the door opened.

But the door didn't move.

It would have been natural for Spud to glance at Danny, but he was too careful for that. She might be looking through the spyhole. Instead, he knocked again.

'So do you want this bloomin' pizza or what?'

'No, you can have it.'

'You joking, love? I've got Margherita coming out my ears.'

'Go away!'

'Tell you what,' Spud called. 'I'll leave it here. By the door. All right?'

No answer.

164

Spud bent down and laid the pizza box on the ground right in front of the door. Still without acknowledging Danny's presence, he turned and headed back down the corridor. The light clicked off before he'd walked even four metres, but he kept going in the darkness until he reached the end of the corridor.

Danny stayed very still. He could just make out Spud's silhouette in front of the door leading to the stairwell. He could smell the pizza. He could hear traffic in the distance, and the pumping of his own heartbeat.

Thirty seconds passed.

Forty-five.

Movement on the other side of the door. A kind of scratching sound. He pictured their target up against the door, looking through the spyhole.

He readied himself.

A click. The door opened.

Some situations required a scalpel. Others a hammer. This was a hammer situation. He had only the fraction of a second between the target opening her door and putting her head out into the corridor, to strike. He swung himself round, his right heel digging into the pizza box, and thrust his latexed hands as hard as he could against the door. It thumped against the body on the other side. Danny lunged into the room, where the light was dim but still brighter than what he was used to. He grabbed the woman's hair with his left hand, then slammed the right over her mouth. Just in time. She tried to scream, but all that came out was a muffled yelp.

In an instant, Spud was there, carrying not only Danny's rucksack but also the crushed pizza box. He shut the door behind him, laid the stuff on the ground, then dug around in the rucksack for the second SOCO kit. Moments later he was gloved, masked and hatted, just like Danny, who still had his hand firmly over the girl's mouth.

Spud pulled his handgun and stepped up to her. 'See this?' he whispered, and he tapped the suppressor that he'd fitted to the barrel of the Glock. 'Most people think it makes the gun silent, like on the telly.' He shook his head. 'It doesn't. Not really.' He pressed the barrel into the soft flesh of the girl's neck. 'But if I shoot you like *this*,' Spud added, 'that's *really* going to make a difference. You'd be amazed how much sound the human body absorbs close up. Very messy, but *very* quiet. They'll only know you're dead when they start smelling you by the stairs in about three days' time. Understood?'

The girl nodded vigorously.

'Good. So when my mate here moves his hand off your mouth, you're not going to make a sound, right?'

More nodding.

Slowly, Danny released his hand, ready to snap it back if the girl screamed. But she didn't.

'Lie on the floor,' he said. 'Hands on the back of your head. You'll be dead if you move a fucking muscle.'

Trembling, the girl did as she was told, and Danny looked round the room.

It was a bedsit, with a kitchenette area in one corner, a single bed against the far wall. A laptop on the small kitchen table, with a webcam clipped to it. A single window looked out onto a light well. They'd clearly arrived just in time. Tasmin Khan, or what-ever the hell she wanted to call herself, had been getting ready to leave. Permanently. A chest of drawers had all three drawers open, and looked like it was vomiting clothes. Two rucksacks lay on the bed, each of them crammed full. Tasmin Khan wasn't just leaving. She was leaving in a panic, and a hurry.

'Kill the lights,' Danny said.

Spud did so. The room fell dark, the only light being a faint greyness from the direction of the light well. Danny stepped over to it, satisfied that he was sufficiently camouflaged by the darkness. If anybody was watching from the windows on the other side of the light well – and at this time of night he doubted it – they might be able to see figures moving about, but they wouldn't be able to identify the intruders. It was a sash window, and Danny was able to raise the lower pane to create an opening about a metre square. Outside, the rain was heavy. Good thing too. More camouflage. He returned to where the girl was lying on the floor, knelt down and spoke quietly, very close to her ear.

'Nice gaff, this,' he whispered. 'Did you bring your mate with the funny eyes back here? Give him a good time before you blew the poor bastard up?'

'I don't know what you mean.'

'Save it, Tasmin. Or should I call you Nicki? I heard a rumour you like big strong men. At least that's what you told your boy on Facebook. Well, here's the good news: you've got two of them in the room with you.'

'You're going to rape me, you *pig*?'

'Not really my scene, darling. I'm just going to ask you a question, and you'd better fucking answer. Where's Abu Ra'id?'

'I don't know,' she breathed.

'Fair enough,' Danny said. 'Kill her.'

Spud pressed the silencer against her neck.

'*No!*' she hissed.

'Where's Abu Ra'id?' Danny repeated.

'I *can't*,' she said loudly. Too loudly. Spud pressed harder.

'Let's keep our voices down, shall we?'

'I can't,' the girl whispered. 'He'll kill me if I do.'

'Then you've got a problem, because we'll kill you if you don't.'

She twisted her head to look at him. 'You'll kill me anyway,' she hissed.

Danny gave her a bleak smile. 'Maybe not,' he said. 'We've got friends in high places. You help us, we can make sure that they help you.'

'Can't promise you'll get away scot-free,' Spud butted in, 'but if you're lucky, you might avoid spending the next twenty years being fisted by the dykes in Holloway.'

'I don't know what you mean,' she spat.

'Well, put it this way. Right now, this fella and me, we're your best friends. And best friends tell each other everything.' Danny pulled his own gun and pressed it into the soft flesh of her cheek. '*Where's Abu Ra'id?*'

She was trembling, almost too scared to speak. But when she did speak, it wasn't what Danny wanted to hear. 'You won't kill me,' she said. 'Not as long as I know something you want to know.'

'Wrong answer,' Danny said. He looked around the room, then stood up and fetched a pair of grey tights from the floor.

'What are you doing?' the girl demanded.

Danny knelt back down over her and, with the fingers of one gloved hand, forced her lips and teeth open. She tried to bite him, but he was too strong. He stuffed the tights into her mouth.

'All right mate,' he said to Spud. 'Break her arm.'

Spud didn't fuck about. With one swift movement, he grabbed her right arm and bent it sharply back at the elbow. There was a cracking, splintering sound. The girl's body went into a rictus of shock, and though she tried to scream again, the tights stuffed in her mouth muffled everything.

Danny let her get used to the pain for a moment. Then he said: 'There's one arm left. After that we get to work on the legs. And after *that*, we've got all sorts of tricks up our sleeves. So I'll ask you again: where's Abu Ra'id?'

With a rough yank, he pulled the tights out of her mouth.

Her breath was juddering. He held the material a couple of inches from her mouth in case she tried to scream, but she was clearly past that. 'I . . . I . . . saw him this morning,' she whispered.

'Where?'

She closed her eyes and didn't answer.

'Okay, mate,' Danny said. 'Do the other one.'

'*No . . .*' she gasped. '*Please . . . don't . . .*'

'Then give me an address. You've got five seconds.'

'He'll kill me.'

'Four seconds.'

She whispered something in Arabic. Her face screwed up in torment.

'I've had enough of this,' said Spud.

'*I'll tell you*,' she spat. '*I'll tell you, okay?*'

'Now,' said Danny.

'There's a block of flats ... Docklands ... the big glass one ... overlooking the river ...'

'There's a lot of big glass towers in the Docklands. What's it called?'

She screwed up her face again.

'*What's it called?*'

'Hertford Tower,' she whispered. 'The penthouse.'

Danny stared at her, implacably.

'You're lying,' he said. 'Break the other arm.'

'*No* ...' she whimpered. 'I swear I'm telling you the truth. I *swear* it.'

Spud reached out for the good arm and started bending it back. Danny could tell there was another scream coming, so he quickly stuffed the tights back in her mouth. Then he held one finger up in Spud's direction to tell him to stop.

'One last chance,' he said. 'What's the address?'

He removed the tights again. The girl whimpered pitifully. 'I'm telling you the truth,' she whimpered. 'Hertford Tower, I swear, the penthouse. But you'll never get in ... it's guarded ... armed men ...'

Danny nodded slowly.

'How big is the apartment? Does it take over the whole floor?'

'Yes ... apart from the bit around the lift. But you need a special code to get the lift there anyway ... and the men guarding it have guns ...'

'Good girl,' Danny breathed. Then he reinserted the tights for a final time. He threw Spud a questioning look.

'Let's do it,' Spud said. 'Through the window.'

The girl's body tensed up. She used her good arm to try to push herself to her feet, but it was a pathetic attempt and only took a single shove from Spud's gloved hand to push her down again. Danny hurried over to where the rucksack was sitting next to the pizza box. From inside, he pulled a copy of the *Evening Standard* he'd bought at the service station, its front cover plastered with pictures of the horror in Piccadilly. He opened it up, removed some of the inside pages that showed more images of devastation, then rubbed the front page over the girl's wriggling head to smear it with her DNA. He gave half a thought to forcing her to write a suicide note, expressing her distress at what she'd done, but quickly discarded that idea. Too obvious. The scene they were going to leave behind would have to tell the story.

He laid the sheets of newspaper around the floor, then turned back to Spud and the girl. 'Take her feet,' he said.

Seconds later, they were carrying her to the open window. She weighed almost nothing, but she wriggled like an eel out of water. Danny was holding her by her upper arms, but he knew not to squeeze too hard. The broken arm was fine – by the time they'd finished with her, it would be just one broken bone of many. Entirely unsuspicious. But bruising would indicate a struggle, and if they wanted it to look as if Tasmin Khan had thrown herself from the window in a moment of unbearable guilt, that wouldn't do.

They reached the window. A desperate, animal grunting was coming from the girl's throat. It was still muffled by the material of the tights, but they had to come out before the guys dispensed with her.

'Ready?' he asked Spud.

'Ready.'

It happened quickly. Danny yanked the tights from her mouth. She screamed. And then the SAS men posted her through the open window.

She fell head first. The scream faded quickly, and ended abruptly.

Danny and Spud moved quickly away from the window back to the door, stopping only to pick up the crushed pizza box and the rucksack, where Danny stowed the saliva-contaminated tights. Spud ripped off his mask, hairnet and gloves. Danny kept just the gloves on as he opened the door for his mate, who stepped out into the unlit corridor, then looked back and gave Danny the all-clear. Danny exited, closed the door silently behind him, then stowed his gloves. They walked calmly but with purpose towards the stairwell.

Where they stopped.

Voices below them.

'Did you hear it?' said a woman's voice. 'Like a scream?'

A man said: 'Probably just a cat. They make that noise some-times.'

'First time I ever heard a cat sound like that round here.'

Footsteps. Ascending. Danny pointed upwards. Silently, the two men moved up to the fourth floor.

They heard the footsteps stop beneath them, then head along the corridor towards flat 38. There was a lessening of the dark-ness: they'd pressed the light switch down there.

'We can't get stuck up here,' Danny said. 'Let's move.'

Carefully, they crept back down again. The two neighbours were standing at the open door to flat 37, deep in conversation with the occupant. They didn't notice Danny and Spud disap-pearing down the stairwell.

Two minutes later, they were back in the Discovery, their clothes sopping wet from the rain. Spud sat in the passenger seat, the crushed pizza box on his lap. He opened it up and removed a mangled slice of pizza. Danny gave him a look. 'A man's got to eat,' he said as he crammed the slice into his mouth. 'Want some?'

Danny shook his head. He checked the time: 04.37. He drummed his fingers on the steering wheel and stared at the rain-spattered windscreen.

'Let's go for him,' he said.

'Who?'

'Who do you think? Abu Ra'id. Let's go for him now.'

Spud swallowed his mouthful of pizza. 'We should check with Hammerstone first, mucker.'

'We haven't got time,' Danny said with sudden vigour. 'Who knows where he'll be by the time they've given us the go-ahead? If we don't nail him, these bombings will go on and on. We can kill as many of his foot soldiers as we want, he'll always find more. And while we've got a lead on his location . . .'

Spud closed the pizza box. He looked like he'd lost his appetite.

'Listen,' Danny persisted. 'You said yourself how *easy* it's been, nailing these three.'

Spud shrugged. 'Maybe we're just good at it, mucker.'

'Oh come on. They're just cannon fodder. Abu Ra'id's been sprinkling them in our path to keep us too busy to get our hands on *him*.'

'We're two guys. It'll need more than just us to make a hard arrest on a major terror suspect. Fuck knows what sort of close protection he'll have around him.'

'Then answer me this,' Danny said, an aggressive edge in his voice. 'How come Abu Ra'id is still even in the country? Why haven't they kicked him out months, years ago? You really believe all that human rights bullshit?' He gave Spud a piercing look. 'Who's Abu Ra'id got in his pocket? Do you *really* expect the authorities to bring him down?'

'*Jesus*, Danny. I thought *I* was the one that liked a conspiracy theory. Listen to yourself. We can't just go round killing people without the say-so from the headshed, okay? They'll throw the fucking book at us. We go back to the safe house, we inform Hammerstone what we've just learned, then we wait for instructions. End of.'

Danny felt every muscle in his body tense up. But he knew Spud was right. He was getting too emotional. In this job, there was no room for it. You had to be cold and hard-headed. And if you weren't able to do that, you had to rely on your mate to do it for you.

He started the car and pulled out into the empty road. They drove in silence back to Battersea, the air in the vehicle thick with the stench of cold pizza and the unspoken tension between them.

They arrived back at the safe house at 05.00 on the nose. Five minutes later they had saved a draft e-mail on the Hammerstone account, confirming they had a lead on the location of Abu Ra'id and stating his potential location.

Thirty minutes later, they had their instructions. Hereford had mobilised a unit. Danny and Spud were to RV with them at Hertford Tower.

The Regiment was on its way.

TWELVE

The Docklands. A bleak network of roundabouts and building sites hardly improved by the grey light of dawn. Immobile cranes and half-built structures dominated the riverside. It seemed to Danny that everywhere he looked there was a speed or security camera looking down at them from a lamp post. On one of them sat a seagull, somehow lost upriver and looking for all the world like it was watching the black Discovery drive past.

Rising up from the centre of this concrete jungle, however, were the impressive towers around Canada Square. Looking up, Danny recognised company names – HSBC, Citigroup, KPMG – affixed to the upper floors of these immense buildings. 'More crooks round here than in Belmarsh,' Spud muttered, and Danny nodded his agreement. As they spoke, a shard of red sunlight broke through a threatening sky and reflected brightly off the mirror and glass structures that dominated the skyline. Canary Wharf glowed like blood in the dawn.

They left the Discovery in an open-air car park where a grizzled old man in mittens, scarf and a threadbare woollen hat accepted twenty quid for the day. Then they walked the almost deserted streets towards the glass and steel skyscrapers that were the beating financial heart of London. Danny's every sense was on high alert. Of all the locations in the capital, this was surely at the highest risk of attack. There would be undercover security personnel here, without question. Maybe even private security, employed by the banks. Danny and Spud certainly didn't want to get mixed up with them.

Hertford Tower. It had to be at least 200 metres high – there was even a wisp of cloud curling round the upper levels. There were countless panes of glass – it wasn't even possible to estimate how many apartments there were in the block. Danny and Spud stood casually at opposite corners of the plaza that faced on to the tower. The plaza itself was 50 metres by 50, with a large fountain in the middle and a line of Boris bikes along the far edge. Along either side of the plaza, more for decoration than timekeeping, was a series of analogue clocks on posts, like three-metre-high lollipops. Perfectly synchronised with each other and with Danny's watch, they read 05.37. Even though it was early, men in suits and women in winter coats and fashionable scarves were walking briskly across the plaza, clearly on their way to work before the financial markets opened. Like Danny's and Spud's, their breath steamed in the early morning cold. Many of them held cups of coffee from Starbucks or Costa. Cafes on the side of the plaza were already opening, their interiors glowing an inviting yellow against the half-dark of morning. Danny and Spud were the exceptions in their leather jackets, jeans and Gore-Tex shoes. Under other circumstances they'd be suited and booted too, in order to blend in. But not this morning. Things were moving too quickly for that.

Danny kept his eyes on the main entrance. Distance: 35 metres. There were lights on in the lobby, but so far nobody had entered or exited. He was aware of Spud walking along the far side of the plaza, before disappearing along one edge of the building. Two minutes later he heard his mate's voice in his earpiece. 'Goods entrance at the back. Main gate locked. For now at least.'

'Roger that. Keep eyes on.'

Time check: 06.15. Danny's every sense was on high alert, his lack of sleep pushed to a far corner of his mind. He looked at the left-hand side of the building. It faced on to a one-way street, but there was no traffic and hardly any pedestrians walking that way. He craned his neck so that he was looking at the top of Hertford Tower. The shard of sunlight that had lit up the building had been an anomaly. Now the clouds had rolled back in again. The penthouse level was still visible, but shrouded in a murky haze. His eyes focused as best they could on the top floor. Was Abu Ra'id up there, hiding in plain sight in the heart of the financial district? It seemed too obvious a location, but so did any location when you knew what it was concealing. Just look at Bin Laden.

'Where the fuck *are* they?' Spud said over the radio.

Time check: 06.21. Danny suppressed a surge of frustration. This was taking too long. They should have come here earlier, under cover of night, barged in on the fucker while he was sleeping . . .

He looked up again. The sky was empty. There was nothing to suggest that this was anything other than an ordinary day.

He felt for his weapon under his jacket. Not that he needed it yet. It was just good to know it was there. Then he turned his attention back to the atrium of the tower. The human traffic in and out became more frequent. City types, mostly, suited and barking into their phones as they hurried out of this expensive residence. Almost exclusively male. But nobody suspicious. Nobody . . .

He blinked. Fifteen metres away, to his ten o'clock, standing just by the fountain in the centre of the plaza with two broad-shouldered men flanking her on either side, was a woman he recognised. Black hair, grey roots. As Danny looked at her she was blowing her nose into a piece of tissue, which she then shoved into the sleeve of her dark overcoat.

Their eyes met. Victoria Atkinson said something to her two bodyguards, then walked over towards Danny.

'What the hell are you doing here?' Danny demanded. 'This could go noisy. And if anyone recognises you, you'll blow the whole thing.' He avoided eye contact, even though he knew it was ridiculous. If anyone was watching them, their RV would have been noted.

'I'm relying on you,' she said. Her northern accent sounded full of cold. 'Abu Ra'id *cannot* leave that apartment alive. He's extremely clever. He'll try to talk his way out of it, and on past performance he'll probably succeed. If he leaves this building alive, the victims of these bombs will *never* have justice.'

Movement in the street along the left-hand side of the building. An unmarked Transit van had just pulled up. Danny felt his face twitch. 'Get back to Bill and Ben over there,' he said. 'And stay clear of the building. The Regiment's here.'

Victoria looked anxious. She swallowed hard, then scurried back to her two bodyguards. Danny spoke into his radio.

'The workmen are on site,' he said cryptically. 'Repeat, the workmen are on site. Making contact in thirty seconds.'

A double-click of the pressel was Spud's only reply.

He was alongside the Transit now. He made no eye contact with the driver, but walked round to the back and knocked three times on the rear doors. They opened immediately. Danny slipped inside.

It was crowded. Seven men in black ops gear: dark trousers and T-shirts, ops vests laden with their radio equipment, and weaponry: frags, flashbangs and ammo. Three of them already had balaclavas over their heads, the remaining three were just about to apply them. Danny recognised Ripley's face and gave him a nod. It felt like weeks ago that he'd last seen him, not four days. Each of the guys had their assault rifles strapped to their bodies by a piece of cord. Ripley handed Danny an ops vest, rifle and balaclava of his own. He pulled off his jacket and got kitted up, discarding the earpiece that kept him in touch with Spud and inserting a new one. In less than thirty seconds they were ready to move.

Danny spoke into the new radio. 'This is work party one, do you copy?'

A momentary pause. Then Spud: 'Loud and clear. Work party two online.'

'Entry in forty-five seconds.'

One of the guys banged on the back wall of the Transit. The vehicle immediately pulled away, accelerating sharply. There was a violent bump as it mounted the kerb, a swerve and then a screech as the Transit came to another abrupt halt.

'*Go! Go! Go!*' Danny shouted.

In an instant, all eight of them spilled out of the back of the Transit. Danny took a second to absorb his surroundings. They had stopped ten metres from the front entrance to Hertford Tower. A second Transit was facing theirs and another eight men were swiftly debussing. Danny recognised Spud not by his face, which was now also covered with a black balaclava, but by his civvies – like Danny, he was the only one of his eight-man team not in full black ops gear.

He turned his attention to the foyer of Hertford Tower. A man in a suit had been walking through the main door, but at the sight of the special forces unit just metres ahead of him he was standing frozen, staring at them. Danny ran towards him. 'Get back into the building!' he roared. '*Now!*' The man dropped his briefcase and fled back into the foyer.

Danny pointed at four of his team. 'Mark the exits,' he instructed. They instantly took up positions, fanning out three metres apart and dropping down onto one knee in the firing position. As Danny ran to the entrance, he was aware of the sudden commotion the arrival of a heavily armed Regiment unit had created in the plaza. Pedestrians were running to the edges of the square, congregating in groups as if that made them safer. Some twats were, predictably enough, holding up mobile phones to take photographs – hence the balaclavas. There was some shouting on the edge of Danny's awareness, and one woman even screamed. He segregated himself from those noises as he burst into the foyer.

There were seven people here. Four men in suits, two women and a concierge in a uniform behind a marble counter. Danny looked over his shoulder. Four members of his team were there. He pointed at one of them. 'Get the civilians on the ground,' he ordered. Then he turned his attention back to the concierge. He was a young guy, mid-twenties maybe, with a thin moustache and dark skin. He looked utterly terrified, and his eyes were darting around as if he was looking for an exit.

He was in for a bad morning.

Danny covered the ten metres between himself and the concierge at a sprint, only half aware of the harsh barks of his team forcing the civilians to the ground at gunpoint. As he ran, he dislodged his Glock from his belt. He ran behind the marble counter and saw three black-clad members of the unit swarming to the far side of the atrium, each securing one of three exits at the back, the grey shutters of what looked to be a service elevator, and a door that led on to a flight of stairs going upwards. He grabbed the concierge by the front of his uniform and saw that he was dialling a number on the mobile in his right hand.

'Drop it,' he growled. The concierge did as he was told. The phone thumped to the floor.

'Is there a separate elevator for the penthouse?'

The concierge's nostrils flared. Danny could smell cigarettes on his breath and see sweat dampening his temples. He stuttered, barely able to get the words out. 'N . . . no.' He pointed nervously across the room towards the main elevator on the far side, 25 metres away. A large, verdant pot plant stood right next to it.

'Is there a service elevator?'

The concierge nodded.

'Does it go to the penthouse?'

'N . . . no. Sir.'

'Stairs?'

'No sir.'

'What's the code for the penthouse?'

The concierge shuddered, but didn't reply. Danny didn't fuck around. With a single swipe of his arm, he cracked the concierge's head against the marble counter. The concierge howled.

'The code!'

The concierge was whimpering now. 'Five Three Eight Nine.'

'Who's up there?'

'I don't know ... I *swear* I don't know.'

Danny gave it a moment's thought. He didn't trust this concierge. If Abu Ra'id had been hiding out in the penthouse of this building, the chances were high that the concierge was complicit.

'You're coming with me,' he said. He dug his Glock into the man's side, then manoeuvred him out from behind the counter towards the elevator.

Spud was already by the lift doors with two other masked men. Danny and the concierge were five metres away when the doors slid open. The lift contained a middle-aged woman with two young children. She screamed when she saw the armed men. 'Get out! *Get out!*' Spud barked at her. He yanked the panicked woman out of the lift, and she dragged her children along with her, all three of them whimpering. Danny chucked the concierge inside, then entered the lift with Spud and the two others. There was an electric panel on the side of the elevator. Danny pressed the touchscreen to take the lift to the penthouse. A numeric keypad appeared.

'Type the code,' he told the concierge. 'If the lift doesn't take us straight to the penthouse, you're dead.'

Trembling, the concierge punched in four numbers. Five, Three, Eight, Eight. Different from the code he'd given Danny at the desk. But this was clearly the correct one, because the doors slid shut and the lift started to ascend.

The concierge was breathing heavily, but otherwise it was silent in the elevator as the Regiment men prepared for the doors to open. Danny stood at the back, his Glock still pressed hard into the concierge's guts. The other three stood in front of them, with their rifles pointing directly towards the door, weapons set to semi-automatic, fingers resting lightly on the triggers.

Twenty seconds passed.

Tense silence in the elevator. None of them had seen a layout of the penthouse. They had no idea what would greet them when the lift doors opened. It was possible that they'd have a direct shot at Abu Ra'id the moment the lift stopped. They needed to be ready to take it.

Thirty seconds passed.

A gentle lurch of the stomach as the elevator came to a halt. Danny glanced at the line of lights above the door: the letter P was illuminated.

A pause that felt like it went on for ever.

The doors hissed.

Danny immediately assessed what was in front of him. The elevator did not appear to have opened inside the penthouse itself. Instead they were facing on to some kind of foyer or corridor. Five metres deep. Ten metres in length. A door at the end to their right.

And two men.

One was Middle Eastern, the other white.

Were they hostile? Abu Ra'id's bodyguards? For a split second it was impossible to say. They clearly had no idea of the commotion that was going on downstairs. They were slouched lazily on a leather sofa four metres away against the wall of the corridor. One of them was reading a newspaper, the other twiddling with his phone. A look of sudden horror struck their faces at the sight of four masked men, heavily armed, facing them from the lift.

The white guy dropped his newspaper. His hand darted into the inside of his jacket. He was clearly reaching for his weapon.

Which was the last thing he ever did.

It was Spud who nailed him. A single shot to his chest which, from this close range, threw him back up against the wall and left a red stain on the paintwork when he tumbled forward. The second man tried to scramble over the side of the sofa, also pulling a weapon from inside his jacket: a pathetic, clumsy manoeuvre that was brought to a sudden halt by a second round. It hit him in the side of the face, splashing another flash of red against the paint, before the man's dead body thumped awkwardly to the floor.

The lift pinged.

They stepped carefully into the corridor, Spud and his two companions covering left and right, checking that there were no threats they had missed from inside the lift, before giving Danny the nod. Danny pushed the concierge out into the corridor, then followed. Aside from the sofa and the two dead bodies, there was nothing here other than a large pane of glass at one end of the corridor which looked out over the Docklands, and the door on the opposite side to the lift, five metres to their right. Next to the door was another keypad.

Spud's two companions ran to the door and knelt down on one knee, covering it. Danny grabbed the nearest dead body and chucked it over the threshold of the lift just as the doors started to shut. They hissed close, then made a clicking sound as they sandwiched against the bleeding body, opened up and then repeated their attempt to shut.

Hiss, click.

Hiss, click.

Danny turned to the concierge. 'Have you been inside the penthouse?' he demanded. 'Do you know the layout.' It put Danny on edge, entering a potentially hostile situation, without at least knowing the geography.

The concierge shook his head. Maybe he was lying, but they didn't have time to find out.

'Open it,' Danny said.

Speechless with terror, the concierge closed his eyes and nodded obediently. Then he moved towards the keypad and, with a trembling hand, punched a code into it.

The door clicked open.

'On the floor, hands on your head,' Danny told the concierge.

The man immediately dropped to his knees. But his eyes flickered over to where one dead guard remained slumped over the sofa. He clearly thought he might be able to lurch over towards him and grab the weapon he'd been going for as the unit had nailed him. The concierge flung himself towards the sofa, but of course he never made it that far. With a single step, one of the team grabbed him by the back of his collar. No need to make use of his weapon on this joker: the masked man delivered two brutal blows, one to the concierge's jugular, the second to the pit of his stomach up towards the ribs. The concierge collapsed, twitching in silent agony, while the SAS man plasticuffed his wrists behind his back. The fucker wouldn't be making a nuisance of himself again.

Silence.

Danny and Spud edged towards the open door. They moved with total quietness. Their rifles were pressed hard into their shoulders, their fingers resting lightly on the triggers.

Spud gently, silently, kicked the door open. A strong, fragrant scent immediately hit Danny's nose. Someone had been burning incense in here very recently.

And maybe still were.

Dead quiet. Danny could hear his pulse.

It was dark in there. They could have done with NV, but they had to make do with their natural vision. Danny discerned a long corridor, twenty metres, which bisected the apartment. There was a suitcase leaning up against the wall about five metres in on the right. Danny immediately marked it as a possible explosive threat. Either that or it belonged to the bodyguards. Or maybe someone else in the apartment?

Several doors led off the corridor. Danny counted them: four on either side. Without lowering their weapons, they stepped inside.

They moved silently. Danny opened each door one by one while Spud covered him in the corridor. The first room on the right was a bedroom. Blackout blinds down. A double bed against one wall – a divan, ruffled sheets. Recently used, but with no space underneath to hide. A closet, empty.

Danny made no noise as he emerged, but nodded at Spud to indicate: room clear.

First door on the left. Same deal.

Second on the right, second on the left. More bedrooms. More unmade beds. But: rooms clear.

Two bathrooms. Huge. Marble. Towelling robes hanging by the door. One of them still had condensation on the mirror. But empty. Room clear.

Noise. For a moment it made Danny start, until he realised it came from outside: the grind of a chopper's rotors. He pictured a military helicopter hovering round the summit of the building, a side gunner at a minigun in case anyone tried to escape on to the roof. But there seemed to be no escape route. No second exit as far as he could tell.

Which meant Abu Ra'id would be in one of these final two rooms. And possibly alerted to a threat by the sound of the chopper.

The further they crept along the corridor, the darker it became. Every room had its blackout blinds down, but now Danny's eyes were more accustomed to the darkness. The final door on the right-hand side led to an enormous sitting room with modern white sofas and a bar area in the corner. Danny's eyes picked out a glass table full of framed pictures. He'd like to know who they were of, but that would have to wait.

Because there was still no sign of Abu Ra'id.

And now only the final room remained.

Danny and Spud exchanged a glance. Then Danny nudged the door open and, weapon primed, entered.

He recognised the room immediately. It was in here that the execution video had taken place. There was a tiled floor and a dining table, and the blackout blinds were shut here as they were everywhere else.

Otherwise it was empty.

The thudding of the helicopter grew louder as it circled this part of the building. Danny stepped across the room and pressed a button on the wall that raised the blackout blinds. Sure enough, he saw a Merlin hovering no more than ten metres from the window, and beyond it the grey sprawl of London against an equally grey sky.

He lowered his weapon and turned to Spud. 'We're too late,' he said meaningfully. 'Should have got here earlier.'

Spud ignored that and spoke into his radio. 'The apartment is clear. No sign of the target, repeat, no sign of the target.'

They left the room. Looking back along the corridor, they could see their mates still on one knee, covering the entrance to the flat. And as they walked towards them, Danny became aware again of the noise of the elevator doors, opening and closing against the bloodied body he'd dragged over the threshold.

The lift area itself was a mess. Blood still oozed from the two dead bodies littering the place. It dripped down the wall and there was a red smear across the floor where Danny had dragged his man to the elevator. Now he dragged him back again so the doors could shut. Immediately, the lift descended. Danny felt inside the jackets of the two guards for their weapons. They each had identical Browning Hi-Powers, idiotically unlocked given where they were stashed. He made them safe before laying them out on the ground again. Spud went through the formality of checking that their targets were fully dead, while the chopper continued to circle outside.

Two minutes passed. The SAS guys covered the concierge's

eyes and mouth with packing tape, then removed their bala-clavas. The lift hissed open. Two figures walked out.

Danny straightened up when he saw them. Victoria Atkinson stepped briskly out of the lift. As her eyes fell on the bloodied corpses, she looked immediately bilious. She removed the tissue from her sleeve and pressed it to her mouth.

Alongside her was Harrison Maddox, Hammerstone's CIA liaison. He looked altogether less concerned by the sight that awaited him, merely glancing at the corpses and the terrified concierge with a raised eyebrow and taking care not to step in the streak of blood that smeared the floor.

'We can do this downstairs, Victoria?' Maddox said. 'If you'd rather.'

Victoria waved her handkerchief at him dismissively. 'I'm quite all right, thank you, Harrison.' She looked at Danny and Spud in turn. 'Perhaps we could go inside?' she said. 'Your col-leagues here can watch the door.'

Danny shrugged. 'Nothing to watch,' he said. 'The flat's empty. He's gone.'

'If only we could question the guards,' Maddox said with heavy sarcasm in his voice. 'But they seem to be a little past it.'

'Yeah,' Danny said coolly. 'They do, don't they?'

The conversation was cut off by the ringing of Maddox's mobile phone. As he took the call, Danny and Spud led the two spooks into the dining room where the execution video had taken place. The blinds were still up here, and as they entered they saw the circling chopper peel off and head towards the river. Victoria looked a bit giddy. 'I don't have a very good head for heights,' she admitted. She looked around. 'Forensic teams will need to come in,' she said. 'Check he was actually here.'

'Not much doubt of that,' Maddox said. 'I've just received word that a figure in a burka left the building just before five o'clock this morning. There's footage on the foyer's CCTV. No doubt our friend the concierge will be able to tell us more.'

'I'd be interested to know how you found that out before me, Harrison?' said Victoria. The American simply shrugged. Neither of them seemed to notice the look Danny gave Spud: a look that said, *I told you so* ...

Danny left the room. He couldn't face listening to the spooks' arguments, and there was something else he wanted to check. He entered the sitting room, and walked up to the glass table with the framed pictures. There were five of them, and they all showed the same family dressed in traditional Middle Eastern clothes. The father had a very obvious crooked nose. He selected the one that showed this feature the most clearly, then carried it back to the others.

'So what now?' Spud was saying. 'He obviously knows we're after him. He's going to go to ground.'

'We've got something,' Danny said, holding up the picture.

'Should you be touching that?' Victoria asked. But she accepted it from Danny when he handed it to her.

Danny watched her carefully. Her eyes narrowed. Recognition. And maybe a hint of a smile.

'Friend of ours?' Danny said.

'Oh, yes,' Victoria said. 'He's *very* well known to us. This is a Saudi businessman called Muhammad Al-Sikriti. He's an occasional donor to the Holy Shrine mosque. We've been trying to link him to Abu Ra'id for some time now. Without success.' She turned to the CIA man. 'Muhammad Al-Sikiriti. Name *mean* anything to you, Harrison?'

'Of course,' Maddox said, clearly trying to restrain himself.

'Mr Al-Sikriti is also well known to the American administration, but for different reasons,' Victoria said. 'Oil, isn't it, Harrison? No wonder he's entertained so many American trade delegations. I do believe we have several pictures on file of him shaking hands with the President ...'

'You've absolutely no concrete evidence that he's anything to do with Abu Ra'id.'

'Not yet,' Victoria persisted. 'But if it turns out that this flat is linked in any way to Mr Al-Sikriti, presumably you won't mind if we inconvenience him with a little extraordinary rendition. Pack him off in a Hercules to one of your black camps in northern Poland. I'm sure he'll be a mine of information. Never mind if he's one of the unfortunate majority who don't survive the questioning . . .'

'Al-Sikiriti can't just disappear off the face of the earth. The political fallout would be . . .'

'Funny, isn't it,' Victoria interrupted quietly, 'how keen you are to violate a suspect's human rights, *unless* they have the one thing that talks.' She rubbed her fingers together to indicate cash.

'I'm not saying you shouldn't question him,' Maddox said. 'I'm just saying he has to survive the process, and remain intact. If anything happens to him, my government *will* deny all involvement. That's a political reality, and it's out of my hands.'

'Did you hear that, gentlemen?' Victoria said. 'He remains intact. Otherwise our American cousins will be *very* upset.'

'Where is this Al-Sikriti now?' Danny asked quietly, happy to put a stop to the barbed sniping of the two spooks.

'He's in the place where the Saudi playboys love to come to spend their wealth and do all the things they can't do in their own country,' she said.

'Right. And where's that?'

Victoria looked out of the window.

'London,' she said.

THIRTEEN

In the morning they slept.

Having arrived back at the safe house, Danny gave himself two hours' shut-eye that felt, when he woke, like it had only been two minutes. He and Spud had hauled their arses out of bed at 14.00hrs, when they returned to the basement of Paddington police station. Fletcher, their police liaison officer, was waiting for them. He looked even more put-upon that the last time they'd seen him.

'Come on in, come on in.' He beckoned them with his soft West Country accent when they appeared at his doorway. As they stepped inside, Danny saw that the piles of paper on his desk had grown even higher. 'Been busy since we last met?' Fletcher asked. 'On second thoughts, don't answer that.' Danny recalled that it had been Fletcher who gave them the key to the safe house opposite the flat of the first bomber. He'd have put two and two together by now regarding that hit, even if he hadn't joined up the dots with respect to the others.

'Have Hereford sent through everything we need?' Danny asked.

'Yes, yes.' He paused. 'Probably shouldn't ask, but is this all to do with the bombings?'

Poker face from both SAS men.

'Quite understand, lads. Quite understand. But if it is, you're doing a better job than us. Not a man to spare and still we don't have a handle on what's going on.' More silence. Fletcher smiled. 'Immune to compliments, I see.'

'Found your intruder?' Danny asked, to move the conversation on from questions they didn't want to answer.

Fletcher looked at them blankly.

'You mentioned it last time,' Danny reminded him. 'That bird with the intruder up on Praed Street. And you had that hit and run on that fella walking up to the university. Gengerov, or something?'

Fletcher shook his head. 'Too much on my plate,' he said. 'Far too much.' He rummaged around on his chaotic desk before holding up a set of printouts – A2-sized architectural drawings. 'The Park Lane Hotel, thirteenth floor,' he said. 'Took the liberty of checking, the whole floor's taken by a Saudi Arabian gentleman by the name of Muhammad Al-Sikriti. Must be quite an entourage he has, and costing an arm and a leg.'

'He can afford it,' Danny said. 'Did you find out about the floor above?'

'All rooms taken, I'm afraid. We could probably put pressure on the hotel to clear one of them for us, if you think that's necessary.'

Danny and Spud looked at each other, and imperceptibly shook their heads. They couldn't guarantee the current occupants wouldn't kick up a fuss – or even that they weren't part of Al-Sikiriti's entourage. Putting in surveillance on Al-Sikiriti from an adjacent room or a room above was a possibility, but in this instance, the wrong call.

Fletcher handed over some photographs. They all showed the same man, but in different clothes. In one he wore full Arab headgear – a white headdress with a red band. In another, he wore just a *dishdash*, and in a third he wore a plain Western business suit. He was easily distinguishable, however, not so much by the thick black hair that covered the top of his ears, but by a slightly crooked nose that looked almost as if it had once been broken.

'If I had his money, I'd get my hooter fixed,' Spud commented. He looked up at Fletcher. 'Anything else arrive for us?'

Fletcher nodded. He turned and, from behind his desk, pulled a metal case the size of a small tool box. He handed it over to Spud who rested it on the copper's desk and unclipped the lid. From inside he pulled what looked like an ordinary black flash-light, about a foot in length. Fletcher blinked at it in surprise. 'Could have fitted you out with a torch easily enough, fellas,' he said.

The SAS men said nothing. Spud returned the torch to its box and held out his hand to shake Fletcher's. Danny did the same. Their police liaison was a good man. A bit naive, perhaps, but a good man nonetheless.

The Park Lane Hotel was not a place for jeans and a leather jacket. From Paddington, Danny and Spud headed to Oxford Street, where Danny got himself suited and booted. 'Nice threads,' Spud said with just a hint of sarcasm as he emerged from Selfridges. Danny's grey suit jacket was too tight around the shoulders, and he could have done with a shave. Otherwise, he looked the part. And most importantly, his Glock and radio pack were invisible under the suit. He bought a packet of Marlboro Lights and a lighter from a kiosk nearby. He wasn't a smoker, but loitering outside a building as if on a fag break was always good cover.

From Oxford Street, they headed to Park Lane. Spud took the wheel of the Discovery, driving steadily down from Marble Arch and pulling up about 20 metres from the corner of the Park Lane Hotel.

'Hope the fucker shows his face sooner rather than later,' Danny said.

'Trust me,' Spud replied. 'He will. These rich Arabs come to London for the hookers and marching powder, not to look at the rain from their hotel window.'

'Well, let's hope he hasn't ordered in.' Danny checked the

time: 15.47. He gave Spud a nod, then jumped out of the car. The Discovery immediately pulled back into the line of traffic. Spud had a boring few hours ahead of him, circling round Hyde Park Corner and Marble Arch, driving up and down Park Lane, maybe parking up for a while in view of the hotel entrance until he got moved on. They'd keep conversation to a minimum over the radio, only checking in with each other occasionally, or when they actively had something to report.

Danny walked towards the entrance to the hotel. This wasn't his first visit to the Park Lane. Two years previously he and a couple of other guys had been here bolstering a BG team babysitting a delegation from the Afghan government. He remembered that back then, like now, there was a line of black cabs queueing up at the entrance to drop off and collect guests. Back then they had been a strange mixture of businessmen and well-heeled families with bags from Hamleys and Harrods. There were no children here today. Hardly surprising. Who'd bring their kids shopping to a city under siege?

Danny passed unnoticed through the revolving doors, past a fat old bloke with an improbably young woman holding his hand, and into the foyer. He examined the space. High ceilings with chandeliers. A glossy black grand piano with a young Chinese guy playing cocktail music. Waiters carrying tea trays to guests lounging around on leather sofas. His first thought was to pick out the hotel's surveillance cameras. If he could stay clear of them, so much the better. But he soon saw a number of small inverted domes on the ceiling, each with three cameras pointing down at different angles. The place was properly cased. There was no way to stay hidden.

His eyes picked out the lift – 30 metres away to his ten o'clock – then selected a sofa that faced directly towards it but on the far side of the seating area. A copy of *The Times* was on the glass coffee table in front of him. He grabbed it and idly started thumbing through its pages, keeping one eye on the lift as he turned over images of destruction in Piccadilly and, on page four, the familiar face of Abu Ra'id staring out at him.

'May I get you anything, sir?'

An obsequious waiter with slicked hair stood by his side.

'Coffee,' Danny said. 'Black.' And he went back to watching the elevator.

A click in his covert earpiece. 'You in position?'

'Roger that,' Danny replied, scratching his nose to hide the movement of his lips. 'Could be a long afternoon.'

Five minutes passed. Danny's coffee arrived. He didn't touch it for a full ten minutes. All his attention was on his surroundings as he picked out individual male faces from the guests milling around the foyer. Their numbers were fluid. At one moment there would be perhaps 30, the next 70. Danny continued to scan them carefully, only finally stopping to pour himself some coffee so he wouldn't stand out.

After 45 minutes he was aware of the waiter hovering again. He looked up impatiently.

'May I fetch you some more coffee, sir?'

Danny's eyes went back to the lift. 'Yeah,' he said. 'Great.'

And then, just as the waiter was bending down to retrieve his used cup, Danny said: 'Actually, no.'

The lift doors had opened. A small crowd of people were emerging.

There were eight of them. Three women, two men, three kids. They all wore traditional Arabic dress. Danny's eyes picked out the faces of the two men. One of them had the distinctive crooked nose he was looking for. He spoke into his covert radio as the waiter walked away. 'I've got eyes-on the target.'

'Alone?' came Spud's voice.

'Negative. He's got half his fucking family with him.'

The lift doors shut, but the little group of eight Saudi nationals didn't move more than a couple of metres away from it. The two men were deep in conversation. As he chatted away, Al-Sikriti put one hand on the arm of one of the women in what looked like a genuinely affectionate gesture, and the woman smiled at him. The remaining two women were fussing over the three children, who all looked rather surly and bored.

The lift doors opened again. Three more men emerged. Eleven surveillance targets in total. They also wore Arabic dress, but it was much plainer. They were pulling suitcases behind them.

'Shit,' Danny breathed. He nonchalantly pulled a twenty from his wallet and dropped it by his coffee things, then stood up and spoke into the radio again. 'They've got their fucking suitcases with them. Looks like they're leaving. Get ready to follow them.'

The group of eleven Saudis were walking towards the exit. Danny followed them from the other side of the foyer. Al-Sikriti was talking in an animated fashion to the children, gesturing extravagantly. The children's faces suddenly lit up at this attention from their father. They even laughed. When they reached the exit, Al-Sikriti and his family held back while the three men in plainer clothes took the suitcases outside.

Danny walked past their little group, close enough to hear them chatting together in Arabic, before exiting the hotel. Directly ahead of him were two Mercedes, black, dark windows. The boots of each car were open and the assistants in plain *dishdashes* were loading the suitcases into the vehicles. The front and rear doors on the hotel side were all open, and two liveried chauffeurs stood by each car, waiting for their passengers. Danny hooked round to the right and pulled his packet of Marlboros and the lighter from his pocket. He cupped his hands against the breeze over the end of a cigarette, and lit up. Acrid smoke filled his mouth. He inhaled it deeply. And he kept eyes on the Mercedes. If Spud was going to follow whichever vehicle Al-Sikriti climbed into, he'd need the plates. Though by the look of things, the family were heading to the airport. So much for hookers and marching powder. This guy looked well and truly under the thumb.

The family emerged. Danny took another drag on his cigarette. He picked out Al-Sikriti again. He was embracing one of the women. Then he bent down and did the same to the children.

'Hold up,' Danny said into his radio. 'I think the target's staying here.'

Sure enough, thirty seconds later the women and children, along with the three male assistants – nine of the surveillance targets in all – had climbed into the cars. Al-Sikriti and the second man stood on the kerbside as the chauffeurs closed the doors on the family, then got behind the wheel. The two-car convoy pulled away. Danny snapped his attention back to Al-Sikriti. The jolliness in his demeanour had fallen away, replaced by something more serious. Wordlessly, he and his companion walked back into the hotel.

Danny stubbed his cigarette and followed. Back inside the foyer he watched as the two Saudi men returned to the lift and disappeared inside. Once more, Danny took a seat on one of the leather sofas.

Once more, he ordered coffee, and waited.

Another hour passed. Danny only pretended to sip his coffee. Too much liquid and he'd need a piss – not possible, when there was only him conducting the surveillance. The pianist finished playing. The clientele changed. Their clothes became more formal: women tarted up for dinner, blokes wearing evening suits. He was aware of two waiters eyeing him from the far side of the foyer. They were clearly talking about him, perhaps discussing whether they should ask him to leave for sitting here so long for only the price of a couple of coffees. He was beginning to think that he should get Spud to swap places with him, when the lift doors opened again.

A less sharp observer would have missed him.

Al-Sikriti looked completely different. The formal Arabic garb had gone. Instead he wore an immaculately cut grey suit with a pale pink shirt, open at the collar. His hair was waxed into place. He was accompanied by the same guy, who was similarly dressed. And on either arm, a girl. One brunette, one blonde, neither much older than eighteen, both of them wearing short, tight dresses that hugged their thighs and pushed their breasts skywards. They both wore diamond necklaces that glittered in the light from the chandeliers, and they gazed at Al-Sikriti like adoring puppies.

You sleazy bastard, Danny thought to himself, unable to stop a momentary flash of grudging admiration.

Al-Sikriti, his mate and the two birds cut through the throng in the foyer as they headed to the exit. Danny got on to the radio. 'He's leaving. Looks like you were right – he's all *Miami Vice* with a couple of pros on his arm.'

'Surprise surprise,' Spud said. 'There's a limo waiting at the entrance. Looks like our man's planning to have it large tonight, now the ball and chain's on a flight back to the desert.'

Danny followed them outside. It was dark now, and already cold enough for his breath to steam. He took up the same position as before, and once again lit a cigarette. One of the hotel doormen stood at the back door of a waiting limo. The two girls giggled as they bundled into the back. Al-Sikriti slapped one of them on the arse as she disapeared into the car. Al-Sikriti turned to the other man, his face suddenly more serious, and gave him some kind of instruction. The other man nodded, looked rather wistfully towards the open door through which the two girls had disappeared, and turned to walk back into the hotel.

As Al-Sikriti climbed into the car, Danny strolled past. He saw a bucket of champagne which the girls were already pouring, and a blacked-out screen between them and the chauffeur at the front. He tried to get a glimpse of the chauffeur from outside, but the front side windows were also blacked out and before he could get an angle through the windscreen, the limo slid away from the hotel. Danny watched it go – not overtly, but from the corner of his eye. As it turned into Park Lane, Danny saw the unmistakable shadow of a black Land Rover Discovery pull out behind it and keep its tail.

Danny dropped his cigarette and stubbed it out with his foot. He walked away from the hotel and started pacing the length of Park Lane. Spud was on the case now. As soon as Al-Sikriti and his escorts had reached their destination, he'd let Danny . . .

'Okay, mucker,' came Spud's voice over the earpiece. 'Prince Charming and his two fairy godmothers have just debussed outside the Golden Flamingo casino.'

'They going in?' Danny asked.

'Yep. They must have been expecting him – some flunky's just come out to open the car door.'

'I'll be there in ten minutes.'

'Stick a monkey on red for me,' Spud replied. 'I'm feeling lucky.'

Danny's mate gave him the address. Sure enough, ten minutes later, Danny was on the outskirts of the West End, standing outside the Golden Flamingo. It was nondescript: an ordinary doorway in a Regency terrace with nothing more than a brass plaque the size of a letterbox to indicate the nature of the establishment. It was clearly a private casino. The door was locked, so Danny had to ring a bell to get access. He didn't have to wait more than five seconds for the door to swing open. A neat little man with thinning hair gave him a patronising smile.

'May I help you, sir?'

'Here for a flutter,' Danny said.

'Unfortunately, sir, this is a members-only club.'

Danny nodded, then pulled his security services ID from his back pocket. 'Here's my membership card,' he said. The doorman took it, and an uncertain look crossed his face. He didn't look any more eager to let Danny in, so Danny leaned in and spoke close to his ear. 'One phone call, mate,' he blagged, 'and I'll have ten police cars pumping neon light outside your front door for the rest of the night. Could be bad for business. Or you could just let me in, and you'll hardly know I'm here. Choice is yours.'

The doorman's eyes narrowed. He stepped back and held the door open for Danny, who walked confidently inside.

The casino smelled of brandy and perfume. The main room was about 30 metres by 20, with eight different card and roulette tables dotted around, and a long bar against the far wall, all brass and optics and low lighting. There were perhaps 50 people here, and there was a low buzz of excited chatter around the tables. In an instant, Danny noticed three cameras directed down towards the card tables. He knew that somewhere, in a back room, gaming surveillance officers were watching those tables carefully for cheats, or anyone who seemed to be having too successful an evening. There was a good chance they'd have facial recognition software running. Anyone who walked out of here with too much of the casino's money would find themselves tracked down and encouraged back with promises of booze, complimentary gaming chips, even women. The casino would just want them back through their doors, because everyone loses eventually.

And the gaming surveillance officers wouldn't only be in the back rooms. They'd be milling around the tables themselves, keeping a steady, undercover eye on the punters. But Danny felt confident that none of these surveillance officers would be interested in him, so long as he stayed quietly at the bar, and showed no interest in the tables.

Within seconds, a girl had approached him. She was no more than seventeen, fully dolled-up with tits practically spilling out of a glittering halterneck top.

'Not seen *you* here before.' she said, her voice husky.

'Not tonight, love,' Danny gave a blunt reply. The girl showed no sign of offence, but wandered off into the casino in search of other game.

Danny ordered an orange juice, remembering at the last minute not to look surprised that it was on the house. Standard practice, since the casino far preferred tipsy punters to sober ones. Then he scanned the room, looking for Al-Sikriti. His target had a roulette table to himself – just him, the two girls, and a croupier spinning the ball and expertly divvying up the chips on the baize. Each girl had an arm draped on one of Al-Sikriti's shoulders. Occasionally, one of them would whisper something in his ear, and nuzzle him as she did so. Al-Sikriti himself was giving it the full playboy routine. He handed one of the girls a little pile of chips and encouraged her as she placed them all on red. The croupier spun the wheel and the girl clapped delightedly as her winnings were doubled. Al-Sikriti took back the larger pile of chips, then placed one of them in the girl's cleavage. She gave him a kittenish smile, then kissed his cheek.

Danny didn't allow himself to stare too closely at the target. If Al-Sikriti moved, he'd be on him, but until then he needed to remain inconspicuous. Out of habit, he checked the room for exits: there was the main entrance through which he'd come, and two doors leading to the male and female cloakrooms. Other than that, just a door behind the bar which he assumed would lead to a goods entrance. He scanned the room again. It crossed Danny's mind that, unhindered as Al-Sikriti was by any kind of close protection that Danny could make out, it would be just a minute's work to follow him into the gents, force him into a cubicle and beat out of him the intelligence that he needed. But he remembered Maddox's instruction: this had to be deniable, and they couldn't leave a mark on the fucker. Danny would just have to be patient.

His eyes took in bored, rich women dripping with gaudy jewellery, losing thousands at the tables just to pass the time. Old, ugly men surrounded by improbably beautiful young women. On the far side of the room, the dapper little man who had let Danny in was eyeing him suspiciously. Danny ignored that and sipped on his orange juice.

And waited.

Thirty minutes passed. Al-Sikriti's luck had changed. The same girl who'd had so much luck on red lost twice that amount on black. As the Arab's luck changed, so did his expression. He looked petulant and shooed the girl away from the table. She immediately left Al-Sikriti's field of view, wandering round the other tables for ten minutes. Danny followed her with his eyes. There was something about her features that reminded him of Clara. Perhaps it was the way a tendril of blonde hair curled loosely round her neck, or the slight upturn of her nose. Whatever it was, it distracted him. He felt a familiar, gnawing anxiety at the idea that she might have found some other bloke by now. He didn't like that idea. When all this was over, maybe he'd call her. Apologise . . .

When the girl returned to the roulette table, the Arab's luck had changed once more. He let her sit next to him again, and was rewarded with a suggestive stroke of his immaculately suited arm.

It took 65 minutes for Al-Sikriti to grow bored of the tables. He clicked his fingers in the air and a member of the casino staff appeared from nowhere. Al-Sikriti said something to him, and he signalled to the dapper man at the entrance. The two girls made their way to the ladies. Clearly, they were preparing to leave.

Danny left his half-drunk orange juice on the bar and headed to the exit. Out on the street, the temperature had dropped another couple of degrees and there was a mist in the air that shrouded the yellow street lamps. Al-Sikriti's limo was parked up outside, hazard lights on, facing to Danny's left. The dapper man who had let Danny in trotted out behind him and opened the rear passenger door, ready for his important client.

Danny crossed the street. He looked back to the limo. The driver's window, which was on the road side, slid down. Sitting behind the wheel was Spud. He winked once at Danny, then raised the window again.

Movement at the entrance to the casino. Al-Sikriti and the two women were emerging.

'Where's the chauffeur?' Danny said into his radio.

'Last time I looked?' Spud said. 'Unconscious in the gutter. Won't wake up for a while. Meet you at the end of the street?'

'Roger that.'

Danny picked up his pace, then crossed the road again. On the edge of his vision he was aware of Al-Sikriti and the girls, 30 metres away now, climbing into the car. He hurried along the street. Twenty seconds later, the limo passed him, its windows all blacked out, its engine humming softly. It pulled up to a halt alongside Danny. A black cab was directly behind it. The driver beeped in frustration at this delay, then quickly overtook. Danny approached the nearside passenger door. He heard a click as Spud switched off the central locking. He took his black balaclava from the pocket of his suit and swiftly pulled it over his head.

Then he opened the door.

Inside, the party was in full swing. The two girls, sitting together opposite Al-Sikriti, were necking, their tongues thrust down each other's throat as they put on a show for the sleazy businessman. Al-Sikriti himself was reclining on his seat, a glass of champagne in his hand, his shirt unbuttoned to reveal his hairy chest, his belt unfastened and his fly undone.

Danny bundled into the car and took a seat next to Al-Sikriti. The girls stopped kissing. Al-Sikriti sat up straight, spilling his champagne as he did so. All three of them looked outraged at this sudden intrusion.

Then Danny pulled his weapon.

One of the girls screamed. Danny pointed the Glock in their direction.

'Goodnight, girls,' he growled. He jabbed the weapon towards the door. The two women didn't need telling twice – they practically scrambled over each other to get out of the car, their high heels twisting on the ground. Once they were outside and hurrying back down the street, Danny leaned over and pulled the door shut. Then he knocked twice on the screen dividing the driver's area from the back of the limo. He heard the sound of the central locking closing again. The limo started moving. At the same time, the tinted screen slid down to reveal Spud, balaclava'd, behind the wheel.

Al-Sikriti was sweating. His fist was clenched round his champagne glass, and he looked as though he might crush it.

'How much do you want?' he said, his voice thin with nervousness. 'You tell me how much you want, I give it to you. I have money here.' His free hand edged towards his jacket.

'If at any point I can't see both your hands,' Danny said, 'I'll kill you right here.'

Al-Sikriti froze.

Spud continued to drive. Danny didn't say a word. Al-Sikriti's terrified imagination would be doing half his work for him. He and Spud kept their silence, for several minutes, all the way round Marble Arch and along the park towards Bayswater.

Al-Sikriti broke it, in a stuttering voice broken by fear. 'You ... you like girls?' he said. 'You like *those* girls? I get you as many as you want. They do anything. *Anything* . . .'

Danny shook his head. Al-Sikriti fell silent again.

Danny took his phone from his pocket. He set it to record. Then he looked over his shoulder. 'Pass it,' he told Spud.

With one hand on the wheel, Spud stretched over to the passenger seat and passed the black torch they'd picked up from Fletcher's office. Danny stowed his weapon and instead brandished the torch. He leaned forward and held the torch about five inches from Al-Sikriti's face. Then he pressed a button on the top.

Suddenly a grating electrical sound filled the car. Al-Sikriti's face lit up with a harsh white light, and Danny saw in the windows the reflection of a violent, three-inch-long electric spark. He let it buzz for a few seconds, then removed his finger from the button.

'This is a taser,' Danny said, as Al-Sikriti gulped for breath. 'Fucking high voltage. Cause cardiac arrest, now and then. Brain damage too, if I go at it really hard.' He leaned in towards the Arab. 'But the worst thing about them is that they *really* ... *fucking ... hurt ...*'

Al-Sikriti shook his head. 'Please,' he said. 'Please, I'll give you whatever ...' He spoke good, precise English, but tinged with a Middle Eastern accent.

'Abu Ra'id,' Danny said. 'Where is he?'

The question immediately silenced Al-Sikriti. His expression changed. There was suddenly less panic in his face, but more fear – a deep-seated fear, Danny sensed. He wasn't going to talk without persuasion.

He did it suddenly, jabbing the torch hard against Al-Sikriti's left arm, and switching on the taser as he did so. Al-Sikrit's body went into spasm. He screamed, and the sound merged horribly with the loud electric buzz of the taser, muffled slightly by his clothes, the spark invisible now that the torch was pressed against a body.

One second.

Two seconds.

Three seconds.

Off.

Al-Sikriti was gasping. There were tears on his cheeks, though his eyes were clenched shut. Danny gave him a moment to recuperate. He needed to be thrifty in his use of the taser. Al-Sikriti was no good to anybody unconscious. Ten seconds passed. Danny's victim opened his eyes. Danny held up the taser and zapped it in front of the Arab's face. Al-Sikriti started as if the machine had been touching his skin. Two seconds later, a foul smell filled the air.

'Did you shit yourself?' Danny asked.

Al-Sikriti nodded.

'Say it,' Danny instructed. 'Say, I shat myself.'

'I shat myself.'

'Dirty fucker,' Danny said, as insultingly as he could. Then he thrust the taser against his victim's arm again.

Al-Sikriti's second meeting with the taser, administered as Spud drove them through Notting Hill, lasted a little longer than the first, and his scream was a little hoarser. By the time Danny removed the device, his limbs were still jerking, like echoes of the main spasm. Danny leaned over to him, ignoring the disgusting smell from his trousers. 'If you don't tell me what I want to know,' he said, his voice muffled through the balaclava, 'I'll zap your cock.' He thrust the taser towards his victim's open fly, and Al-Sikriti quickly covered his groin with his hands.

'Move your hands,' Danny instructed. Al-Sikriti did as he was told. 'Abu Ra'id was staying in your flat. Now he's gone. Where is he?'

Al-Sikriti's eyes widened. He shook his head. 'I swear, sir. I do not know . . .'

Immediately, Danny thrust the taser into Al-Sikriti's groin and gave it a two-second burst. Not too long, because he knew the bastard was prone to piss himself, and he wasn't sure how the moisture would affect the electrical contacts. But he didn't need any longer, because as the grating electrical sound died away, Al-Sikriti was saying something. A single word, repeated in a harsh, reluctant whisper. At first Danny couldn't understand it. It sounded obscure. Arabic, perhaps. But gradually, as Al-Sikriti repeated it, the sound crystallised.

'Yemen,' he said. 'Yemen . . . Yemen . . .'

'Yemen's a big place. You'll need to do better than that.' He zapped the taser in the air to underline his point.

'All I know,' Al-Sikriti said, 'is that he took a boat to France last night. An airplane was waiting for him there, to take him to

Sana'a. Al-Shabaab have a camp north of there, in the Sana'a governate, where he will seek sanctuary . . .'

'How far north?'

'I don't know. I swear, they keep it a secret.' And as Danny approached him again with the taser, he squealed: '*That is all I know . . .*'

His final statement had the ring of truth. Danny believed him. He looked over his shoulder at Spud. 'Let's get out of here.'

Spud indicated right, turned off the main drag and then turned into a dark side street where he pulled up. Danny put the taser down and picked up his phone. He stopped recording, then scrubbed back a little and replayed the recording.

'. . . *take him to San'a. Al-Shabaab have a camp north of . . .*'

Danny scrubbed further back.

'*I shat myself.*'

'*Dirty fucker . . .*'

Danny pressed 'pause'. 'Make a fuss about this, that tape goes straight to every business partner of yours we can find. Got it?'

Al-Sikiriti nodded, the fear on his face giving way to unchecked hatred.

'No, I don't think you do.' Danny pulled his gun and put it to Al-Sikriti's head. 'Trust me, friend. If that cunt Abu Ra'id gets even a whisper that you've spoken to us, I'll start with your wife and then with your kids. I'll give you a couple of weeks to get used to them being dead, then I'll do you. You won't see me, you won't even know I'm there till you get a bullet in your brain. Understood?'

Another terrified nod.

Danny had nothing more to say. Spud switched off the central locking and the two men debussed, pulling off their balaclavas as they stepped out of the car. Danny gave Spud the taser. Spud stuffed it into his bag as they walked swiftly away from the limo back towards the main road.

'Not sure that's quite how he expected his evening to pan out,' Spud said.

'Why did he leave it so late?'

Spud looked at his watch, confused. 'It's not even midnight,' he said.

'Not Al-Sikriti. Abu Ra'id. Why did he only skip the country this morning?'

Spud shrugged. 'Because he's a fucking idiot?'

'If he's such an idiot, why can nobody catch him?' He looked at the phone that was still in his hand. 'They need to hear this,' he said. 'Let's get back to the safe house and make contact.'

Spud nodded. The two SAS men melted away into the night.

FOURTEEN

They'd been told to RV at Hammerstone House at 06.00 the following morning, but Danny and Spud were early. They stood in the biting frost of dawn, watching the headlamps of a convoy of four vehicles trundle slowly up the long driveway. The cars crunched on to the gravel in front of the house. They came to a halt, but the headlamps still blazed brightly. The faceless silhouettes of four chauffeurs stepped out and opened the rear doors, releasing four more figures from the back seats. Even though he couldn't make out their faces immediately, Danny identified each one by the shape of their silhouettes and their gait. Victoria, shorter than the others and briskly shuffling. Chamberlain, tall and broad of shoulder. Harrison Maddox, lean and with a relaxed yet purposeful stride. And Buckingham, who waited for the others to step forward into the lamplight before revealing himself and keeping to the back of their little quartet. Everyone's breath steamed. As they drew near and their faces became visible, Danny saw that each one was etched with tiredness and concern.

Buckingham had a key to the house. Nobody spoke as he let them in. They traipsed through the darkness into the same room where they'd had their first meeting. Buckingham turned on the lights. Everyone except Danny and Spud squinted as their eyes recovered from the sudden shock. None of the spooks removed their greatcoats, or even pulled their hands from their pockets. But Danny sensed that, with perhaps the exception of Chamberlain, they were eyeing the two SAS men with a certain wariness that he hadn't noticed before. Which figured, he supposed. They knew what Danny and Spud had been up to since their last meeting. And, of course, they had heard the recording of his little chat with Al-Sikriti.

Victoria cleared her throat. 'I think I speak for us all,' she said, 'when I congratulate you both on your work.' The others gave no indication that they agreed with the sentiment, but stared stonily at them. 'We're quite convinced that Abu Ra'id has left the country for fear that he might be next on our list. A dangerous threat to the security of this country has been removed. We fully expect a cessation of the atrocities. Or at the very least a pause.'

'So job done?' Spud demanded.

Each of the four spooks gave them a startlingly similar look: a thin, humourless smile.

'Not yet,' Victoria said. She cleared her throat again. She nodded in Maddox's direction, and the CIA man returned the gesture. 'We need to make sure that the threat is eradicated. Permanently.' She looked from Spud to Danny, then back again.

Danny wasn't stupid. He knew what was coming.

'Hugo, you've been liaising with our Yemen analysts. Would you like to tell us what you know about the Sa'ada Governate?'

Buckingham stepped forwards. Even his handsome features were marred by tiredness. He refused to catch Danny's eye, and spoke instead to the company at large. He was unable to hide from his voice the smugness of a man who was aware that he knew what he was talking about.

'It's bandit country,' he said.

'I think we'll need a little more to go on than that,' Victoria said primly.

Buckingham inclined his head. 'The intelligence we've ... *you've* ... gleaned from Al-Sikriti certainly makes sense,' he said. 'Yemen is by far the poorest country on the Arabian Peninsular, and a fertile training ground for Islamist militants – Al-Qaeda, historically, but in recent months Al-Shabaab groups have crossed over from Somalia, and their training camps have been appearing in remote areas to the north of the country – especially in the Sa'ada Governate. It's a rigorously Islamic region, mostly of the Zaydi Shi'ite persuasion. Al-Qaeda and Al-Shabaab are Sunni, or course, but they're attracted to this area because of its lawlessness. It's quite out of the control of the Yemeni central government – almost like a breakaway state in many ways.' Buckingham cleared his throat, then gathered his thoughts for a moment before continuing. 'The Yemeni government makes all the right noises about stamping down on these camps, and have in the past liaised with the United States military as well as the Saudis to launch missile attacks on them. But they're in a jolly difficult situation. These Islamist groups are well funded. They don't just appeal to the religious sensibilities of their recruits, they *pay* them, which is something the Yemeni government simply can't compete with. The government knows that if it removes this source of income from the very poorest parts of the population, it risks having an uprising on its hands.'

'Typical Middle Eastern politics,' Chamberlain butted in.

'In fact,' Buckingham said, 'Yemen has more in common with Afghanistan than with its Arabic neighbours. Equally tribal, and the local elders often have more influence over their armed civilians than the government itself. The bottom line is that these training camps can turn up almost anywhere, often without the knowledge of the central government.'

'We have people on the ground in Yemen, of course' – Victoria took up the briefing – 'as do our friends in Langley.' She looked over at Maddox, who didn't respond. 'They're putting the feelers out as we speak, trying to establish exactly where this training camp might be.'

'Problem solved,' Spud said with a shrug. He looked at Harrison Maddox. 'You Yanks will have some drones in the area. Doesn't sound like anything a couple of Hellfires won't sort out.'

That thin-lipped look again from the spooks. A moment of silence. Danny could tell that they had a different strategy in mind.

'Bloody important,' Chamberlain said, 'that Abu Ra'id gets what's coming to him. Hard to be sure you've got the right fellow when you make an indiscriminate strike from the air. Could have nuked Abottabad at the drop of a hat, but who'd have been able to confirm we'd got Bin Laden?' He chortled slightly, as though the idea of nuking an entire Pakistani city was an amusing one.

'What I think Piers is trying to say,' Harrison Maddox continued in his slow American drawl, 'is that we need men on the ground to identify Abu Ra'id and eliminate him. It's then up to the Yemeni administration whether they want to take out the whole training camp or not.'

Danny looked at each of the Hammerstone quartet in turn. They were staring implacably at him and Spud. He walked over to the window and looked out. The headlamps of the four cars were no longer burning, but the sky was a fraction lighter now. A steel grey.

'You'll need sixteen men,' he said. 'Minimum. And that's assuming your intelligence guys can find out the exact location of the camp.' He turned. 'But I'm guessing that you haven't dragged us here if you were thinking of a major operation like that.'

Another silence.

'It's out of the question,' said Buckingham finally. 'The footprint of this operation needs to be small. Instructions from on high.'

Danny walked up to him. 'Oh yeah? Just *who* on high?'

Buckingham sniffed. He maintained steady eye contact with Danny. 'Important people,' he said.

Suddenly Chamberlain was there, standing between them. He gave Buckingham a warning look, then turned to Danny. 'You'll report to Heathrow at 08.00,' he said, easily falling back into the role of a rupert issuing orders. 'Both of you. There'll be Regiment representatives there to brief you further.'

'Just like that?' Spud murmured.

Chamberlain gave a bland smile. 'Happy landings, gentlemen. We've every faith in you.' He looked over at the others. 'England's finest, eh? Couldn't be in safer hands.'

If they were encouraged, the Hammerstone quartet didn't show it as they exited the chilly room. Outside the house, Danny and Spud watched them wordlessly climb into the back of their chauffeur-driven vehicles, then file slowly down the driveway before turning out of sight.

'Small footprint?' Spud said. 'Important people? You believe all that shit?'

Danny shook his head. 'No,' he said.

'Maybe this is just what E squadron's like.'

Maybe. But it wasn't the first time he didn't know the whole story. Wouldn't be the last either. Occupational hazard. They had their orders, and unless they wanted to find themselves up in front of a military tribunal, they had to follow them.

'Let's go,' Danny said, and together they climbed back into the Discovery and drove away.

08.00hrs

There were parts of Heathrow to which the public had access. There were parts for which only members of the aviation services were authorised. And there were parts that few people ever got to see. This Portakabin, a restricted area in the shadow of Terminal Two, was one of them. A white Transit van was parked up alongside it, next to which was Danny and Spud's Discovery. A member of D squadron – Danny recognised the face but couldn't put a name to it – stood at the entrance, his assault rifle slung across his body. He gave Danny and Spud a nod of greeting, but remained rooted to the spot. It wouldn't do for any unauthorised personnel to enter this Portakabin, not least because its contents made a mockery of the security procedures thousands of holidaymakers were undergoing at that very moment.

Danny and Spud were there. So too was their ops officer Ray Hammond. He watched unsmilingly as the two Regiment men dealt with the hardware laid out on a table in front of them.

There were two rifles: HK416s. Danny and Spud stripped one of them down each, until each weapon was no more than a tight bundle of grey metal, wrapped in grey rags to stop the moving parts rubbing against each other. The guys each had a sturdy North Face holdall, about three foot in length. They each stowed their bundle and returned their attention to the rest of the gear. Their Regiment-issue Sig P266s were laid out – these too they wrapped up and stowed. Ammuntion for both weapons: 5.56s for the rifles, 9mm for the handguns, neatly packed in small cardboard boxes. Lengths of bungee cord to strap the rifles to their bodies. Fragmentation grenades, two each. Flashbangs, same number. A single Claymore mine – Spud took it in his holdall. Sand-coloured hessian backed with strands of wire so that it could be shaped into whatever form they needed for desert camouflage, but now folded into a neat square. A trenching tool. A pack of silvery thermal sheeting – the only thing that could hide an OP from thermal imaging devices.

'What's with that?' Danny asked.

'We've had trouble with the Yemeni government in the past,' Hammond said. 'They have their own spy planes. Wouldn't put it past them to shop your location to the bad guys if they see you. Chances are you'll have to put in an OP. Use that if you want to stay totally hidden.'

Danny continued to work his way through the gear. There was worn paper mapping of the area they were heading for. Radio packs. A GPS handset, a Leica NV spotting scope, and two sets of night-vision goggles. Empty ops waistcoats, ready to be filled once they were on the ground. A sat phone each, of course, and a compass. A fistful of MRE packs. A thin wad of American dollars – $2,000 each. Ridiculously, this was the only thing Hammond made them sign for. Like the kind of people they were likely to encounter would want to issue receipts.

Once the holdalls were full, Danny and Spud zipped them up. Hammond handed them each a white sack. The sacks were printed with diplomatic stamps. The guys placed their holdalls in the sacks, then tightened the cords at the top and secured each one with a padlock. From now on, these diplomatic bags couldn't leave their sides.

Hammond handed each of them their passports. These too included full diplomatic stamps that would get them across the UK and Omani borders with no questions asked. 'The BA flight to Muscat leaves at 09.00,' Hammond said. 'You clear on your movements when you get there?'

The guys nodded.

'We've cleared a flight path with the Saudis along the Saudi-Yemen border. You'll RV with one of the Sultan's Chinooks when you get there.'

'Who's going to fly it?' Danny demanded. Because, orders or no orders, if they thought he was going to let some unpractised Omani pilot fly them the length of the Yemen for a covert insertion, they could fuck off.

'We've got an SF flight crew coming in from Iraq,' Hammond said. 'You'll RV with them on the Oman-Yemen border at midnight. They'll airlift you into Saada.'

Hammond moved over to another of the tables, where several piles of documents were neatly laid out. 'The main town in the Saada Governate is Ha'dah. Population, about fifty-thousand, but that's just a guess. There are thousands of IDPs in the area because of the conflict over the past few years. The town itself is situated on a mountain plateau, about 1,800 metres high. Where they drop you depends on how deserted or otherwise the road that leads up to it is. The town itself is occupied by Houthi militia. They've pretty much declared independence from the rest of Yemen. Officially there's a truce between them and the government. In practice, they're as bad as the fucking Taliban. Funded by the Iranians and Hezbollah. Trigger-happy. Give them a wide berth. Once you reach the town, you'll have to make contact with a local schoolteacher, name of Hamza. He's on the Yanks' payroll and so far as we can tell he's just about the only guy in the vicinity who speaks English.'

'Does this Hamza know where the training camp is?'

'Claims to. The CIA say his credentials are good. He's been feeding them accurate information for the past three years, and gave them a lead on a Somali terror suspect who was hiding out in the area. SEAL unit went in to nail him, confirmed that his intel was good. But he's getting greedy now. Wants a cash payment before he spills any more beans about Abu Ra'id. Five hundred US – quite a lot of moolah out there, and if he's asking for it, chances are he's confident of his intel.'

'Either that,' Spud said, 'or he's trying to rake it in while he's in the Yanks' good books.'

'That's a possibility. I certainly wouldn't trust him too far. He might be a CIA tout, but he's still Yemeni, still very devout. So far as we can tell, his motivation for supplying us with this intel-ligence is complex.'

'Sounds to me like he just wants a payday,' Spud said.

'There's a bit more to it than that. He's a Shi'ite muslim, unlike AQAP.'

'AQAP?' Danny asked.

'Al-Qaeda in the Arab Peninsula. Al-Qaeda and Al-Shabaab are Sunni Muslims. The Sunnis and the Shi'ites have major the-ological and political differences. You're heading to a principally Shi'ite area. A lot of the population in the north don't like the idea of AQAP and Al-Shabaab operating in what they see as Shi'ite territory, so they seem happy to screw them over.'

Hammond directed their attention to a sheet of aerial mapping. With his finger he traced a built-up area set on top of a mountain plateau – clearly Ha'dah. He followed a line eastward where the terrain fell down sharply on to a flat desert region. 'This is the area where the camp is most likely to be situated,' Hammond said. 'Very wild, very dangerous – Bedouin, bandits and not much else. Terrible roads. Hardly anyone goes there. Hardly anyone *dares.*'

'Looking forward to it already,' Spud muttered.

Hammond handed them each a pale blue armband with the letters UN emblazoned in white. 'Your cover story, if it comes to it, is that you're a couple of UN medics and you've heard there's a Western couple in the area who need medical aid. But for fuck's sake don't leave those things lying around. If the UN find out you've got them, there'll be hell on earth.' He shook his head. 'It's madness,' he said. 'Two guys. The CO's already appealed to the Director Special Forces. Hit a brick wall. It's . . .'

Danny could tell he was about to say the word 'suicide' but held back at the last minute.

'The CIA seem pretty keen on this Hamza fella,' Hammond continued, 'so you need to make sure he stays intact. We don't know where he lives, but he'll meet you outside the central mosque in Ha'dah when the call to prayer starts at dawn tomorrow – which will be just after 05.00. It'll be up to you to get the information from him.' A dark, uncomfortable look crossed Hammond's face. 'When you locate Abu Ra'id,' he continued, 'take him out immediately. As soon as he's dead, you need to phone in confirmation – before you leave the camp or anything. I'm sorry, lads, but London's adamant about this. They can't risk you being taken out before they know for sure that the bastard's dead.'

'Good to hear our welfare is the first thing on their minds,' Spud said.

Hammond pointed at their diplomatic bags. 'You've got GPS

beacons fitted to your radios,' he said. 'We'll track you every step of the way. We'll know where you are at every moment in real time. If you send us a distress signal, we can be in-country from the Gulf of Aden in a few hours, and fuck the fallout. But assuming everything goes to plan, you'll need to find a secure location to lie up, and we'll get you picked up as quickly as we can.' He looked at his watch. 'You'll need to board any minute.'

As Hammond spoke, Danny's personal mobile vibrated in his pocket. He took it out: number withheld. He was on the point of dismissing the call when he caught a lairy look from the ops officer – a look that said now's not the time for taking calls. Danny found himself accepting it just to make his point.

'Yeah?' he said.

A pause.

'Decided to pick up, did you?'

Danny felt himself grow tense. He stormed out of the Portakabin, past the Regiment guard and out onto the tarmac. A passenger aircraft roared overhead as it took off. Danny just caught a flash of Aer Lingus green on its tail.

'What is it, Kyle?' he shouted over the noise.

He heard his brother sniffing, then a coarse cough that sounded like he was bringing something up.

'Kyle?'

'Saw that bird of yours on Wednesday.'

Now it was Danny's turn to fall silent. He'd been doing everything he could to keep Clara from his mind. Now he almost felt as if she was standing next to him.

'Stay the fuck away from her,' he said. 'I mean it, Kyle. You lay a fucking finger on her, I'll . . .'

'Take it easy, take it easy, nothing happened, we just bumped into each other.' Danny saw the guard staring at him, and flashed him an aggressive look. Kyle coughed again. His voice changed. 'I'm in trouble, bro,' he said. He sounded like he meant it. 'These Poles, they don't take no for an answer. I'm in deep.'

'How deep?'

'Five large.'

'Fuck's sake, Kyle,' Danny breathed.

'They've done me over once already. Couple of broken teeth. Think my nose might be bust and all.' He coughed for a third time. 'I need some help, bro . . .'

Another plane roared overhead. 'What did you say?'

'*I said I need some help. They're not fucking around!*'

Danny wanted to throw the phone to the floor. It was typical of Kyle to put him in a position like this. To beg for money that Danny knew would be spent as soon as it landed in his brother's wallet. He paced the tarmac for a moment, ignoring the sight of Spud appearing at the door of the Portakabin, watching him carefully. For a moment he felt himself wavering. He thought about their father, who lived alone and disabled in a small Hereford flat, and who would always beg Danny to help his brother. If he was here now, he'd beg the same as usual. But then he remembered how Kyle, drunk and high on a cocktail of drugs, had attacked their father before ending up in prison for a stretch. As it always did, that memory sent every ounce of sympathy he might have had out the window.

'Forget it, Kyle. You got yourself into this mess, you get yourself out again.'

Silence.

'You're a piece of shit, Danny. You know that? Always were, always will be.'

Danny made to hang up. But before he did, he said one more thing. 'Stay away from Clara, Kyle. If you don't, trust me, the Poles will be the least of your worries.'

Kyle was snorting contemptuously as Danny hung up. He spun round and looked aggressively at Spud. 'What?' he demanded across the seven or eight metres' distance between them.

'Nothing, mucker,' Spud said calmly. 'We just had word. They want us to board. Let's get moving, eh?'

PART THREE

Desert Warriors

FIFTEEN

When the Regiment moves, it moves quickly.

A member of the BA staff – a young guy with a pimply face and clearly no idea who his charges were or what they were carrying – collected Danny and Spud, along with their diplomatic bags, from the Portakabin. He asked no questions as he ushered them through security as members of the diplomatic service. Their security teams barely looked at their bags, let alone screen them. Danny and Spud spent five minutes in a comfortable lounge set aside for their use before a pretty air stewardess with a brown bob, a bit too much make-up and a good tan let them on to a waiting 747. They were the first to board and as they entered the aircraft they turned left to the business-class cabin. Danny and Spud were each given a double booth – one seat for them, one for their bags. As the regular passengers filed on to the plane, a few cast an envious glance at these two guys who seemed to have been afforded special treatment. But once the aircraft was airborne, they were too busy with their menus, glasses of champagne and re-runs of *Top Gear* to pay them any mind.

Danny instructed an air hostess not to disturb him until they were landing, then pulled a blindfold over his face and reclined his seat so it was fully flat. He had long since taught himself to grab some shut-eye whenever and wherever he could, knowing that he couldn't always be sure when he'd next have the chance. He slept deeply for three hours. When he woke, he looked out of the window. He saw a blood-red sun setting across a mackerel sky. And on the ground, through the half-light, he saw dots of orange – flames, licking from the oil fields of the Middle East. Iraq, he surmised, or Kuwait. He thought how you only ever really got a sense of the vastness of the Arabian peninsular from the sky. He felt an uncomfortable twist in his stomach at the thought that he'd slept over Syria. He recalled its war-torn towns. The blood and destruction. He tried to put it from his mind. What had Clara said, about remembering the things he was supposed to forget? He felt a pang at the thought of her, and at the thought that they were heading into very hostile territory. If something happened to him – something terminal – Clara would never know how he really felt about her. She'd probably hate him for the rest of her life. When he reclined again on his seat, his sleep was not so deep.

Wheels down, 20.30 local time. The pretty air hostess ushered Danny and Spud off the aircraft before anyone else had the opportunity even to stand up. They received a few more curious glances this time, as they hauled their heavy diplomatic bags along the aisles. A blast of heat hit them as they alighted on to the waiting stairs, at the bottom of which was a middle-aged man in a lightweight suit who reminded Danny of Buckingham. He stood next to a black Range Rover, passenger doors open. 'Tim Johnston,' he said, holding out his hand. 'British Embassy. You're cleared for security. There's a welcoming committee from the Omani military at the other side of the airfield. Allow me to escort you.'

Danny and Spud nodded and climbed into the back of the vehicle, still clutching their bags. They drove in the opposite direction from the large, brightly lit modern terminal building. The embassy guy clearly knew better than to ask them what they were doing, so the two-minute journey passed in silence. A couple of hundred metres up ahead, Danny saw a helicopter standing alone on the tarmac – a Puma, with the red and green markings of the Omani military. A three-man flight crew loitered alongside it. They wore standard desert camo, with *shemaghs* covering their heads or wrapped round their necks. As the Range Rover approached, one of them – clearly the pilot – disappeared inside and by the time they pulled up 20 metres from the chopper, its rotors were already starting to spin.

The embassy guy leaned over from the front passenger seat. 'Best of British, gentlemen,' he said, and once more Danny was reminded of Buckingham. But he put that from his mind as he and Spud debussed and ran across the tarmac. A few words of greeting with their Omani escorts and the two Regiment men climbed up into the Puma. They'd barely been on the ground ten minutes before they were airborne again. The golden, sprawling lights of Muscat disappeared as they found themselves plunging through the dark night of the southern Arabian peninsular.

It took two and a half hours to cross the length of Oman to its western border, including a 25-minute refuelling stop at a military base somewhere en route, during which time Danny and Spud sat quietly out of view in the shadowy interior of the Puma. They passed the journey in silence, drowned out by the regular thunder of the chopper's rotors as it slid unobserved through the skies with its secret cargo. Occasionally, through the windows, Danny saw the lights of a settlement far in the distance, or headlamps on a deserted highway, but their flight path was clearly taking them across vast, uninhabited stretches of land. He found he was keeping a lid on a sudden feeling of excitement. It felt good to be abroad again. Good to be on unfamiliar territory. You could get lazy in London. Out here, living by your wits was the only option.

And it was intriguing, if nothing else, to know that they were about to set foot in the Goat Farm.

Danny and Spud had heard people talk about the Goat Farm. They all had, back in Hereford. It was a military camp near the south-western shore town of Salalah, where the Sultan's special forces were trained, usually under the grizzled eye of ex-Regiment personnel. The Regiment had form in this part of the world. In the early seventies, communist guerillas from South Yemen had been involved in the Omani Dhofar rebellion. The SAS had dispatched nine personnel to help train the Omani special forces. They had come under attack in what became known as the Battle of Mirbat, where nine guys had held their own against a force of more than four hundred. Two of them died – one from having his jaw blown off. But that savage battle itself was a piece of Regiment history, and from that day to this, the SAS were welcome in Oman.

The Puma started to lose height. Danny looked through the window. He estimated that they were less than a thousand feet high. He could see the lights from a network of evenly spaced symmetrical buildings, and also the orange glow of what looked like a large open fire. A minute later his vision was obscured by brown-out as the chopper came in to land, kicking up clouds of desert dust. Thirty seconds after that, they were on the ground.

The Omani flight crew opened up the doors for them. Danny and Spud shook their hands, then jumped out. The rotors were slowing down, but they were still surrounded by whirling clouds of dust that obscured their vision and stung their faces. As he peered through the cloud, however, Danny saw a bright light and, standing in front of it, the silhouette of a sturdy, broad-shouldered figure standing in wait. Clutching their holdalls – which were still wrapped in the white diplomatic bags – they ran from the chopper towards the figure. The dust settled and the noise eased off as the rotors powered down.

'Evening, kids,' said a voice. A deep voice, slightly hoarse, with a definite London accent. Danny shielded his eyes from the light surrounding the silhouette – emanating from the headlamps of some sort of armoured vehicle – and found he could just make out the man's features. The face was deeply lined and weather-beaten. The eyebrows were dark, the hair ruffled. He wore camouflage gear, and it crossed Danny's mind that here was the sort of bloke who'd look out of place wearing anything else. He stepped towards them, hand outstretched.

'Welcome to the Goat Farm,' he said.

His name was Roberts, and in the minute it took him to lead Danny and Spud towards a single-storey corrugated-iron building with a noisy petrol generator outside, he'd given them the lowdown on his career: 20 years in the Regiment, 20 years in the employ of the Sultan, helping to train up the Omani special forces. The Goat Farm was the closest thing he had to a home.

'Don't get me wrong, kids,' he said as he let them into the building. 'Made some good friends out here. Don't suppose I'll ever go back to Blighty.' He switched the light on. 'But it's good to see someone from home now and then.'

Danny's eyes smarted from the light. When they relaxed again, he saw that this was little more than a warehouse. Shelves along the walls, full of boxes of God knows what. Even more boxes piled up at one end. Sand on the floor, where it had blown in through the door. He looked back at Roberts and saw that his face had a pale white scar along the jawline. Roberts caught him looking at it. '*Jambiya* scar,' he said.

'What's that?' Danny asked.

'*Jambiya*? It's a knife. Yemeni men hang them by their belt. It's a status thing. The markings on the hilt indicate how important they are. And they're not afraid to use it.'

'You spent much time in Yemen?'

'Wish I hadn't, kid. Where you headed?'

'Ha'dah.'

'Might have guessed. Worst place in the whole stinking country. Full of toughs beetling around on their pissy little motorbikes, and they don't just carry *jambiyas*. They've all got a piece of some kind. More AKs in Ha'dah than frickin' tooth-brushes.' Roberts fetched an unmarked bottle of an amber liquid and three dirty glasses from one of the shelves. 'You want some?'

The guys shook their heads.

'You're as bad as the fucking Arabs. Except they're off their tits on khat half the time.' He poured himself a good couple of inches of whatever firewater it was, then knocked it back. 'Give me Scotch over that shit any day,' he said. He turned and walked over to one of the boxes on the floor. 'See,' he called back to them, 'the trouble with your khat is that it gives you the horn of a rhino, but stops you getting it up.'

From the box, he pulled a bundle of clothes, then carried them back to where Danny and Spud were standing.

'About six o'clock, the men all get together and start chewing the weed. They call it the hour of Solomon, because everyone's so high they think they're the wisest fucker in town. Course, they're just speaking bollocks. And dancing. Don't forget the dancing. All good men together.' He dropped the clothes in a pile at the guys' feet, then danced a comical little jig that petered out into a wheezing chuckle. He took another swig of his drink. 'The fellas have got a thing about perfume, too. That's how I got this.' He touched the scar on his face. 'Accused some rosewa-tered Yemeni twat of being a nancy boy when he was twerking with his buddy. Fucker came at me with his *jambiya*. Messy busi-ness. Messier for him, of course, but that's another story.' He poured himself a second Scotch and left Danny and Spud to rummage through the clothes.

There were two *dishdashes* there, and matching *shemaghs*. But before they put them on, Danny and Spud turned their atten-tion back to their diplomatic bags. They undid the padlocks and pulled out the holdalls. They removed their stripped-down rifles and started piecing them together. The air was filled with the dull clunk of metal on metal. When they were complete, they extracted their ops waistcoats and fitted them over their

T-shirts, before filling them with grenades and ammunition and affixing their radios. As they worked, Danny was aware of the grizzled form of Roberts watching them with something approaching envy. He sensed the old-timer wished he was still on the job.

They fitted bungee cord to their rifles and slung them so they were hanging along the side of their bodies, then fitted their Sigs into their waistcoats. Only then did they pull their *dishdashes* over their clothes and wrap their *shemaghs* around the lower part of their faces and the top of their heads, so only their eyes and nose were fully visible. A sharp-eyed observer might notice their boots, but that was a risk they'd have to take. It was much too hard to move around quickly in desert sandals. Roberts threw them an embroidered shoulder bag each. 'Can't schlep round Yemen with a fucking Bergen,' he said. 'Decant what you need into those.'

Once they were dressed, Roberts eyed them up and down, then gave an approving nod. He downed the remnants of his glass. 'Follow me,' he said.

He led them back out of the hut into the warm desert night. He looked up to the sky. 'About midnight,' he said, clearly reading the time in the stars. A truck had driven up to the Puma and was refuelling it, but the guys turned left. Up ahead was a large bonfire. Danny could hear it crackling, and could make out the silhouettes of about ten men sitting round it. He could tell that they too were wearing *shemaghs*, and assumed that these were members of the Omani special forces for whom the Goat Farm was home. But Roberts led them away at an angle from the fire, and as he walked, he pointed towards the sky. 'Bang on time,' he said. 'We'll have to give you the grand tour next time you come.'

He might have been an old-timer, but his eyes were still good. Danny peered upwards. The stars were incredibly bright, millions of pinpricks swirling in the blackness. And against them, it was impossible to tell how far away, a black form hulking in the sky.

They saw the incoming Chinook before they heard it, but the distant buzz of the twin rotors hit their ears just a couple of seconds after Roberts spoke. The pilots were clearly flying blind, relying on night-vision goggles, because the chopper itself emitted no light. The great black silhouette against the stars grew bigger, closer. The roar increased. A couple of minutes later, the Chinook was coming in to land on a sparse LZ 50 metres from where Danny, Spud and Roberts were standing. Another two trucks immediately screeched up to start refuelling.

'Fun to slum with you, kids!' Roberts shouted. He clapped them on the shoulder. 'Now get the fuck out of here.'

Danny and Spud ran towards the open tailgate of the Chinook. The swirling clouds of dust stung their eyes and those parts of their faces that weren't covered up by their *shemaghs*, but Danny could still make out the long shape of the aircraft and a faint glow above the twin rotors as airborne sand sparked against them. As they ran up into the chopper, the familiar stench of aviation gas hit Danny's nostrils, a dirty, greasy smell but a strangely comforting one. Up ahead, a grey Toyota Tundra was parked in the middle of the aircraft, fastened to the sides by lengths of sturdy rope. Left-hand drive, Arabic plates. Two men stood by it, both wearing head cans and boom mikes – a loadie and an engineer. There were no words exchanged: the loadie simply jabbed his finger towards a bench that ran along the right-hand side of the chopper. Danny and Spud headed towards it and took a seat. Two headsets were hanging from the side of the chopper. They plugged themselves in and immediately heard the pilot's voice: British, with that easy confidence all pilots seem to have: 'We'll be airborne in ten minutes, lads. Flight time approximately three hours, subject to what we find when we approach our destination. I'll keep you in the loop.'

To Danny's right was a small window. Through it he could see the bonfire, though the glow was diffused by the brown-out around the Chinook. Spud was looking straight ahead. Steely.

Focused. Just like Danny. Because they both knew that the op started here.

Movement at the far end of the chopper. The tailgate was closing. The loadie and the engineer took seats opposite Danny and Spud. A moment later, they felt the Chinook rise into the air. Not high. In the darkness, Danny's only point of reference was the fire. He estimated that they were about 30 metres up when the Chinook suddenly turned and they started plunging through the Middle Eastern night.

The pilot's voice in their headsets: 'We're heading north up the Oman-Yemen border,' he said. 'When you feel us turn again, that means we're entering Saudi. We've got permission to be in Saudi airspace along the northern Yemeni border, but the border's still fluid. We'll be flying blind the whole way.'

A hiss in the headphones, then silence. Just the dull, repetitive thud of the Chinook's rotors, as it carried Danny and Spud towards their destination.

02.30 Arabia Standard Time
They had been airborne for two and a half hours. Danny's muscles were stiff, his backbone aching from contact with the hard side of the Chinook. The headset burst into life again. 'Entering Yemeni airspace in five,' he said. 'We're hoping to use the cover of a high-walled wadi to get us close on target.'

Sure enough, five minutes later the Chinook banked to the left, then suddenly lost height. Danny looked out of the window. There was a moon now, and by its silver light he could see, perhaps 20 metres from the chopper, a craggy wall zooming past, and the faint shadow the Chinook cast against it. He found himself unconsciously checking for the bulk of his weapon under his *dishdash*. This was dangerous territory. Chinooks had been put down by RPGs in safer areas than this. He found himself thinking about a Seal team who had taken a hit while inserting into the mountain regions of eastern Afghanistan.

They'd suffered the biggest loss of life in the force's history, and that was before a single man had set foot on the ground.

Twenty minutes passed. The pilot again: 'We're fifteen minutes out. We're about to leave the wadi.' Danny pictured the maps he'd examined back at Heathrow. Ha'dah was on a mountain, so they would need to make a steep climb. 'We'll approach from the north, which is the least populated region,' the pilot continued. 'We're going to try to put you down on the road, but we'll need to find a deserted spot, so get ready to hop and pop when we give you the word.'

The loadie and engineer stood up on the opposite side of the chopper. The loadie indicated that the guys should remove their cans, while the engineer went about unstrapping the Toyota from the bonds that held it fast in the aircraft. While he did this, the tailgate lowered. A rush of new air filled the aircraft. Danny and Spud approached the vehicle. Danny could feel the aircraft gaining height and through the opening tailgate he saw not the earth any more, but an inky skyful of stars. He opened the driver's door of the vehicle and climbed inside, while Spud took the passenger seat. There were still two ropes securing the vehicle – the engineer would release them when it was time to alight. Danny's hand felt for the gearstick. It was locked in first gear, handbrake on. The key was already in the ignition. He pressed down the clutch and turned the key. The engine started immediately. He didn't turn on the headlamps, but he did lower his window.

The chopper had stopped gaining height now. The loadie appeared by the door. 'Thirty seconds!' he shouted through the open window. And as he spoke, the chopper twisted 90 degrees clockwise. Through the open tailgate, Danny could see a narrow, winding mountain road. He estimated that they were 30 feet above it, but then they started a sharp, almost vertical descent. The road came up to meet them. There was a jolt as the chopper touched down. The engineer released the final two cords.

Danny pressed the accelerator and lifted the clutch up to its biting point, one hand on the wheel, the other on the handbrake. The Toyota felt like it was straining to escape from the chopper, its engine groaning loudly. Suddenly the loadie was by their side again.

'*Go!*' he shouted, and he thumped the top of the Toyota three times.

Danny let the clutch up. The vehicle shot forward, like a stone from a sling. It practically bounced on to the tailgate ramp, and sped down from the chopper. A second later, he felt the crunch of rubber tyres on a rough surface. And as he checked his rear-view mirror, he saw that the Chinook was already rising, its tailgate still down.

The flight crew had done their job. Danny and Spud were on their own now.

SIXTEEN

Danny looked ahead.

He only had ten metres of visibility before the road veered sharply upwards and to the right. To their left, a sheer drop. To their immediate right, a craggy rock cliff face. He eased the Toyota forward, hugging the cliff face as he went. The noise of the Chinook died away. He caught a glimpse of it from his left-hand side, curling away in the air as it headed back to the wadi. The flight crew would remain in the vicinity for 20 minutes in case they had a distress call from the guys as a result of a hot insertion. But then it would be gone.

'There,' Spud said. Danny looked ahead to his right. There was a fissure in the cliff face, a cave in the shape of an inverted V, just wide enough for their vehicle. Danny edged past it, then locked the steering wheel down to the right and reversed off the road and into the cave. The Toyota's rear-view camera illuminated the back of the cave on a dashboard screen. Danny backed up as close to it as he could. It meant the front of the Toyota was set back about three metres from the mouth of the cave. He killed the engine. Wordlessly, Danny and Spud exited the vehicle. They extracted their rifles and both bent down on one knee in the firing position, two metres apart, their weapons pointing out of the cave.

No sound of the Chinook now. No sound of anything. A dark, ominous stillness. Danny felt the warmth of the Toyota's engine against his back and he realised he was sweating as heavily as if it was midday. There was even sweat between his finger and the trigger of his HK, but he kept it lightly resting there as they waited to see if their arrival had disturbed anybody in the vicinity. And if it had, to deal with them.

They stayed in that position for a full ten minutes. Danny used the time to get his thoughts straight. This was very hostile territory. A lawless region where nobody would feel bound by any kind of rules of engagement. If Danny and Spud were caught in the town of Ha'dah, they would do everything in their power to stick to their cover story that they were UN medics who'd been told that there was a Western couple in the town who needed medical aid. But it was hard to explain away a covert assault rifle, and their captors would get the truth out of them eventually. When that happened, it would be bullet-in-head time. Yemeni bullets, Regiment heads.

Ha'dah would not be massively populated. Newcomers would stand out. Newcomers with white skin even more. Danny pulled his *shemagh* further up his face as he ran over their objectives once more. Sneak quietly into town under cover of night. Locate Hamza and get from him the information he claimed to have about the training camp where Abu Ra'id was located. Then get the hell out of there, just as quietly. If everything went according to plan, they'd be on the road out of Ha'dah not much past dawn, unnoticed and hopefully unfollowed.

Danny's eyes picked out the scene ahead of him: the dark frame of the cave mouth, the road no more than five metres wide, the star-filled sky and, extending into the distance, the flat lowlands beyond the mountain. The plough was low in the sky, and he used it to calculate their orientation: they were facing south. In that direction were the pirate-filled waters of the Gulf of Aden, and beyond that, the war-torn land of Somalia. It was weird to think that less than 24 hours ago, they were in the damp air of Hammerstone House. Nothing damp about the terrain round here. This was tough, craggy desert territory. And

it was populated by tough, craggy desert dwellers. A large proportion of whom would be armed, because weapons were more
common than toothbrushes in this part of the world ...

'Shall we go?' Spud said.

Almost immediately he spoke there was a buzzing sound off
to the right. Twenty seconds later, a figure on a small motorbike
whizzed past. Danny held his breath, waiting for more bikes.
More potential threats. But the threats didn't come, and after
another five minutes the guys got back into their vehicle. They
eased out of the cave and turned right. Danny switched his
headlamps on: they lit up a pot-holed, stony road. They moved
on, keeping a careful, steady 20 mph, Spud still clutching his rifle
– cocked and locked, with the barrel pointing down into the
vehicle's footwell.

The road didn't deviate. There were no junctions or forks. It
simply wound and snaked up the mountain. They saw no other
traffic, and no pedestrians. Down on the flats, however, many
miles distant, were the occasional glows of fires dotted around,
and other lights that moved.

'Bedouin trucks?' Spud suggested.

'Maybe,' Danny replied. He checked his watch. 03.00hrs. He
didn't reckon there were many people moving around down
there on honest business. The vehicles they could see might be
Bedouin, but they might just as easily be government forces, or
militants. He wondered if one of the fires indicated the location
of Abu Rai'd's training camp.

They drove for a further 20 minutes and passed nobody. Then,
as Danny turned another steep corner, he saw an old mud-
walled hut on the side of the road. It was barely bigger than the
Portakabin back at Heathrow where just a few hours ago their
ops officer had been briefing them, but as the Toyota's headlamps landed on it, they saw that it was deserted and dilapidated,
with one end totally crumbled away into nothing, the remnants
of the rubble covered with rough green and brown scrub. It was

a perfect place to hide the vehicle, since driving into the hostile town of Ha'dah in an unfamiliar four-by-four was a sure-fire way to alert the locals to their presence.

Danny pulled the vehicle off the road and slowly manoeuvred it over the rubble and into the old hut. He killed the lights, then he and Spud debussed. They exited the hut and stood on the road, checking that the vehicle was sufficiently hidden. When they were satisfied that nobody could see it from the road, Spud pulled his GPS unit from his bag. They waited 30 seconds while it triangulated. 'We're about three clicks from the edge of the town,' he said. He pointed along the road to indicate the direction they needed to walk, though he needn't have: it was either up, or down.

They trekked in silence. A high cliff still loomed on the right-hand side of the road. They hugged this for cover. The temperature had dropped now that they'd gained height, but their brisk pace kept them warm. At 03.45hrs they turned another curve in the road, still hugging the cliff face, and suddenly saw the imposing outline of Ha'dah silhouetted against the stars up ahead, the bulk of it perhaps a kilometre away from their position. Danny removed his NV kite sight, and used it to scan the scene ahead.

Despite the green haze of the NV view, there was something medieval about the shape of the buildings that comprised the outskirts of Ha'dah. They stood on the rocky outcrop like a collection of minor fortresses from another century, and it struck Danny that they probably had remained unchanged for hundreds of years. They were perched on a rocky plateau, with weathered rocky banks leading up to it. An ancient stone staircase carved into the mountainside curled up towards them, while the road itself wound round to its right. It would be far safer to cover the final kilometre to the town by road, Danny decided. Here they would be camouflaged against the high cliff walls, whereas if they took the stone stairs they would be exposed in open ground.

The buildings themselves, those that he could see, all had flat roofs, and numerous holes for windows evenly distributed. They were tall, unusually tall, four or five storeys high, which added to their somewhat wobbly, precarious appearance. Along the edges of each roof was evenly spaced, fussy detailing, and at the foot of the buildings were plenty of trees, a reminder that despite the endless sands of the deserts over which they'd just flown, this was a more fertile region. The town was not big – certainly less than a kilometre from edge to edge. Danny could take it all in with a single sweep of his night sight. And from here he could see no movement, nor even any light. Ha'dah was sleeping.

A sound pierced the air. It was a howling dog, coming from the direction of Ha'dah. A second dog barked in response, then both fell quiet.

Movement. It was just on the edge of the kite sight's field of vision. About halfway up the old stone staircase was a man. He was sitting down, but had what looked like a rifle at right angles across his lap. Some kind of lookout. Distance: 100 to 120 metres.

Danny passed Spud the sight. 'Eleven o'clock, on the stairs,' he said. Spud took it in, then handed back the sight with a grim expression.

'Shall we take him?' Spud breathed.

Danny thought it through for a moment. He judged the conditions. A little over 100 metres between them. No wind. The shot was do-able. But the noise of even a suppressed weapon would echo off the mountainsides and might alert more armed men to their presence.

Perhaps they should go for the silent kill. One of them could approach with a concealed blade, while the other took a covert position and covered with his firearm. But there was a chance that the guard would be missed. They had no idea what time he was due to finish his stag. Perhaps he had a family waiting for him back home who would raise the alarm if he didn't return.

No. Killing him was the wrong call. They would just have to

sneak past him. Danny looked at the guard through the sight again. The man didn't have his eyes on the road, but was picking at his fingernails, not watching carefully. If they continued to hug the cliff, he reckoned they could pass him without being seen.

'Keep going,' he told Spud. 'If he sees us, we'll deal with him.'

They crept forward. Danny stopped every ten metres to check on the guard through his kite sight. The guy just sat there with his weapon and didn't move. Three minutes later they had advanced 50 metres and passed his field of vision, and the Yemeni guard didn't know how lucky he was to still be alive.

Danny checked the time. 04.32. Dawn – the hour of their RV – would arrive just after 05.00. 'We need to move,' he said. Spud nodded, and they continued their approach.

04.47hrs

They had covered the final kilometre to the edge of Ha'dah in ten minutes.

Ha'dah had a distinctive odour about it, a mixture of wood smoke, dirt and rotting food that Danny could smell even through the thick, musty material of their *shemaghs*. This was not a 21st-century town. Danny knew that hardly any of the houses up ahead would have proper plumbing. As for electricity, forget it. They stood now beneath the low branches of a sprawling tree. To their left were four small, squat dwellings with white domed roofs. Towering above them, no more than 20 metres from their position, was one of the large square buildings Danny had examined from a distance. Its walls were made of hard-baked mud bricks, and the windows were little more than black openings. Light now glowed from two of them – faint, yellow and flickering, almost certainly from a candle or an oil lamp. To the left of the building, a road led up at a slight gradient. It was the only road that they could see that led into the town.

Movement up ahead. Danny caught his breath. He scanned

the road through his night sight. An animal stared back at him. Too gangly for a dog. Lean and hungry-looking. It suddenly turned and scampered away.

'Hyena,' Danny breathed.

As he spoke, the stillness in the air was broken. From within the small town came a strong voice, the low chanting of a *muezzin* calling the faithful to prayer. It seemed to curl and echo round the buildings with its familiar words. *Allahu Akbar, Allahu Akbar, Ash-haddu an-la ilaha illa llah . . .* That sound meant that dawn was almost upon them. Their RV needed to take place in the next ten to fifteen minutes. Then they could get away from the town as quickly as possible, pick up their vehicle and get off the mountainside. The Regiment men stepped out from under the camouflage of the tree, their *shemaghs* and robes covering their features, and started walking purposefully up the street.

At first they followed the sound of the voice as it wailed above the top of the buildings. One moment, however, it sounded like it was coming from the north, the next from the south. After five minutes of pacing the narrow roads of Ha'dah, another way of locating the mosque presented itself. Men were appearing in the streets – only a handful at first, but after a few more minutes Danny had counted more than thirty. Some wore full-length, loose-fitting robes, with a jacket on their upper half. Others wore a kind of wraparound kilt with a shirt. Some of them had their heads wrapped in turbans, others with *shemaghs* not unlike Danny and Spud – though the Regiment men put their heads down and scrupulously kept their distance rather than rely just on their ability to blend in, and occasionally took cover in dark doorways to avoid passing groups of more than two or three men. Most of the locals wore the scabbards around their waists that Roberts had warned them about back at the Goat Farm. They were all hurrying in the same direction. Danny and Spud kept to the shadows, and followed.

The central square of Ha'dah was not large. Perhaps 35 metres by 35. As they entered it from the south-west corner and lurked in the shadow of a deep, overhanging balcony, they saw the mosque on the far side. Night was becoming dawn now, and in the steel grey light Danny saw that the mosque's tower – a good 20 metres higher than the surrounding buildings – resembled nothing so much as a small lighthouse. The sound of the *muezzin*, his reedy drone still calling the faithful, rang out from the tower. At ground level, a large wooden door was open and an inviting glow emanated from inside. Men were hurrying into the mosque, paying little attention to each other at this early hour and not even seeing Danny and Spud, who had melted into the shadows and were staying very still and unassuming. The rest of the square was unwelcoming. There was nothing that resembled a shop, or even a dwelling. Just randomly spaced and rather rickety-looking wooden doors a little higher than a man leading into the buildings on four sides, all of them closed. The ground was strewn with dust and chunks of stone the size of Danny's fist.

Danny recalled Hammond's words at the briefing back at Heathrow, about Hamzah, their contact. *He'll meet you outside the central mosque in Ha'dah when the call to prayer starts at dawn tomorrow.* He looked around for their contact, but saw nobody who looked like they were waiting for an RV. Perhaps they were too late? If so, they were fucked. They didn't know what this Hamza character looked like, or where he lived. And even if Hamza was his real name, the chances of the locals responding well to the enquiries of two British men – or even understanding them – were vanishingly small. They would have no option but to abort the mission: leave town, hide up and call for a pick-up.

The wailing voice of the *muezzin* suddenly stopped. Two stragglers hurried inside the mosque and the doors creaked shut. The glow from inside the mosque escaped through the gaps round the door, and almost immediately a muffled chanting came from behind it. Danny and Spud continued to survey the square. It was deserted. Their contact was a no-show.

Danny felt a spike of suspicion. Had they been lured here? Was it a trap? He tucked one hand into his *dishdash* and pulled his Sig. Spud, next to him, did the same. Danny peered up to the windows of the buildings looking over the square. He saw nothing, but it was, he realised, very easy for anyone to hide in those gloomy holes. Walking across the square would make him too exposed. If they were going to search the vicinity, they'd need to stick to the edge of the square. To the shadows. One of them needed to go alone, while the other kept watch, weapon ready, alert for any threats.

'Cover me,' Danny breathed.

A gentle click as Spud quietly cocked his weapon.

Danny trod very quietly, moving lightly on the balls of his feet as he traversed the side of the square opposite the mosque. At the far corner he looked back. Spud was only just visible in the shadows, but he was there and that was all Danny needed to know. Still gripping his weapon he turned 90 degrees and started heading up along the eastern side of the square towards the mosque.

Danny had covered ten metres when he saw a man. He was directly diagonal from Danny's position, hiding in the north-western corner of the square about five metres from the entrance to the mosque, a dark figure in the shadows pacing nervously. He'd been invisible from their original positions.

Danny was almost definite that the guy hadn't seen him. He remained absolutely motionless for a second, then made a quick gesture to Spud, pointing first to his eyes and then in the direction of the figure. Then he continued to skirt around the edge of the square.

When he reached the front wall of the mosque he didn't turn left towards the contact. Instead he took a right, his plan being to edge round the back of the mosque and approach him from the other side. As soon as he was clear of the square he sprinted, intent on getting to his target before he wandered off. Twenty metres north, before taking a left and boxing round the back of the mosque. There was a dog here – a lean, dark-haired mongrel with a white patch round its left eye, ribs visible under its meagre body. It chased him for a few metres before losing interest and scampering back towards where it had been. Danny took another left and hurried down the western side of the mosque. When he reached the front corner he stopped and listened.

The contact was still pacing. Nervous footsteps, up and down, just a few metres away by the sound of it. Fucking amateur should keep still if he's on edge, Danny thought to himself. But the man's footsteps crunched on the rough ground. Back and forth. Back and forth. Back and ...

In an instant Danny swung round, his weapon raised. He saw a young man with a short wispy beard and thick, glistening lips. White *dishdash*. Red *shemagh* tied with a cord around the forehead. Colourful sheath hanging in front of his groin. Danny's sudden, unexpected appearance clearly terrified him. He looked like he was going to shout out. But before he could, Danny had wrapped one arm around his head, covered his mouth with his free hand, and pressed his Sig against his skull.

Hammond had said their contact's English was good. So if this was Hamza, he'd understand what Danny was about to say.

'Make a sound and I'll kill you.'

The man was trembling. He nodded his head vigorously. Danny noticed with satisfaction that he clearly understood English. The chances of him being their contact were good.

'When I remove my hand, you're going to tell me your name. You'll whisper it, and if you do or say *anything* else ...' He made a double clicking sound in the corner of his mouth. He paused, for a couple of seconds, then slowly moved his hand.

'Hamza,' the man whispered.

Danny quickly covered his mouth again.

'Okay, Hamza. My friend's waiting for us at the corner of the square.' He pointed with his gun in Spud's direction. 'You're going to walk there, I'm going to walk behind you. Don't try and run away unless you can run faster then twelve hundred feet a second, because that's how fast a bullet from this gun will travel and I'll have my weapon on you all the time. Do *anything* that makes me nervous, it'll be the last thing you know about. Got it?'

Hamza nodded again.

Danny removed his hand and pushed Hamza towards the square. He was flat-footed and noisy as he walked, but the sound was drowned by a sudden swell in the muffled chanting from inside the mosque. They moved along the edge of the square towards where Spud was waiting for them. He eyed Hamza up and down with a single unimpressed glance.

'This him?'

Danny nodded.

Hamza was twitchy. Nervous. He rubbed his clenched hands as though he was washing them with invisible soap and water. 'My house is not far from here,' he said in a dry voice. 'We must go there.'

Danny and Spud exchanged a questioning look. They wanted to get out of Ha'dah as quickly as possible, but maybe it was best that the exchange of information and money took place off the streets. Spud nodded his approval. 'Okay, sunshine,' he said. 'Let's go.'

Hamza's house was on the western edge of Ha'dah, and accessed via a maze-like network of rough side streets. He had a donkey tethered to a post just outside, whose head was swarming with flies. 'Yours?' Danny asked. Hamza nodded.

Inside it was a poor place, made of the same mud bricks as the larger buildings, but only a single room, about ten metres by eight. A thin mattress and blanket at one end served as a bed, and next to it a small stove fitted to a beaten-up old propane canister. No chairs or tables, no sign of running water or a toilet. There was a small saucepan of food on the stove, and the air smelled of goat meat and fenugreek. And on the mattress, the bulky form of a sat phone. Hamza's CIA handlers were clearly keener to ensure he had a means of staying in touch with them, rather than anything in the way of luxuries.

Danny pointed at it. 'You should keep that hidden,' he said.

Hamza nodded, and stuffed the sat phone under the blanket. 'May I offer you food?' he said. 'Tea?' He was stooping slightly, and still soaping his hands.

Danny shook his head. He knew he was probably offending their contact, but to accept food from him would be foolhardy. They had their MRE packs which they knew hadn't been tampered with.

'You know why we're here?'

'Of course, sir.'

'So where is it?'

'Where is what, sir?'

'The training camp, shit-for-brains.'

A venal look crossed Hamza's face. 'You have something for me first?'

Danny shook his head. 'You don't get shit until you tell us where the training camp is.'

Hamza's nose twitched.

'I don't know, sir.'

Danny blinked. 'What do you mean, you don't know?' There was a dangerous edge to his voice.

'But I know a man who does,' Hamza said hastily, his face brightning as though this was excellent news.

The two Regiment men were silent for a moment. The donkey brayed noisily outside.

'Go on,' Danny breathed.

'His name is Ahmed. I heard him talking during the khat chew.'

Danny's heart sank. 'The hour of Solomon,' he muttered.

Hamza grinned. 'Yes!'

'When everyone spouts bollocks,' Spud added.

Hamza's face fell into a frown. 'No,' he said. 'No, sir. Many important things are discussed during the khat chew. Serious things. The man I am talking about, Ahmed, he hears things from all over. He is one of the older men in the village. Everyone respects him. Even the Houthi leave him alone.'

'I want to know exactly what he said,' Danny stated. '*Exactly*.'

Hamza took a moment to gather his thoughts. 'You have to understand,' he said. 'Ahmed, like many in Ha'dah, longs for the days of the Zaydi kings to be returned, for the Yemen to be ruled by a Shi'ite majority. He has no time for the Sunnis, and makes it his business to know when they trespass upon what he believes to be the land of the Zaydi Muslims.'

'Thanks for the history lesson, pal. I still don't know what he said.'

Hamza soaped his hands even more vigorously. 'That a famous British cleric was arriving in the lowlands. That he was to be given sanctuary at a training camp of the Sunni jihadi. And he even said where the camp was.'

Danny and Spud looked at each other, then back at the joker in front of them.

'So where *is* it?'

Hamza lowered his head and looked suddenly rather embarrassed. 'I do not remember,' he muttered.

A moment of silence. Then Spud swore under his breath. 'You were fucking stoned, weren't you?' he said in disbelief.

Hamza gave them an apologetic look. 'It was the khat chew,' he said, as if that explained everything.

'For fuck's *sake*!' Danny exploded. Spud had murder in his eyes. Their chances of ducking quickly and unseen out of Ha'dah were crumbling. At a stroke, their op had become ten times more dangerous. Danny felt himself grabbing the tout by his throat, throttling him. Seconds later, Spud was there, removing Hamza forcibly from Danny's grip but not treating him much less roughly. He threw the tout roughly to the ground.

Danny stood bleakly over him. 'How do we find this guy?'

Hamza loooked terrified and started jabbering. 'I do not know where he is during the day . . . but at six o'clock – at the hour of Solomon – he will be where he always is, at the khat chew near the marketplace. I will take you there.' His eyes brightened as he tried to put a positive spin on things. 'You can join in! You will like it very much, the khat. It makes you feel . . .'

Hamza didn't get a chance to explain how it would make anybody feel, because Danny kicked him so hard in the guts that he started to cough and wheeze violently. 'If I see you *anywhere* near that shit while we're still around, you'll be chewing your own fucking teeth.' He turned to Spud. They exchanged an anxious look.

Time to make a call. Should they split now and call off the op? Or risk staying in Ha'dah for another 12 hours, where strangers, surely, would be noticed?

Danny and Spud locked gazes for ten seconds.

'We stay here till six,' Danny said finally. 'All three of us. Then we go find this Ahmed character.' He gave Hamza a contemptuous glance. 'And if Howard Marks here tries to leave, we nail him.'

'It'll be my pleasure.'

Hamza cringed on the dusty ground.

'Two hours on, two hours off,' Danny said. 'I'll take first stag.' He looked over at the thin mattress on the ground. 'You take the four-poster, get some kip.'

And without another word, Danny sat cross-legged on the ground and aimed his rifle purposefully at the door.

The day passed slowly. When it was Danny's turn to rest, he slept soundly and awoke to find Hamza conked out on the ground. He lay there, snoring, for most of the morning. Outside it was much noisier than it had been at dawn. Even here on the out-skirts, Danny could hear men shouting to each other, the occasional tinny buzz of a motorbike, and footsteps passing Hamza's tiny residence. Every few hours, the brittle sound of the call to prayer drifted over the town.

At midday they opened a couple of MREs and shovelled cold, stodgy sausage and beans into their mouths straight from the foil parcels. At 16.00hrs they did the same. An hour later, Hamza roused himself. He looked like shit. His hair seemed to have grown twice as greasy as he slept and his teeth had a dark green tinge to them. He had a slight tremor in his hands, like an alcoholic in need of a drink. Maybe he was after a hit of khat. Danny found himself thinking about Kyle. It made him feel faintly sick to think that the success of this mission might rely on a junkie like his brother.

Hamza gave Danny an insincere smile. His eyes were darting around the room, though, and on the exit. Despite what Danny had said about nailing him if he tried to leave, the truth was that they couldn't kill him. It wasn't just that he was a CIA tout and the ruperts would make their lives hell if they did. The whole op now depended on this twat leading them to the man who had the information they needed. No Hamza, no mission.

The tout walked over to the far side of the room where he opened the drawer of a small desk. He took out a packet of tobacco and cigarette papers, and with a gesture offered them to Danny. Danny shook his head, and Hamza started rolling himself a cigarette.

'Where's the marketplace?' Danny said.

Hamza was concentrating hard on his cigarette. 'Not far from here,' he said. 'It's in the western quarter of the town. It will take maybe five minutes to get there. I know a back way. Less people.'

He grinned again, revealing his khat-stained teeth. But the grin soon fell away when he saw the fierce look Danny gave him. He took a lighter from the desk and lit up. He inhaled deeply and allowed smoke to steam from his nostrils.

'Here's what's going to happen,' Danny said. He'd been

planning their next move while he kept stag. 'You lead us into the marketplace. Me and Spud will lead your donkey.'

'What for?' Hamza asked.

'There'll be lots of other people with donkeys, right?'

Hamza nodded.

'So it'll help us blend in. Once we're there, you stand outside the place where the khat chew happens. You don't go in.' Hamza's face fell, but he didn't dare say anything. 'When this Ahmed character leaves, you go up to him and shake his hand so we know who he is. Then you come straight back here.'

'Here?' Hamza looked deeply uncertain.

'Does he speak English?'

Hamza shook his head, then brushed a strand of greasy hair from his face.

'Then you have to translate.'

'But . . . what will you *do* with him? You will not hurt him? He is respected. An elder. If he thinks I have done something to . . .'

'He'll be fine.' Hamza didn't need to know that was probably not true. 'We'll give him some money for his information. He'll be very happy.'

'What about *my* money?' Hamza said.

'You get *your* money when we get the information we need, and not before.'

Hamza's eyes narrowed, but he mastered that calculating look and started soaping his hands once more. 'Of course, sir,' he said.

Danny stepped up to him. 'Don't make a fucking mistake, pal,' he breathed.

'No, sir,' Hamza replied quietly. Close up, he stank of sweat. 'No mistakes.'

The guys made their preparations, wrapping their *shemaghs* around their faces, stowing everything they didn't need in their embroidered bags. At 17.45hrs, they gave Hamza the word. Their contact gave them a craven little bow, then stepped out of the front door of his house. Danny and Spud allowed him a 30-second start. At the last moment, Danny stepped over to the desk and looked in the drawer. There were several pouches of tobacco and cigarette papers here, all with Arabic writing, and a stash of lighters. Danny and Spud helped themselves.

'You think we're okay bringing Ahmed back here?' Spud said. 'Maybe we should find somewhere deserted, take Hamza and Ahmed with us, interrogate them somewhere out of the way.'

But Danny had already considered that. 'I reckon Ahmed's going to take a bit of persuading to talk. Hamza's on edge. He might run to get help. I'd rather have him where I can control him. And anyway, we don't know the geography well enough. We should get off the streets as quickly as possible, before someone notices us and starts asking questions.'

That was good enough for Spud. They left the tiny house, untethered the donkey and followed Hamza, Spud leading the beast behind him.

By day, Ha'dah was a different town. Immediately they stepped out into the street, Danny clocked four armed men. They each brandished a Kalashnikov, and one of the gunmen couldn't have been more than 13. It was hard to be sure, but Danny didn't have them down as Houthi militants – they didn't have the swagger of someone who thought they were in charge. He reckoned that these were regular Yemeni civilians who just happened to be armed. A small part of him wondered where these weapons came from.

That question was soon answered.

The marketplace that Hamza had talked about was not a single location. Rather, it was a sprawling mass of stalls lining the streets in a random, hotch-potch fashion. The first stall they passed was little more than a black blanket laid out on the ground. Behind it, a boy no older than 12 sat cross-legged. And sitting on top of the blanket was a selection of firearm ammunition to rival the armoury at Hereford. There was everything here, neatly packed in pristine brown cardboard boxes the size of Danny's fist – 9mm rounds, 5.56s, even .50 cals. As Danny had predicted, there was another donkey behind the stall. What he hadn't predicted was that it would be carrying a basket over its back which held a stash of old Russian fragmentation grenades. The kid behind the stall didn't look at all excited by his wares, but was tracing patterns in the dust with his forefinger. Twenty metres further down the same street, the hardware got a little more serious: two men stood behind a rickety wooden table on which lay two rocket launchers and five RPGs. One of them shouted out in Arabic to Danny, and tried to catch his eye. Danny just lowered his head and walked on by.

The market stalls didn't just have weaponry on display. There were stinking piles of dried shark meat heaped up in wicker baskets – again, some of them carried by donkeys – and colourful spices. Saffron strands, ground turmeric and fenugreek seeds were stacked in neat little piles. An elderly man with a deeply lined face and intensely blue eyes presided over a tableful of small glass vials of assorted perfumes, whose pungent stink caught in Danny's throat as he passed. There was street food – big dishes of lamb and rice, and women cooking large, thin flatbreads over glowing braziers.

And people. Hundreds of people, milling around these little side streets, bartering at the stalls. All the men wore knives at their waists and at least a third of them had rifles or handguns on display. Danny did his best not to lock eyes with anyone, not only because he needed to keep his attention on Hamza, who was walking about 15 metres ahead of them, but also because he could feel the tension in this place. Establishing eye contact with one of the locals would just make them look at Danny and Spud a little closer. And that was the last thing they wanted . . .

They'd only been walking for four or five minutes when Hamza led them into a square about the same size as that in which the mosque was situated. The surrounding walls were high – three storeys at least – and dotted with the same regular window-holes that he'd seen elsewhere, many of them with shadowy faces peering out. There were perhaps 50 people milling around the square itself, almost exclusively men, and all dressed similarly to Danny and Spud, in robes and *shemaghs*. Most of them had *jambiyas* swinging by their waists. In one corner was a pick-up truck, its doors all open and five young Yemeni men – all armed – loitering in the back. They didn't look particularly aggressive – more like the Ha'dah version of London kids hanging out at a bus stop. Hamza barely seemed to notice them as he crossed the square to where a painted green wooden door stood open. In front of it were a few rickety tables, around which sat a collection of Yemeni men, some of them young but mostly very old, with their distinctively lined faces and wary eyes. They had bowls of tea in front of them, and one of the older men was smoking *shisha* from a water pipe.

Hamza looked back, his face anxious, and picked Danny and Spud out from the crowds. The guys avoided eye contact and instantly peeled away from each other. Danny took up position on the eastern side of the square, Spud led the donkey to the opposite edge where he made a show of checking the animal's teeth and ears. Danny pulled the tobacco from the deep pockets of his robe and started slowly to roll cigarettes. As good a way as any to blend in – he noticed that well over half the men in the square seemed to be smoking – although he couldn't risk actually smoking his creations because that would mean removing his *shemagh*. Together they formed a three-man triangle, each of them fifteen metres apart, with Hamza at the leading corner. Their Yemeni contact looked longingly through the door – this was clearly where the khat chew was taking place – but with another glance at Danny, he took a seat at one of the tables and called for tea.

Danny stood quietly, his back up against a rough stone wall, his fingers busy with the tobacco. He noted all the exits to the square: the street at his ten o'clock, by which they'd entered, and two others leading off at a diagonal on either side of the cafe, at one o'clock and three o'clock. It was impossible to know how long it would take before this Ahmed character emerged. Until he did, Danny and Spud – who was now scratching the donkey's ears while he kept one eye on Hamza – needed to melt into the background. The *shemagh*, still wrapped round Danny's face to hide his white skin, made his breath hot and moist. His eyes flickered between Hamza and the armed kids in the pick-up, but as before he avoided full eye contact with anybody.

He didn't trust this Hamza character. Didn't trust him not simply to say whatever he thought they wanted to hear, just to get his money. He saw no evidence of a khat chew. No evidence that this was anything other than a street cafe, with old men drinking tea. He needed to investigate further.

Time check: 18.03. Danny stepped towards the tables. Hamza had some tea in front of him now. He lifted the bowl and put it to his lips, watching Danny over the brim as he approached. Danny was a couple of metres in front of the line of tables when he heard the music: scratchy Arabic beats coming from inside the building, with a voice wailing – tunelessly to Danny's ears – over it. He approached the door and looked inside. There was a single room, large and dark. About fifteen men sat in a circle, remonstrating with each other as vigorously as they were chewing. To the left of the circle, three other men were dancing. The colourful scabbards round their waists jiggled as they did so. Danny remembered Roberts's description of life in Yemen: this looked like a khat chew, all right. He retreated, and under the watchful eye of both Hamza and Spud, returned to his position by the wall.

Five minutes passed.

Suddenly, Danny became aware of a commotion around the exit to the square at his nine o'clock. A small group of men entered – Danny counted five of them. The locals in the square parted to give them passage, and even the kids on the pick-up seemed to sit a little straighter. There was a lull in the general conversation as the newcomers strutted further into the square. They wore mismatched clothes. Three of them wore camouflage gear – either a jacket, or trousers, or both. The other two were more traditionally dressed but wore heavy bandoliers of rounds like necklaces. Each of them had the ubiquitous AK-47 strapped to their bodies, and they had an arrogant swagger. To Danny they looked like jokers. But jokers with assault rifles could do a lot of damage, as the locals clearly knew well. Hamza shifted nervously in his seat. Only the older tea drinkers appeared unmoved by the arrival of these overbearing youngsters, and stared at them impassively while sipping at their bowls of tea.

One of the newcomers was clearly the leader. He wore full camouflage and instead of a *shemagh* had a kind of low fez, white with purple Arabic lettering. Danny could tell he was looking for trouble. He was jutting out his chin and trying to catch the eye of anyone he could. If his gaze descended on any of the locals, they would step backwards from him, bowing slightly. The young man took up a position in the centre of the square, looking around for someone to pick on.

His eyes fell on Danny.

There were about eight metres between them. Five or six locals blocked the way, but they were clearly tuned in to the situation and melted away as it became clear that the swaggering militant had chosen his target. They locked eyes. The militant had a wispy beard like Hamza's, and a hooked nose. He was chewing something, probably khat. Not a good sign.

A crackling in Danny's ear. Spud. 'I've got line of sight, mucker. I can take him if you say the word.'

Danny looked beyond the young man. Sure enough, Spud had stepped a few paces from the donkey and had manoeuvred himself further along his stretch of wall. He had one hand in his *dishdash*, ready to pull a weapon. He could put this fucker down, no question, but a single round wouldn't just kill the tough – it would kill their chances of hooking up with Ahmed as they fought their way out of the area.

The square was practically silent now, apart from the noise of Arabic music coming from where the khat chew was taking place. The young man took a step towards Danny. He called something out in Arabic. Danny couldn't understand him, so he didn't reply. Instead he raised both palms in a gesture of concil- iation, knowing full well that Spud had his back.

This seemed to amuse the young man, who didn't understand that Danny was calculating which of his buddies to kill first as and when the situation turned noisy. His lip curled into an unpleasant grin, and he moved his hands so that they were gently resting on the rifle that hung round his neck.

'Just say the word, mucker,' Spud breathed.

Five seconds passed.

An unfamiliar voice echoed round the square.

It came from the direction of the pick-up. One of the kids had stood up and shouted something. Danny didn't understand the words, but he could easily discern the aggression behind them. The militant stopped in his tracks. He turned round swiftly and barked an instruction, before striding back towards his cronies. Danny felt himself relaxing. The guy seemed to have forgotten all about him. The buzz of conversation resumed slightly, though there was still a nervous edge to it.

More commotion by the pick-up. Three of the newcomers had climbed up on to the vehicle. They were dragging one of the kids – Danny assumed this was the one who had shouted out – down on to the ground.

Scuffling. Shouting. The militants had surrounded the kid and now they were bundling him away from the square, down the street to Danny's nine o'clock. Danny looked over at Spud. Now that the threat had passed, he was edging back towards his orig- inal position. And not a moment too soon, because Hamza had just stood up. Three men had emerged from the room where the khat chew had been taking place. Traditional Yemeni dress. Greying beards – they were older than Hamza, but not as old as the craggy-faced men drinking tea. In their fifties, perhaps, though it was hard to tell from a distance. What was easy to tell was that they were swaying slightly.

Hamza instantly stood up and approached the middle of the three men. He grabbed his hand and started pumping it vigorously. Even as he did this, he looked over at Danny, unsubtly indicating that he'd marked his man: this, clearly, was Ahmed. He had a strange, sharp face. His beard was shorter than the others, and trimmed in a square, angular fashion. Bright blue eyes that contrasted with his dark skin. But his face looked as weathered as the rocky mountainside on which this town was built. Ahmed looked rather startled as Hamza shook his hand. Danny could tell that he barely knew who Hamza was, and he pushed him away with a sharp word. He and his two mates turned to the right, and headed towards the street that led off from the far corner of the square.

Immediately Danny started cutting across the crowd. Five seconds later he was alongside Hamza. 'Take your donkey and get back to your house,' he said. 'No detours. If you're not there when we get back, you can forget about your money.'

The agitated Hamza nodded, then scurried away. Spud was already on Ahmed's case, trailing him by five metres. Danny drew up alongside him with several large strides. This narrow street was much less busy than the square had been. Ahmed and his companions walked three abreast. Five metres up ahead, two women in full burka dress stepped aside to let them pass. Another fifteen metres beyond that was a small spice stall laid out on the ground.

Ahmed and his two mates stopped by the stall. They chatted for twenty seconds, then the two friends started talking to the stallholder while Ahmed continued, alone, up the street.

Danny and Spud picked up their pace. Danny's every sense was on high alert. They had no props now to help them blend in – no donkeys or cigarettes. They had to get to Ahmed and persuade him to come quietly to Hamza's place before somebody noticed them.

They passed the spice stall five seconds later. Danny thought he caught a whiff of perfume coming from Ahmed's mates. He kept his eye on the target, ten metres away now. Nobody between them.

Five metres. He and Spud moved purposefully. They turned to each other. Looked ahead. A couple of kids etching a picture on the ground with stones, twenty metres away. Behind, nothing, though Danny could hear the roar of a motorbike engine from the square they'd just left.

He turned to Spud. They nodded at each other, then they pulled their Sigs.

In less than a second, Ahmed had Danny's handgun pressing into the side of his belly. Danny got a noseful of stinking perfume that made him want to puke. He took a firm hold of Ahmed's elbow as a look of outrage crossed their target's face.

'*Taala ma'ana*,' Danny breathed.

You're coming with us.

A sudden flow of Arabic escaped Ahmed's lips. He was clearly furious about this imposition. But whatever he was saying, he was cut short when Spud held up his Sig.

'*Taala ma'ana*,' Danny repeated, jabbing the gun sharply.

Ahmed looked like he was going to spit. He held his head up high, and for a tense moment Danny thought he might be about to shout out for help. But although he kept a condescending look on his face, he fell silent. Danny nodded at Spud. His mate stowed his weapon and locked arms with Ahmed. Danny kept his Sig out, but hidden under the sleeve of his robes.

They walked. Ahmed continued to talk, but he had enough sense not to try anything stupid. They took a left turn, which

Danny calculated would take them west, back towards Hamza's place. Ahmed didn't shut up, but that was okay. As long as he was speaking, he wasn't running. And even when they passed other people in these largely deserted side streets, he didn't cry out. It was clear that the threat of Danny's Sig was doing the trick. Either that, or the fucker's head was still muddled from the khat chew.

Time check: 18.30. They turned a corner to see Hamza's house 20 metres ahead. The donkey was tethered outside. Hamza was next to it, fitting a nose bag of food to its head. They watched him for a full minute before he noticed the SAS men and their captive. When he did, he looked shocked, as though they'd appeared from nowhere. He gave an anxious nod, then disappeared inside.

Spud forced Ahmed toward the house. Danny followed.

SEVENTEEN

Danny reckoned this was going to be a four-finger job. Maybe five. If Ahmed had been sober, he'd perhaps have got away with a crack on the head and a few sharp words. But he wasn't, so he wouldn't.

Both Yemeni men were face-down on the floor of Hamza's room. Spud had his heel on the back of Hamza's neck, Danny on the back of Ahmed's. Each man had his Sig drawn, and aimed at the back of his target's head.

It was clear that Ahmed spoke no English. It was also clear that the khat had dulled his sense of fear. He was jabbering away in Arabic, his tone offended. Argumentative. He stank of a pungent perfume that made Danny want to puke.

Danny didn't bother with threats. Not yet. It was much more important, first off, that Ahmed knew he was serious. He bent down and, with one rough tug, pulled his prisoner over on to his back. He laid his Sig on the floor and covered Ahmed's still-wittering mouth with one hand. With the other he grabbed the little finger on his prisoner's left hand. He noticed that the fingernails looked manicured, a strange contrast to Ahmed's craggy, weather-beaten face. Ahmed was an ugly old fucker, but clearly vain. Danny also sensed that that there was no strength in the man's arm. He might be a respected elder, but he was physically weak.

Danny didn't hesitate any longer. With a sudden yank and a crack, he rammed the little finger 180 degrees backwards.

Ahmed's eyes widened in sudden shock. A second later, the pain kicked in and he tried to scream. But with Danny's hand over his mouth and his neatly cropped beard, all that came was a muffled wail.

'No!' Hamza cried out. 'You must not hurt him!'

Danny ignored that. 'Tell him I break another finger for every lie he tells me. After that I start on his teeth.'

'Or what's left of them,' Spud butted in.

Hamza anxiously clutched a handful of his own hair. Ahmed nodded in a terrified fashion.

'I need the exact location of the training camp where the British cleric is hiding.'

Hamza asked the question, his tongue tripping over his words. Danny slowly moved his hand away from Ahmed's mouth. There was a hoarse, throaty sound, then Ahmed spat in his face. Danny slammed his mouth over Ahmed's mouth again, then yanked back his manicured ring finger, before slamming his fist down on both broken bones just to be sure he got his message across. Hamza turned away so he didn't have to witness this sudden violence.

'Why don't we just do his knee-cap?' Spud suggested.

Danny shook his head. 'Don't want the fucker to bleed out on us.' In truth, Danny knew that a serious gun wound like that in a backwater like this could be a death sentence. Not acceptable when they needed to get their information out of the old boy. He surveyed Ahmed's hand. The two broken fingers were pointing out at different angles. He grabbed the middle finger and bent it back so that it was almost at breaking point. Then he addressed Hamza once more. 'Ask him again,' he said.

This time, when Danny removed his hand, Ahmed was more compliant. He spoke quickly, his voice high-pitched through the pain. Hamza waited for him to finish talking before he translated. 'He says ... he says he doesn't really know, only that it's in the lowlands somewhere.'

Crack. Danny yanked the third finger back, only just managing to get his hands over Ahmed's lips a fraction of a second before the scream came. This time Ahmed's muffled squealing lasted a full thirty seconds before dying away.

'Where is it?' Danny demanded implacably.

Hamza looked like he was going to cry as he popped the question. Danny removed his hand. This time Ahmed's gasping Arabic monologue was more extensive. 'You follow the road down the mountain,' Hamza translated. 'Where the road forks, you go left. There is a track that heads north by a grove of acacia trees. Follow that track into the valley. That is where you will find them.'

Danny and Spud looked at each other. A look that said: do we believe him?

Danny did. You learned an instinct for these things after you'd done it a few times. And it was very hard to lie to a man who had been trained to lie to anyone, no matter what they threw at him.

He stepped away from Ahmed, but Spud kept his foot on Hamza's neck. He cocked his weapon. 'Let's finish them off,' he said.

'Not him,' Danny said.

Spud gave him a look that said: what the fuck?

But they had their orders. Hammond had said it explicitly: Hamza was the CIA's man and he needed to stay intact.

The same didn't hold true for Ahmed. The chances of him keeping quiet about the two British men asking for directions were zero. Which left them with only one option.

Ahmed had his eyes closed as he writhed on the ground clutching his broken fingers. So he didn't see Danny standing above him, pulling his suppressed weapon and aiming it at the old man's head.

A single head shot. The round thudded into Ahmed's head. The body jolted and fell still. Blood oozed from the wound.

Spud took his foot off Hamza's neck. The tout scrambled to his knees. 'You said he'd be okay,' he started to say, but then bent over and started retching by his bed.

Spud strode up to Danny. 'We should nail him too,' he breathed. His eyes flashed angrily. 'He doesn't fucking like what you've just done.'

Danny hesitated. Maybe Spud was right. But they'd had a direct instruction: the tout stays intact.

'We've got our orders,' Danny said. 'We keep him alive.'

'It's the wrong call. I don't trust him.'

'Trust me, he's going to have his hands full,' Danny said. He fished the wad of American dollars from his ops vest. He peeled off five hundred bucks – a fortune in a backwater like this, he reckoned – and dropped the notes on the floor in front of Hamza. Important to pay him, because an aggrieved tout would be much more likely to screw them over. Then he bent down to where their Yemeni contact was still prostrate on the ground. 'Get rid of the body tonight,' he said. 'And make a good job of it. If anyone finds him here, they'll think *you* killed him. And a word of advice, pal. Don't do *anything* that makes us want to come back.'

Hamza looked at him with utter terror and hatred. Danny felt another twinge of uncertainty. But he'd made his decision. He nodded at Spud and then, to the sound of Hanza's continued retching and occasional sobbing, they stowed their weapons, wrapped their *shemaghs* back round their heads, stepped over the fresh corpse and slipped out of the tiny residence and back into the dark streets of Ha'dah.

Time check: 19.32. Danny could sense Spud's anger at the call he'd made, but they were professional enough not to let it get in the way of what they had to do now: get out of Ha'dah, unob- served and quickly. The sun was setting, but the streets were still busy. Danny felt incredibly self-conscious of his heavy boots under his robes, but they both kept moving. As Danny and Spud headed south towards the road they had followed into the village, it became obvious that this was the hour when the toughs of Ha'dah walked out. It seemed that on every corner there was a group of swaggering militants, barely distinguishable from the kids who had made their presence felt in the square less than two hours ago. They hurried on in the shadow of the vast, fortress-like, mud-brick buildings. The call to evening prayer echoed over the rooftops. The *shemaghs* over their faces barely smothered the twin stenches of sewage and dried fish that hung in the air. Danny controlled his pace carefully – not so fast that he looked suspicious, nor so slow that he risked being picked out by one of these armed, trigger-happy kids.

They reached the main road that headed back down the mountain in about twenty minutes. They saw a single vehicle go past – a beaten-up old pick-up much like the one that they'd seen in the square earlier. Curious eyes looked out of the windows at them as they trekked along the cliff-face side of the road. Danny estimated that they could make their vehicle in about half an hour if they weren't held up. He checked over to his right. From here, he could see the outline of the stone staircase where they had crept past the guard the previous night. At that exact spot, he could just make out the outlines of two animals – he couldn't tell if they were dogs or hyenas – sniffing the air. No humans tonight. At least none that they could see.

Spud looked anxiously over his shoulder, then cast Danny a dark look. There was unspoken tension between them. 'We should have nailed him.'

Danny didn't reply. He'd just heard, from somewhere up behind them, the sudden buzzing of motorbikes. The two men shared a glance. Then they upped their pace. Danny couldn't shake the feeling he might have just screwed up. Badly.

Twenty metres further along the road they found another crevice in the cliff, smaller than the one into which they'd driven the Toyota, but big enough for the two of them. At Spud's insistence they ducked inside. Forty-five seconds later, the buzzing of the motorbikes became suddenly louder. A convoy shot past the opening of the crevice. Danny counted five of them. It was impossible as they whizzed past to discern their features accurately, but they all wore rifles across their backs.

'Reckon they're looking for someone?' Spud asked sarcastically. The buzzing of their bikes died away. Spud's face was like thunder. 'How far to the vehicle?' he said.

'Ten minutes. If we leg it.'

They made it in seven. As they approached the Toyota's impromptu hideout they slowed their pace and drew their weapons. Their camouflage was good, though. A couple of minutes later Danny was behind the wheel again, easing the Toyota out of the tumbledown hut and on to the road. He realised they'd barely seen any vehicles in Ha'dah. Certainly none like this. They were going to stick out on the road if anyone was following them. He turned right and, carefully manoeuvring the vehicle inches away from the sheer drop at the edge of the road, started winding their way down the mountain. By his side, Spud was checking over his Sig. There was a deep frown on his forehead. He looked like he expected to have to use it. With one hand on the wheel, Danny pulled his own handgun and stowed it in an open compartment just by his knee.

The road twisted and turned as they passed the location where the Chinook had set them down the previous night. Once more Danny was aware of lights moving around on the desert floor far below them, but the bulk of his attention was on the road, every sense alert as his eyes flickered between what was ahead, and the rear-view mirror.

Ten silent minutes passed.

Suddenly the road straightened out, and Danny slammed his foot on the brake. Glaring at them from the darkness ahead were five individual headlamps: a row of three, then a row of two, evenly spaced across the five-metre-wide road.

Motorbikes. Distance to the first row: fifteen metres.

An ordinary roadblock? If so, perhaps they could avoid a fire-fight by paying their way through.

The light of the Toyota's headlamps battled with those of the bikes. In the resulting glare, Danny could only see the outlines of the riders. But he could make out the shape of their robes, and the angular silhouettes of the weapons slung across their chests. He realised that one of the bikes had two riders. They climbed off, and the driver pushed his passenger forwards into the no-man's-land between the bikes and the Toyota, before getting back on his bike.

Spud swore under his breath when they saw his face. Hamza. He peered towards the Toyota, clearly dazzled by its headlamps. He was obviously trying to identify the drivers, but couldn't because of the glare. He turned round and made a gesture with his arms that said: I don't know if it's them.

The Toyota's engine purred. Danny revved it once. Thoughts flicked through Danny's mind. Had Hamza taken exception to their brutal treatment of Ahmed? Or had he been planning to rat on them all along?

'Still think we should have left that fucker alive back there?' Spud murmured.

Danny didn't answer. The situation was what it was. There was no right or wrong decision: only what they *had* done and what they *hadn't*. But they both knew what to do now.

Two of the front row of riders stepped off their bikes, leaving their vehicles propped up at an angle, the headlamps still burning. They stepped past Hamza towards the Toyota. Hamza himself scurried back behind the second line of motorbikes, but all Danny's attention was on the approaching men. Even their sil-houettes had that self-assured gait Danny recognised from up in the village. His hand felt for the Sig in the compartment by his knee. He gripped the handle and with the press of a button wound down his side window. He heard Spud doing the same.

The night air – warmer now that they were lower down the mountain – hit his face.

The figures continued to approach. They were seven metres away now, side by side directly in front of the Toyota. Danny could make out their features. They were young, no older than twenty, and their black beards looked barely grown. Their faces were pictures of suspicion and contempt, but they had a confidence about them that comes with a loaded weapon.

Three metres from the front of the vehicle, the figures peeled off to either side, one towards Danny's window, one towards Spud's. Like policemen on an American highway, they each placed a hand on the top of the vehicle, then leant in to look through the open window.

They didn't even have time to speak.

There was a fraction of a second between the firing of the two handguns: Spud's first, then Danny's. They shot each of the Yemeni bikers full in the face. Because of the proximity of the target, Danny felt a blowback from the shot, and a flat slap of wetness against his fist as blood spattered from his target's face. The impact of the rounds forced the two targets to fall back a couple of metres, clearing the Toyota sufficiently that Danny and Spud could swing the doors open and throw themselves out of their seats before the remaining three targets even had time to get their weapons ready to fire.

Immediately, there was shouting from the direction of the enemy targets. One of the bikes fell to its side as the driver jumped off it. Danny's foot crunched down on the shin of the man he'd killed as he took cover behind the open door, dragging his HK out of the car with him. The pistol was fine in confined space, and even over the 15-metre distance between them and the bikes. But the rifle would be more accurate over distance if the enemy tried to flee, and a harder-hitting round was always preferable if you wanted to be sure of putting your man down.

Chaos in the enemy ranks. Shouting. Two shots rang out. One of them flew over the top of the Toyota. The other slammed into the side door protecting Danny. He felt the car shuddering violently, but noted that the bullet hadn't fully pierced the door. That didn't mean the next one wouldn't, though.

Two more loose rounds. No doubt that these were amateurs but they were still well armed, even if they were firing randomly. They needed to be put down, quickly.

It was Spud who took the third one out. Unlike the enemy's loose fire, his was a single, well-aimed shot from his rifle as he peered round his open door and fired on the remaining target in the front row. There was a clatter as both the man and his bike fell to the ground. They heard more alarmed shouting, and a revving of bikes. Clearly the remaining two guys were preparing to flee.

Danny pushed himself up so he was looking through the window of the open door, the butt of his rifle pressed hard into his shoulder, safety switched to semi-automatic. Both bikes were facing in on each other as their riders attempted to turn. Distance: 20 metres, and he thought he could just make out Hamza five metres beyond that. Each of the two targets on motorbikes was lit up now – by each other and also by the Toyota. They weren't even firing back.

'*Go left!*' Danny shouted the instruction to Spud. The only words either of them had spoken since the firefight had begun. Then he gave himself a couple of seconds to aim at the guy on the right.

The two SAS men fired once in perfect unison. Their rounds found their targets unerringly. Both men slumped to the ground, their bikes falling on top of them.

Which left Hamza. His silhouette had turned and was running away from them, down the road.

Danny felt a sudden flash of anger. He jumped out from behind his door, his rifle in the firing position. He covered the

15 metres between the Toyota and the bikes in seconds, avoiding the corpses as he sprinted after the tout.

Hamza was 20 metres down the road and sprinting like his life depended on it, which it did. Danny calmly got down on one knee, gave himself a second to line up the sights, then took the shot. It echoed off the mountainside, and Hamza crumpled to the ground.

A pause. Then the sound of screaming. The tout was down and wounded, but still alive. Danny stood up and found Spud next to him.

'You were right, I was wrong,' he said. Then he sprinted the 20 metres to Hamza, whose screaming had grown less intense. He'd hit the tout in the lower back and he was bleeding out fast. Hamza took a sharp intake of breath as he looked up at Danny, the whites of his eyes glowing in the darkness. He managed to shake his head as Danny raised his weapon, but the Regiment man wasn't going to make the same mistake twice.

He fired a fourth single shot at Hamza's head. The body juddered and was still.

No time to hesitate. Danny bent down and grabbed Hamza's body by its legs. He was aware of Spud killing the engines on the motorbikes as he dragged the corpse towards the steep incline at the edge of the road. He rolled him down the mountainside, out of sight.

Jogging back up to Spud's position, he saw that his mate had already done the same thing to two more of the Yemeni dead. Together then cleared up the rest, before sending their bikes plunging off the road after them.

They were grim-faced as they got back into their vehicle. There was no guarantee that there weren't more of these fuckers coming, or that Hamza hadn't told anyone of their destination. And they sure as hell didn't want company when they were trying to creep up on Abu Ra'id.

They needed to get off this road quickly. Without another word, they continued the journey down the mountain.

Time check: 22.05hrs

The winding road had evened out. They were at the foot of the mountain. The headlamps of the Toyota revealed fast-moving, parched scrubland on either side. Danny had Ahmed's words in his head. *Where the road forks, you go left.* But so far there had been no sign of the road forking. It just kept on going straight.

Twenty minutes passed. Half an hour. Danny pulled over and killed the lights. Then he took a look round with his night sight. The terrain was perfectly flat for as far as he could see. The occasional boulder. Patches of low scrub. The gnarled tree 200 metres to the north. In the distance, glowing like fireflies in the green haze of the night vision, he could see the headlamps of other vehicles moving around. But with no point of reference, it was impossible to tell how far away they were. He climbed back into the car. He could tell Spud was still pissed off with him, but at least he was calm.

'Anyone following?' he asked.

'Not that I can see.'

They continued along the road for another ten minutes.

Twenty.

The fork in the road suddenly appeared out of the darkness. The right-hand fork was by far the better kept. Off to the left, the terrain appeared pot-holed and undulating. At the apex between the two forks there lay the skeleton of some animal, its bones dry and pitted. There were no signposts, of course, or any indication that this was the way they needed to go. The two SAS men merely looked at each other and nodded their mutual consent that this was the right path. Danny stepped out of the car again. He looked down at the ground and saw fresh tyre prints. 'Someone's passed this way recently,' he said. 'A four-by-four.'

'Abu Ra'id?' Spud asked.

Danny shrugged. He performed another sweep with his kite sight. Nothing. But they should still take precautions.

'I'm going to go blind.'

Spud grunted his agreement. Danny immediately killed all the lights on the Toyota. From his kit bag, he removed his set of NV goggles and fitted them over his head. Spud did the same. The darkness dissolved and the world turned a shade of green. The goggles illuminated everything. The stars were riotous overhead, the stony ground of the desert terrain almost more detailed than it would have been in daylight with the naked eye. Danny took the left fork, and eased the Toyota on to this new road. The tyres trundled and crunched noisily over the imperfect surface.

Danny couldn't do more than 20 mph. Not on this road surface and wearing NV. In any case, it was desirable to keep the engine noise as quiet as possible, since they didn't know what was waiting up ahead. Danny concentrated on keeping the revs low and steady, while Spud kept looking all around, scouring the terrain for possible threats, and checking that nobody was following them.

Nobody was. At least, not so far as they could tell.

Time check: 23.25hrs. They had been going along this stony road for more than an hour. The diesel tank was half full. Danny concentrated on remembering Ahmed's instructions: *There is a track that heads north by a grove of acacia trees. Follow that track into the valley. That is where you will find them.* So far, there had been fuck-all. Just flat, featureless terrain.

'Up there,' Spud said suddenly.

Danny stopped the vehicle and looked. Sure enough, about 100 metres up ahead, there was a break in the featureless expanse. A collection of low trees. They moved forward again, and as they grew closer Danny saw the trees in more detail: gnarled and squat. They drew up alongside this acacia grove, and stopped again. Just beyond the grove, a smaller track bore off to the left. Danny climbed out of the car and removed his compass from his ops vest. He stepped ten metres from the vehicle so the metal wouldn't compromise the compass reading, then took a bearing. Sure enough, this smaller road headed north. Just like Ahmed had said.

They moved even more slowly now: a steady, quiet ten mph. The terrain changed. It was no longer as flat as it had been since they left the mountain. It undulated, and Danny realised that they were heading downhill again, with terrain sloping up on either side. They continued like this for another half hour before it became quite clear that they were heading down into a valley.

'Stop,' Spud said.

Danny braked. He had seen it too. An orange glow low in the night sky, seen through a V shape in the terrain to their left. A distant fire. He pulled off to the side of the road and killed the engine. The two men emerged from the vehicle. They didn't need to speak. They both understood that now was the time to approach on foot.

It took them five minutes to prepare themselves: to repack their bags and check over their weapons. There was no cover for the vehicle – it would have to stay where it was, ready for them to pick up when the time came to extract. If all went well, they would put some miles between themselves and the camp, find somewhere to lie up, and call for a pick-up. For now, they kept their NV goggles on their heads, slung their bags over their shoulders and started to hike, following the road but keeping 20 metres to its left-hand side so they could easily go to ground if another vehicle came their way.

The terrain was empty. The air silent. The only sound was the light crunch of their footsteps on the dry ground. They continued in single file, Spud first, Danny second, spaced ten metres apart to avoid presenting a bunched-up target to any unseen threat. The valley shape became increasingly pronounced, though after 15 minutes' walking the road started to incline upwards. They followed it to the brow for 200 metres. Before he reached it, Spud got down on all fours and crawled the final 10 metres. Danny did the same, because to present oneself on the brow of a hill was a surefire way to reveal yourself. When he was alongside Spud, they peered over the brow to the terrain beyond.

'Bingo,' Spud breathed.

Yeah, Danny thought. Bingo.

They were looking at the training camp. There was very little doubt about that.

Danny had been expecting something ragged and temporary. Amateurish. What he saw came as something of a surprise. It was nestled about 100 metres to the left of the track, and perhaps half a click from their current position. It comprised perhaps a hundred tents, spaced out in a neat square, ten columns of ten, with a walkway of five or six metres between the columns. Regimented. Orderly. In the centre of the camp was a large fire and Danny could just make out the silhouettes of people milling around it, though from this distance it was hard to say how many, and of course impossible to see their faces.

He counted eight technicals dotted around the camp. One of them was circling it, its headlamps beaming brightly. Danny could make out the outlines of top-mounted weapons on the vehicles, and instinctively knew from their shape that these were .50-cal machine guns. There wasn't much in the way of a ground assault that hardware like that couldn't defend the camp from. On the far side, a stretch of very flat ground – ideal, he realised, for markmanship and demolitions practice. But there were no such things going on at this time of night. Everything was quiet and, aside from those few people around the fire, everything was still. On the south side of the camp, which was the edge closest to them, a herd of goats seemed to be tethered to a post.

'Fucker could be in any one of those tents,' Spud whispered.

'Don't know why they won't just send in a drone and bomb the whole lot.'

But Danny understood why: because wiping out the training camp like that would give the Firm no assurance that Abu Ra'id was dead. And they *really* wanted him dead.

'We need to lie up,' Danny said. 'Get a visual on Abu Ra'id when it's light. See which tent is his.'

'That could take days.'

'Got anything better to do?'

Spud gave him a sour look, then scanned the surrounding area. 'Over there,' he said, pointing to the terrain on the western edge of the camp. Here the ground sloped up sharply from the plateau of the camp. It was dotted with the occasional tree and small collections of boulders. The incline lasted about 100 metres, before flattening out slightly at the top. They could dig themselves in up there and have a good view of the camp. Whether they'd be near enough to get a positive visual ID on Abu Ra'id was a different question, but it was about as close as they could safely get and remain covert.

'Let's do it,' Danny said.

The truck circling the perimeter of the camp was facing away from them as they crawled over the brow of the hill. They descended another ten metres so that when they stood up they wouldn't be visible against the skyline. When the truck turned in their direction the guys went to ground, lying perfectly still on the stony incline. The headlamp beams didn't hit them directly – there was just a slight lessening of the darkness – but they knew that as long as they stayed motionless, they'd remain unobserved. When the circling truck turned again, they skirted along the incline that surrounded the camp until they reached their position. From this angle, they could see that there was a second pathway bisecting the camp at right angles to the first. It meant they had a decent view of all the open spaces of the camp from here.

They selected a space to the side of three boulders well out of range of the pick-up's headlamps. It gave them something to crouch behind while they prepared to dig in. Spud removed his trenching tool from his pack and started hacking at the hard, stony desert floor. In 15 minutes he had sweat dripping from his face, and had dug out a hole a couple of metres long, 30 cm deep and a metre wide – large enough for them both to lie in side by side, along with their bags. Danny unwrapped the foil thermal sheeting – Hammond's words of warning about Yemeni spy drones ringing in his ears – and then unfolded the wire-backed hessian. The two men settled down in the hole, with the thermal sheeting sandwiched between their backs and the hessian camouflage. They got some scoff inside them, then Danny extracted the kite sight from his bag and trained it on the camp.

He had a direct line of sight to the fire. It was burning low now, and there seemed to be fewer silhouettes around it. He lowered the sight, and checked the time: 00.45. They wouldn't get a positive ID on anyone till daylight. Until then, they needed to rest up.

'I'll take the first stag,' he suggested to Spud.

Spud grunted his agreement. Seconds later he was fast asleep. Danny lay motionless in the pit, his ears on high alert, his brain turning over. If everything had gone according to plan, Abu Ra'id would be resting up just a couple of hundred metres from their position. Danny couldn't wait to get a bullet in him and extract. It would be tough locating a place to lie up in this featureless terrain while they waited to be collected, but he figured they'd find a wadi nearby where they could hide, make a call for a pick-up and sit it out for however long it took for them to be airlifted out of here.

He realised he'd been thinking about Clara. Funny, he thought, how you think about home the most when you're furthest from it. With Abu Ra'id, the last man on his hit-list, dead, and the threat to London eliminated, maybe he could get back with her again when he returned.

Would she take him back? He knew, in his gut, that she would.

He comforted himself with that thought as he waited for morning to come.

05.03hrs

Danny felt a sharp nudge in his ribs. He knew from the musty warmth under the camo that the sun was rising. His eyes flickered open.

Spud was eyeing the training camp through the spotting scope. He was lying very still.

'What is it?' Danny breathed.

Very gently, Spud passed the scope over to Danny. 'Eleven o'clock,' he breathed. 'About seven metres north of where the fire was.'

Danny put one eye to the optic and pointed it in the direction Spud had indicated. He saw three blurry figures. He carefully focused the scope and they eased into sharp focus.

Two of them were facing him, cross-legged on the ground, while the third stood in front of them, his back to the OP. He had his right arm raised, his finger pointing to the sky. And although Danny didn't recognise the faces on the two cross-legged men, he felt a strange, prickling sensation down his back as he held his breath and focused in on the third. He was tall, with a plain robe and a white headdress. He looked as though he was preaching.

He stayed standing for a minute. Two minutes. Three.

Then the cross-legged men stood up. They shook hands with the third man, before wandering away towards a nearby tent.

At which point the third man turned.

For a heartstopping moment, Danny thought the man was looking directly towards them. But then it became clear that in fact he was gazing up at the beauty of the desert sky at dawn. He smiled.

Danny recognised him, of course. The black beard that reached down to his chest. The neat, perfectly proportioned, handsome features.

'Abu Ra'id,' he breathed.

'Damn right,' Spud replied. 'Abu fucking Ra'id.'

EIGHTEEN

The hit on Abu Ra'id couldn't happen during the day. They needed to enter the camp covertly, carry out the hit covertly, and leave covertly. That required the cover of night. That didn't mean Danny or Spud liked the idea of waiting. If Hamza had told anyone else of their destination, they could expect company. Either that, or someone might arrive from Ha'dah to tip Abu Ra'id off. Danny silently cursed himself for not listening to Spud. Not knowing who might arrive to blow their cover made every minute feel like an hour. A sick, anxious feeling gnawed at Danny's gut.

'Wish we could just snipe the fucker from here,' Spud said. But that wasn't an option. They didn't have the right hardware to take such a shot, it would only give away their position and anyway, their orders were very precise: make the kill at close quarters so you can be sure the bastard's dead. But there was no question about it: they had to make the hit the following night. The longer they delayed, the higher their chance of being compromised.

Their target remained outside until an hour after sunrise. Various people from around the camp approached him. The militants seemed to be taking their turns in receiving an audience from the cleric. They were like clones: bandoliers of ammo, black and white *shemaghs* covering their heads. 'Might as well have a sign round their necks saying "terrorist cunts",' Spud said. Danny welcomed his sarcastic asides. Spud was his old self, which meant that Danny's fuck-up of the previous night was forgiven, if not forgotten.

By 07.00hrs the desert sun was already very hot. As Danny watched carefully through the spotting scope, he saw Abu Ra'id disappearing into one of the tents, presumably to protect himself from the fierce glare of the rising sun. Danny made a mental note of which tent it was: the sixth of ten rows, six columns along from the right. He reported that location to Spud, then kept the scope trained precisely on it, in case Abu Ra'id emerged and repositioned himself.

He didn't, but as the morning wore on there was a great deal of other activity around the camp. Each tent seemed to house three or four men. They queued up at the fire – which was smoking heavily – to be given some food, before congregating on the flat ground at the northern end of the camp. Even from their OP, which was a good 400 metres away from this training area, Danny could hear the barking of instructors, followed by the retorts of weapon fire. There were wooden structures here – scrambling ropes and precarious-looking climbing frames. Take away the dry desert heat and the fact that these were jihadi insurgents in the making, and it could have been a British army training exercise on Salisbury Plain. Four of the technicals circled the camp with their .50 cals mounted on the back, but it was clear nobody really expected any intruders. Why would they? Who would be crazy enough to hunt them out in this bleak, unforgiving pocket of desert? It seemed significant to Danny that the machine guns were aimed upwards. These militants clearly expected any threat to come from the sky, not the surrounding area. Not for the first time, he remembered Hammond's warnings about Yemeni drones.

Midday. The heat had massively increased. Danny found himself lying in a clammy puddle of his own sweat. He and Spud drank sparingly from their bottles, but they were losing water far more quickly than they were drinking it. Danny ignored his parched throat and the sore itchiness as his skin chafed against his sweat-soaked clothes, and kept his full attention on Abu Ra'id's tent. Even when Spud took over on the scope, Danny watched with his naked eye, to the accompanying retorts of gunfire that echoed over the dry desert terrain. The pounding midday sun made him feel slightly dizzy, but he still kept eyes-on. Abu Ra'id didn't emerge. Several other men entered the tent at intervals throughout the day, but they always walked out alone. Abu Ra'id himself stayed put.

'You think the fucker's still in there?' Spud said.

'Sure, unless he's dug a rabbit hole,' Danny said with a hint of sarcasm in his voice.

'What if he's not alone in the tent when we go in?' It was an issue. The tents were about six metres by eight in size – comfort-able enough for four or five guys.

'Then we take out everyone who is.' Simple as that.

Nothing changed until the late afternoon, when the heat of the sun started gradually to diminish, even though the warlike sounds of the camp did not. At 16.58hrs there was a flapping at the entrance to Abu Ra'id's tent, and the familiar figure of the cleric stepped outside. Immediately, two men ran up to him and accompanied him to the fire in the centre of the camp, which had stayed smouldering despite the heat, the air above it a smoky, wobbly haze. They sat cross-legged together by the fire, and didn't move as the sun sank slowly behind Danny and Spud's OP, filling the Yemeni sky with astonishing streaks of pink and orange.

Danny and Spud barely noticed the beauty of the sky. All their attention was on the target. As night fell, the retorts of gunfire eased off. The jihadi students returned from the open plain of the desert to the camp. Most of them retired to their tents. A handful – maybe fifteen, it was difficult to count in the poor light, even through the spotting scope – sat round the fire with Abu Ra'id. The cleric was on his feet now, one hand raised. He seemed to be preaching again. He pointed to the sky, then used his hands to indicate an explosion. Obviously a warning against evil Westerners and their weapons of destruction. 'They'd better not listen to him talking for too long,' Spud said. 'They might end up with the urge to cut their own throats. Fucker has that effect on people.' He paused. 'Come to think of it, maybe they should just chat away. Make our job easier.' The flames were visible again now, and Danny found himself wishing he could share their warmth. The temperature had dropped dramatically in their little OP. His sweat-moistened clothes were clammy. 'Roll on midnight,' Spud said, his parched voice cracking slightly.

In the event, the camp fell quiet long before that. At 21.58, the figures around the fire suddenly stood up. Danny was watching through the scope, the green haze of Abu Ra'id's bearded face bang in the centre of his field of view. Everyone dispersed, heading off to tents around the camp. Abu Ra'id returned alone to the one in which he had spent most of the day.

The only movement now came from the pick-up truck with the mounted .50 cal, which had resumed its circling of the camp. A slow trundle, regular and bluntly predictable. 'Could be a decoy?' Spud said. 'They've got better security outside my fucking local.' He sniffed. 'Mind you,' he said, 'that *is* Catford.' A similar thought had crossed Danny's mind, and for the last half hour he'd been scanning the surrounding terrain, searching for other, more sophisticated threats. He saw none, and told Spud so. 'They chose this place because they don't expect anyone to come here. And if someone does, they expect them to be mob-handed. That's why they've got the fifty-cals.'

Spud grunted. 'Then let's get down there,' he said. 'Show them how wrong they are.'

Danny shook his head. 'We'll give our brave little soldiers time to settle down after lights-out,' he said.

'Had a feeling you'd say that.'

'We know where Abu Ra'id is. And I haven't seen anyone else getting into his tent. I doubt he's going anywhere tonight.'

Midnight came and went. There was no movement in the camp except for the circling technical. 01.00hrs. 01.30hrs. Not until 01.45 did they agree to make their advance.

They couldn't use a firearm for the hit. Even suppressed, the retort of one of their handguns would echo round the camp just like the gunfire they'd heard earlier in the day. As they crawled out of their cramped, stinking OP, they both checked the knives they had tucked into their ops vests. Sharper than razors. As Danny went through the rest of his gear, he was aware of Spud taking a shit ten metres to his left, before burying the result. He checked the time. 01.53.

'Ready?' he said as Spud returned to the OP.

'Ready.'

Both men lowered their NV over their eyes. The world changed. The stars in the night sky burned hot. Danny's field of view increased to a full 180 degrees thanks to the fly-like side optics in his goggles. You could see better through these things than with the naked eye. The circling truck passed in front of them, from left to right at a distance of 100 metres. They waited, crouching low, until it had turned left to trundle along the far end of the camp. Then they advanced.

They moved in convoy, Danny in the front, Spud seven or eight metres directly behind him. Danny had his weapon slung across his chest, his hands resting lightly on it. He didn't *want* to discharge any rounds, but the potential for contact was high and if he needed to, he would.

Fifty metres to the first column of tents. Zero movement, except the pick-up which was now moving up the far edge of the camp. Danny increased pace. They needed to be among the tents for cover by the time the truck completed its circuit. His breath sounded loud in his own ears, his footsteps regular and noisier than they actually were.

Twenty metres to the nearest tent.

Fifteen.

Movement.

Shit.

Danny held up one hand. Both men came to a halt and slowly, quietly, hit the ground. They were in open ground, ten metres from the perimeter of the camp. The pick-up circling the perimeter was moving along the top end. Two minutes, Danny estimated, before their path was lit up by its headlamps. Fifteen metres up ahead, a man had emerged from the nearest tent. Plain robe, wispy beard, young. He looked directly out in Danny and Spud's direction, his eyes glinting in the NV like a cat's in torchlight.

He squinted.

Had he seen them?

No. He turned and walked ten metres in the opposite direction towards the centre of the camp. Then he lit a cigarette and stood there smoking it with his back to them, gazing up at the stars.

Sixty seconds till the truck lit them up. Enough for this guy to finish his fag and go back to bed? Unlikely. But this figure was directly in their way, 25 metres from their position. There was only a fifty-fifty chance that they could creep up on him unseen and unheard. The second he clocked them, he'd raise the alarm. But to take him out now with a gunshot would spell the end of the op.

Decision time.

The guy was still smoking.

They couldn't wait. They had to creep past him. And if there was a chance of him seeing them, they'd have to deal with it ...

Danny raised a silent arm and pointed at a bearing of 30 degrees clockwise, away from the path that would lead them past the guy with the cigarette to Abu Ra'id's tent. Slowly, he and Spud pushed themselves to their feet. The figure still had his back to them as they trod silently out of his potential line of view. They reached the tents, skirted round one and started heading down the aisle parallel to Abu Ra'id's. His was in the sixth row along, which meant they had to pass another four tents. The tents were about six metres wide, the space between them roughly the same. Danny crept past one of them.

Two.

A noise. Danny froze, holding his breath. It came again – a low groan. He exhaled slowly. Just someone moaning in their sleep.

The pick-up was approaching their part of the perimeter. Danny could hear the low buzz of its engine, and his NV grew brighter in the light-spill. He crouched down on the far side of one of the tents and sensed Spud doing the same thing by the tent behind him. Distance between them: 12 metres.

Footsteps.

The lone figure had turned and was walking back towards the perimeter, towards the truck. He passed barely five metres from where Danny was crouching, but his focus was clearly on the truck itself. Like most people, he failed to see what he didn't expect and walked straight past the heavily armed intruder.

Voices. Arabic. They spoke for maybe 30 seconds before the truck continued its circuit.

Then nothing.

Danny remained very still, listening hard for any movement. There was none.

Thirty seconds. He slowly pushed himself to his feet again.

The figure seemed to come from nowhere, turning round the corner of the tent behind which Danny was crouching, suddenly facing him full on. Danny felt a surge of adrenaline as he let go of his rifle and felt for his knife. But he could tell he was going to be too late. The young jihadi's face was a picture of sudden alarm and he was opening his mouth to shout a sudden warning.

It never left his lips.

Spud had appeared behind the target. One firm, broad hand covered his mouth and nose. The other whipped a blade in front of his neck and, with two clean, deft flicks sliced into the flesh on either side of his Adam's apple. There was barely a sound from Spud's victim as a sudden fountain of blood erupted from his jugular. Danny stepped quickly forward and grabbed his legs and wrists so they couldn't make a noise as he flailed during his body's death throes. He lifted the feet a few inches off the ground and held the squirming man tight as blood flowed, less violently now, from the twin wounds on his neck.

He took 30 silent seconds to die.

When his body was still, they laid him quietly on the ground, parallel to the nearest tent. Then they crouched silently again, fully aware that they might have disturbed someone beneath the adjacent canvas. But nobody emerged. Once more everything seemed still. Danny pointed again in the direction of Abu Ra'id's tent. Estimated distance: 20 metres. Seconds later, they were advancing once more.

They met no more obstacles as they approached their target. The truck was moving along the far edge of the camp but it was almost 100 metres away and posed no threat now that they were in the thick of things. The threats came from closer at hand. The slumbering jihadis – perhaps four or five of them per tent – were doubtless armed. Disturb them, and things *would* go noisy. Danny and Spud were better equipped and better trained. But the numbers were not in their favour, and they knew a contact could become a bloodbath. The Regiment men, however, were expert at moving in silence. Slow, firm steps, feeling for loose ground with the tips of their toes before placing a full footstep.

A minute later, they were outside Abu Ra'id's tent.

Speaking wasn't an option. Not this close to the target. But that was okay. Danny was holding his breath anyway. They moved as one, in sync with each other. The tent itself was about half a metre higher than Danny, six metres in length and three in width. Its entrance was merely a loose piece of canvas, unpegged, unfastened, hanging motionless in the still desert night. Gaining entry would be straightforward. Exactly what would happen when they were in that enclosed space was anybody's guess. One thing was for sure: here, in the heart of enemy territory, they would have to be swift and silent. They expected their target to be alone in here, but if there were any others, there was going to be a sudden bloodbath. They'd need silently to take out anyone who was still awake first, before killing the rest in their sleep.

Danny and Spud stood on either side of the entrance. Danny held up three fingers.

Two.

One.

Go.

Spud entered first, Danny a fraction of a second behind him.

The interior of the tent was sparse. The only ground cover was a sheet of rough hessian. There was a thin mattress along the far end with a single figure lying asleep upon it, his chest rising and falling in slow regular movement. Danny picked out the man's features and instantly identified them, beyond question, as belonging to Abu Ra'id.

They had their man.

At his foot end, to the side of the mattress. Next to it, a book – a Qu'ran, maybe? And lying on the book, a data stick. Aside from that, the tent was empty.

Heart pounding, Danny quietly loosened his knife. Spud did the same. The best way to keep quiet was to murder the bastard in his sleep.

They were seconds away from ending this.

Spud stepped forward, blade in hand. Danny turned towards the target's feet, ready to hold them tight while Spud slit his throat. A speciality of his, and even if the target woke with the pain, he wouldn't be able to cry out if he had a severed trachea.

They were big men in a cramped space, but they moved with slow, silent precision, knowing that to take out the target while he slept was their quietest and safest option. They closed the gap between them and the sleeping Abu Ra'id to four metres.

Three.

Which was when their target's eyes opened.

For a split second, nobody moved. Three statues, frozen with indecision.

Abu Ra'id's head turned to look at them. His piercing eyes, bright in the NV, stared first at Spud, then Danny. His face was acutely familiar, not only from their briefings but from news reports on the TV back home, and pieces in the newspapers. Now, though, even through the green haze Danny could see a riot of unfamiliar emotions in them. Astonishment. Fear. Fury.

Panic. And panic could be noisy.

The SAS men hurried forwards, Spud to the head end, Danny to the feet. It felt to Danny like everything was happening in slow motion. As he collapsed to his knees, he saw Spud bending over the target's head. His left hand fell towards Abu Ra'id's mouth. His right swiped the knife across the top of the chest to his throat.

Spud's left hand was mere inches from Abu Ra'id's face when a sound escaped their target's lips.

It was not a cry of alarm. Not a shout for help. The cleric was not even begging for his life. He simply breathed a single word.

'*Hammerstone.*'

Danny froze again for a split second. Then, almost by instinct, he stretched out his arm to stay Spud's knife hand.

Too late.

The sharp blade slid easily through the cleric's wiry beard and into his throat. The beard itself hid the flow of blood but it was clear from the sudden stiffening of the body that Abu Ra'id was mortally wounded. His body started to shake, and there was a muffled sound from his mouth, against which Spud was now pressing his broad hand while he pushed the edge of the knife blade further into the cleric's butchered throat to silence him completely.

They held the writhing body fast and still.

In a matter of seconds it was a corpse.

Silent.

Motionless.

Unlike Danny's mind, which was suddenly spinning.

Hammerstone.

He and Spud looked at each other, raising their NV goggles in unison.

'Did he just say what I thought he said?' Spud breathed.

Danny didn't even answer. Just gave a short nod. Too many things were falling into place.

He tried to keep a clear head. What were their orders? To phone in confirmation of Abu Ra'id's execution before they'd even left the camp.

Why? Was it really in case they were killed while extracting? Or for some other reason?

Think.

Their radio packs were fitted to their ops vest. Should they make the call? There was no doubt that they wanted to get the hell out of there as quickly as possible. Already Spud's hand was heading to his radio.

Hammerstone.

'Don't phone it in,' Danny said.

'Why the fuck not?'

'Just *don't.*' He paused a moment, staring down at his own radio. Both his and Spud's unit contained a GPS tracker – Hammond had told them so – which meant their handlers could locate their position to the nearest metre.

If Danny and Spud had learned something they shouldn't, their handlers knew exactly where to kill them.

'That other bloke you just nailed,' Danny said. 'Get his body.'

'*What*? You crazy?'

Crazy? Maybe.

Maybe not.

Hammerstone.

'You want to get out of here alive, we need that body. And quickly, while it's still warm.'

Even in the darkness of the tent, Spud couldn't hide the look on his face: a look that said quite plainly that he thought Danny was losing it. But the truth was that for the first time in days, everything was clear. Without another moment of hesitation, Danny moved towards the entrance of the tent, re-engaged his NV, and looked over his shoulder.

'Cover me.' He stepped outside.

Their silent, lethal work didn't appear to have disturbed anyone. The technical had completed another circuit of the perimeter, but a quick scan told Danny that the coast was clear. As Spud stepped out of the tent, handgun primed, Danny hurried past the lines of tents to where they had left their first casualty. The corpse was still there, a sticky pool of blood surrounding its head. Danny picked it up, and heaved it over his shoulder before loosening his own handgun. Then he hurried back to Abu Ra'id's tent and carried the second body inside. Spud joined him.

'Take out your radio,' he told his mate as he laid the body down on the floor.

Spud did as he was told with obvious reluctance. Danny took his own radio and laid it on the corpse's chest. He jabbed his finger to indicate that Spud should lay his on Abu Ra'id's body.

'I'm going to phone it in now,' Danny said. 'I give it a minute after that before it goes noisy. Get ready to run.'

'I hope you fucking know what you're doing, mucker.'

Danny grabbed the data stick from the side of Abu Ra'id's

bed and stuck it in his pocket. 'Me too,' he said. He crouched down at his radio and punched in his access codes. He didn't speak into the handset, but instead speedily inputted a text message.

Target down. Preparing to extract.

Then, leaving the radio on the corpse's chest, he turned to Spud.

'Head for the OP,' he said.

Spud nodded. He looked like he was beginning to understand what Danny was doing. He engaged his NV and stepped out of the tent. Danny followed.

'*Run!*' he hissed.

Danny and Spud sprinted side by side towards the edge of the camp. They pounded past the tents. Danny heard shouts. Scuffling. Figures flickering on the edge of their vision. They were compromised, only it didn't matter now because in a matter of minutes he knew that everyone in this training camp would be dead.

Including them if they didn't get the hell out of there.

Thirty metres to the edge of the camp. Somewhere behind them, skywards, there was a noise. A buzzing sound, like some distant, angry bee. It was punctured by the sound of a firearm being discharged. Badly aimed – a round flew several metres over their heads – but clearly intended for them.

'*Keep running!*' Danny yelled. The muscles in his legs were burning. His lungs too. The edge of the camp was only 20 metres away, but there was a massive commotion behind them as tens – hundreds – of militants awoke, disturbed by their presence.

A second round. Closer this time – it flew just inches above Danny's right shoulder as they cleared the edge of the camp. Danny risked looking back. The camp was ablaze with torches.

Distance to the OP: 150 metres. Open ground. They had no option but to run.

The two SAS men thundered up the sandy, rocky incline.

They covered the first 50 metres in 15 seconds. They weren't being followed, yet, but he clearly saw three of the technicals screeching round the perimeter of the camp. Any minute now, they'd come under heavy .50-cal fire.

They sprinted again. From behind, Danny heard the distinctive bark of an AK-47 — a single shot at first, then a burst of rounds. An explosion of sand five metres ahead of them as the rounds hit the ground.

'*We need to take cover!*' Spud roared as they carried on sprinting.

'*To the OP!*'

'*Bollocks! That won't protect us from fifty cals . . .*'

But Danny shook his head. '*We need to get under the thermal sheeting. Now!*'

'*What the fuck for?*'

Distance to the OP: 25 metres. Danny didn't have time to explain. The two men just carried on sprinting.

They were only ten metres from the OP when it happened.

There was another burst of AK fire from the direction of the camp. Most of the rounds went loose, slamming on to the desert floor a metre to Spud's left. Most, but not all. Spud lurched and fell forwards, so heavily that Danny knew he hadn't tripped. He'd been hit.

Time slowed down. Danny threw himself to the ground by his mate, just as a third burst of fire flew low over their heads. '*YOU OKAY?*'

Spud wasn't. He was gasping for air, trying to say something but unable to get the words out. Danny looked over his shoulder. The three technicals were turning to face them. Any second now they were going to open up, and a sustained burst of .50-cal fire would turn them both to mincemeat.

Danny had no time to think. He was acting on raw instinct. He pushed himself to his feet, leaned over and pulled Spud up from the ground. His mate was a heavy lump, and Danny heard himself shouting with the strain as he hauled the wounded Spud over his shoulder and staggered the final ten metres to the OP. The grisly sound of Spud trying to get air inside him made Danny feel cold and sick. He kicked off the hessian covering and thermal sheeting from the OP, then lowered his mate quickly down into the hole. Spud's gasping sounded panicked as Danny rolled in beside him and covered them with the flimsy, silvery material of the thermal sheeting and the hessian camo, leaving just the tiniest gap between the front edge of the sheet and the ground so he could observe what was going on down below.

Danny stared desperately down at the camp. The three technicals were facing them now, spaced only a few metres apart. The distance between them was 150 metres, but that was nothing for a .50 machine gun. They'd clearly seen where Danny and Spud had hidden themselves, and were preparing to rain down their fire on that exact location.

'I . . . can't . . . breathe . . .' Spud gasped.

'Take it easy, buddy,' Danny said, his voice hoarse and grim. 'We're going to get you out of here.'

But as he spoke, there was the thunder of machine-gun fire. Danny could see the flashing of the barrel as it swept a broad arc from left to right. A fraction of a second later, the sand exploded 15 metres in front of them, the arc of the gun repeating itself on the ground as the rounds landed.

A half-second pause. The gunner continued to fire, sweeping from right to left this time, and aiming closer. This time the rounds landed just seven or eight metres from their position. Sand showered their OP. Danny pressed himself closer into the ground as the drilling noise of the weaponry shuddered right through him. But that deafening sound was not nearly so awful as Spud's desperate, pained gasping next to him.

'Stick in there, mate!' Danny shouted.

But his voice was cut short by a sudden explosion.

The ordnance had come from the sky. Danny had just caught the trail, as clear as tracer fire through his NV. It had landed precisely in the centre of the camp, mere metres from the location of Abu Rai'd's tent. There was a blinding blast of white light, and the ground itself shuddered violently as a shock wave emanated from the epicentre of the hit. A wave of intense heat followed, then the sound of falling shrapnel surrounded them. Through the noise, Danny could faintly hear screaming: the blind, agonised screaming of men who were on the brink of death and wished they could hurry it along. He peered out from under the thermal sheeting and saw, glowing in the green haze of his NV, a scene of utter devastation.

The entire camp was ablaze. Every tent was burning and so too were several of the militants, who were running around in unspeakable agony. The technicals had been overturned, and there were hunks of burning metal as close as 30 metres away from the OP. Suddenly, as though someone had turned the volume down, the screaming stopped and the flailing, burning figures fell still. Danny could tell at a single glance that there would be nobody left alive down there.

And a single thought rang in his head. *We left our radios broadcasting a GPS signal on two warm bodies. Someone thinks we're still down there. That strike was meant for us.*

Shrapnel had stopped falling now, but the impact had kicked up a great sand cloud which was still swirling around them. And it was through the hazy filter of this cloud that Danny saw the drone. It was hovering maybe 50 metres above the camp, an indistinct green blotch in his field of view. It seemed to be concentrating at first on the area in the very centre of the camp, but after about ten seconds it started to spiral outwards. Sinister. Quiet. Covering the whole area systematically.

'Don't move,' Danny breathed. 'There's a UAV up there looking for us.' He didn't know if Spud was listening or could understand. But he did know he had to keep talking to his mate to give him the best chance of staying conscious. He closed the gap so that they were completely covered by the thermal sheeting.

'We have to keep under the sheeting. They'll have thermal imaging. That's why we left our radios on the dead bodies.'

'I ... I can't breathe ... *can't ... breathe ...*'

Silence. Just the distant flickering of flames in the demolished training camp.

Danny gingerly peered out from under the thermal sheeting. The sand cloud had cleared and, so far as he could tell, the drone was no longer in the vicinity.

His mind was spinning. *Abu Ra'id name-checked Hammerstone.*

Spud's breath was coming quicker. Shallower. He needed immediate attention, but Danny didn't dare move. Not just yet. He kept talking, doing his best to keep the anger from surging.

'We should have known,' he said. 'That's why they sent us out here on our own. This isn't a two-man job, but it's easier to kill two guys than a whole fucking squadron. And they wanted us out of the way if – or when – we found out the *one* thing they didn't want us to know.'

A pause. Spud was trying to say something. 'Hammerstone ...' he breathed weakly. 'Working ... with Abu Ra'id.'

Another silence.

'*Don't fucking leave me here ...*'

A secondary explosion suddenly filled the air – some kind of ordnance down in the camp that made the two men start as it ignited.

More thoughts spun through Danny's head as he hunkered down again. If Hammerstone was running Abu Ra'id, if it was an *official* thing, would it *matter* if Danny and Spud knew about it? They were buttoned up with the Official Secrets Act anyway. But if it was only one of them, maybe two, and they were keeping their little game secret from the others ...

He left the thought hanging, as a sinister, rattling sound came from Spud's chest. He peered out again.

The drone had gone, and he knew none of the militants could

have survived that hit. Danny's focus now was his friend. He pushed away the thermal sheeting and the hessian cover, then gently rolled Spud on to his side so he could see his back. His clothes were wet with blood. Danny took his knife and sliced the clothes open to get access to the entry wound. But as one half of his brain concentrated on Spud, the other was working away in the backround.

If one of the Hammerstone group was cosy with Abu Ra'id, they might have been behind the London bombings . . .

Concentrate. Danny knew it had been an AK-47 that had hit Spud. That meant that the entry wound the size of his fingernail had come from a .762 short. The bleeding wasn't as bad as it could have been, but there was a more serious issue. The position of the entry wound in the lower back and Spud's struggled gasping suggested that the round had become lodged in his left lung. And it sounded like the lung was collapsing.

'Agony . . .' Spud managed to say. Then, more quietly, 'Morphine . . .'

'No can do, mate.' Morphine was a respiratory depressant. It would slow Spud's breathing down, which was the last thing he needed.

Danny rummaged in his bag for his med pack. He needed to keep his focus on Spud, but he coudn't help the faces of the four Hammerstone spooks appearing in his mind. The clearest of all of them, with his absurdly handsome features and cold, calculating stare, was the man Danny hated more than anyone else in the world: Buckingham.

If one of them was worried we might learn they were involved in the bombing, no wonder they want us dead.

First things first. Stop the air escaping from the lung.

He removed a waterproof adhesive patch and stuck it carefully over the entry wound. Spud's body jolted when the patch made contact, but he didn't shout out. Danny knew he was barely conscious. And if he didn't stop the lung collapsing, his mate only had minutes to live.

But it was going to hurt.

There were two cannulas in his med pack. Hollow, wide-bore needles, four or five inches long, with a soft plastic casing and a valve at one end. Danny took one of the cannulas, then rolled Spud on to his back and ripped open his clothes to gain access to his rib cage. Spud's thorax was rising and falling in short, sharp bursts as he tried to breathe. But with only one working lung, he was struggling badly. Danny's fingers traced the left-hand side of his rib cage. The lower rib felt broken, but it was the gap between the ribs that Danny was interested in. He held the point of the cannula against the ridge between the two lower ribs.

'Sorry, buddy,' he breathed. 'This will be bad.'

With a single, firm movement, he pushed.

The needle slid easily through the skin and into the centre of Spud's left lung. Spud's back arched slightly and his limbs shook with the sudden pain. No shouts, though. Spud just didn't have the breath for it. Danny felt sweat dripping into his eyes. He wiped it away, then turned his attention back to the cannula. Slowly, carefully, he eased the needle out of Spud's abdomen, leaving only a couple of inches of the plastic coating sticking out of the body.

Spud's face was pale and screwed-up with agony, but his breathing eased slightly, which told Danny he had stopped the bad lung from collapsing completely. But there was still a .762 in there, and the lung cavity could fill with blood any moment. This was a serious wound. It needed proper medical care. But there was no one around to give it. Except Danny.

Danny realised his hands were covered with Spud's blood. He looked over towards the smoking wreckage of the training camp, then back down at his injured mate. He tried to assess his options. Spud was in a shit state. He needed a medic. But Danny couldn't call for one because their radios would have been destroyed in the drone strike.

The drone strike. Even if they *could* call in their position, it would simply invite another attack. Because someone had just used the GPS signal beaming from their radios as a marker for a Hellfire missile. Someone had just tried to kill Danny and Spud after they'd confirmed Abu Ra'id was dead. Then a drone had hovered over the impact site to make sure nobody was escaping. But Danny and Spud had managed to hide from the drone. Which meant that whoever had just tried to kill them most likely thought that they'd succeeded.

Danny looked at his blood-soaked hands again. For someone supposedly dead in the hostile wilds of the Yemeni desert, he at least was very much alive.

Unlike Spud. Danny felt his blood temperature rising. Thanks to Hammerstone, they were stuck in the middle of nowhere, and his mate was on the brink.

NINETEEN

There were five of them in the room.

Tessa Gorman, Home Secretary, looked at each of the other four in turn. With the exception of Hugo Buckingham, who was as well presented as always, they looked tired. Victoria Atkinson had dark bags under her eyes and, unless Gorman was mistaken, dried milk on the lapel of her tweed jacket. Piers Chamberlain's usually immaculate comb-over was ruffled. Harrison Maddox wasn't even wearing a suit, but had arrived in a plum-coloured jumper with leather elbow pads, almost as though he was making a point about the lateness of the hour.

'Well?' Gorman asked briskly. 'Let's hear it.'

Atkinson cleared her throat. 'Abu Ra'id is dead, Home Secretary,' she said.

Silence. Gorman closed her eyes and inhaled slowly.

'You're sure?'

'Quite sure.'

'Where?' she asked.

'Yemen, Home Secretary. Two operatives from 22SAS were in-country.'

'You've had confirmation from them?'

Atkinson nodded. 'Yes, but they unfortunately didn't make it out alive. Abu Ra'id was hiding in an Al-Shabaab training camp. The Yemeni administration clearly got wind of it at the same

295

time as us. They launched a drone strike while our people were on the ground.'

The Home Secretary looked at Harrison Maddox. 'Your people should never have sold them those things.'

'Impossible to predict an event like this, Home Secretary,' Maddox said.

'We can keep those details from the press, of course, depending on how you want to present it,' Atkinson said.

Keep it from the press? And let Yemen take the credit? Out of the question. She was sick of opening up the newspapers and reading a barrage of criticism regarding *her* failure to extradite this hate-spouting cleric. If she could intimate that the British government was involved, it could be worth another term in office, and all thanks to her. You never know, she might even get a crack at the Exchequer. 'I think the public deserves to know when a soldier dies defending our liberty,' she said.

'Can't mention 22, of course,' Chamberlain said. 'We can name-check their parent regiments. That's the way we do things.'

Gorman was barely listening. She felt as though a weight had been lifted from her shoulders. 'This is excellent news,' she said. '*Excellent* news. There's no doubt that he was behind the bombings?'

'None at all, Home Secretary,' Buckingham said.

'So I can tell the PM that we have our man?'

'Absolutely.'

'Good. *Good.*' She looked around the room. 'There'll be honours for this, ladies and gentelemen. I'll see to it myself.' She stood up and headed briskly for the door. But before exiting, she stopped and turned. She picked out Hugo Buckingham. 'These two soldiers,' she said. 'Friends of yours, weren't they?'

Buckingham bowed his head slightly. 'In a manner of speaking, Home Secretary,' he said.

'I'm very sorry for your loss.'

'Thank you, Home Secretary,' said Buckingham. 'They were good men. I know they'd appreciate the sentiment.'

Gorman nodded. Then she turned and left the room. It had been a hell of a couple of weeks, but things were looking up and she couldn't wait to get on the phone to the PM and tell him the good news.

00.00hrs GMT

Clara was woken by the wind. It howled bitterly as the rain thudded against her bedroom window. She sat up quickly in the darkness, sweating.

It was a relief to be awake. Her dreams had been troubled. She had seen herself by the bedside of dying children, both here and in a faraway country. She had seen Danny too, his face dirty and his clothes torn. She couldn't shake the feeling that he was in some kind of trouble.

She felt for the glass of water by her bed. But before her fingers touched the glass, there was a noise. A single bang. It sounded like a door slamming shut.

She froze, clutching the bedclothes. Her eyes turned towards her bedroom door. Had the sound come from her own flat? The thought made the fine hairs on her arm stand up.

It's just the wind, she told herself. Nothing more. She reached for her water again and took a sip.

The second bang came as she was settling down on her pillow. She clenched her eyes shut and didn't move, dread creeping through her limbs. But then the wind howled again. That's all it was, she reminded herself. The wind.

She forced herself out of bed. She was naked, so she groped in the darkness for the dressing gown on the back of her bedroom door. The cord was missing – she'd used it to hold up her hair while she was having a bath – so she held the front of the dressing gown together with one hand while she crept out of the bedroom to check the rest of her flat.

It was the kitchen door that had been banging, she soon realised. She'd left the kitchen window open after burning the toast she'd grabbed for supper. As she shut the window, she saw her hand was shaking slightly with relief. She poured some milk into a cup and warmed it in the microwave. Then she moved into the front room, cup in one hand, hem of her dressing gown in the other.

She hadn't closed the curtains before going to bed. Rain was lashing against the window. She stepped up to it, her eyes fixed on the blurred glare of the yellow street lamp on the other side of the road. Her breath misted the window as she looked out, barely able to see across the road for the rain sluicing down the window pane.

She blinked.

At first she thought her eyes were deceiving her. Visibility was poor, and after all, who would be standing out in *this* weather? But as she stepped to the left, away from the misted area, she saw it clearly: a figure, standing in the rain under the street lamp. He – or she – had on a heavy coat with a hood. Rain dripped from the front of the hood, and the figure's features were hidden. But he was looking towards Clara's house. Motionless. Untroubled by the elements.

For ten seconds, neither Clara nor the watcher moved. Then Clara stepped backwards. She was barely able to control her limbs. The dread had seeped back into them and she found herself short of breath.

She put her milk down on a coffee table, then hurried back into her bedroom. Under the bedclothes, she considered calling the police, but quickly rejected that idea. They'd tell her she was over-reacting. That the person she had seen had every right to be where he was. *Don't be so stupid*, she told herself. *You're over-reacting. Look again and he'll have moved on. He wasn't watching you. Of* course *he wasn't.*

Why would he be watching you?

A tight knot of panic hung in Danny's stomach. Spud was flitting in and out of consciousness. Right now, his eyes were rolling. His breathing sounded a little better, but it was impossible to tell what was going on inside his lung cavity. Danny kept him in the recovery position while he desperately tried to work out his next move.

Moving Spud was almost impossible. A tab across desert terrain on hard rations and scant water was tough enough for an able-bodied soldier. For Spud it was out of the question.

But they *had* to move. Whoever had sent that drone in thought they were dead. If they found out otherwise, they'd want to finish the job off, and it wouldn't take long to locate them, especially with Spud in this state. And the chances of them surviving another hit were zero.

He'd considered going to see if one of the technicals from the training camp was still operational. But a single glance at the burning, twisted hunks of metal dotted around the camp told him that was a no-go, and any fuel down there would have burned up in the strike, no question.

Maybe he should leave Spud. His chances of survival were slim, in any case. But Danny quickly rejected that idea. You stuck by your mates. No matter what.

His mind turned to the abandoned Toyota. It was almost out of juice, but at least he could use it to get them away from the blast site before working out his next move. He didn't like the idea. Firstly it would mean leaving Spud alone while he went to fetch it. Secondly, if the Toyota wasn't found in the vicinity, it might suggest to someone that they'd escaped. But it seemed like his only choice.

04.10. The flames had subsided in the burning, devastated camp. Danny prepared to trek towards the Toyota. He took his spotting scope and scanned the surrounding area. As he did so, he saw movement to the north-west. Distance, about a kilo-metre, maybe slightly less. Headlamps approaching.

Danny re-evaluated. He knew dead bodies always attract parasites. Sometimes those parasites take human form. He re-camouflaged himself and Spud in the OP, and carefully watched this new arrival through his scope. The vehicle stopped 30 metres from the edge of the camp. Two men emerged. They wore traditional Arab robes and headdresses. One of them carried a long-barrelled rifle. From here it looked rather like an old-fashioned musket. The vehicle, so far as Danny could tell from this distance, looked in pretty poor shape – an old Land Rover, dented and rickety.

'Bedouin,' he breathed. Here to scavenge over the bomb site.

More options had suddenly opened out. He could nail these two newcomers and nick their vehicle. Head north over the Saudi border, a journey of about 100 kilometres. Danny gave that a moment's thought. He had mapping of the area and could easily find their route. But he was a stranger in a hostile land. His mate was badly wounded. What if they ran out of fuel, or needed water, or medical supplies? Much better, he decided, to have some locals on the payroll.

Option two: for a price, Danny reckoned these two could be persuaded to offer a taxi service. Maybe they knew somewhere Danny could get medical help. Failing that, perhaps they could find someone with an aircraft. That way Danny could get them out of the area and stand a fighting chance of getting Spud some proper medical attention. He made a quick calculation in his head. They had $2000 each, minus the 500 Danny had given their tout. Hardly a fortune. But enough, perhaps.

Decision made.

He needed to move quickly. It was 15 minutes since the Hellfire had hit. These two were the first on the scene, but there would be others, and soon. Not to mention that two Regiment guys presumed dead in action would raise alarm bells in Hereford and Whitehall. There was a good chance of a unit being airlifted in to destroy any evidence of Danny and Spud ever having been in-country. If they found them here, alive and well, whoever had just tried to kill them would surely be tempted to give it a second shot. No. For now staying 'dead' was their best – their only – option.

Spud groaned. 'I'll be back in a minute, mucker,' Danny said.

He emerged slowly from the OP. It was still thickly covered with sand from the explosion. He engaged his rifle, pressing the butt deep into his shoulder and aiming it at the two locals who were now treading carefully towards one of the burning tents. Distance: 60 metres. Danny was clearly unobserved. These two men seemed to have nothing on their minds except looting – though what they thought they could extract from this smouldering wreckage was anyone's guess. They stood by the gently flapping remnants of a tent, silhouetted against the glowing ash. Even when Danny was ten metres away, his weapon trained directly on the two men, they failed to notice him.

'*Salam*,' Danny called.

The two men spun round instantly. The guy with the musket started to raise his weapon, but instantly lowered it again when he saw that Danny had them at gunpoint. He was an elderly guy with a grizzled beard and hard, suspicious eyes. His companion was younger, but had similar features. They looked like father and son.

'Drop the gun,' Danny said. And then, when it became clear that the old guy hadn't understood him, he repeated himself slowly. 'Drop ... the ... gun.'

Unsmiling, the old guy laid his weapon at his feet.

'Bedouin?' he asked.

The old man nodded without expression.

Good. The Bedouin were wanderers. They travelled across the desert with no respect for boundaries or borders. In the books Danny had read as a kid he had learned that they traditionally travelled on foot or by camel, but times had changed and so had the Bedouin. Some of them had cars now. Danny pointed at the Bedouin's rickety old vehicle. 'Medicine,' he said. 'My friend needs medicine.'

The Bedouin looked blankly at him.

Danny cursed under his breath, then tried again. 'Saudi?' he suggested. 'You take me and my friend to Saudi?' He risked lowering his gun, then spread out his arms to indicate an aircraft. 'I need to find someone with a plane. You understand that? A plane?' He removed some of the cash he had stashed away and waved a hundred-dollar bill under the old guy's nose. That got his interest. 'Saudi,' he repeated.

The two Bedouin conferred for a moment. But only a moment. The older guy turned back to them, pointed at the note and then held up two fingers.

'No way, buddy,' Danny said. Right now, their cash was more valuable to him than his weapons. Much easier to buy their way out of the desert, than shoot their way out. 'That's all you get.'

The Bedouin shook his finger. '*Itneyn*,' he said. *Two*.

Danny swore again and removed another note. It did the trick. A smile spread across the older guy's face to reveal a mouthful of missing teeth, hitting Danny with a blast of halitosis that almost knocked him down. 'Saudi,' the man said in a croaky, lizardy voice. '*Asdiqa*.'

It was an Arabic word Danny understood. It meant 'friends'.

The Bedouins' smiles had quickly disappeared when they saw Spud. Having driven their vehicle up to the OP, they watched uncertainly as Danny pulled his mate up to his feet, taking care not to dislodge the cannula sticking out of his rib cage, then put Spud's arm round his neck and held him upright. Spud was having a moment of lucidity. 'Don't . . . don't leave me,' he whispered.

'You've got to walk ten metres. Can you do it?'

It took a full minute, with Danny supporting Spud as he made micro-steps towards the vehicle. It took another two minutes to get him laid out on the back seat, lying on his side. Danny fetched their bags and weapons, shoved them into the Land Rover, then perched uncomfortably on the edge of the seat and held his mate in place.

'Let's go,' he told the Bedouin.

The vehicle stank of animal shit and petrol. The back seats were hard, uncomfortable. The young guy drove. Spud lost consciousness again as they headed north. Danny's thoughts turned to Abu Ra'id. He checked his pockets for the black data stick. It was still intact, and Danny realised he *had* to find out what was on it. Then he saw the young Bedouin man eyeing him in the rear-view mirror. He tucked the data stick back in his pocket and gave his new companion a cool look.

They travelled in silence. Danny wished he could discuss their situation with Spud. His thoughts were so half-formed. Could it *really* be the case that Abu Ra'id was in league with Hammerstone? What would any of the four members of the security services plausibly have to gain from terror hits of such grotesque magnitude in the middle of London?

London. It seemed like half a world away as Danny looked through the window of the bleak, parched, night-time desert terrain. It *was* half a world away. He found he missed its pan-icked, rain-hammered streets. A picture popped into his head of himself and Clara, walking down one of those streets a few nights previously.

Clara.

A sickness twisted in his gut, like he'd been punched. He swore at himself for not thinking about her earlier. Because if they – whoever they were – had tried to kill him, Clara's life was surely in danger too. He knew how these people worked. How they *thought*. Danny hadn't mentioned splitting up with Clara to anyone. They would automatically assume that he might have mentioned something to her – spilled the beans about the nature of his trip to Yemen, expressed some kind of suspicion.

And these were suspicions that somebody, somewhere *really* didn't want to be common knowledge. They would go to any ends to keep them quiet.

As the Land Rover trundled over the bumpy desert ground, he realised he had to do the one thing you must *never* do when you're trying to stay off the grid: make contact with someone.

And he realised something else. He *had* to get back to the UK. Quickly. There was no way Spud would be able to make that journey. At some point, no matter how badly Spud begged him not to go, Danny would have to leave him.

'How far to the Saudi border?' Spud directed his question at the old Bedouin man. But he just gave one of his toothless grins, nodded foolishly and repeated the word 'Saudi'.

The unease in Danny's gut doubled. He hoped to God this old boy knew where he was going.

05.45hrs AST
Sunrise.

The desert seemed to glow in orange and pink. There was a settlement of some kind about 500 metres up ahead. The Bedouin were clearly heading for it.

'Hold it right there,' Danny said. And when the younger man driving failed to take his foot off the gas, he raised his handgun. 'Stop!'

The vehicle came to a sudden halt. Danny pointed through the windscreen. 'Where are we going?'

The Bedouin man grinned. '*Asdiqa*,' he said. *Friends.*

Danny looked down at Spud. His breathing was a little more regular, though his face was still creased with pain. Danny stepped out of the car and scanned the area ahead through his scope. The buildings were low, single-storey, and made of mud-baked walls. He counted six of them, though there could have been more hidden from his view. There were also three tents made of a dark, brown canvas. Two meagre camels were tied to a post, and in the centre of the settlement was what appeared to be a well. A bent old woman in black robes was pumping water from it into a plastic container.

He got back in the car and nodded at Spud to indicate that he thought it looked okay. The driver set off again. Danny noticed that the old boy kept glancing at him in the rear-view mirror with his stony eyes. '*Asdiqa*,' he repeated, quite unnecessarily. *Friends.*

'I get the message, pal,' Danny muttered. He wasn't at all convinced by his claims of friendship – not least because he'd paid this fucker two hundred bucks to get them to an airfield, and this was a piece-of-shit village in the middle of nowhere.

By the time they reached the settlement, more people had emerged from the nearest building: three men, who stood in a line, staring at the new arrivals with undisguised suspicion. Danny examined each one. They didn't appear to be armed. True, they could have concealed weapons beneath their robes, but there were no bulges or awkward stances. He looked around. Featureless desert terrain as far as he could see. Open ground that made exit strategies limited. The Land Rover came to a halt ten metres from where the three men were standing.

Danny climbed out of the vehicle again. The sight of this armed SAS man – his boots visible under his robes, NV goggles still on his forehead and a bag slung over his shoulders – had a marked effect on the men. Their stony faces suddenly changed to expressions of alarm, even anger. They started shouting questions in Arabic at Danny and Spud's companions. Danny held back as the old Bedouin man walked towards the trio, arms held up in a calming gesture. He started talking quickly while Danny remained by the Land Rover, clutching his rifle.

A couple of minutes of animated conversation followed. Danny became aware of more people emerging from the various buildings of this settlement – women and children mostly, clearly curious about these unexpected arrivals. They hung back in the heart of the settlement, watching quietly.

The old Bedouin man turned and walked back towards them. He was accompanied by one of the three men, an unsavoury-looking guy with one eye that pointed off in the wrong direction. He pointed to himself. 'Yasser,' he said by way of introduction.

Danny nodded, but didn't offer his own name.

'American?' asked Yasser.

'Yes,' Danny replied. 'American.'

'I know man with airplane,' Yasser said. 'Three hours from here. We go tonight.'

'Not tonight,' Danny said. 'Now.'

Yasser grinned at this hilarious suggestion. 'Not now,' he said, waving his index finger. 'Too dangerous. Tonight. You pay me.'

'I already paid him.' Danny pointed at the old Bedouin guy.

Yasser gave an apologetic tilt of his head. But he clearly wasn't going to yield.

'How much?'

Yasser's eyes narrowed. He pointed at the NV goggles that Danny still had resting on his head. 'You give me those,' he said.

Danny gave that a moment's thought. Truth was that their gear was worth less to them than their money. 'Okay,' he said. 'But not till we get there. And any funny business . . .' He held up his rifle meaningfully.

Yasser smiled again and his wonky eye seemed to roll. 'No funny business,' he said, chuckling. 'No funny business . . .'

12.00hrs AST

They had offered Danny and Spud an outbuilding by way of shelter from the sun while they waited for nightfall. But there was no way Danny was going to enclose themselves among these people they hardly knew and trusted even less. Instead, he laid Spud down in the scant shade of the Land Rover, his weapon close at hand, accepting water in a wooden bowl on an hourly basis from the old woman they'd seen drawing it from the well, and doing what he could to get some down Spud's neck. The brutal midday heat drew the liquid out of their bodies as fast as they replenished it, but at least here they had a full view of the settlement, and of any threats that might emerge. The old woman had looked at Spud with a critically maternal eye. Minutes later she had brought him a wet cloth to place across his forehead. It wouldn't make any difference, of course, but Danny gave her a nod of thanks. And Spud stayed remarkably stable, given his circumstances.

When he wasn't tending to his mate, Danny had spent the morning scanning the sky. In the bright, clear sunlight there was a chance of catching the metallic glint of a drone high overhead. So far, nothing – but that didn't mean they weren't being watched.

Was he being paranoid? Maybe the drone strike had just been a fuck-up. A blue on blue. Wouldn't be the first time. But he knew that wasn't the case. Someone meant to kill them, in case they'd found out the truth about Abu Ra'id.

But who? He found his thoughts drifting to Harrison Maddox, the Yank in Hammerstone. He remembered when they'd all met for the first time, the way Maddox had spoken to the others. Like he was pissed-off with the British for not going the Guantanamo route. Was it possible that the Yanks were bank-rolling Abu Ra'id? A couple of spectaculars in London just to get the Brits back on side in the war on terror. And now that the job had been done, they'd roped a couple of stooges into nailing the fucker before wiping their fingerprints off the crime scene with a drone strike? It would be fucked up, but Danny knew enough of the way the world worked to know governments had justified worse things to themselves.

He remembered being stuck in the car with Buckingham.

Remembered the poison he'd started dripping in Danny's ears about Harrison Maddox. *Plenty of rumours circulating in the Firm. Not beyond the CIA's capacity to get into bed with the right sort of terrorists, you know, if it suits their purpose. Keep everyone on their toes, and if the occasional atrocity reminds their allies why they're fighting a war on terror, well, who's counting?*

He tried to rid his head of Buckingham's voice. But it wouldn't leave him. *Not the only one of our American cousins who takes a dim view of our government's sudden change of heart with respect to supporting the Americans' intervenionist foreign policy.*

Or maybe it was one of the others. Danny stared into the distance as he remembered something else Buckingham said. About Victoria Atkinson, and how she ran an intelligence station in Riyadh, back in the day. How she'd met her husband out there. And how she'd gone AWOL for six months in the middle of her stint. Could she have been radicalised in that time? She'd come back with an Arabic boyfriend, married him, you could guess the rest . . .

Caused a bit of gossip behind her back over at Thames House. Nasty. Not as if having a Muslim husband is a handicap, eh? Sure he's been thoroughly vetted. Clean as a whistle . . .

Then there was Chamberlain. He remembered what Buckingham had told him about the former Regiment man keeping some funny company. Nutcases who wanted to transfer power to the army if and when Islamic extremism got out of control. *Not too many people take them very seriously, naturally, but they're a vocal minority and recent events haven't exactly harmed their argument.* Could Chamberlain have roped Abu Ra'id into helping things along a bit?

Maddox. Atkinson. Chamberlain. It seemed they all had a motive for aligning themselves with Abu Ra'id. But their motives were all different, which fitted with Danny's instinct that Abu Ra'id's connection was not to Hammerstone as a group, but to an individual member.

And what of Buckingham? Had he chosen Danny and Spud for this mission because he thought he could control them? Had he fed Danny all that information about the other three to divert his suspicions? Was Buckingham – greasy, self-serving, treacherous Buckingham – capable of encouraging Abu Ra'id to carry out these attacks, then despatching Danny and Spud to kill him so he could mop up all the glory?

Deep down, Danny knew the answer to that: that Hugo Buckingham was capable of just about anything.

He pulled the data stick from his pocket again. Did it hold any answers? He had to find out.

11.00hrs GMT
Clara was glad to be on the late shift. After her broken night staring at figures through the window of the front room, she had slept in and only crawled out from under the duvet at midday. She had shaken off the night terrors now, and was pulling on her raincoat. Her shift would take her through till midnight. She was glad of that. She wanted to be out of the house.

As she stepped into the rain, she glanced towards the lamp post opposite the house. There was nobody there. She felt foolish for being scared last night.

She had planned to walk to the hospital, but as she approached the Edgware Road, the rain became even heavier and she decided to take a bus. They, at least, were running, even if the Underground was still down. There was a 332 approaching the bus stop. She picked up her pace and ran towards it. A taxi honked her as she hurried across the road, then splashed her as it passed. Her lower legs were soaked, and she felt bedraggled as she knocked on the already closed door of the bus, mouthing at the driver to open up and let her in. He pretended not to see her, and the bus drove off.

'Thanks!' she shouted after him. '*Thanks very . . .*'

She fell silent.

He was standing on the other side of the Edgware Road, beneath the canopy of a small shop that sold cheap electronics. His hood was up and his face obscured. He didn't move, but there was no doubt in Clara's mind that he was watching her.

She had been warm from running. Now she was icy cold. A tiny part of her brain told her that she should run across the road and confront him. But that part of her brain was overruled by good sense.

She turned and ran, her flat shoes flapping in the puddles, the rain soaking her face, and dripping down her neck.

18.50hrs AST
Sunset.

The woman had spent the afternoon baking flat bread on hot stones. She offered some to Danny, along with a bowl of tough goat stew. Or maybe it was camel. It tasted like shit, but he chucked it down his throat anyway. It was fuel, and he couldn't run on empty. He didn't risk trying to feed Spud, though. His mate was too weak to swallow solids, so he just continued to trickle water down his throat.

When he had finished eating, Yasser approached with a kid who he introduced as his son. The boy couldn't take his eyes off Danny's weapons, but he seemed harmless enough. Yasser was a different matter. He chewed as he walked, and Danny instantly recognised the spaced-out look on his face. His wonky eye looked even wonkier. Danny controlled the now-familiar surge of anger, and suppressed an irrational desire to nail him and take his vehicle. But if he did that, he'd never find Yasser's mate with the plane. Danny needed this guy's intel, not his driving skills.

'Let's get . . . out of here,' a weak voice said, 'before they . . . ask us to . . . fucking dance.' Danny looked at Spud and grinned. His mate's eyes were open, just. He was a tough little sod.

'We're going to find you some proper help, mate,' he said.

But Spud had closed his eyes again, and didn't respond.

Of course, Danny wanted to get moving too. The longer they stayed in one place, the easier they were to find. Yasser refuelled the Land Rover from an old jerry can, sloshing a good proportion of the fuel over the desert floor, then invited them to take their seats in the back. Easier said than done. It took five minutes to get the semi-conscious Spud back into the Land Rover again. But as soon as he was in place, and Danny had loaded himself and the gear up, they were on the move again.

They travelled faster than the previous night. The khat-addled Yasser was heavier on the gas than their previous chauffeur. Danny had to tell him to ease off – the faster they went, the bumpier the journey, which was no good for Spud. Sweat-soaked and sand-stained, Danny gazed into the desert night, scanning for strange lights from one window, occasionally checking Spud's pulse. It was weak, but regular – unlike his breathing, which had started to become more erratic again.

Two hours passed in silence. The lights, when they came, came from straight ahead.

Yasser slammed on the brakes. Spud groaned as his body jolted forwards. The driver looked over his shoulder. The khat seemed to have worn off. He looked sharper now.

'You have money?' he demanded.

'Why?'

Yasser pointed at the blinding headlamps 15 metres up ahead. Two figures had emerged from the car in front. Their silhouettes were approaching.

Suddenly, the headlamps went dark. Danny blinked heavily as his eyes adjusted. The figures were alongside the car now. Yasser opened his window to talk to one of them. Danny glimpsed a *shemagh* round the man's head, and a weapon slung round his neck.

Fight or pay? Danny's money was certainly precious. But to leave a trail of bodies would be a marker that they'd passed through this way. And besides, who knew what the darkness was hiding. With Spud out of action, Danny could be taking on more than he could manage. He pulled another 100-dollar bill out and handed it to Yasser. Yasser clicked his fingers to indicate that he needed another, which Danny reluctantly gave him.

Conversation in the front. Not friendly. But efficent. Yasser handed over the cash, and the two self-appointed toll merchants stepped back. Yasser moved off again, driving round the vehicle that was still bang in front of them. Danny engaged his NV and looked around. Fifty metres on either side he saw the green glow of five other trucks, with human figures standing round them.

Looked like he'd made the right call.

'How much further?' he growled.

'We cross the Saudi border in ten minutes,' Yasser said. 'Then, a half hour. Be patient, my friend. You will be there very soon.'

TWENTY

They called it an airfield. That was generous. It was little more than a flat run of hard-baked earth, three miles west of a barely used highway in southern Saudi Arabia, with a tiny breeze-block building at one end.

But it *did* have an aircraft.

Danny stood by the Land Rover and surveyed it from a distance of 500 metres through the NV he was shortly to give up to Yasser. It looked like an old Cessna 172. Single-engine. High fixed wing. Nothing to write home about. But good enough. He looked at the building. There was an old saloon car parked up outside it, which suggested to him that there was somebody inside. Other than that, nothing.

If Spud had been okay, now would have been the time to ditch Yasser and the kid and approach on foot. But Spud wasn't walking anywhere. He turned to Yasser, who was still behind the wheel. 'Kill the lights. I'm going to walk, you're going to drive next to me. *Very* slowly, so the engine doesn't make a big noise. Understand?'

Yasser nodded.

'If you try to drive away without me, I'll shoot out your tyres, then I'll shoot you and your boy.'

Another nod, more nervous this time.

Danny raised his rifle and surveyed the building through the sight. No movement. No personnel as far as he could see. He

313

kept the rifle raised as he started walking across the open ground, the vehicle creeping along beside him.

Five minutes later, they were 250 metres out. Still no movement, no sign of life. Yasser was doing a good job of keeping close, slow and quiet.

A hundred metres out.

Fifty.

Danny stopped and held up one hand. The Land Rover came to a halt. Danny scanned the area again for threats. Nothing. It was dead quiet. He walked round to the passenger side of the Land Rover, opened the door and pulled out Yasser's kid.

'You stay here with my friend,' Danny told Yasser. 'Only drive up when I give you the sign.'

Yasser was sweating profusely. 'My son . . .' he said.

'He'll be fine, so long as you do what I say.'

Danny nudged the kid towards the building with the point of his rifle. The boy was trembling and looked like he might shit himself. But that was fine by Danny. It would keep him on message.

They covered the final 50 metres in about a minute. All the while, Danny had the back of the kid's head and the building in his sights. He kept scanning for movement. There was none.

As they came within 20 metres of the building its finer details came into view, not that there were many. A wooden door on the near side, a tumbledown shack on the other that looked like an outdoor toilet. Danny grabbed the kid by one shoulder and pushed him to the ground. 'Lie down,' he said. 'Don't move.'

The terrified boy did as he was told. Danny left him cringing on the desert floor as he completed a circuit of the building to check there were no other exits. No personnel they hadn't seen as they approached. The toilet shack stank of shit, but was empty. Elsewhere, the stench of aviation gas hung in the air. Danny approached the main door. Slowly, he reached out and turned the door handle. It was unlocked. He engaged his NV, pulled his Sig, and quietly opened the door and stepped inside.

He heard the occupant of the building before he saw him. His snores resonated around the shabby, cramped single room. There was an old stove at one end, a cluttered desk with a blinking laptop, the outline of what looked like a large mobile phone, and a low bunk along the far wall, where the snoring was coming from. Danny stepped quietly up to it. A man lay there, fully dressed and foul-smelling. He was very thin, and even in the dark Danny could make out his plainly East African features. Somali. Possibly Ethiopian.

He bent down and put one hand over the man's mouth.

His eyes shot open. Danny pressed his Sig against the man's forehead. 'You speak English?' he whispered.

The man nodded.

'Sit up very slowly.'

He removed his hand from the man's mouth and allowed him to sit up.

'You the pilot?'

Another nod.

'Sober?'

A shrug.

'Where's the nearest hospital.'

'Three hundred miles. Very bad road.'

Danny swore. He didn't think Spud had it in him to make that kind of journey.

'Can you get me and my friend to an international airport? No questions asked?' Because they were more likely to get medical help near a major airport.

'You have passports?'

'I'd rather not show them.'

The man's lips curled into a distasteful smile. 'For no questions asked, it will cost you,' he said.

Danny nodded, then stood up, pulling the man up with him. 'What's your name?'

The man gave him a steady look. 'Brian,' he said. Clearly a lie. 'I can take you to Addis Ababa. I know people there.'

Danny gave it a moment's thought. From Ethiopia, he would be able to get a flight to Paris. But Addis Ababa was a major hub. Chances were, their immigration systems would be up-to-date. Danny didn't *think* their passports would be tagged, not if the security services had them down as KIA. But the fewer up-to-date airports they presented their ID at, the better.

'Where else?' he demanded.

'Eritrea,' Brian said. 'Massawa Airport.'

Eritrea. Danny gave himself another moment to think. He knew there were rumours that the Eritreans were supplying Al-Shabaab with arms. Under the circumstances, it felt like a high-risk destination. But relations with the East African state and the West were strained. That meant the chances of them sharing immigration information were small.

'And do you "know" people at Massawa?' Danny breathed.

'Of course.'

'Can we get medical help there?'

'For a price. Who are you?'

Danny thought for another moment. 'Do they have flights to Europe?'

Brian shrugged again. 'Frankfurt, maybe.'

Germany. From there, he could hop a flight to southern Ireland. Sneak over the border and take a ferry to the mainland. Complicated, but it would avoid having to show his ID at a UK border. Because if anyone *was* still looking for him and Spud, *that* would be where security was tightest.

Hardly risk-free. The moment he presented himself at any international border he'd be looking over his shoulder. But there was unfinished business back home. He'd have to take some risks.

He led the man outside. The kid was still flat-out on the desert floor. Danny raised one arm in the direction of the Land Rover, which immediately started trundling towards them. He turned to face the pilot. 'How much?'

'Who did you kill?' Brian avoided the question.

'What do you mean?'

'People come to me, usually it's because they killed someone. So, who did you kill?'

'You, if you don't answer the question. How much to Eritrea?'

'A thousand.'

'That's too much. I don't have it.'

Brian thought for a moment. Then he pointed at Danny's rifle. 'You have other weapons?' he asked.

'Maybe.'

'Show me.'

Ordinarily, Danny would have stonewalled a request like that. But he and Spud only had $3,100 between them, and their weapons were fast becoming useless. Spud was past using them, and Danny would almost certainly have to ditch them before they got on to a commercial airline. He held up his Sig, then pointed out the fragmentation grenades, flashbangs and ammo in his ops waistcoat.

'Okay,' Brian said. 'And how much cash?'

'No cash,' Danny said, thinking on his feet. 'Weapons only.'

Brian shook his head, a sickly smile on his face.

'Fine,' Danny said. He put his Sig to Brian's head. 'I can fly a plane. I'll just kill you and take your aircraft.'

Brian's smile dropped. 'Wait,' he said quickly. 'Okay, no cash, just the weapons.'

'You don't lay a finger on them while we're still here,' Danny said. 'I leave them in your hut. They're yours when you get back.'

Brian nodded reluctantly as the Land Rover pulled up alongside them. He peered into the back passenger window and stared at Spud for a few seconds. 'Is he going to live?' he asked.

Danny gave him a cold stare, but didn't answer. 'Take him to the plane,' he told Yasser.

Two minutes later, Danny, Yasser and Brian were carefully lifting Spud out of the back seat of the Land Rover and into the Cessna. There were two seats at the rear of the cockpit. Danny laid Spud across them. His mate groaned sharply as Danny positioned him at a 45-degree angle, and his shallow breathing was now more of a hoarse rattle. He checked the cannula. It was still sticking out from Spud's rib cage, but the skin around it had turned several shades of red and yellow. It didn't look good. Danny knew that infection could set in at any moment. It would spread through Spud's weakened body in hours. He needed major surgery. He needed antibiotics. He needed everything Danny couldn't supply him with.

Once Spud was secured, Danny jumped back down off the Cessna where the others were waiting for him. He unloaded his gear from the Land Rover, then removed his NV goggles and handed them over to Yasser. Yasser looked immensely pleased as he gathered up his new toys in his arms. Less so when Danny pulled out his handgun and grabbed the Bedouin kid by a clump of his hair. He turned to Yasser. 'I've seen where you live,' he said. 'If you tell anybody about us, I'll come back.' He put the gun to the kid's head. 'Understood?'

The kid looked like he was about to scream. Yasser nodded his head violently, and his eyes spun like marbles in a glass.

'Get out of here,' Danny said.

They didn't need telling twice. Father and son scrambled back into the Land Rover and seconds later they screeched off.

'How long till we take off?' Danny asked Brian.

'I need a half hour,' Brian said, 'to check the plane.'

Danny gathered up their gear. 'The rounds from one of these rifles will puncture your fuel tank,' he said. 'You try to leave without me, that's what'll happen. I'm going to wait for you in the building. Call me when you're ready.'

Brian gave one of his laconic shrugs, then turned to his aircraft. Danny jogged towards, and entered, the hut. It still stank, even without Brian in it. He looked around in the darkness, his eyes resting on the cluttered desk. He knew what he was looking for.

The laptop looked old and bulky, but it was the handset next to it that attracted Danny's attention. It was three or four times the size of an ordinary mobile, with a chunky black aerial and – he could only just make this out – the word 'Iridium' in white lettering on the front. A sat phone.

He paused for a moment. He had a chance now to call Hereford. Get a casevac set up. Spud might stand a chance then. But he knew that wasn't really an option. Whoever had tried to kill them back at the training camp had gone to a lot of trouble. If they popped up on the grid now, they'd be dead men. It wasn't an option.

It took twenty seconds for the sat phone to power up. Its pale green screen glowed in the darkness as Danny punched in the code for the UK, followed by a number he knew well.

A pause. Then a ringtone.

Ten seconds passed.

Twenty.

A voice. Male. Groggy. Suspicious.

'Yeah?'

'Kyle, it's me.'

Silence.

'What the f . . .'

'Shut up and listen to me carefully. There's a couple of grand hidden in my flat. Some of it's in dollars, but if you do what I say, it's yours. I'll tell you where it is now. And when I get back, I'll sort out your problem with the Poles. That's a promise.'

Danny could hear him lighting up a cigarette at the other end of the phone.

'Back from where?' his brother asked.

'Away. I can't talk for long. It's Clara.'

'Yeah, the posh bitch. What about her?'

He sounded shifty. Danny didn't know why.

'I think she's in danger. I want you to go to her. Take her somewhere safe till I get in touch again. Use the money if you have to. Find a B and B in Wales or somewhere.'

Another pause.

'Don't be so fucking stupid,' Kyle said.

'What do you mean?'

'I mean, don't be so fucking stupid. Like that blonde bitch is going to waltz away with me just because I say she should. Fuck's *sake*.' Kyle's voice grew fainter. He sounded like he was hanging up.

'Wait,' Danny hissed. 'Kyle, *wait!*'

Silence.

'What?'

'Tell her this,' Danny breathed. 'Tell her, I'll stop remembering the things I want to forget. She'll understand.'

More silence. And then, a cynical laugh. 'Pass me the fucking puke bag.'

Danny mastered the anger that was rising in him. Even from a distance of thousands of miles, Kyle could wind him up. 'Listen to me, Kyle,' he breathed. 'Do this and your problems are sorted. But if you don't, trust me, you'll wish the Poles had got to you first.'

The laughter died away. Danny could picture his brother's hard, avaricious features.

'Where's the money?' he said.

'The wardrobe in my bedroom. Under the floor.'

'Key?'

'You'll have to break in. It doesn't matter. And Kyle, at some point in the next twenty-four hours, someone might tell you I'm dead. Don't tell them I'm not.'

Kyle fell quiet again. When he did speak, he sounded somehow more subdued. 'You in trouble?' he said.

More than you can possibly imagine, Danny thought. But he said: 'Keep her safe, Kyle. I fucking mean it.' And then he hung up.

Danny threw the sat phone back on to the table, then ran out to check on the plane. He could still see Brian walking around it, so he hurried back to the table and turned his attention to the old laptop. It took a full two minutes to power up. Danny pulled Abu Ra'id's data stick from his pocket then plugged it in. A yellow folder appeared on the desktop, simply named 'Folder 1'.

Double click.

The folder opened, to present a single Quicktime file.

Double click.

Abu Ra'id's face. Calm. Unflustered. A plain backdrop. Danny recalled the last, horrific video the cleric had been involved with and for a moment wondered if this might be something similar. But moments after he clicked the 'play' button, he realised that this wasn't a message for the world.

It was more personal than that.

The sound quality of the video was poor. A hissing in the background, and Abu Ra'id's voice was muffled. But they could still understand him.

'If you are watching this,' the ghost of Abu Ra'id intoned, 'then my life is in danger. Perhaps I am already dead.' A pause. Abu Ra'id stared hard into the camera. 'Do not weep for me. I go to a place where my rewards will be great. You will join me, when the time is right.' The cleric cleared his throat, then continued. 'If they have come for *me*, they will come for *you*. With this message I give you a weapon with which to fight them.'

Outside, Danny heard the sound of the Cessna's propellor firing up. He increased the volume on the laptop.

'The governments of the West are riddled with treachery and dishonour. You know that this is true. I have taught you how they will be your friend one moment, your enemy the next. How they will destroy you with their bombs, and then shake your hand. The Taliban were once their friends. Then they were their mortal enemy. Soon they will be their friends again.' Abu Ra'id's lip curled, as if this inconstancy made him feel nauseous. 'There is someone in the security services,' he continued. He shook his head, almost apologetically. 'I do not know their identity. They have been clever enough to keep it a secret. But for the past six months I have been in contact with this person. Everything I have done, I have done with their full knowledge. They have their reasons for wanting the streets of London to be filled with terror.'

There was a moment of juddering on the film. Abu Ra'id disappeared for a few seconds, leaving Danny to stare at the background. Then he suddenly appeared again, and continued talking almost immediately.

'We correspond by draft e-mails left on a Gmail account. They are instantly discarded the moment they are read. Only my contact and I have the address and the password, but you will find them in the name of God.' A piercing stare. 'You need only send an e-mail stating what you know. My contact will be terrified of this becoming known. They will see to it that you are not harmed.' He continued to stare straight at the screen. 'You must not tell them anything about me. And if this weapon does not work, you know what to do.' A fierce glint entered his eyes. 'You *know* what to do.'

He disappeared again. The video stopped.

Danny frowned. He realised that ever since they'd left the training camp, he'd been silently hoping that he'd been wrong. That it had all just been a dreadful mistake they'd been lucky enough to survive. But this message – for his wife, Danny assumed – was confirmation. The smoking gun. The faces of the Hammerstone quartet swam in Danny's mind. Victoria, with her Muslim husband and the mysterious six-month gap in her CV. Chamberlain, with his right-wing sympathies and links to the royal family. Maddox, attached to the CIA whose motives and activities were a mystery to everyone but themselves.

And Buckingham. Treacherous, sleazy Buckingham, who would do anything to advance himself . . .

'What you doing with my computer?' Brian's voice from the doorway. Aggressive.

Danny pulled the data stick away from the USB port and closed down the laptop. 'You ready?'

Brian looked like he was spoiling for an argument, but a dangerous look from Danny subdued him. He nodded, then pointed at Danny and Spud's weapons. 'You leave them here?'

'Go and wait by the plane. I'll meet you there.'

Brian reluctantly left the hut. Danny removed his waistcoat and piled his weapons by the door. He kept his money, his and Spud's passports, and his medical pack. At the last minute, though, he grabbed back his pistol. He'd have to ditch it before getting off the plane in Eritrea – there were no diplomatic bags now, and they couldn't simply cross borders armed to the teeth. But he'd feel a little less naked for a little longer if he had at least one firearm. He walked out to the airfield. Brian was climbing into his plane, so Danny jogged towards it.

Danny didn't trust their pilot even remotely. Nobody trustworthy would be running an operation like this. But right now, Brian was all he had.

20.00hrs GMT

It had been a quiet shift at the hospital. Good thing too. Clara was in no state to think clearly. But now that it was time to go home, she found that she didn't want to. She spent longer than usual changing out of her hospital gear into her ordinary clothes, which were still damp from her sprint along the Edgware Road that morning. When her colleagues called goodnight to her as she left the wards, she barely heard them. And as she approached the exit to the hospital, she drew a deep breath to steady her nerves, before stepping out once more into the drizzle.

It was cold now, as well as wet. Her damp clothes seemed to

draw any warmth from her bones. But her pulse was racing nonetheless. She had already decided that she was going to take a taxi home, but there didn't seem to be any as she stood on the edge of the pavement. As the minutes passed, she just grew colder.

'Thought you'd never turn up,' said a voice immediately behind her.

She started and spun round. Shock turned to distaste as she recognised Kyle's face.

'What do *you* want?' She turned again and made a show of craning out her neck to look for a cab. 'I'm not giving you any more money. I know you wasted it.'

'Don't need your money, love,' Kyle replied in a maddeningly insulting tone of voice. 'Got a message for you, that's all.'

'Somehow I don't think so.'

'Stuck-up bitch, aren't you?'

She ignored him. She caught sight of the orange 'For Hire' light of a black cab about 50 metres up the road and raised one hand to flag it down.

'It's from my brother.'

She blinked, then lowered her hand. 'What?'

'Gone deaf as well?'

'Why can't Danny give me his own messages.'

'Because he's a twat. Trust me, love, I've known him a lot longer than you.'

'I've told you once not to . . .'

'Do you want to know what he said, or not?'

She inhaled deeply to calm herself. 'Go on,' she said, her voice level.

'You're supposed to come with me. You're in trouble.'

She blinked again. 'What do you mean? What sort of trouble?'

'What am I, Derren fucking Brown? I don't know. He wants me to keep an eye on you, anyway.'

'*You* keep an eye on *me*?' Clara frowned. She looked directly at Kyle. 'Have you been following me?' she asked. 'Loitering outside my house?'

Kyle gave her a disgusted look. 'Fuck's sake,' he said. 'You think I haven't got better things to do with my time?'

Not really, Clara thought. That silent answer clearly showed in her face. Kyle spat on the pavement, just short of her feet. 'Fine,' he said. 'I don't give a shit either way.'

Kyle turned to walk away.

And that was when Clara saw *him* again. He was on her side of the road this time, standing in the shelter of a bus stop about 20 metres beyond where Kyle had his back to her. She just caught a glimpse of him through the oncoming pedestrians. Hood down. Face obscured.

'Wait,' she called out. Kyle carried on walking, so she ran after him and grabbed his arm. Her mind was a riot of suspicion and panic. She knew she couldn't go home now, and yet she didn't trust Kyle. 'How do I know you're telling me the truth? Where's Danny? Why don't we call him?'

He gave her a dark look. 'He's out of the country.'

She felt a shiver, because she knew what 'out of the country' meant to Danny.

A strange expression crossed Kyle's face. Like he couldn't decide to say what he was about to say. She looked over his shoulder. The hooded figure was still there, no longer facing them but standing with his head down. 'He spouted some bullshit about, I don't know, forgetting things he shouldn't remember, some crap like that. Fucker was talking bollocks if you ask me.'

But Clara had caught her breath. She grabbed Kyle by the arm again. 'Is he safe?'

For the briefest moment, the look of arrogance fell from Kyle's face. 'No,' he said. 'I don't think he is.'

'We have to warn someone.'

The old Kyle immediately returned. 'Do what you want,' he said. 'But I don't think he'd thank you.'

'What do you mean?'

'Look, my brother was always a fucking Walt, so if you want my advice, take everything he says with a pinch of salt. But he reckons someone thinks he's dead, and we can't say we've heard from him.'

She stared at him in horror. And then, from nowhere, a single word came into her mind. *Buckingham*.

'What?'

'It doesn't matter.' She looked over his shoulder again. The hooded man was still there. She grabbed Kyle's arm and started dragging him in the opposite direction. 'Where are we going?'

'Changed your mind, have you?'

'Somewhere safe. Not my place. Not yours. Somewhere we can hide, until Danny gets in touch.'

'I can find a place,' Kyle said. 'But there's somewhere we need to go first.' He sounded shifty. Untrustworthy.

'Where?' Clara demanded.

'Hereford,' said Kyle.

'Hereford? Why?'

Kyle stopped walking. He had a greedy, avaricious look on his face. She recognised that look from when she'd given him the money a few days previously. 'Take it or leave it,' he said, a nasty twist in his voice.

She looked at him. Then she looked back along the pavement. She couldn't see the hooded figure anywhere. She wanted to keep it that way.

She nodded her reluctant agreement. 'Okay,' she said. 'Hereford.'

They hurried on through the rain.

TWENTY-ONE

It was a turbulent flight. Hot desert air hit the moist ocean atmosphere at the western coast of Saudi Arabia, causing treacherous pockets where the tiny Cessna 172 would drop 50 feet without warning. Danny had flung himself from enough planes not to be a nervous flyer, but he was aware that they were hardly in the hands of an SF flight crew. All he could do was hope this dodgy geezer who called himself Brian knew what he was doing.

Danny wasn't properly strapped in. Instead, he was crouched down beside Spud, holding his mate firmly to minimise the effect of the turbulence. Every time the aircraft bumped, the semi-conscious Spud made a retching sound. He was clearly in excruciating pain, and the movement wasn't helping things. Now and then his eyes opened, and he'd mutter something Danny couldn't understand. His speech was slurred and getting slower. Not a good sign.

He turned and tapped Brian on the shoulder. The pilot looked back at him. 'Call through to Massawa,' he instructed. 'I need a medical team on the ground as soon as we land. Can you do that?'

'How much money will you pay?'

'A thousand dollars. More if my friend lives. I'll come back and pay them.'

A pause.

'I thought you didn't have a thousand dollars.'

Danny didn't hesitate. He just pulled the Sig and pressed it to the back of Brian's head. 'Just make the call.'

Brian did as he was told, jabbering away over the radio in Arabic as Danny kept the gun on him. Lights along the edge of the land distinguished the coastline from the sea. Once they were over water, he made out the lights of several ships. The southern stretches of the Red Sea. He wondered if any of the ships were Royal Navy. An uncomfortable thought crossed his mind: that if they were, *they* could be the enemy now.

The eastern coast of Eritrea passed below them, less clearly lit than that of Saudi. And after that, vast stretches of blackness as they passed over the desert lands of that country. There were no bursts of sound from Brian's radio. The airspace of East Africa was not policed and regulated. Fly an anonymous plane over the UK and a Tornado squadron would be on your tail in minutes. But it was easy to fly in and out of these countries, on whatever business, without anybody noticing.

As they flew, Danny replayed Abu Ra'id's video in his head. The cleric's words sickened him, but not so much as the thought that a member of the security services was in some way involved in the London bombings. The faces of their four handlers swam in front of his eyes again. Who was the guilty one? How would they ever find out?

They had been airborne for 90 minutes when Spud said something Danny understood.

'It's . . . it's the Yanks.'

Danny looked over at Brian. He was wearing ear-protecting cans in the cockpit, so they could talk securely.

Danny thought about what Spud had said. It was possible, sure. Likely even. It was common knowledge that the CIA would do almost anything to protect their interests. But Danny couldn't shake the memory of Buckingham in the car after their first meeting at Hammerstone, sticking the knife further into each of his colleagues with every sentence. Laying a false trail with every word.

He said nothing of this. He realised he needed the e-mail

address and password Abu Ra'id used to contact his handler. He recalled the cleric's words on the tape. *Only my contact and I have the address and the password, but you will find them in the name of God. You know where to look.*

Riddles. Impossible to solve. Danny had to get his hands on Abu Ra'id's missus – the White Witch, or whatever the fuck they called her. Not easy, given that he was currently in a tiny Cessna between two continents, nursing a wounded man who could be hours away from death.

No, Danny thought. Not easy.

But not impossible. He just had to get back into the country first.

Danny looked out of the window to see a tiny sprawl of lights perhaps 20 miles in the distance.

'Massawa!' Brian called from the cockpit. 'We land in ten minutes.'

The plane banked sharply. 'Go easy!' Danny shouted. But as he did, Spud made a harsh choking sound. His face, already pale, turned several shades whiter. He started gasping for breath again, just as he had done moments after he'd been shot.

Something had happened. Danny stared at his friend for a moment. *What was wrong?*

Internal bleeding, he decided. The round inside him must have moved. The lung cavity was filling with blood. Spud was going to suffocate if Danny didn't do something. They couldn't wait ten minutes. Spud just didn't have it in him. Danny needed to bleed him.

He quickly grabbed his med pack and pulled out the second cannula. He ripped the tear in Spud's clothes open wider. The skin round the first cannula had deteriorated. Danny could see networks of blue and red capillaries spreading out from the hole. Spud's gasping became worse. His body started shaking violently. Danny couldn't put it off any more.

He pressed the sharp end of the wide-bore cannula deep into

the rib cage, an inch or two to the left of the first. Spud didn't even seem to notice what he'd done. Holding the plastic tubing firm, he removed the metal needle. As soon as it came out, a jet of blood spurted from the cannula. Ordinarily a bad sign, but not in this instance. The effect was immediate as the blood-letting reduced the pressure on the bad lung. Spud drew a long intake of breath. His eyes flickered open for a moment. His lips started moving. Danny realised he was trying to speak. He sealed the new cannula with the adjustable valve at the open end to stop the blood flow, then he shuffled up to Spud's head so he could hear him better.

Spud's words were slower and more indistinct than ever. 'Find ... the fucker ... who did this to me ...' he breathed.

Danny felt his jaw setting. He nodded, even though Spud had closed his eyes again and couldn't see him do it. Then he turned to look over his shoulder at Brian.

'*Get us on the ground!*' he roared.

Brian gave him a slow, confused look.

'*NOW!*' Danny shouted, and he waved the gun in Brian's direction again.

Instantly, the Cessna's engines changed pitch and they started losing height more quickly. Danny felt Spud's pulse. It was horribly weak. But he was at least breathing as the Cessna continued to lose height. 'Stay with me!' he shouted at Spud, but his mate was clearly past hearing. So instead he shouted at the pilot again: '*Get us on the fucking ground!*'

Five minutes later, the wheels touched down. Danny knew they were hitting the runway too fast, but Brian was a decent pilot and although the landing was bumpy he kept control of the aircraft as it rapidly lost speed. Spud was entirely unconscious as they taxied off the runway. From a corner of his eye, Danny saw a passenger aircraft coming in to land behind them – a sharp reminder that from now on, staying off the grid would be a lot harder. The aircraft came to a halt a good 150 metres from the main terminal building. It was a low, concrete building, not much bigger than the squadron hangar back at Hereford. Unlike Hereford, it was surrounded by squat palm trees, their leaves motionless in the still night air.

'Where's the medic?' Danny shouted. '*Where's the fucking medic?*'

He didn't have to wait for an answer. At that moment, he saw something that, for the first time in days, gave him a surge of hope. A van was speeding across the tarmac towards them. On one side it had the familiar markings of the Red Cross.

Danny didn't hesitate. He jumped down from the Cessna as the van pulled up alongside them. Two guys jumped out, one black, one white. The white guy looked Danny up and down, clearly surprised by the state of his blood-stained clothes.

'Where's the patient?' he asked.

'In the plane. He has a bullet wound. A .762. I think it's entered his left lung. I've inserted one cannula to stop the lung collapsing, a second to bleed it when the cavity filled with blood. He's in a bad way.'

'How did it happen?'

'Bandits in Ethiopia,' Danny lied easily. The medic didn't question him.

'Does he have any ID?'

Danny shook his head. He didn't want to give them Spud's name or passport. The last thing he could do to prolong his mate's life was preserve his anonymity. 'Can you get him out of the airport?' He pressed a thousand dollars into the medic's hands, and the medic nodded. Then he and his colleague opened up the back of the van and pulled out a stretcher bed. Two minutes later, Danny had helped them manoeuvre the uncon- scious Spud out of the plane and on to the bed. The medics were already fitting a saline drip to his arm and an oxygen mask to his face. They hurriedly loaded the stretcher bed into the back of the van. The black guy climbed in with Spud. The last

Danny saw of his mate, it was impossible to tell at a glance whether he was living or dead.

'Coming?' the white medic asked Danny.

Danny stared at the van. Then at the medic.

'Look after him,' he said. 'I'll be back for him, when I can.'

The medic didn't question Danny's decision. There clearly wasn't time. He hurried to the ambulance, jumped behind the wheel and screeched off.

Danny took several deep breaths, trying to calm his nerves. Had he made the right call? Would Spud stand a chance with these Red Cross doctors? Was it possible that word of this anonymous injured man arriving on an Eritrean airfield would make it back to the security services? Danny didn't know the answer to any of these questions. All he knew was that the decision was made, and that now he had to concentrate on getting back to the UK, and doing exactly what Spud had asked him to do: finding the fuckers that had put them in this situation.

He turned to Brian. 'What now?' Danny demanded, the tension clearly audible in his voice.

'Now,' said Brian, 'we wait.'

They didn't have to wait long. Within a couple of minutes, a lone airport official appeared, walking across the tarmac to the plane. Black skin, shaved head, sunken yellow eyes. Hi-vis jacket and handgun at his belt. Brian walked up to meet him, and they stood talking by the wing for perhaps 30 seconds. Some money changed hands and the official smiled. Brian approached Danny. 'You owe me a hundred dollars,' he said.

'I already paid you,' Danny said.

'Okay,' he said. 'I'll take my money back from him, and *he'll* take *you* through passport control, not round the back way.'

Danny frowned. Fucker had him over a barrel. He handed Brian another $100. That put Danny's funds down to two grand. Brian grunted gracelessly, then gestured at the airport official to join them.

The official looked Danny up and down. No doubt he appeared strange, with his grubby, blood-stained *dishdash* hiding his camouflage gear and boots. But he didn't say anything. He just made a little clicking sound in the corner of his mouth, and indicated that Danny should follow him. Danny turned to Brian. A nod from each of them was the only farewell that was required. Moments later, he was trudging across the tarmac with his new companion. When Danny looked over his shoulder, the Cessna was already on the move. Danny's senses had slipped back into top gear. He scanned the area around them, checking that they weren't being unduly watched. And as they neared the terminal building, he instinctively looked upwards, searching for CCTV or any other type of surveillance. Nothing. For now.

The official led him round the side of the terminal, through a locked metal door to which he had a key. Danny found himself in a narrow corridor with scuffed walls and strip lighting. Their footsteps echoed as they paced down it towards a second locked door. The official opened it, then stepped back. Danny peered through: the concourse of Massawa International Airport. Far from busy at this time of night. A few bored-looking officials milling around. Check-in desks on the far side: closed. Ticketing booths for Eritrean Airlines and Nasair: closed. A couple of white backpackers sleeping on rows of plastic seats. And perhaps 50 Eritrean nationals, waiting for passengers on the plane Danny had seen landing to come through security. There were a few shops along the edges of the concourse – souvenirs, Bureau de Change, even a clothes shop – but their facades were covered with metal shutters. And there was a grotty cafe, but all the chairs were stowed on top of the tables.

'Go! You go!' the airport official said. He tried to push Danny forwards. Danny shook him off impatiently, but then stepped from the corridor on to the concourse. The door shut quickly behind them. He was on his own.

Danny looked up at the departures board. There were no

flights leaving until 06.00 – Eritrean to Khartoum, Nasair to Dubai. At 10.15hrs, however, an Eritrean Airlines flight was listed to Frankfurt. Flight time, 5 hours 54 minutes. It meant he could be in Europe around 14.00 local time.

Would Spud still be alive by then? Danny didn't know. A silent rage boiled up inside him. He felt he wanted to do something. To *hurt* someone.

But he couldn't. All he could do was wait.

The early morning hours passed in a blur of tiredness. Danny realised he hadn't slept since he and Spud had been lying in the OP above the training camp, more than 24 hours ago. Eritrean airport officials and travellers blurred in and out of focus. As waves of fatigue crashed over him, he felt himself nodding. Every now and then he'd wake with a start and look round for Spud. But with a guilty, angry pang he remembered Spud wasn't there. God only knew what was happening to him.

He woke suddenly for a final time at 06.55hrs, when he looked blearily over towards the ticket desks. Both the Eritrean Airlines and the Nasair desk had a uniformed woman attending them.

The ticket to Frankfurt cost 499 Eritrean nafka. It was sold with only the most cursory glance at Danny's dirty clothes and his passport, though the guy at the Bureau de Change who converted his dollars scrutinised the passport a bit more closely. No computers though, Danny noted with satisfaction. So far, he reckoned he was still under the radar.

In the cafe he bought a cup of thick, powdery coffee and cellophane-wrapped biscuits hard enough to break your teeth on. When the clothes shop opened at 08.00 he bought cheap linen trousers, sandals and a loose-fitting T-shirt. In the other shop he found razors and shaving foam, which he took along with his new clothes to the rancid toilets at one end of the concourse. He changed in a cubicle with shit stains round the toilet rims, dumping his old clothes behind the cistern. Back in front of the sinks he shaved his face and, in a last-minute decision, his head. He drew strange looks from the Eritrean men who came in for a slash as he flicked clumps of hair into the sink. Better, though, to get strange looks here than in Frankfurt.

Back on the concourse, his gate was being called. He presented his ticket and passport to the flight attendent. She checked them, and made a handwritten note of the passport number. But then, with a smile, she ushered him through.

Danny boarded the brightly coloured Airbus as the morning sun was rising in the African sky. The aircraft was only half full, so he had a row of seats to himself. And by 10.20hrs he was airborne again, high above the parched landscape of East Africa and heading north. He didn't look back out of the window. He didn't have the heart. He felt a deep guilt at leaving Spud behind, even though he knew he'd done his best for him.

For now, he decided to sleep again. To refresh himself for the next stage of his journey.

09.00hrs GMT

'What are we doing here?' Clara asked.

They had taken the first train to Hereford. Now they stood outside Danny's flat. Clara looked up and down the street, all around. She had been doing that all night, as they nursed paper coffee cups at Euston. The police presence at the station was high. Clara found that a comfort. At no point had she seen the hooded figure and she was beginning to wonder, as she always seemed to when morning came, if seeing him again had just been some kind of coincidence.

'I'm going to break in,' Kyle said. His hands were shaking. Delirium tremens, she diagnosed at a glance. Kyle was craving a fix of something.

'Don't be stupid,' she said. 'I've got a key.' She hurried up to the front door and let them in, ignoring the voice in her head that asked her why on earth she was still carrying Danny's house key after he'd finished with her.

It was dark in the flat. All the curtains were closed, and there was an unpleasant mustiness. Once inside, Kyle shot down the corridor towards Danny's bedroom. 'What are you doing?' she called. He didn't answer. When she followed him into the room, she found that he had opened the wardrobe and was on his knees, pulling up the floorboards inside. 'Kyle, what the hell are you ...'

She fell silent. Kyle had three wads of bank notes in his fist and a look of unrestrained greed on his face. He started stuffing the money into his pockets. When he was sure he had it all, he followed Clara back along the corridor to the front door, which was still ajar. She opened it wider.

And gasped.

He was there. On the other side of the street. Despite the hood, she could make out a little more of his face this time. Dark eyes. A hooked nose. And was that a stud in his lower lip?

She slammed the door shut. 'I'm being followed,' she whispered.

Kyle frowned. 'What do you mean? You're as bad as him.' His hands involuntarily went to the pockets where his money was.

'There's a gate in the back garden. It leads to an alleyway. *Run!*'

She pushed past him and hurried back to the bedroom where French doors led to the garden. They were locked. No sign of the key. She grabbed a pillow from the bed, held it by one hand against the glass pane in the door, then kicked it as hard as she could. The glass splintered. Two more kicks and it was in shards around her feet. 'Come *on!*' she hissed at Kyle, who was hanging back, staring stupidly at her.

They picked their way through the jagged remains of the window pane. Clara winced as a shard scraped against her scalp, but she kept on moving, dragging Kyle along behind her.

Danny's garden was untended and overgrown. The back gate was open. They hurried through it, out into the alleyway behind the row of houses.

Left or right? She knew that both directions ended out in the street. Left emerged further away from Danny's front door. If her stalker suspected that she was escaping round the back, he'd expect her to take that route. So she turned right.

Kyle was wheezing and out of breath after just a few metres. Clara pulled him along. He was red-faced and coughing as they emerged on to the street. She looked carefully around.

No sign of the stalker. She turned to Kyle.

'Where can we go?' she demanded. 'Not your place. Somewhere nobody can find us till Danny gets back. Do you know somewhere?'

A shifty look crossed his face. 'Yeah,' he said. 'I know somewhere. You won't like it.'

'I don't have to *like* it,' Clara snapped. 'Is it far?'

'No,' Kyle said. 'Not far. Follow me.'

She followed.

14.15hrs Central European Time

Frankfurt International Airport. Eritrean Airlines Flight 592 from Massawa touched down on to a rain-slicked runway. A bendy bus transferred the passengers from the aircraft to the terminal building. Danny felt a twist in his stomach as he stepped off the bus. Armed police, everywhere. But he told himself that was to be expected. All of Europe would be on high alert after what had happened in London.

He kept his head down as he stepped into the terminal building. He knew there would be CCTV everywhere. Impossible to spot them all. Better to spend his time making sure he went unobserved.

There was a long queue at passport control. Most of the other passengers from Massawa went into a separate line for non-EU citizens, but Danny joined at least 50 others waiting to present their passports. There were five people between them in the queue. Danny instinctively looked around, checking where the exits were in this huge immigration hall. He saw plenty, but he knew, of course, that they were of no use to him if everything turned to shit. The exits were guarded, and he was unarmed.

It took a full 20 minutes before Danny was called up to have his passport checked. He walked up to a grim-looking German woman and handed over his passport. Was it his imagination, or did the woman glance disapprovingly at his dirty hand, little knowing that this wasn't ordinary grime, but a mixture of gun residue and dried blood.

She scanned the passport. Danny couldn't see the screen of her terminal, but found himself scrutinising the contours of her face. He noticed a sudden tightness around her eyes. He tensed up.

She looked at the photograph, then directly at Danny. She frowned. The images were different, since Danny had shaved his head.

Back at the photograph.

Back at Danny.

'*Willkommen in Deutschland*,' she said, handing the passport back.

'*Danke schoen*,' Danny mumbled.

He forced himself to keep a steady pace as he walked away from the immigration desk. Ten metres to his right, an armed police officer. But the cop paid him no attention. Relief crashed over Danny like warm water. He was through.

Next stop, southern Ireland.

1500hrs GMT

'What is this place?'

Clara didn't know which part of Hereford they were in. All she knew was that it wasn't a good part. To get here, they'd passed through an area of bleak parkland. Clara had noticed, just metres from the swings and slides, a metal bin for depositing used needles, on which someone had sprayed a single graffiti tag. Raddled-looking mums sitting nearby, wiping their running noses on the sleeves of threadbare clothes as they watched their pale children on the roundabout, none of them wearing enough clothes to protect them from the biting cold.

Now Kyle was leading them along a terrace of run-down houses. Condemned, most of them, with graffitied steel casements over the windows and building-control signs warning passers-by not to enter on grounds of safety. A few cars lined the streets, but almost without exception they had missing tyres or broken windows. A supermarket trolley lay on its side in the middle of the pavement. Even though it was broad daylight, an urban fox sat in the road, watching them intently. Somewhere in the distance, just on the edge of her hearing, she sensed the throb of a drumbeat. But there was no music in this street. It was silent.

The house outside which they stopped looked worse than the others. The ground-floor windows were covered in bolted steel mesh. On the first floor, the panes were smashed and the frames rotten, leaving the interior of the house open to the elements. There were slates missing from the roof. The chimney stack was crumbling.

The door, however, was slightly open.

Kyle walked up to the door. He pushed it open with his foot and stepped inside. Clara looked over her shoulder. There was no sign of anyone in the street. She followed Kyle inside.

The first thing that hit her was the smell. She could discern cannabis and booze, but that wasn't the half of it. There was a lingering stench of vomit. Also, sewage. And lacing it all together, the sweet, sickly smell of infection. The doctor in her knew before she had even taken a second step over the threshold that this was a house of the unwell.

It was dark in here, and very cold. She knew that there could be no electricity, but looking up she saw that neither was there a light fitting in this narrow hallway. Just a bare wire hanging from the ceiling. Instinct told her that if there had ever been a bulb and fitting there, they had been stolen and sold long ago. Same went for the light switch and even, she noticed, for the radiator that had once stood against the wall between the sawn-off ends of two copper pipes. The house had been stripped of anything of value, then graffitied so heavily that she could see nothing of the walls.

'I don't like it here,' she breathed.

Kyle shrugged, then threw her own words back at her: 'You don't have to like it.'

Clara clenched her jaw as she followed Kyle further into the house, up a flight of stairs with a thin, sticky carpet. At the top of the stairs he turned right. They entered a large bedroom – in fact, it looked like two rooms knocked together. It was even colder in here. The windows were broken, as she'd seen from the pavement, and the carpet in front of them was wet where the rain had seeped in. Which was presumably why the sleeping bodies had congregated at the far end of the room. She counted them: six people, bundled up under thin blankets.

Clara heard herself say: 'What is this place?' But even as she said it, her eyes fell on the paraphernalia that surrounded the sleeping bodies. Teaspoons. Candle stubs. Small Calor Gas stoves. Dirty swabs of cotton wool. And needles, maybe ten of them, lying on the ground, with no sign of sealed foil wrappers to show they were sterile. Three upturned milk crates were dotted around the room in place of chairs. The walls were graffitied just as heavily as downstairs, and there was a stench of urine that suggested someone had relieved themselves in here recently. There was a poster on the wall showing a picturesque French village, but that too was graffitied.

'We can't stay here,' she breathed.

'Why the hell not?' Kyle said. 'Nobody's going to come looking for you in this place.'

'What about the police?' she said. She didn't know why, but the thought of the authorities finding them put a chill through her.

Kyle snorted. 'Don't be stupid. Police don't want anything to do with this lot.' And Clara supposed that was right. Especially now, when all their resources were focused on the terror alert. She'd heard people say on TV that there'd been a crime spike since the bombings, as the understaffed police force tried to prioritise their workload. But these people, she surmised, had been here since long before the bombings. They probably didn't even know the atrocities had happened.

'How do you *know* about this place, Kyle?'

But that wasn't a question Kyle wanted to answer. He indicated a patch of floor, empty except for a couple of old cigarette packets and a crushed tin of Tennants Super.

'Make yourself at home,' he said.

16.00hrs CET
Aer Lingus from Frankfurt to Dublin.

He felt a strange sensation when, from his window seat, he saw the coast of southern Ireland slip into view. Home turf, or as near as. Why, then, did it seem threatening? On ops, you knew your friends from your enemies. Now that he was heading home, he felt like the two had merged into one.

Except for Clara. He knew, implicitly, that he could trust her. He loathed himself for putting her in the care of his brother. He just hoped – prayed – that for once Kyle had managed to man up.

17.00hrs GMT. Touchdown. Another excruciating pass through passport control. But no hold-ups. Danny stepped out into the damp Irish air, exhausted, his face grim. He felt no sense of triumph at having got this far unobserved. No satisfaction that all he needed to do now was board a ferry from Dublin to Holyhead, a route Danny knew would not even require him to show his passport. Just anger. Raw, burning anger as his thoughts turned to Spud back in Eritrea. Had he made it? Danny had no way of knowing.

Someone, he told himself, was going to pay.

But first he had to bottle the anger. To use it. He forced himself to concentrate on his own situation. On Clara. And on Hammerstone. His job was only just beginning, and there was only so long that he could remain off the grid.

By 20.00hrs, he was on the Holyhead ferry. He stood on deck, sheltered from the rain by the overhang of a deck above him. Danny had often discussed with his Regiment mates how this was an easy route for terrorists or criminals to slip into the UK unnoticed. He'd never thought that one day it would be him doing it. In the distance, the west coast of Wales slipped into view as Danny carefully thought through his next move. He needed three more guys, he decided, if he was going to smoke out his enemy. People he could trust to keep their mouths shut – to help him out and not let anyone know that he'd made contact.

Ripley was the first name on Danny's list. He was a good man. Trustworthy. More to the point, Danny knew his home number. He was also a petrolhead. Danny and the improvised team he was going to put together would need transport. Ripley could bring some of his motorbikes.

Barker was second on the list, assuming he was out of hospital after his flesh wound from the dealers in Horseferry Mews. And there was that mate of Barker's who'd had the brother killed in the Paddington bomb. What was his name? Hancock? Danny reckoned he could get him on side if he thought it was to do with the terror attacks.

He decided he'd make contact from a public pay phone as soon as he got in to Holyhead. Arrange to meet with the guys in London the following night. That would give him time to make a few more arrangements.

Not to mention one other crucial thing. He had to pay a visit to the White Witch.

PART FOUR

RV

TWENTY-TWO

Midnight

Clara felt sick.

Sick with fear. Sick with disgust. And just plain, ordinary sick.

She was huddled in the corner of this revolting room, hugging her knees, with nothing to protect her from the cold that came in through the window but the clothes she wore.

Kyle had disappeared 20 minutes after they arrived here. She'd tried to persuade him not to leave her, but he'd simply spat a few obscenities and left anyway. The six junkies were all unconscious and she'd been terrified to find out what their reaction to her would be when they woke up. In fact, they'd barely looked at her. She'd soon realised why: it seemed they all still had gear on them, and they were far more interested in getting that into their veins than in the petrified newcomer shivering in the corner of the room. They all awoke at different times, and immediately went about the business of cooking little sachets of brown powder in teaspoons over candle flames, and sending themselves back to oblivion. The doctor in Clara wanted to stop them. But good sense prevailed. She knew that to stand between one of these addicts and their next hit would be asking for trouble.

Kyle had returned a couple of hours later. He stank of booze and he had a bottle in his pocket. He had thrown Clara a packet of crisps, but otherwise barely acknowledged her. Starving, she had wolfed down the food while Kyle sat on the other side of the room, sipping frequently from his bottle of Teacher's.

'We can't stay here,' she'd whispered.

'Fine,' came the reply. 'Fuck off.'

She'd remained just where she was, of course. She was scared to stay, but she was even more scared to leave.

Just as the light was failing, one of the junkies woke up. He had pale, sallow cheeks and terrible acne, especially round his lips. His hands shook. He stared, bleary-eyed, across the room. First at Clara. He eyed her up and down. Not a lascivious stare – Clara had an intuition that the drugs had long since pushed any thought of sex from his mind – but a calculating one. Did *she* have any drugs? Any money? What could he *get* from her?

The junkie turned his attention to Kyle. A flash of recognition registered in his eyes. 'Back again?' he asked in a thin, reedy voice.

Kyle ignored him. The junkie snorted dismissively. Everyone fell silent, while the junkie looked between the two of them.

'Got anything for me?' the junkie had asked Kyle.

'You've got a fucking nerve.'

Whatever that meant.

Ten minutes passed. Then, suddenly, the junkie stood up. He was unsteady on his feet, and his hands were shaking worse than ever. He left the room. Clara heard his uneven footsteps going down the stairs. The door slamming. Silence again.

'How does he know you?' Clara had asked. But she'd received no answer. Just a shifty look, and another pull from the bottle of Scotch.

Now it was midnight. Dark in the room. Colder than ever. She was shivering. Kyle had fallen asleep, the bottle empty in his fist. Clara's thoughts were darker than the room. How had she ended up here? What was she *doing*? Panic gripped her. She wished, more than anything, that Danny was here. To take her away from the horror of it. But he wasn't. The only person she had was Kyle, and he was the last person in the world she could trust.

She heard voices outside the house. For some reason they made her jump and she realised she hadn't heard anybody in the street since she arrived here. This was a place people avoided. A now-familiar cold shadow of dread passed over her. She found herself, almost involuntarily, standing up and creeping towards the broken window. She peered through it.

There were three figures on the pavement outside the house. She couldn't see their faces, but one of them had the same lanky gait as the junkie who had left that evening. She strained to listen. She could hear two different voices. At first she couldn't make out what they were saying. Then she realised why: they weren't speaking English. She tried to work out what language it was. It sounded harsh and angular. Russian, perhaps? Or Eastern European?

She swallowed hard. She was no linguist, but she suddenly knew, beyond doubt, that they were speaking Polish.

She hurried over to Kyle and shook him. 'Wake up. *Wake up!*'

Kyle groaned and lashed out.

'Wake *up!* The Poles are here!'

Kyle opened his bloodshot eyes. He stared at her, uncomprehendingly.

'*The Poles are here!*'

Kyle's expression changed. He was scared. He scrambled to his feet. 'How did they find me?' he slurred.

'That junkie, of course,' Clara hissed. 'He knew you.'

Kyle was looking around the room, searching for exits like a hunted animal. But there was only one: the main door. He headed towards it, clearly thinking only of himself and not of Clara. He stumbled over one of the milk crates and cursed as it clattered noisily.

Then he stopped.

There were footsteps coming up the stairs. More than one set. Kyle looked around the room again. To the window. Back to the door. He shrank against one of the walls. Clara found she was holding her breath.

Ten seconds passed.

Figures in the doorway.

They entered the room.

They were broad-shouldered men. Shaved head. Donkey jackets. Through the gloom, Clara could see that one of them had a tattoo on his neck. It was the head of a black raven, and the sight chilled her. He stepped further into the room and gave Kyle a look of total contempt. The junkie was loitering in the door frame, clutching his shaking hands together.

The tattooed Pole put one hand into his jacket. He pulled out a flick knife, which he opened with a well-practised move. Then he strode up to Kyle, grabbed the front of his clothes with one big hand, and pressed him up against the wall. He rested the blade of the knife against his cheek.

There were a few seconds of absolute silence.

'Where's my fucking money?' said the Pole, his voice slow, the English almost incomprehensible beneath the Polish accent.

'I . . . I've got it,' Kyle whispered. He slowly put his hand in his pocket and pulled out a fistful of the notes he had taken from Danny's wardrobe. The Pole looked over at his mate, who had fat lips and a pockmarked face. He walked up and took the money from Kyle. He counted it out with quick, well-practised fingers.

'*Piecset*,' he said, and stuffed the money into his pocket.

'Five hundred not enough,' said the Pole. 'You still owe me five *thousand*.'

'I'll have it soon,' Kyle said. 'I promise.'

'Promise, promise, promise!' the Pole shouted. 'All you ever do is promise.' He flicked the knife quickly downwards. Kyle hissed in pain as a streak of blood appeared on his cheek.

Clara gasped at the sudden violence. The Pole turned to look at her.

'Is that girl?' he asked the junkie in the doorway.

'That's her,' the junkie said.

The Pole nodded at his mate again, who turned and started walking towards Clara.

Clara felt a sudden fire in her gut. 'Don't you *touch* me,' she said, jutting out her chin in defiance. The Pole just grinned. He stretched out one big hand and grabbed her by the throat. Clara's reaction was instant. She raised her knee sharply into his crutch. The Pole swore as he doubled over, letting go of her neck as he did so.

Clara looked quickly towards the door. The junkie was still standing there, but she knew she could push her way past him. If she moved now, she could escape. But then she looked over at Kyle. His face was bleeding, and he wore a pitiful expression of terror. She thought suddenly of Danny, and of how she couldn't leave his brother here to the mercy of these two awful men. She started striding towards him, her intention to grab him and pull him from the room.

That was her mistake.

The man she had disabled recovered quickly. He grabbed at her legs as she moved. Clara fell hard to the floor.

After that, she didn't stand a chance.

He grabbed her hair first, clutching a big clump and twisting it sharply round until she whimpered with pain. With his free hand he struck her a vicious blow on the cheek, then pulled her up to her feet by the hair. Another crushing blow to the face and a third to her left breast: a pain so sharp and sudden that it drew the breath from her lungs and forced her into silence. Just to be sure, though, the Pole put his free hand over her mouth, as his tattooed mate spoke to Kyle.

'You have forty-eight hours,' he said. 'Midnight tomorrow. If I don't have my money, your girlfriend . . .' He swiped one fore-finger across his neck. 'I stick her in hole and piss on her. Then I come do same to you.'

He spat in Kyle's face. Kyle slumped to the ground, one hand pressed over his bleeding cheek. The tattooed Pole turned to his mate and said a single word in Polish. Clara felt herself being thrust towards the door, past the sallow-faced junkie who was suddenly jabbering nervously. 'We had a deal, mate. What about it? What about our fucking deal?'

From the corner of her eye, Clara saw the tattooed Pole throw a small, sealed plastic bag on to the floor. The junkie dived towards it and started scrabbling around to pick it up. It was the last thing Clara saw of the room. The Pole pushed her roughly towards the stairs.

Down them.

And out into the night.

TWENTY-THREE

Ripley had sounded shocked to hear from Danny when he'd called from Holyhead. It wasn't just that he'd been speaking quietly to avoid his missus overhearing the phone conversation. Ripley hadn't said as much, but Danny could hear in his voice that the guys had been told he and Spud were goners. But he'd agreed to do as Danny asked.

'Where and when?' Ripley asked.

'Tomorrow night. On the south side of the Thames between Vauxhall and Lambeth bridges. Bring Barker and Hancock. And seriously, mate – don't tell *anyone* you've heard from me.'

'You've got some fucking explaining to do, pal,' Ripley said. But Danny knew he'd keep his word.

But there was still a lot to do before his RV with his SAS mates.

From Holyhead he'd made it by train to Birmingham, where he needed to change to get to London. Before getting on a train to Euston, though, he'd headed out of Birmingham New Street station and found a Save the Children charity shop, where he'd bought fresh clothes. Jeans. A jumper slightly too small for him. A waterproof jacket and a black woollen hat. A pair of trainers to replace the sandals he'd bought in Massawa. He even found an old balaclava, threadbare and bobbled, which he bought for 50 pence. Because you never know.

Next to the charity shop was an angling store. Danny had bought a cheap torch with a red filter, intended for night fisherman who didn't want to compromise their night vision. Then he'd headed to the central library to use an internet terminal. He googled the White Witch. Abu Ra'id had said his wife would find the username and password for the account he shared with his contact 'in the name of God'. It was clearly a code of some sort. Something that was meaningful only to them. Danny didn't have the time or inclination to puzzle over what he meant. If this woman had intelligence that he needed, he was going to have to find a way to make her deliver it to him.

Information about the White Witch was freely available. Real name Amanda Ledbury. Born 23 October 1982 to British parents. Converted to Islam at the age of 17. Attended University College London where she studied politics and theology, and met Amar Al-Zain, the man who would later style himself Abu Ra'id.

He started digging a little deeper. Internet chat rooms were filled with praise or bile for this woman. Praise from the Islamists, among whom rumours abounded that she was behind a grenade attack on some football fans in a Kenyan bar during the previous world cup. And bile from almost everyone else – Muslim and non-Muslim alike – who deplored how she was able to live on housing benefits in a large detached house in Ealing with a cleric who preached hate against the very society that was supporting them. Who were disgusted at her ability to fight her way through the courts using a team of lawyers paid for by legal aid. Who couldn't understand why she and her husband were allowed to stay in the UK, even though it was the country of their birth.

A conversation replayed itself in his head.

'Personally, Harrison, I'm extremely pleased my children can grow up in a country where the rule of law can be relied upon, and extended to all our citizens, regardless of . . .'

'Regardless of how many people they're planning to kill, Victoria?'

The sentiment on these forums was more in line with

Harrison Maddox's than Victoria Atkinson's, but Danny didn't want opinions. He wanted an address. And after 20 minutes of clicking through links and scanning the chat rooms, he'd found one. The user who had supplied it called himself SwordOfTruth. A quick glance at his profile told Danny that he held views even the EDF would consider extreme. For the briefest moment, he found himself thinking about Piers Chamberlain. But then he turned his attention back to the screen. In a barely literate call to action, SwordOfTruth supplied Amanda Ledbury's address in the hope that like-minded psychos would stalk her house and give her 'what she had coming'. Danny memorised the address: 13 Princess Park Gardens, London W5. He checked the location on Google Maps, then zoomed in on satellite view, as close as he was able. He'd seen that it was a detached house with a perimeter fence. No obvious point of access other than the doors and windows.

Or was there?

He zoomed in on a small patch at the rear of the house, and smiled grimly to himself.

Next he googled the names of the four Hammerstone spooks. Within 15 minutes he'd found a decent picture of each one of them, which he'd printed out on the library's colour printer. Then he'd cleared the browser history and left the library.

SwordOfTruth had made him think as he headed towards the train station to get the next train into London. His plan was to break into the White Witch's house. But that wasn't going to be straightforward. She'd have received death threats. No question. That meant there was a possibility of a police presence outside the house. And if the police weren't on-site – Danny remembered DI Fletcher's complaint that they were unable to follow up half the crime being committed in London in the wake of the bombings – there was a very good chance that the security services would be watching her. He'd need to be careful.

He arrived at 13 Princess Park Gardens at 23.30hrs. It was a detatched house in a quiet residential street in north Ealing, a 15-minute walk from the Tube station. There was a single light burning on the first floor of the house which suggested someone was at home, though he couldn't be totally sure. Similar detached houses on one side, a terrace on the opposite side, with an alleyway heading round the back much like the one behind his own flat in Hereford. Like the mob whose comments he'd read on the internet, Danny found himself wondering how a hateful couple like Abu Ra'id and his missus had managed to arrange their lives so that they were living in a place far bigger than they needed or deserved. He thought of his own little flat in Hereford, and of the number of times he'd been called upon to risk his life for his country. It wasn't right.

He dragged his mind back to the job in hand.

The house itself was different from the others that surrounded it. More secure. The two-metre-high wooden fence that extended along either side of the front garden had also been erected across the front, serving as a barrier between the pavement and the garden. A wooden gate in the middle. Closed. Locked, he assumed. There was razor wire along the top of the fence, but not above the wooden gate – which meant the razor wire might as well not be there at all. The fence and gate were about 2.5 metres high. Easily scaleable. But Danny wasn't going to do that. Not yet.

He was on foot, standing at the corner of Princess Park Gardens where it met a busier street with a parade of shops about 50 metres further along. He was a metre from the alleyway entrance on the even-numbered side of the road. The road was lined with cars. A sign on the kerbside indicated that this was a residents' permit area. Sure enough, the car by which he was standing – an old blue Fiat Panda – had a permit fixed to the windscreen. Danny wasn't a smoker, but he'd bought himself a packet of Marlboro and a box of matches because he knew that if he was pulling on a cigarette, the eyes of any casual observer would be drawn to that rather than his own features. He lit up and started walking down the street, hands in his pockets, woollen hat pulled down over his ears. The rain had let up for a moment, but he sensed it would be back fairly soon.

He clocked them within seconds. Five cars down, right outside Number 10, there was a Renault Laguna. It was too dark to see through the front grilles and tell whether they hid a siren, but he didn't have to. Two guys sat in the front. One of them was drinking from a paper coffee cup. The other was looking out of the passenger window towards the White Witch's house. They had no residents' permit. Instead, they'd propped up a blue disabled parking badge in the windscreen. But these two guys, both in their early thirties, didn't look disabled to Danny. They looked like undercover cops. Or spooks. One or the other. They weren't even trying to be majorly covert. Probably just there to put the shits up the White Witch every time she left the house.

Danny took all this in at a glance. He didn't let up his pace, and he didn't stare unnecessarily at them. He simply walked past, having marked out his most immediate threat to gaining entry to number 13. Scaling the door was out of the question. Not with them watching. And if they were any good at their job, they would be able to see him jumping the wall on either side of the garden – even if it wasn't razor-wired.

At the far end of Princess Park Gardens he turned right, stubbing out the half-smoked cigarette with his foot. If there was a terrace backing on to it, maybe he could break through from the other side. When he turned right again, he found that there *was* a terrace, but there were no side entrances for him to enter.

He couldn't walk back along Princess Park Gardens. Any surveillance professional worthy of the name would notice him. Danny knew *he* would, in their shoes. He considered his options. Clearly he needed a distraction of some sort. He thought through his arsenal of tricks. He could make a 999 call, phone in a fake sighting of somebody with a firearm in the area. He quickly rejected that idea. Sure, it would trigger an armed response, but not necessarily from the two surveillance guys. Perhaps he could make a different kind of call, stating that he'd just seen two guys bundle a struggling six-year-old kid into a Renault Laguna on Princess Park Gardens. It would certainly get a reaction from the police, but it would take a matter of seconds for them to realise that the surveillance guys hadn't *really* abducted a child, and a matter of a few seconds more before they twigged that someone was playing them.

The bottom line was this: Danny couldn't rely on the surveillance guys leaving their car. That meant that the distraction would have to come to them.

Which gave him an idea.

The alleyway behind the even-numbered side of the road stank of bins and rotten rubbish. The ground was muddy and wet from the incessant rain. As Danny paced along it, he heard the scurrying sound of rodents rushing out of his path. The alleyway turned 90 degrees. Danny kept a steady pace: if he ran, he might arouse the suspicions of anyone watching from rear windows of the row of houses. He continued to the far end. He knew he was back at the top of the street now, and recalled that the surveillance guys were parked up outside number ten. He doubled back on himself, counting off the house numbers as he passed their rear gardens – two, four, six, eight – until now he was standing outside the garden gate of number ten.

It was a rickety old gate. One solid shoulder-thump and it would probably break open. But Danny wanted to make as little noise as possible so he scrambled over it instead, cursing under his breath as a splinter of wood ripped into his palm, but ignoring it.

A narrow garden, about 50 feet long. A neat lawn. Flower borders on either side. Your typical, boring suburban garden with a wooden shed at the end. It was unlocked, so Danny stepped inside.

He could smell it at once. The thick, greasy stench of petrol.

He groped around in the dark and felt the handles of a lawn-mower. He collapsed them so he could more easily lift the lawnmower up. Then he felt for the twist-off cap of the petrol tank. He undid it, then lifted the whole lawnmower. His muscles strained as, within the cramped confines of the shed, he turned the lawnmower upside down. He heard the trickle of petrol pouring from the tank on to the wooden floor of the shed.

He stepped back towards the door. Backwards out into the garden. Then he took the box of matches from his pocket, lit one and threw it inside. The petrol ignited immediately, making a low popping sound as blue and yellow flames filled the shed. Danny hurried back over the garden gate into the alleyway. He followed it back up to the top of the Princess Park Gardens. He had already decided that he wouldn't simply wait for the fire engine to come. The occupants of number 10 were probably asleep. They might not even notice that their shed was on fire. He turned right out of the alleyway, then right again on to the wider road. He only had to walk 30 metres before he came across a pay phone outside a parade of shops.

He dialled 999.

'Which service do you require.'

'Fire. Number ten, Princess Park Gardens, Ealing.'

He hung up.

It took five or six minutes for Danny to hear the sirens of the fire engine. By this time, he was loitering on the corner of Princess Park Gardens again, on the odd-number side this time, out of view of the two surveillance guys. Twenty seconds later he saw the fire engine approaching. It sped past the parade of shops, then turned left into Princess Park Gardens. Danny hurried down the pavement alongside it, brightly lit by the neon blue lights. But that was okay, because the vehicle blocked the line of sight between him and the surveillance guys. And he noted with satisfaction that it stopped bang outside number 10:

a huge, immobile barrier between the two men in the car and the front gate of number 13.

He couldn't hesitate. The sirens would draw attention, and he estimated he had about 20 seconds before one of the surveillance guys got out of the car to get eyes on their target again. He sprinted to the gate, jumped up and heaved himself over the top. He landed catlike on the other side just as the sirens fell silent. The neon still flashed, lighting up the front of the White Witch's house, but here, at the foot of the high wooden fence, where the unkempt grass was higher than his knees, he was out of sight.

He caught his breath. There were voices shouting out on the street as firemen alighted from the engine. He zoned them out. All his attention now was on the house as he worked out how he was going to break in.

It was a fairly old brick building. Victorian, maybe. A bit shabby. The garden was overgrown. Three windows on the top floor. Two on the ground, one either side of the door. As he watched, a light appeared in the top-left window. Through the curtains he saw a silhouette. It stood very still for perhaps ten seconds, watching through the window, then melted away. That told him where his target's bedroom was. He knew he wanted to break in round the back, but not until the light was out again, and the fire engine had moved on.

He didn't move for a full 30 minutes. Not one muscle. Out on the street was all the commotion that went with extinguishing the garden fire. A second siren arrived – police, he supposed – but Danny's only focus was on staying motionless and hidden. Moisture seeped through his clothes from the wet grass, but he'd spent longer than this hiding out in far worse conditions. The noise on the other side of the fence died away. The figure disappeared from the bedroom window and the light switched off. Danny gave it another ten minutes. Then he advanced.

He kept to the perimeter of the garden, where the fence afforded a little bit more camouflage. The high grass made a slight swishing sound underfoot, but he kept it to a minimum by careful pacing. He boxed round the side of the house, then quickly crossed the grass until he was outside the back door. It was a dump here. Old cardboard boxes, made soggy by the rain, were piled high against the back wall of the house. A foul smell filled the air from bin bags full of rotting refuse. Danny had the impression that Abu Ra'id's missus was a prisoner in her own house. He gave the back door a cursory examination. Two mortice locks and a single pane of glass. Hard to open, and it would make an unnacceptably loud noise if he shattered the window. He looked around for the entry point he thought he'd seen on Google Maps.

He found it in seconds.

Danny didn't imagine that the old brick coal bunker had been used for decades. It was a couple of metres wide, a couple deep and maybe a metre high. Right now it was covered with slimy, wet old bin bags, which Danny carefully removed to one side. On the top of the bunker was a rusted metal plate with an iron handle. He yanked it.

Stuck.

Danny climbed on top of the bunker and yanked it again with a bit more force. This time it worked loose, but made a harsh grating sound as it came off in Danny's hands that sounded all the louder because he needed to be quiet, and sounds could travel a long way through a quiet house – even up to the White Witch's bedroom, if that's where she currently was. He crouched down and remained motionless for two minutes. Then, when he was sure he hadn't disturbed anyone, he took his red torch and shone it down into the bunker. It was about two metres deep. He lay the grate so that it was half covering the hole, then jumped down into the bunker.

Silence.

There was no coal here. Probably hadn't been for years. Rodent droppings all over the floor. And an opening, only a metre high and half a metre wide, into the basement of the house.

He was in.

The basement was high enough to stand in, and completely empty. A flight of wooden steps on the far side. Danny crept up them. A door at the top. He extinguished his torch and tried it.

Unlocked.

He stepped out on to the ground floor of the house, and closed the cellar door quietly behind him.

It smelled damp. Musty. Dirty. He was in a hallway. To his right, the kitchen, which looked out over the back garden. To his left, a staircase heading up to the first floor, and a door to the front room. He paused, concentrating hard on the quietness of the sleeping house as he fixed his next move in his mind. He didn't know for sure that the White Witch was alone in the house, and although it seemed likely, he knew his interrogation of her needed to be as quiet as possible. He didn't want anybody walking in while he got to work on her. Best place was her bedroom: a hand over the mouth while she was asleep would stop her screaming when she realised there was an intruder in her house.

A minute passed. Everything was quiet. He got ready to creep up the stairs.

But then there was a sound.

Footsteps up above. Light spilled down the stairway.

Danny quickly evaluated his options. Head back down into the cellar? No: harder then to tell when the coast was clear. Kitchen? If she came downstairs, it was most likely that's where she'd be heading. He fixed his eyes on the other door. Decision made. He headed towards it. To his left he saw a shadow stretching down the stairs, cast by someone standing at the top. He had a horrible intuition that she'd heard him.

He silently opened the door and stepped into the room beyond.

A poky sitting room. His eyes picked out the shape of a sofa by the window. A fireplace with a large picture above the mantle. TV in one corner. A rug on the floor. The same stale smell that pervaded the whole house. He hurried over to the sofa and crouched down beside it. As long as it stayed dark, he'd be hidden. If she turned the light on, things would hot up.

Footsteps down the stairs.

The hallway light came on, spilling into the room through the few inches where the door was ajar.

From his hiding place he briefly saw a figure pass the crack in the door.

He felt his jugular pulsing. If there was going to be violence, he wanted it to be on his terms. At the moment, it wasn't.

A clattering sound in the kitchen. She was looking for something.

Footsteps again. They stopped outside the front room. The door slowly opened.

She was standing there. A silhouette in the door frame. He could clearly see the shape of her head, the folds of her dressing gown.

If he moved, she would see him.

She made a sucking sound through her teeth. Danny's eyes flickered round, looking for a weapon. They fell on the picture over the fireplace. The light spill from the door was shining on it now. It wasn't a picture at all. It was an Arabic symbol.

A symbol he had seen before. Recently.

He tried to place it, but couldn't.

Suddenly, the woman turned. It seemed she was satisfied that there was no intruder in the house. She switched the light off and clumped up the stairs.

Silence, and darkness, filled the house once more.

Danny waited a couple of minutes before moving again. He slipped out of the front room and silently climbed the stairs.

He knew which was her room, because he'd seen the light

from outside. At the top of the stairs he walked along the landing until he was there. The door was slightly open. He peered in. He could see the bulk of her body beneath her blankets. Distance to the bed, five metres. If he crossed it quickly, he could have one hand over her mouth before she screamed.

He inhaled slowly.

Then he moved.

She was awake. He could tell that by the way she started before he was even halfway across the bedroom floor. But before she could make a noise, he was looming over her. Even in the darkness he could see the whites of her eyes as she stared up at him. He slammed one hand down on her mouth before she could make a noise, even though he sensed that she hadn't been going to scream.

Only her head was visible above the blankets. Her body, however, was very still. Tense. She was no looker. Pasty skin. Spots. Greasy black hair matted to her forehead. A rank smell of stale sweat.

'Listen very carefully,' Danny breathed. 'Your fella's dead. I watched him having his throat cut. His little friends with the big bombs are dead too. I killed the fuckers myself. Nasty way to go, all of them. And I *will* kill you, in a way that will hurt more than you can imagine, if you don't do exactly what I tell you to.'

She made no attempt to speak.

There was a lamp on the bedside table. No lampshade, just a bare bulb. He reached over with his spare hand and twisted the bulb from the lamp. He threw it to the floor, then switched the lamp on and held the bulb socket an inch from her cheek. 'Make a sound,' he said, 'and you're toast.'

No response.

He gingerly lifted his hand from over her lips. No sound. She just stared straight up at him.

'Abu Ra'id left you a message. You want to hear it?'

A pause.

In the split second that followed, Danny realised now what the clattering sound in the kitchen had been. She'd fetched herself a weapon. The White Witch thrust upwards with one hand and the point of a sharp kitchen blade pierced her duvet. Danny knocked it away easily enough with his free hand, but this woman wasn't giving up without a struggle. She managed to sit up. The duvet fell away, revealing her flabby white breasts. She tried to stab at Danny again with her knife – a hopeless gesture that Danny easily deflected for a second time. But she leaned forward as she did it, and the flesh of her breasts pressed against the exposed bulb socket that Danny was holding in his right hand.

The electric shock was sudden and immediate. The White Witch's body jolted violently, and so did Danny's because his right arm was suddenly in contact with the woman's chest. He let go of the lamp just as her limbs flailed momentarily out of control. Her legs jarred upwards, and her right arm, which still held the knife, slammed back inwards towards Danny.

Danny's faculties were blurred by the shock. He instinctively knocked the knife hand away yet again, but it was an awkward movement, pushing the knife back towards the White Witch's chest. She saw it approaching and tried to twist out of the way, but in doing so her skin came in contact with the bulb socket for a second.

Danny barely saw what happened. All he knew was that there was another violent jolt, and a second later, there was blood all over her stomach. The White Witch looked down in horror to see the blade sticking into her belly.

A moment of silence. The lamp fell away from the bed and clattered on the floor. Then a mouthful of blood erupted from the White Witch's lips and spattered over her pasty, pale breasts.

'Shit,' Danny breathed. '*Shit!*'

Danny grabbed the knife and pulled it from her body. Blood pissed out over the sheets. He quickly laid her out onto her side, but the whites of her eyes were rolling upwards now. Her breath came in short, sharp gasps. Danny was reminded of Spud. But Spud was tough. The White Witch wasn't. She was on the way out.

'He left something for you,' Danny whispered quickly. 'He said you'd find it in the name of God. What did he mean?'

No reply.

'*What did he mean?*'

She was unconscious. Perfectly still. Bleeding out.

Danny stared at her. Then he looked at his own hands. Blood. Everywhere. He realised his DNA – DNA that was undoubtedly filed away on a system somewhere – was smeared all over this gruesome scene.

He staggered back from the bed, blood dripping from his hands. The White Witch wasn't dead yet, but she would be soon. An involuntary, mirthless laugh escaped Danny at the grotesque way she'd met her end. Then the horrible reality fell in on him. His enemies – whoever they were – would realise that *he* was alive just as soon as forensics got to grips with this scene. After everything he'd gone through in the past few days, he was fucked.

He staggered back to the stairs and hurried down a lot less stealthily than he'd climbed them. Still swearing under his breath, he walked past the open door into the front room.

Suddenly he stopped.

He turned again, and looked through the open door.

A memory flashed in his mind. He was at Hammerstone, watching the grisly video of the young man Abu Ra'id had almost persuaded to slice his own throat. In the background was a canvas with an Arabic symbol on it. He heard Spud's sarcastic voice. *Looks like a bird's arse.*

His eyes traced the shape of the symbol above the fireplace. A 'w' shape, followed by an 'i', with strange markings above.

It's the Arabic for Allah, Buckingham had said. *A very sacred symbol to the Muslim community.*

Danny blinked.

What had Abu Ra'id said? *Only my contact and I have the address and the password, but you will find them in the name of God. You know where to look.*

Allah. The name of God.

He stepped into the room again, his eyes flickering towards the curtains. The surveillance guys didn't know he was here. They didn't know their subject was dead. He reckoned he could allow himself a couple of minutes to act on his hunch.

It was a square frame, about 60 by 60cm. He lifted it off the wall and carried it down into the basement – the only place in the house he felt secure using his torch. He laid it on the ground, face down, and scanned the backing board. No marks of any kind.

The board was stuck into the frame by strips of brown tape. Danny scraped them off with bloody fingernails, leaving traces of the woman's gore over the board. When it was loose, he pulled it out and turned it over.

There was a white sticky label on the inside of the board. In neat, handwritten letters, it bore the words 'username' and 'password'. And next to each of these, a 16-digit alphanumberic string.

Carefully, Danny peeled it off, taking very good care that it should remain intact. He secreted the sticker in his trouser pocket.

A strange calmness had come over him. He'd got what he came for. Now he needed to get the hell out.

He knew that as soon as he tried to scale the garden wall, he risked being seen by the surveillance guys. If they saw him, they'd make chase. He exited back through the coal bunker, his shoulder muscles burning as he hauled himself through the opening and into the garden. He hurried straight up to the front gate. It was deadbolted on the inside. Danny thought for a moment. Then he pulled his threadbare balaclava out of his pocket and pulled it over his head. He unlocked the bolts and pushed the door open. Then he stood to one side, out of sight.

He estimated it would take 60 seconds for one of the surveillance guys to come and see what was happening. In the event they were slower off the mark. It was a full minute and a half before a figure appeared. He didn't quite enter the garden, but loitered in the frame of the gate for a fraction of a second. But that was all Danny needed. He grabbed the man and slammed his head against one of the fence's uprights. He knew instinctively how hard to do it – enough to knock him out, not so hard as to do him any permanent damage. He was just doing his job, after all. The guy slumped to the ground. Danny reckoned he'd be unconscious for about a minute. That gave him enough time.

If the second was following any kind of SOP, he'd still be in the vehicle. Danny ran out of the gate and across the door to the car. Sure enough, the second guy was sitting behind the wheel, his window open. At the sight of the balaclava'd man approaching him, he started to panic, quickly grabbing the wheel and fumbling for the keys. But Danny got there first. He leant over. 'Your mate needs an ambulance,' he lied. 'Urgently. You can either follow me, or help him. Up to you.'

With that, he walked round to the pavement and hurried back up to the top of the road. He ripped the balaclava off as he turned right, out of sight. He knew the surveillance guy wouldn't be in pursuit. He had time to disappear into the shadows.

But that was the only comfort he had. Now the clock was ticking. It was only a matter of time before his presence in that house was confirmed. When that happened, every last policeman and security agent in the country would be looking for him. Because one of the Hammerstone quartet – and he had a very good idea which one – would know he was on to them. And if they wanted to pin a murder on him, it would be child's play.

Which meant that now, he really did have no choice other than to use the information contained on a dog-eared sticky label to smoke out his enemy.

Before his enemy got to him first.

TWENTY-FOUR

03.00hrs

London could take your breath away at night, Danny had always thought. The bridges and the buildings all lit up. You could feel safe here, surrounded by all that strength.

But not tonight. Not Danny. Tonight London felt like the enemy, just like Ha'dah had.

The stretch of the Albert Embankment between Vauxhall Bridge and Lambeth Bridge was quiet. Danny walked past the MI6 building, brightly lit up even though the hour was early. But he was equally aware of MI5 on the other side of the river in Thames House. He looked ahead. Thirty metres away he saw three broad-shouldered men, one of whom had his arm in a sling. They were looking out over the river. Danny watched them for a moment. He saw Ripley, in his trademark biker's jacket. Barker in the sling, a reminder of their encounter with dealers what seemed like an age ago. And next to Barker, Hancock, who had a shock of bright orange hair that almost seemed to glow in the riverside lamps.

They'd made their RV in time.

An old tramp staggered past them. Ripley was looking impatiently at his watch. Danny let the tramp pass before he approached them.

Barker and Ripley eyed him warily. There were no fond greetings. Far from it. 'There's a piss-up tomorrow,' Ripley said. 'The lads wanted to give you and Spud a good send-off. You coming?'

Danny ignored the sarcasm. 'Busy,' he said. 'So will you be.'

'Where's Spud?'

Danny suppressed the cold twist of anxiety. 'I don't know,' he said. 'He might be dead.'

'So do you feel like telling us what the hell . . .'

'The reason you thought *I* was dead is because someone wants me that way. Spud too, and they might have succeeded on that count.' Danny gave Hancock a piercing look. 'Whoever it is, I think they were involved with the bombings.'

A steely look crossed Hancock's face. 'Go on,' he said.

'They've tried to kill me once and they'll try to kill me again. I need your help. Can I trust you?'

The three men looked at each other. 'What do you want us to do?' said Barker.

That was enough for Danny. He pointed towards the MI6 building, then across the river at Thames House, impressively lit up in the darkness. 'Surveillance,' he said.

'On who,' Ripley demanded.

'Four people. Their names are Victoria Atkinson, Harrison Maddox, Piers Chamberlain and Hugo Buckingham.' He reached inside his pocket and handed out the printouts of the Hammerstone quartet that he'd made in the library in Birmingham.

'One of this lot's my target. I just don't know which one yet. I need your help to smoke them out. Each of these people works out of a different building. Atkinson's MI5, so that's Thames House. Maddox should be at the American embassy. Chamberlain has an office at the MoD building in Whitehall. And Buckingham's MI6.'

'How do you know all this?' Ripley asked.

'A little bird told me.' The little bird was Buckingham, of course, after their first Hammerstone meeting, but the guys didn't need to know all about that.

'Come morning, each of us is going to keep eyes on one of

those buildings. We'll ID each one target as they enter their place of work. Once they're inside, I'm going to do something that's going to make one of them want to get to an RV. Each person needs following when they leave. Barker, you'll follow Atkinson from Thames House. Ripley, take Maddox from the Embassy. Hancock, you'll follow Chamberlain from the MOD building.'

'And you?' Hancock asked, his face intent and one eyebrow slightly raised.

'I'll take Buckingham,' Danny said quietly.

'No prizes for guessing who *your* money's on,' Ripley breathed.

Danny ignored that. 'Did you bring the bikes?'

Ripley frowned. His collection of motorbikes was his pride and joy. 'They're in the back of the Transit. I'm parked up a couple of blocks away.' He looked shiftily around him. 'Look, mate, they're nice bits of kit. Do you *really* have to use them?'

'It's that or Boris bikes,' Danny said.

Ripley looked at him like he'd just taken a shit on the pavement. 'I don't want a single fucking dent in *any* of them,' he said.

Danny was already looking at the bag Barker was holding.

'Did you get the phones?' he asked.

Barker nodded. 'Five of them. Samsungs. Pay as you go. Couple of gigs of data each. That's six hundred quid you owe me, mucker. Hope you're good for it.'

'I don't understand why you need five,' Ripley said. 'There's only four of us.'

'Give me two,' Danny said. For their own safety, the less they knew, the better.

Barker handed round the phones. They spent five minutes plugging in each other's numbers.

'All the bikes have a phone holder,' Ripley said as he tapped at the screen of his phone. 'Fucking use them, eh guys? I don't want you crashing my bikes because you've got your fucking phones in one hand.'

No answer from the others.

'And there's a chain and padlock for each one,' Ripley added, his voice increasingly anxious. 'Fucking big ones. Do me a favour and lock the bikes up if you leave them. I don't want some shit-kicker turning up and ...'

'We communicate by text,' Danny interrupted him. 'Every message goes to all of us. That way we can stay in the loop. Did you manage to bring any weapons?'

'Yeah,' Ripley said, the old sarcasm back in his voice. 'Just walked into the fucking armoury and checked them out.'

'Doesn't matter,' Danny said. 'Let's get the bikes, then find somewhere to sit it out till dawn. You need to study these images, commit them to memory so you can recognise the targets the moment you see them. We'll set up surveillance as soon as the sun comes up.'

Clara didn't know where she was.

The Poles had shoved her into the back of a four-by-four. How long ago had that been? Twenty-four hours? More? The guy who had grabbed her hair had taken the wheel. The other man, the one with the tattoos, had sat next to her, his flick knife just inches from the side of her midriff. Clara had been too frightened to take any notice of their route. She had considered trying to jump out of the car, but as soon as the driver saw her glancing towards the doors, he'd switched on the central locking.

'I'm not his girlfriend, you know,' she'd whispered after they'd been driving for ten minutes. 'He doesn't care about me.'

The Pole had given a mirthless little snort. 'You better hope he does,' he said. He pulled a phone from his pocket, punched in a passcode and started swiping until a photograph filled the screen. He held it in front of Clara's face. At first she couldn't tell what she was looking at. Then she did, and her stomach turned. It was a close-up of a gun wound. A shoulder, she thought, shattered, blotched and bloody. The Pole swiped again to reveal an image that showed the victim's entire body. A woman. Blonde hair, like Clara's. Sprawled on the floor, semi-naked, her lifeless limbs spread out.

'Want to know what we did to her before we killed her?' the Pole had asked.

Clara closed her eyes. 'No,' she'd whispered.

They had driven for 20 minutes. Clara told herself she wasn't going to scream. It would do no good, and she wouldn't give them the satisfaction. But she'd been screaming inside, especially when the car stopped and the Pole dragged her out of the vehicle.

They were in a different part of town, that was for sure. She'd looked up and seen another house. Detached. Brick. Two storeys. A number three on the door. Not quite as rundown as the place she'd just left, but not far off. Boarded windows. And was that razor wire on the sills?

She'd felt herself being pushed inside, along a dark hallway with peeling wallpaper. A door to the left. Stone steps leading down. The tattooed Pole had pushed her into the basement. There was a light down here, but nothing else. The Pole had thrown her to the floor, then kicked her hard in the ribs. She'd curled up into a little ball, whimpering as the pain coursed through her.

Through her tears she'd seen the second man arrive in the basement. He was carrying something. Clara had only realised it was a roll of packing tape when he started wrapping it around her head, several revolutions covering her mouth and sticking her hair. She'd tried to struggle, but the men were too strong for her. They'd forced her arms behind her body and wrapped the tape around her wrists.

As they left her in the basement, they'd switched the light off. Clara was glad of that. As she had been flailing on the floor, she thought she had noticed russet stains on the concrete. And as she lay there now, she couldn't but remember the picture her abductor had shown her, and wonder if this was where the woman in the image had met her death.

06.00hrs

The skies above London turned slowly from starless black to drab grey. Lights had been burning in the MI6 building all night, of course. Danny stood alone in the shade of a clump of trees, 30 metres from the impressive entrance, on the opposite side of the stretch of Albert Embankment that ran in front of the building. He watched more lights switch on behind the bomb-resistant windows. Behind him, a train trundled noisily past on its way into Waterloo.

The other three had confirmed that they were in place outside Thames House, the MoD building and the American Embassy. Danny himself was perched astride one of Ripley's bikes – a grey Yamaha TDM900. 'Top speed, 139 mph,' Ripley told him proudly as he handed over the keys. 'Crash the fucker, I'll rip your kidneys out and sell them to settle the bill.'

'It'll be fine.'

'And lock it up when you're not using it!' Ripley had called after him. There was a vast, thick chain with a sturdy padlock stowed in the storage box behind the saddle. Danny had no intention of using it. If he needed to move quickly, he couldn't be fucking around with security padlocks.

From this side of the building, he couldn't see the satellite dishes perched on top of the MI6 building, or even spot any CCTV. But he knew they were there. He wondered, too, if there might be plainclothes surveillance operating in the area. The helmet Ripley had given him hid his face, of course, but he remained alert for signs that he was being watched. So far as he could tell, there was no one.

At 7 a.m., as the trains into and from Waterloo became more regular and the traffic on the Albert Embankment started to stack up, employees of the security services started arriving en masse: men in suits, women in smart two-piece office wear, all of them trotting through the cold, dark morning to be swallowed up by the building. Danny looked up, wondering which of those windows, if any, was Buckingham's. But then he snapped himself back to ground level. He couldn't let his attention wander. He needed to keep sharp. And to make sure he saw his target as and when he entered the building.

He stood there for an hour. Watching. Picking out faces from the crowd.

No sign of him.

Just after 8 a.m. the phone he'd clipped to the holder on his bike lit up. A text message, from Hancock to him, Barker and Ripley. It said simply: 'PC'.

Which meant that Piers Chamberlain had turned up for work.

One down. Three to go.

The second text message came through about two minutes later. From Barker this time. 'VA'.

Victoria Atkinson had arrived. Danny's lingering worry that his rough printouts had been insufficient for the others to ID their targets started to ease. He shouldn't have worried. His SAS mates had been trained to observe, and to do it better than anyone else.

The traffic eased off. Fewer London buses, more black cabs. Danny worried that he might have missed seeing Buckingham enter the building during the rush hour. But he was fairly confident he hadn't. He didn't much like surveillance, but he was good at it.

The third text came through at 10.38 a.m., from Ripley. 'HM'. The CIA liaison officer had turned up at the American embassy.

Which left only Buckingham.

He didn't show all morning. By the time midday came around, Danny was cursing inwardly. His strategy relied on them being able to follow each member of the Hammerstone quartet. Trust

Buckingham to screw it up. If Atkinson, Chamberlain or Maddox left their locations before Buckingham arrived, they'd have to be followed from their place of work. The guys were up to it, but it wouldn't be ideal. Not ideal at all.

The afternoon wore on. It turned into evening. There was no word from the others, but that was to be expected: it just meant they had nothing to report. And no news was good news. It meant their other three targets were still in place. But it was 18.00hrs now, and Buckingham hadn't showed. With a sick feeling, Danny started to realise that his plan might be screwed . . .

Only it wasn't. Because at one minute to seven, just as the workers he'd seen arriving that morning were exiting the building to go home, Buckingham arrived. No chauffeur. Just him and a small leather briefcase. He trotted up the stairs and into the building.

Danny quickly sent his text to the others. 'HB'.

The targets were all in place.

He didn't hesitate for a second. Kicking the bike into action, he sped up towards Vauxhall Bridge. The road carried him straight past Victoria, across Hyde Park Corner and along the east side of Hyde Park. The Park Lane hotel, where he'd staked out Al-Sikriti, sped past on his right. But Danny's focus was on what was up ahead. He eased up on to Edgware Road, resisting the temptation to speed. Getting pulled over would be a disaster.

19.23hrs. Danny pulled up outside the dilapidated United Reform Church where, ten days previously, he had ended things with Clara. It had immediately popped into his head as a good place: deserted, but reasonably central. It was a large, red-brick building with old slate tiles on the roof. The mortar between the bricks was crumbling away, and clumps of litter – old crisp packets and Coke tins – had collected against its outside walls. The windows were boarded up and the whole place had an air of neglect.

He left Ripley's Yamaha unchained by the side of the road, then ran up towards the old building.

The door into the building was padlocked, but the lock was rusty and loose. The whole fitting came away after a few good tugs. Danny opened the door and stepped inside.

A single room, about 30 metres by 20. Dark. It smelled of damp. Bird shit covered the floor. A broken window at the far end, about three metres high on the wall. From somewhere, the drip-dripping of a leak. As Danny stepped inside, a flapping sound echoed off the vaulted ceiling and the silhouette of a pigeon tumbled across his vision before landing on the floor ten metres to his left. Otherwise, the place was completely empty.

Danny pulled out the fifth mobile phone Barker had acquired for him. He checked that the 3G signal was good. Then he opened the browser and navigated to the Gmail homepage. From his pocket he took the sticker he'd confiscated from Abu Ra'id's house. He tapped in the username and password for the first time. There was no way he could have risked a trial run before now, for fear that any activity on the account would be flagged. And there was no guarantee, he realised, that these account details would be correct or valid.

He hit 'enter'.

A pause.

Relief crashed over him as an empty inbox appeared on his screen.

Quickly, he hit 'compose'. Then he started typing.

It takes more than a drone strike to kill me.

He saved the message as a draft.

He brought up a new browser page. It took only a few seconds to find a webpage that had archived the text of a standard Nigerian scam e-mail, offering a hundred grand in return for five hundred quid being deposited in a bank account. The sort of thing any right-thinking person would delete without a second glance.

Unless they saw that it came from an e-mail address they recognised, of course.

He copied the text, then pasted it on to a fresh e-mail from the Abu Ra'id account.

He had committed to memory the address from which Hammerstone had sent their instructions. Now he keyed it into the top of the e-mail.

He stared at the screen for a moment, knowing that to hit 'send' would set in motion events whose outcome he couldn't predict. A dodgy e-mail would arrive on the screens of the Hammerstone quartet. Only one of them, he assumed, would recognise the address it came from, and would surely take it as a sign to check the draft e-mail he'd left, purporting to be from Abu Ra'id. With the resources at their fingertips, it would be trivial for them to track the location of the phone that had sent the e-mail.

And then what? Danny didn't know. A hunted animal could be unpredictable. Certainly Danny couldn't stay here. If he'd miscalculated, an armed unit could arrive at any moment and he couldn't risk being in the vicinity. But if he was right, his target wouldn't want to involve anyone else.

He hit 'send'. Then he laid the phone on the ground of the deserted church hall.

He left the building, and jumped back on to Ripley's bike. He performed a roaring u-turn as he headed back towards the Euston Road.

Suddenly he stopped. He checked his watch. 19.31hrs. Instead of turning left on to the Euston Road he roared over it, towards the canal. Thirty seconds later, he had come to a halt again. The Yamaha's engine purred deeply as he looked to his left.

He could see Clara's ground-floor flat on the other side of the canal. There were no lights on. He took that as a good sign. A sign that Kyle had done as he had asked and got Clara the hell out of there, to somewhere safe.

378

But a cold, uneasy feeling in his gut doubled in intensity. Could he trust Kyle? Like hell he could. He wished he could call Clara, just once. Hear her telling him that she was okay. But he couldn't. Not yet. The risk was too great.

For fuck's sake, Danny. You have to get back. He turned again, and floored it back towards the MI6 building south of the river.

Danny was halfway across Vauxhall Bridge when the phone clipped to his bike lit up. It was a message from Ripley.

It said: *Target leaving.*

That meant Harrison Maddox had been the first to move.

TWENTY-FIVE

19.42hrs

Danny's mouth was dry as he took up position opposite the MI6 building again. He texted Ripley: *Don't lose him.*

Thoughts flickered through his mind. *Had the CIA man been the one to take his bait? Had the Yanks been working with Abu Ra'id, persuading him to foment whatever bloodshed he could in London, to keep the wavering Brits on side in the war on terror?*

He had to rely on Ripley tailing the Yank to the very best of his abilities, and reporting back on his movements asap.

Danny turned his attention back to the MI6 building. As a full moon rose behind the blocky architecture, two middle-aged men climbed into separate limos at 19.45hrs and 19.51hrs precisely. Lined faces, expensive suits. Like Buckingham in 20 years' time. But *not* Buckingham.

At 19.55, a second text came through. It was Barker. *VA leaving.*

Keep on her, Danny texted back.

The old suspicions started multiplying in his mind. *The Muslim husband. The lost six months in Saudi. Could Victoria Atkinson really be a sleeper at the very heart of security services?*

It would seem not. Three minutes later another text came through from Barker. *Heading south over Lambeth Bridge.* The opposite direction from central London.

Two minutes after that, his phone vibrated. Ripley. *WW debussing at Canadian Embassy. Looks like a cocktail party.*

Keep eyes on, he texted back. But mentally he struck Maddox off his list before returning his attention to the MI6 building.

Ten minutes passed. The rush-hour traffic on the Albert Embankment started to thin out a little. At 20.20hrs, a message came through from Barker. *VA entered house near Old Kent Road. Family home? Young girl met her at the door. Daughter?*

Victoria Atkinson was home for the evening. Tucking the kids up in bed. It kind of figured.

Piers Chamberlain was the third to leave. Danny received a text from Hancock at 20.28hrs to say as much.

Don't lose him, he texted back as Chamberlain's face swam in front of his eyes. *The royal links. The unfavoured boyfriend who'd died in the first bombing. The right-wing sympathies and the strange conversation they'd had with him in the cafe.*

Three targets were on the move. Only Buckingham was left. Danny's pulse was racing. He felt as if the traffic was driving past in slow motion. Headlamps seemed to blur in his vision. He found that he was not even remotely surprised when a text message came through from Hancock which read: *PC in Mayfair. MILF in a dressing gown opened the door to him. Dirty bastard.*

So Piers Chamberlain was getting his end away.

Which meant he wasn't travelling to Edgware.

Nor was Victoria Atkinson.

Nor was Harrison Maddox.

Buckingham appeared at 20.32hrs.

He was alone, a shoulder bag made of soft brown leather slung in front of him. He had two hands over it, as if it contained something special. He stood at the entrance to the MI6 building for a moment, an expression on his face that Danny found difficult to fathom. He looked around, as though checking that nobody was watching. Then he stepped forwards to the edge of the pavement. He looked right, into the line of the traffic, and raised the forefinger of his right hand. Forty-five seconds later, a black cab pulled over in front of him. It had an advert for cheap calls to Africa on the side. Buckingham leaned in to speak to the driver, then he opened the rear door and climbed inside.

Danny followed.

It took every ounce of his self-restraint to keep a covert distance. When the cab turned right over Vauxhall Bridge towards the centre of town, he felt his pulse quickening as the vehicle remained out of sight for the 20 seconds it took to catch up. And when it ran a yellow light up towards Victoria, he cursed under his helmet as the subsequent red light forced him to wait for a full minute and a half. Impossible to run it: there was a police car over his right shoulder, so even when the light turned green he had to keep himself well within the speed limit.

No sign of Buckingham's cab. Danny swore again. Streets fed left and right off the main road. He had no way of knowing if the cab had turned into one of them. And yet he knew, instinctively, that Buckingham's path would lead up past Victoria and towards Hyde Park Corner, just as Danny's had done earlier. On Ripley's bike he was able to weave through the traffic. Sure enough, as he approached the station he saw the cab up ahead. *Nigeria, 1p a minute.* He manoeuvred up to within 20 metres. The cab continued north-west.

A message came through from Ripley as he was passing the Park Lane Hotel again. *What's ur status?* He ignored it. All his attention was on the cab up ahead. And the scheming, duplicitous, treacherous piece of shit inside it. Of *course* it was Buckingham who had taken his bait. Of *course* it was Buckingham who was heading to the location where he'd left the phone he sent the message from. Buckingham had been involved in this from the beginning. He'd brought Danny and Spud on board because he thought he could control them. And because he knew they'd get done whatever job he gave them. Danny felt sickened at the thought of Buckingham being in league with Abu Ra'id. The cleric's voice replayed itself in his mind as Marble Arch came into view up ahead. *Everything I have done, I have done with the full knowledge of this person. They have their reasons for wanting the streets of London to be filled with terror.* What was Buckingham's reason? To create a monster, then catch him so he could reap the rewards and the praise?

Edgware Road. The cab overtook a bus and slipped out of sight for a moment. Danny swerved out and a car behind him honked its horn angrily. He accelerated past the bus. Green lights ahead. The taxi passed under the Westway. Danny stuck to him. The taxi travelled another 50 metres. It suddenly indicated left before pulling over.

Danny didn't stop. He just continued past the taxi as Buckingham climbed out of the back and paid the driver. He hooked a left into a dark side street and killed the engine on the Yamaha. He ripped off the helmet and hung it from the handlebars. Then he turned and ran back up to the corner of the side street and Edgware Road.

He could see Buckingham approaching. Distance: 30 metres. The little shit looked shifty. He was still clutching his leather shoulder bag. He looked like he was hurrying.

Distance, 20 metres. Danny stayed on that corner, his head down. He didn't want Buckingham to recognise him before he'd made his move. He found himself clutching his knuckles, almost on instinct. He concentrated on the bag. What was in there?

A weapon?

Ten metres. Buckingham seemed to be talking to himself, his lips moving quickly but silently. A couple of kids cycled past on the pavement. Two red buses slid by in quick succession.

Five metres.

Danny raised his head.

'Going somewhere nice?' he said.

Buckingham stopped.

At first he looked behind him. It was as if he hadn't even seen Danny. Or if he had, he'd looked straight through him.

In the distance was the sound of a siren.

Another red bus trundled past.

Buckingham looked forwards again. His eyes fell finally on Danny. They widened.

'You,' he breathed. Then he swallowed hard.

'Not dead enough for you?' Danny asked.

He stepped forwards. Buckingham staggered back, bumping into a couple who were walking arm in arm along the street. The man looked like he was going to say something, but Danny gave him a fierce look and the couple hurried on.

Danny stepped up towards Buckingham and grabbed him by one arm. 'Let's have a little chat,' he said.

He could almost hear the clockwork in Buckingham's brain. 'Bloody good to see you, old sport,' Buckingham said, his tongue tripping over the words. 'We all thought you'd been . . .'

'Conveniently blown up?' Danny suggested.

He dragged Buckingham down the side street.

'You should have let us know you were okay. We could have . . .'

'Sent in another drone to finish us off?'

'Of . . . of course not . . . arranged some sort of . . . help.'

Danny stopped in the shadow of a parked van, manhandled Buckingham so that he was facing him, then kneed him hard in the bollocks. Buckingham groaned as he bent double. Danny raised his knee again, sharply cracking it under Buckingham's chin. Buckingham fell back on to his arse. He was still clutching his leather shoulder bag.

Danny crouched down so they were face to face. 'Let's talk,' he hissed.

A flash of anger entered Buckingham's eyes. 'You've gone too far . . .'

'Too far?' Danny spat the words with contempt. 'I haven't gone *nearly* far enough. How many people were *you* willing to kill, Buckingham? You and your buddy Abu Ra'id?'

Buckingham stared at him, speechless.

'What did you promise him, you piece of shit? Immunity? Money?'

'What the . . .'

'How did you feel when you saw the e-mail, Buckingham? How many alarm bells went off in your head when you thought he was still alive and not dismembered in the Yemeni *fucking* desert with me and Spud.'

Danny's temperature was rising. He felt the anger taking him over. Controlling him. Before he knew what had happened, he'd dealt a cracking blow to Buckingham's pretty-boy cheek. Buckingham fell to his side, a huge welt immediately appearing on the side of his face. Still clutching his shoulder bag, he tried to scramble away, but Danny was already on him. He dragged him up to his feet again, then thrust him up against the side of the van. The jolt made the van's alarm start to blare loudly. Danny hardly heard it. He was too intent on doing Buckingham harm.

'We're going to go somewhere quiet,' he shouted over the alarm, 'and you're going to tell me absolutely . . . fucking . . . *everything*!'

'You're insane,' Buckingham hissed from between swollen, bleeding lips. 'You've lost your mind, Black.'

'What were you going to say to Abu Ra'id when you finally caught up with him?'

'You'll bloody well pay for this – I *don't* know what you're talking about.'

'Bullshit,' Danny growled. 'You're the only one who's responded to the e-mail.'

'*What* e-mail?'

On an impulse, Danny grabbed the leather shoulder bag from Buckingham's arms. It was bulky. Heavier than an ordinary handgun. 'What were you going to do, Buckingham? Finish him off yourself?' He ripped the shoulder bag open.

But he didn't find a weapon. He found a bottle. Champagne.

'What the fuck . . .'

Danny stared at the champagne. Then he looked at Buckingham.

'You're supposed to be *dead*,' Buckingham snapped. 'Why *wouldn't* I go round and offer my condolences?' He tried to straighten his tie – a ridiculous attempt to make himself look presentable, given the mashed-up state of his features. 'She's too bloody good for an oik like you anyway.'

Danny blinked. It took a couple of seconds for him to twig what Buckingham was on about.

'Clara?' he whispered incredulously. He looked again at the bottle of champagne. 'You were going to try it on with *Clara?*'

Buckingham's bloodied face grew redder. 'Well why the bloody hell not?'

A terrible pause.

'I don't believe you,' Danny said. 'You were working with Abu Ra'id all along. *You* were behind the bombings.'

'*What?*'

'You heard me. Abu Ra'id knew about Hammerstone. I heard it from his own lips.' He reached out one hand and grabbed Buckingham by the throat. 'And since you're the most treacherous little cunt I've ever met . . .'

'*It must have been one of the others,*' Buckingham said in a strangled voice. '*Maddox . . . the Americans . . . they're always sticking their nose in . . .*'

Danny shook his head slowly. He'd heard Buckingham's pathetic attempts to shift the blame one time too many.

'*What about Chamberlain?* The man's got more skeletons in his closet than . . .'

Danny squeezed harder. Buckingham's voice petered out as he gasped for breath.

'*Victoria,*' he said, high-pitched, desperate. He started babbling, words tumbling out of his mouth. '*It's all an act, you know. She pretends to be all mumsy and scatty, all that family stuff, but she's ruthless.*'

'Bullshit.'

'You're wrong. She slept her way to the top, you know . . . I heard she shagged half the Russian-speakers in London . . . the academics . . . you know how that lot have all been tapped up by MI6 . . .'

Danny blinked. 'What?' he said, loosening his grip slightly.

Buckingham clearly thought he was getting somewhere. He nodded furiously. *'Fucked them all, just to get her first job at Moscow station . . .'*

All of a sudden, Danny let Buckingham go. The spook doubled over, clutching at his bruised neck. Danny's mind was elsewhere. He was remembering a conversation he'd had, days previously, in the bowels of Paddington police station with DI Fletcher. Fletcher had been holding up a report on his desk. His words rang verbatim in Danny's ears. *'This poor fella, a Professor Gengerov, lectures at one of them universities up Bloomsbury way, cycling to work last Friday just as he has done every day for the last twenty years, some idiot knocks him off his bike and kills him stone dead. We haven't even collected the witness statements yet.'*

A hit and run on the same day as the first bombing. Hidden at the bottom of the pile while the police investigated more important things.

The warmth drained from Danny's body. What if Buckingham *hadn't* been heading towards the RV? What if he *had* been heading to Clara's to get his end away?

Danny staggered back. Had he got everything so wrong? Had his strategy just collapsed around his ears?

No. It was impossible. Buckingham was messing with his head. The little shit was talking now, spitting bile, aggressive bullshit. Danny didn't hear a word he said. His mind was spinning. He couldn't get a single thought straight in his mind.

'You're bluffing!' he heard himself shouting at Buckingham. He stepped angrily towards him, all the stress and tiredness of the past few days crashing over him. He wanted to hurt Buckingham. Badly. The fire was back in his blood again.

Buckingham shrank back.

'*You're fucking bluffing!*' Danny roared again, raising his fists, ready to pummel the cunt to kingdom come.

His phone buzzed.

Not a text message. A phone call.

Danny froze. As the terrified Buckingham cowered once more against the side of the van, he pulled his phone out of his pocket.

It was Barker.

He accepted the call.

'What is it?' he growled.

'Fuck's sake!' Barker sounded out of breath. 'I've been trying to get hold of you.'

'What's the matter?'

'Victoria Atkinson left home about twenty minutes ago. I've been tailing her, but I just *fucking* lost her because my arm's in this *fucking* sling . . .'

Danny blinked. A sudden calmness came over him. Buckingham was scrambling away, running down the street. Danny didn't follow.

'She's driving herself,' Barker said, still breathless, still clearly pissed with himself. 'A green Yaris. She's in a fucking hurry, mucker. Ran three red lights before she even hit the river.'

Danny took a deep breath.

'Last seen?'

A scrambled noise. Barker was breaking up.

'Say again,' Danny said.

Barker came back online. 'Park Lane,' he said. 'Heading up to Marble Arch. I'm sorry, mucker – that's where I lost her. I don't know where she's going . . .'

But Danny did. He killed the phone line and looked down the street. Buckingham had stopped about 20 metres away and was looking back, breathless.

Danny threw the leather shoulder bag into the gutter. There

was the sound of glass breaking. He turned his back on Buckingham, who started shouting again. 'You'll bloody *pay* for it, Black. I'll have you hung, drawn and bloody well *quartered* for this.'

But Danny wasn't listening. He started jogging. His jog turned to a run. Moments later he was sprinting across the Edgware Road, then north, towards the dilapidated United Reform church where he had laid his trap.

He'd been following the wrong scent, but now he was back on track.

He had to get there first.

TWENTY-SIX

Danny stopped at the corner of Station Way. He could see the
United Reform church from this position. Thirty metres distant,
the moon seeming to hang over it, bright and full. He watched
carefully for a full minute, looking for anything suspicious.

Nothing.

His eyes scanned the vehicles parked along the road. They
were all cars. No vans or trucks that would have rung alarm
bells.

A couple of pedestrians walked up the street. But they didn't
look at the church, and soon disappeared.

He checked the roof. No movement.

So far as he could tell, the location was unobserved.

He advanced 15 metres on the opposite side of the street to
the church, then stopped by a bus stop. No shelter, not even a
timetable, and no other passengers waiting.

A vehicle turned into Station Way from the south side.
Headlamps on. As it passed, Danny saw it was a blue Golf. It
continued to the far end of the road and disappeared.

Now a second car had appeared from the opposite direction.
A Mini Cooper. It shot past Danny. As it reached the south end
of Station Way it honked its horn loudly at a third vehicle that
had swung its way carelessly into the road. The third car
approached. It pulled up on to the kerb ten metres short of the
church entrance. The driver killed the lights. Danny squinted, to
see what kind of car it was.

Yaris. Green.

Suddenly the street seemed unnaturally quiet.

Danny inhaled slowly. He leaned against the bus stop and watched the Yaris from the corner of his eye.

A minute passed. Nobody emerged.

Suddenly, the clunking sound of a door opening. A figure climbed out. Short. Dumpy. She closed the door quietly behind her, but didn't lock it. She had a large handbag from which she took something. Danny couldn't see what it was, but by the way she covered her right hand with one side of her coat, he could tell it was most likely a weapon. Victoria Atkinson was armed.

Danny wasn't.

She looked around, her body language nervous. And either she was unskilled in surveillance, or her nerves were getting the better of her, because she didn't even seem to notice Danny loitering by the bus stop, staring at the pavement to hide his face.

She moved, checking over her shoulder with every step.

Ten seconds later, she was at the front door of the church. Danny had left it unlocked. She removed the firearm from inside her coat, pointed it in front of her, and stepped inside.

Danny didn't hesitate. He ran, lightfooted, across the road, then approached the entrance to the church a little more slowly. His every sense was on high alert. If she reappeared, the shock of seeing him could very well cause her to discharge her firearm.

But she didn't reappear. The door was slightly ajar. Wide enough for Danny to slip sideways through the gap.

It took a fraction of a second to take everything in.

A shard of moonlight cut into the church hall from the broken window at the far end. It illuminated Victoria Atkinson, who was standing in the middle of the hall. She was ten metres from Danny, her back towards him, and was staring at the mobile phone that was still on the floor where he had left it. Even though it was no longer raining outside, there was still a dripping sound from the far end. It echoed around the empty room.

Atkinson's shoulder's seemed hunched. Somehow exhausted. Even so, Danny could tell that she was holding out the weapon – a snubnose of some type – in front of her as she stared down at the mobile phone. She was a hunted animal, trapped in a corner. He needed to disarm her as quickly as possible.

He knew it wouldn't be a problem.

He covered the distance in a couple of seconds. Only when he was five metres away did Atkinson become aware of someone else in the hall. She spun round, her gun hand wavering dangerously, shock and panic on her face. Danny plunged towards her, knocking the weapon from her hand before she had time to fire it. It clattered noisily as it went spinning across the floor, while Atkinson collapsed into an inelegant heap.

Danny stood over her. She looked up.

The colour drained from her face. Her eyes widened. Confusion.

Then she closed them.

'I didn't have a choice,' she whispered.

'Everyone has a choice,' Danny said. His eyes flickered towards the gun. It was lying five metres away. He stepped over and picked it up. An S&W 9mm snubnose revolver. It seemed improbable that someone like Victoria even knew how to use it. But he wasn't going to take the chance.

'Get to your feet,' he said.

Atkinson didn't move. 'If you're going to kill me,' she whispered, 'please don't do it here. Let me disappear. I don't want my children to see my body.'

Danny felt a click of satisfaction. He knew that everyone had a pressure point. Atkinson had just artlessly revealed hers. He raised the snubnose and pointed it at her. 'I'll post your fucking corpse through their bedroom window if you don't start talking.'

She stared at him in horror. 'I *didn't* have a choice,' she whispered.

Silence. Just the drip-dripping of water. And outside, the

sound of a car passing. Danny stepped towards the mobile phone and pulled the battery from the back. Then he flung it back to the floor. It clattered noisily. He gave Atkinson a long, uncomfortable stare, but didn't say anything.

'He threatened to kill my family,' she whispered.

A pause.

'Abu Ra'id?'

Atkinson shook her head. 'Of course not,' she breathed. She buried her head in her hands for a moment. When she looked up again, her face was tear-strewn. Mascara was smeared round her eyes. Danny almost felt sorry for her.

Almost.

'Gengerov?' he asked quietly.

The name seemed to go through Victoria like an electric shock.

'You know?' she whispered.

Danny kept a blank face. He couldn't let her see how little he actually *did* know.

'Abu Ra'id told you?'

No response.

'I was young,' Atkinson breathed. 'I didn't understand. Pyotr Gengerov helped me with my Russian so that I could get my Moscow posting.'

She closed her eyes again. 'We fell in love,' she said. 'At least, I fell in love. That's all. I didn't *think* I was being indiscreet.'

'What did you tell him?'

'Nothing,' Atkinson said. 'Really, nothing. Nothing important. But it was enough. Enough for him to . . .' She buried her head in her hands again.

'To blackmail you?' Danny said.

She nodded.

'How long have you been feeding him information?'

A pause.

'Twenty years,' she said. 'He said he would reveal everything if

I didn't keep the intelligence coming. I'd have gone to prison for the rest of my life. And I had . . . I had *children* by then . . .'

She dissolved into helpless tears. Danny paced round her. He knew there was more to come.

'I thought I was getting away with it,' she said once her crying had subsided a little. 'But then . . . Syria happened. Relations between us and the Russians hit rock bottom. And he wanted . . .' She tried to steady herself with a deep breath. 'They wanted names. The names of all British personnel operating undercover in the Middle East and Africa.'

Danny felt himself frowning. He wondered how many of his mates' names would be on a list like that.

'And?' he asked, his voice dangerously quiet.

She shook her head. 'I couldn't do it,' she whispered. 'I swear, I just couldn't do it. But he insisted. He'd always kept my identity secret from Moscow, but now he said if I didn't give him a list of names, he'd reveal my name to Moscow *and* London. And he threatened to harm my family. I believed him. You don't know what he's like. I *truly* believed him.'

Another pause.

'So you decided to kill him,' Danny said.

Bloodshot eyes looked back at him. 'It was for my children.' Her voice cracked as she spoke.

'And Abu Ra'id?' Danny said.

She bowed her head again. 'He was my best weapon,' she said.

'What do you mean?'

A flash of irritation crossed her face. 'Why do you think nobody could ever deport him? He was working for *us*! Our highest-ranking double agent.'

Danny blinked heavily. '*What?*'

'Only a handful of us knew about it. Me, the head of MI6. Four or five others in the security services. The PM, of course. Abu Ra'id was going to deliver the whole network. Or so we thought. He was permitted to orchestrate minor acts of terrorism to keep his cover, but nothing like Paddington or the Trocadero. *Nothing* like that.'

Danny stared bleakly at her. 'Go on.'

Victoria lowered her eyes. 'I *truly* believed he was on our side. We all did. I didn't realise just what he would do for his own cause. When Gengerov demanded that list of names, I asked Abu Ra'id a personal favour. It was all anonymous, of course – he only knew me by a code name – but I needed someone to eliminate Gengerov. He could use his people to do it.'

'How did he know about Hammerstone?'

'He didn't,' she said flatly.

'He knew the name.'

Victoria thought for a moment, then nodded. 'I left him a package in the grounds of Hammerstone House containing all the details he needed to know about Gengerov. I mean, for God's sake, I couldn't just invite him into Thames House. I told him he could engineer some small diversion, to distract everyone's attention from the hit on Gengerov. But I *swear*, I had no idea he would ...'

'That he would get his goons to fit up a bunch of Down's syndrome kids to bomb the fuck out of London?' Danny said.

'I never *thought* ...'

'*No!*' Danny spat back. Images of mutilated bodies in the bombings filed through his head. He remembered Spud the last time he'd seen him, on the brink of death, being wheeled into the back of the Red Cross van. 'You never *thought!*' He paced round her again, trying to work out his next move.

She looked up suddenly, her mascara more streaked than ever. 'I *tried* to fix it,' she said. 'Once Abu Ra'id had shown his true colours, he thought he had a hold over me. He thought now I was implicated in his beastly acts of terrorism, I'd bend over backwards to see he wasn't caught, in case he revealed my involvement.' A steely look came into her eyes. 'He thought wrong,' she said.

A change seemed to come over her. She pushed herself to her feet and brushed down her clothes with her hands.

'Very wrong, as it happens. You don't get to my position without knowing a few people in government that have the Prime Minister's ear. I dropped some hints, let them think it might soon leak out that Abu Ra'id was being kept safe for other purposes. Political dynamite. I knew it wouldn't be long until they issued a kill order.'

'So you needed a hunter-killer unit. Small enough to control, and small enough to eliminate when the job was done, in case they found out the truth when they caught up with Abu Ra'id.'

She stared at him. 'I'm sorry,' she whispered. 'Buckingham spoke so highly of you. And if I didn't bury my tracks, my children . . .'

'Yeah, yeah,' Danny muttered. 'Your children.' He paused a moment. 'Whose was the drone?' he demanded. 'British? American?'

She shook her head. 'Yemeni. I had access to the real-time data for your mission. It's standard practice. I . . . I supplied the Yemenis with coordinates from your GPS units. Anonymously, of course. They didn't want that training camp on their territory, any more than we would.' She grimaced slightly. 'But it seems you got the better of me.'

Danny continued to circle around her, the snubnose firmly in his grasp. 'I can't see any reason why I shouldn't just waste you now,' he said.

Victoria bowed her head. 'Wouldn't you do the same for your family?' she asked finally. Then she looked up at him. 'You've got to help family. It's the only thing we have.'

Danny stopped pacing. Her words cut through him. He thought of Kyle. Of how his brother had *begged* him for help, and how Danny had turned him away. He found that, despite everything, he had a weird kind of respect this woman. She'd fucked up, no doubt about it. But she was a fighter. A kindred spirit.

And anyway, now that he knew her secrets, he had some collateral.

'I'm not going to beg,' Victoria breathed. Her voice was shaking now. 'If you're going to do it . . .'

Danny held the weapon up to her head. Point blank. His finger rested calmly on the trigger.

'Do it quickly,' she whispered.

Danny stepped forward. He allowed the barrel of the gun to touch the back of her skull. 'If I let you walk out of here,' he said, 'the first thing you're going to is find Spud Glover. If he's still alive, the Red Cross will have him in Eritrea. I don't care if you have to use every last member of the military to do it. Whatever it takes, you get him back. Understood?'

He watched the back of her head nod slowly up and down. Her shoulders trembled.

'You've got twelve hours to square things for me with Hammerstone and the Regiment. I want to be able to walk into Hereford HQ first thing in the morning, and if I have to answer too many questions about how we disappeared in Yemen and cropped up in the UK, we might end up telling someone the truth.'

Slowly, Victoria Atkinson turned. Her wide eyes were brimful of tears. Of gratitude or terror, Danny couldn't tell. 'Thank you,' she whispered. She clenched her hands against her chest. There was something pitiful about her. The smeared mascara. The mussed hair. '*Thank you.*'

Danny scowled. 'Get out of my sight,' he breathed.

She stepped backwards, her heel buckling slightly.

'Thank you,' she repeated again. She was unable to take her eye off the firearm, which Danny was still pointing in her direction.

Danny lowered it.

She turned. She upped her pace towards the exit.

And then, suddenly, she screamed.

TWENTY-SEVEN

They had entered the room silently. Two figures. Balaclavas. Jeans and leather jackets. MP5 SDs – permanently suppressed submachine guns. Ideal for close-quarter battle. Quiet. Ruthlessly effective.

Regiment? They easily could be. They held their weapons like pros. But that variant was not standard SAS issue. They might be pros, but they weren't colleagues.

Distance between Danny and the armed men: 15 metres. Victoria was bang in the middle. And Danny knew if he raised his snubnose just an inch, he'd be dead.

A third figure appeared in the doorway. Just a silhouette, at first. He stood there in the shadows. Danny found he was holding his breath.

'Interesting conversation,' said the figure. An American voice. Slow. Kind of polite. Instantly recognisable.

Victoria gasped.

The figure stepped out of the shadow and further into the church hall, the moonlight lighting up his face. The two shooters stayed where they were.

Silence. The water dripped at the far end of the hall. Victoria didn't move.

'Harrison,' she whispered finally.

'Victoria.' Hammerstone's CIA liaison officer inclined his head politely. Then he looked beyond her to Danny. 'I think I told you once that our boys in Delta speak highly of the British SAS. Looks like they're right. I'm impressed you're still alive.'

'I'm impressed you knew where to find me,' Danny said, his voice cold.

Maddox smiled. 'Chrissakes, Black. We've got the full resources of the NSA behind us. We can find anyone, pretty much. We've been tracking you ever since you dragged one of our agents out of bed in southern Saudi Arabia.' A confused look flickered across his face. 'I gotta say, I was *slightly* surprised you didn't think a guy would be operating a Cessna taxi from the Arabian Peninsular to East Africa without us at least *knowing* about it. Touching phone call to your brother, though. Very touching.'

Danny didn't let any expression show on his face. But he felt nauseous.

'Not that we weren't monitoring him, of course. And naturally we had eyes on your girlfriend. Sharp girl. I think she may have noticed our guy, but no harm done. We've even had surveillance on your poor old dad. Not that he can do much in that wheelchair, but there was always a chance you'd get in touch with him.'

Danny felt the skin tightening around his eyes. He remained quiet.

'Had to pull a few strings to make sure you got through immigration in Germany and Ireland, but it wasn't too onerous,' Maddox said. 'We didn't want you languishing in a Frankfurt jail. Not when there was a chance you had information we needed. Our intelligence networks are good, but there are always a few missing pieces of the jigsaw. Now do us all a favour and put that weapon on the ground, would you?'

Danny kept hold of the snubnose. An exhausted look crossed Maddox's face. He pinched the bridge of his nose. 'Drop the fucking gun, Danny,' he said. 'We've kept you alive this far, but now you've given us everything we need on Mrs Atkinson here, it's really no big deal for me to have one of my guys drop you. I've half a mind to let them do it anyway. If I didn't have a younger brother in the military myself . . .'

A pause. Danny considered his options. It didn't take long. He bent down and put the gun on the ground.

'Kick it away,' Maddox said.

Danny obeyed. The weapon skidded ten metres from his position.

'Attaboy,' said Maddox, as though praising an obedient pet.

'What do you want, Harrison?' Victoria said. She sounded waspish again, but couldn't quite stop her voice from breaking.

'Want?' Maddox replied. 'I want the same thing I've wanted ever since I made contact with yourself and those ridiculous lunatics Piers Chamberlain and Hugo Buckingham.'

'*What?*' Victoria insisted.

'You.'

He took a couple of paces forwards.

'You're in a lot of trouble, Victoria,' he said. 'In the days when you were feeding information to Gengerov, six American undercover operatives lost their lives as a direct result. It's not something we take lightly.'

He stepped two more metres towards them.

'He was blackmailing me,' Victoria whispered, but Maddox merely waved her away with an impatient flick of his hand.

'Contrary to your belief, Victoria, we don't just stick people in Guantanamo – or any of our other facilities – unless we're *very* sure they did what we're accusing them of. That's why *you've* been walking free all these years. Oh, for God's sake Victoria, don't look so shocked. Why else would I muscle my way into your silly little cabal? I just didn't expect to nail you so quickly. We've suspected you for some time now, of course, but we've never had the smoking gun.' He smiled blandly. 'Until now. A full confession, straight from the horse's mouth, pardon the phrase. I'm sure the British would be very pleased to get their hands on you when they learn of your involvement in the bombings, but unfortunately for them, we got to you first.'

'I can explain,' Victoria breathed.

Maddox smiled. 'Really?'

'Everything you heard me say was for *his* benefit.' She looked round at Danny. 'You can't expect me to give the full story to an ordinary soldier. You're cleverer than that.'

Maddox held up one hand. 'Enough, Victoria. I don't want to hear your excuses. You're a traitor to your country. Frankly, I can live with that. But you're also an enemy of the United States. You know what that means.'

Victoria's knees buckled. A sob escaped her throat.

Maddox addressed Danny again. 'You'll need to be on your way, my friend,' he said. 'I doubt this is something you'll want to witness.'

Danny stepped forwards. Slowly. Five seconds later he was standing between Victoria Atkinson and Harrison Maddox.

'You're making a mistake,' he said.

Maddox looked exasperated. 'Say, *what?*'

'She fucked up once, a long time ago. Since then she's been blackmailed, twice – once by Gengerov, once by Abu Ra'id. She's not your enemy. It's more complicated than that. You know it is.'

Maddox's brow furrowed. 'What the hell do you care? She tried to *kill* you.'

'Lots of people have tried to kill me,' Danny said.

'Just get out, Black,' Maddox said. 'I don't want my guys here to have to deal with both of you, but if you give me no option I'll just say the word.'

'No,' Danny said. 'You won't. Because I've got three Regiment mates who know where I am, and if I disappear, they won't let it lie. And trust me, we're persistent.'

Maddox stared at him. He looked momentarily unsure of himself. Then, without a word, he put one hand into his jacket pocket. He pulled out a mobile phone. 'Since you've been staying off the grid, I'm sure you've been too cute to check your messages lately,' he said. He punched a few numbers into the phone, then held up the handset. 'Your journalists aren't the only ones who know how to hack a phone,' he said, as Danny's voice echoed round the hall.

This is Danny. Leave a message.

His personal phone that he hadn't even switched on for days.

Maddox punched in another four-digit code to access Danny's messages.

A beep.

A woman's voice: *Message received today at 12.42 a.m.*

About the time Danny was watching the White Witch stick a knife in her own guts.

It was Kyle's voice. He sounded bad.

It's me. You've got to call.

Another beep.

Message received today at 8.03 a.m.

While Danny was conducting surveillance on the MI5 building.

Fuck's sake, Danny. I'm not pissing around. It's important. Call me.

Beep.

Message received today at 7.55 p.m.

While Danny and his mates were tracking the Hammerstone quartet around London.

They've got her, all right? The fucking Poles have got her. His voice was slurring.

High, or drunk, or both. Bile rose in Danny's throat. *I couldn't do anything about it. It's your fucking fault, you should have helped me out with them in the first place. If I don't get them their fucking money before midnight, they're going to . . .*

Kyle's voice petered out.

Just fucking call me, okay? They're not pissing around. She'll be dead by midnight . . .

Maddox lowered the phone. 'So here's the thing, Danny. Either we can stand here shooting the shit while some greasy Polaks get to work on your girl, or you can get the hell out of here and leave us to do what we're going to do anyway. Choice is yours, but make it quickly.' He ostentatiously checked his watch. 'Half past nine. I'd say time's running out, no?'

Danny turned and looked at Victoria. She'd collapsed for a second time. She clenched her hands in front of her, like she was praying. She uttered a single word: '*Please!*' But Danny didn't know if she was talking to him, or to the Americans.

Suddenly he didn't care.

Kyle's voice echoed in his mind. *The fucking Poles have got her. It's your fucking fault . . .*

'Everything *she* promised you,' Maddox said, pointing at Victoria, '*I* promise you. You know I have the influence. Walk out of here and you walk free. And you never know – your girl might stand a chance.'

Danny gave the trembling Victoria a hard stare. 'You're on your own,' he said.

Then he turned again and headed to the exit. He could sense the tension from the balaclava'd shooters as he approached Harrison Maddox. One of them followed him with his weapon as he walked. He knew that, tightly coiled, they'd fire at the merest sign of a sudden movement. He'd been in their position before, after all, and that's what *he* would have done.

But he stopped a metre from Maddox's position.

'Is Spud alive?' he asked. His voice cracked slightly as he spoke.

Maddox looked him straight in the eye. 'We don't know,' he said. 'He dropped off our radar. And that's the truth.'

Danny nodded. Then he stepped out into the night and pushed the door closed behind him.

In the distance he could hear the noises of London. Buses. Car horns. A passenger aircraft cruising overhead. Danny's hand was just reaching for his phone when he heard a different sound behind him: like a fist being thumped on a heavy door. He knew what it was: two suppressed shots from the MP5s.

The Americans weren't fucking around. The target was down.

Danny felt nothing but an icy coldness. The spook had been one in a long line of people to learn how death stuck to Danny Black. It chilled him to think who might be next.

He strode away from the United Reform church. By the time he hit the pavement he was running, while keying Kyle's number into the phone. He pressed the handset to his ear as he ran. It rang five times. Six. He was already sprinting across Edgware Road when a surly voice answered.

'Yeah?'

'It's me.'

'Jesus.' Kyle had the gall to sound offended.

'Can you call the Poles?'

'Yeah, course.'

'Tell them you've got their money.'

'But I haven't.'

Danny swore as he drew up alongside Ripley's Yamaha. 'Just *tell* them, Kyle. Then call me back on this number and let me know when and where the RV is. Don't let it happen for two hours.'

'What? Why the fuck not?'

Danny started the Yamaha's engine. 'Because that's how long it'll take me to get to Hereford,' he said.

TWENTY-EIGHT

Clara tried to work out how long she'd been in that dark, cold basement. Close to 48 hours, she decided. It was impossible to tell, hunched in the dark, trembling with fear. A minute can seem like an hour. An hour like a day. The Poles hadn't brought her anything to eat or drink and the tape was still stuck round her head and wrists. Her mouth was agonisingly dry, apart from the area around her lips, which were perhaps bleeding, though she couldn't tell for sure.

After three hours of confinement she had kicked on the door, her throat making formless noises as she begged to be let out to use the toilet. But they'd ignored her, and she'd been forced to shuffle awkwardly out of her trousers and urinate in one corner of the room. The liquid had trickled towards the centre, and now the stink of it filled her nose.

Occasionally she heard voices above her. Footsteps. They made a debilitating nausea course through her, which barely eased off when the voices stopped or the footsteps faded away. It was sickening to be here, but the thought of what would happen when they came for her was even worse.

When the door at the top of the stone stairs finally opened, a shard of light blinded her. She screwed her eyes shut, determined not to make any sound that suggested she was scared. After a few seconds she looked again. A figure was walking down the stairs. Heavy footsteps. She sensed that it was the Pole with the fat lips and the pockmarked face. He crossed the cellar floor, stopping when his feet touched the wet patch. He spat something in Polish – it sounded like a curse – then walked faster over to the corner where Clara was cowering. He bent down and pulled her up by her hair. She gasped in pain, then felt herself being swung round and thrown to the wet floor.

A boot, on the side of her face, ground her head into her own filth.

Then he grabbed a clump of her hair again, pulled her to her feet and dragged her up the stairs. He stank of booze and body odour.

She found herself in the dark hallway with the peeling wallpaper. The front door to her right. She could tell through the glass panels that it was dark outside.

She was dragged along the hallway and pushed into another room. Brown paisley carpet, a threadbare three-piece suite. Patches of damp on the wall. The Pole with the black-raven tattoo was sitting in here, his huge bulk almost swallowed up by an even more enormous armchair. To his right was an old-fashioned gas fire, all three segments burning. His knife was extended in his hand, and he was twisting it round and round. Clara felt herself being thrown to the floor just in front of the gas fire. The door closed behind her and the second Pole stood in front of it, an ugly leer on his face.

On the floor by the side of the armchair was a newspaper. Slightly crumpled, open at a double-page spread. Pictures of the London bombings, which Clara had all but forgotten in her current predicament. The tattooed Pole nudged it with his right foot.

'They are good for us, things like that. Keep police busy.' He smirked. 'Not so good for you.'

Clara looked away from the newspaper, sickened.

'Looks like your boyfriend doesn't want to pay us,' the Pole said. 'Shame for us, shame for you.' He held the knife up in front of his eyes and twisted it round again. 'More shame for you, though. We both made same mistake, getting involved with junkie like him.' He grinned. 'But *we* get to have bit of fun with you first.' He looked up at his mate. 'Cheaper than hooker,' he said. 'And no pimp to deal with if we hurt her.'

On her knees, Clara looked up at him. She tried to speak, but again, all that came from her taped-up throat was an incomprehensible grunt.

The Pole leaned forwards and placed the tip of the knife into the flame of the gas fire. He kept it there for 30 seconds. Clara couldn't take her eyes off it. Her body was trembling again, and although part of her didn't want to give these monsters the satisfaction of knowing how much they scared her, she couldn't prevent herself from shaking her head.

She'd half expected the tip of the knife to be glowing when it emerged. It wasn't. The blade was just slightly blackened. But as the Pole moved the knife to within a couple of inches of Clara's face, she could feel the heat emanating from it. She recoiled. The Pole laughed. She caught a whiff of his breath, a warm, fetid stench.

The knife grew closer. Right between her eyes, just an inch from the skin.

He pointed it closer to the left eye. Then to the right. 'Eenie meenie minie mo . . .' The nursery rhyme sounded obscene in his rough Polish accent. 'Catch a hooker by her . . . *eye* . . .'

The knife ended up by the right eye. The Pole grinned again, apparently pleased by his childish ditty.

Then a phone rang.

The ringtone was behind Clara. It belonged to the second Pole. Her tormentor inclined his head, then looked up at his mate and nodded. Clara could sense the guy by the door trying to find the phone in his pocket. The ringtone became a little louder as he pulled it out.

He said something in Polish.

The tattooed guy withdrew and sat back on his armchair. He nodded. His mate answered the phone.

'Yes?'

A pause. Clara could just hear the babble of another voice at the other end.

'He's got money,' said the Pole.

Clara felt like collapsing with relief, but something – pride, maybe – kept her upright. She watched her tormentor as he sat in the armchair, staring with a certain disappointment at the burning tip of his knife.

'He says two hours,' said his mate. In other circumstances they would have been comical, speaking to each other in English.

The Pole shook his head. 'Not here,' he said. 'Where disused railway track crosses river. Up from rowing club. Underneath bridge. And he has ninety minutes, not two hours. If he's late, she goes for swim.'

His mate relayed that. Clara heard Kyle's voice arguing at the other end. 'Yeah, yeah,' the Pole said. 'We bring girl.' More arguing, but the Pole soon cut him off.

There was a moment of silence again.

'So . . .' said the Pole slowly. 'So . . . It looks like your boyfriend gives a shit after all.' He leaned forwards again and cupped Clara's chin in his rough hand. 'But you're too pretty to let go. We still have fun with you, once we have our money. And I don't think world will miss piece of shit junkie like *him*, do you?'

He nodded at his mate. Clara felt her hair being grabbed yet again. She was pulled to her feet, then back along the hallway to the door that led down to the cellar. Thirty seconds later she was entrapped once more, surrounded by darkness and the foul smell of her own waste, half of her wondering if she should try to kill herself now by beating her head against the wall to save her the humiliations to come, half of her defiantly wondering if the journey to meet Kyle might offer her some chance – just some small, impossible chance – of escaping these monsters and getting to safety.

*

The screen of Danny's phone lit up. *11.30*, it said. *Where the old railway crosses the river. Near the rowing club.*

Time check: 22.23hrs. He had less than an hour. He cursed. He wanted to call Kyle, tell the idiot to put back the RV. But that would mean stopping the bike and losing precious seconds. He tried to give it a bit more throttle. But there was no more to give. Ripley had been right. The Yamaha maxed out at just shy of 140 mph. Not that Danny didn't try to push it higher. He crouched down over the handlebars, head low, burning down the outside lane of the M4, half blinded by spray from a motorway still wet from the recent rain. The engine screamed, and Danny's head rang with the Doppler effect of trucks honking at him as he wove dangerously around them. He half expected to see the flashing neon of police lights at any moment, and was grimly prepared to outrace them. But for once, luck was on his side. The motorbike ate up the miles.

He pictured the location of the meet. *Where the old railway crosses the river.* Danny knew it well. The railway was disused and the area round the bridge was ordinarily deserted. Close to midnight, the only other people they were likely to see would be winos staggering down the riverside.

That didn't mean things would be easy.

He had no weapon. And no money, of course, to pay these fuckers off.

Worse still, he had no time.

He crouched lower over the handlebars, and continued to speed along the motorway.

23.20hrs

The Poles had dragged her out of the cellar again. The one with the tattoo had groped her, then pushed her along the dingy hallway to the front door. Now they were bustling her back into the car. The guy with the tattoo sat next to her in the back and pressed her head down into his lap so nobody could see her from outside. She squirmed, but the Pole was too strong for her as he pressed her face down into his stinking crotch. She felt a bulge there, and wanted to retch.

Moments later, they were moving.

To keep her mind off the horror, Clara concentrated on the movement of the car. They stopped three times. She heard the click of the indicators on each occasion. They turned left twice, right once. Then a long stretch of straight-ahead driving, during which time her mind lingered on terrifying thoughts. She couldn't tell how long it was before they started to slow down. Ten minutes? Maybe a bit more? The vehicle bore round to the left, and the terrain underneath them became bumpy. They were heading off-road. That only made Clara's nausea more acute, because off-road most likely meant they'd be isolated. Very far from help.

The vehicle stopped. The Pole in the front got out, then closed the door behind him.

Clara started shaking again. Once more she tried to cry out, but uselessly. After a minute or so she found the strength for another burst of intense struggling. It did no good: the Pole kept her pressed down and she wasn't strong enough to wriggle free.

Clara's passenger door opened. Cold air drifted in. The driver said something in Polish, then grabbed Clara by her collar and yanked her up. The windows were misted up inside the car, so it was only once the Pole with the pockmarked face had dragged her outside that she was able to see where she was.

They had parked up at the edge of an area of wasteland. The rain had started again – heavy, driving rain that soaked her in seconds. The ground was covered in low, ragged scrub, through which the vehicle had left distinct tracks – two ruts, with untouched scrub between them. She could see the lights of Hereford glowing in the distance, but there were no houses or other buildings nearby.

On the other side of the car, perhaps 20 metres away, was the railway line, raised up on a steep bank about five metres high. Clara's eyes followed it along to the right, where a bridge carried the tracks over the river. Clara could just make out its gentle curve. A steep bank led down to the water, and in a matter of seconds she found herself being dragged in that direction through the rain by the tattooed Pole.

It was a futile gesture. She knew that even as she did it. But she had to try *something*. She kicked the Pole hard in the shins as they walked. He barked a curse and momentarily let go of her. Clara grabbed her chance. She turned 90 degrees and ran as fast as she could. Even with her hands taped behind her back, her wet, matted hair straggling in her eyes, and even though she could only breathe through her nose, it might have been enough. But after 20 metres, she stumbled on the uneven ground and fell heavily. Unable to break her fall with her hands, she landed heavily on her right arm. A shock of pain thumped through her. She ignored it and tried to scramble to her feet.

Too late.

A sturdy boot from one of the Poles connected just below her rib cage. Air shot from her lungs and painfully through her nose.

Another kick, straight in the thorax this time. She folded up her body, foetus-like.

'Get up,' said an angry, accented voice. She didn't know which one it was. She shook her head and whimpered. Seconds later she felt hot breath near her ear. 'Do that again, bitch, I cut you, and not just on face.' She felt herself being pulled up once again.

Her eyes were blurry with tears of pain and fear as they dragged her back towards the river, holding her more tightly this time, and treating her more roughly. At the top of the bank, they pushed her down. She slipped and stumbled down the wet, muddy earth, her body landing with a thump on the riverside path. The river was hissing as the rain hit it. It briefly crossed her mind to make another escape attempt, but the two Poles were by her side almost immediately.

Bruised and muddy, she stood up. The bridge was 15 metres away. It was a dark brick arch over this narrow stretch of river. The Poles dragged her towards it. Once they were in its shadow, protected from the rain, one of them dealt her another sharp blow to the stomach. She collapsed again and this time she stayed there, bent double and weeping, wanting to scream but unable to make a sound, and suspecting that if she tried to escape again it would most likely be the last thing she did. She peered beyond the bridge. It was dark and gloomy there, obscured by the night and the rain. She could see nothing. Even if she could escape that way, she'd be running blind.

Thunder ripped through the sky. A flash of lightning. She heard them speaking. Low voices. Polish again. They sounded pissed-off and she realised why: Kyle wasn't here. One of the Poles spat on the ground nearby. Then she felt warm breath again, and realised the tattoed one had bent down to talk to her. 'You better hope your junkie boyfriend turns up,' he shouted over the rain.

She shook her head, wanting to explain once more that Kyle was *not* her boyfriend. The Pole had walked away. They were standing on either side of the bridge, the side from which they'd entered, looking out. Clara did the same, first in one direction, then in another.

And as she looked in the direction from which they'd come, there was another flash of lightning. She blinked.

A figure.

It was standing on the towpath about 20 metres beyond the bridge.

Just standing. And watching.

Danny?

For a moment – just the briefest moment – she felt a twinge of hope. There was something about the figure – the slope of his shoulders, maybe, or the shape of his head? – that made her think it was him.

But that moment of hope soon vanished. The figure moved forwards and she could tell, from the stumbling gait and the way the silhouette held itself, that this wasn't Danny but his brother.

Kyle stopped ten metres from the bridge. She saw that his wet face was still smeared in blood from where the Pole had cut him the night before.

'Where's my money?' shouted the Pole.

Kyle wiped his nose with his sleeve.

'Let her go first,' he called. His voice wavered as he spoke.

The second Pole had joined his mate now. They were standing side by side underneath the bridge, looking towards Kyle as he stood bedraggled in the driving rain. They turned to each other and laughed. A nasty, forced laugh that had little to do with mirth. They conferred briefly in Polish, then the second Pole stepped back to where Clara was crouching. He dragged her over to their original position, then forced her to her knees again. His mate pulled a knife, grabbed her wet hair in one hand and rested the blade against the soft flesh of her jugular.

Clara's breath came in short, sharp gasps. She tried to master it, but couldn't.

'Where's my fucking money?' shouted the Pole.

Kyle didn't move. Even with her head yanked back, Clara could see the uncertainty in his eyes.

He took a step backwards.

'You think we're fucking stupid, junkie?'

Kyle shook his head vigorously, but he also took another step back.

'We should just kill her,' the second Pole said, loud enough for Kyle to hear. 'Kill her and stick her in river. No one will find her for weeks.'

Kyle's knees seemed to buckle. Clara simply couldn't stop herself from whimpering behind the packing tape wrapped round her head.

All feeling seemed to drain from her body as the Pole raised the knife slightly, as though preparing to fillet her neck.

Indescribable horror crossed Kyle's face.

Then, suddenly, behind them, coming from the other side of the bridge, there was a beam of light.

It cast long shadows on the towpath, of the Poles and of Clara, that stretched as far as Kyle. Clara could see the elongated shape of the Pole's arm and hand, and of the knife he was clutching.

A moment of silence, broken by Kyle. 'Y... your money,' he called, stuttering. 'Here's your money.'

The Poles seemed to move very slowly. With care. The tattooed one let go of Clara, who collapsed on to the towpath. She saw her two assailants turn round. And beyond them, on the other side of the bridge, the gloomy side, maybe 25 metres away, she saw a single beam of light, like a headlamp, burning through the rain. It hurt her eyes. Dazzled her.

A figure stepped from behind the bike and into the beam of white light. The light distorted its shape, made it seem somehow ghostly as it stepped forward. Clara blinked as the figure stopped and removed a helmet from his head.

He spoke.

Clara swallowed hard. She recognised the voice, of course. She'd recognise it anywhere.

'I've got your money,' he said.

The Poles looked at each other. 'Put your hands up in the air,' said the tattooed one.

The figure paused. He dropped his helmet. Then, slowly, he raised his hands.

Danny took everything in through a filter of incessant rain.

The two Poles, standing side by side, 15 metres from his position.

Clara on her knees, just a couple of metres behind them, her head bound with tape, her wrists behind her back, soaked. She looked like shit, and it made the anger in Danny's blood burn even hotter.

Ten metres beyond Clara, Kyle, shuffling nervously in the rain from one foot to the other. A bad cut on his face. He looked like he was about to leg it.

'Where is it?' called one of the Poles, stepping forwards slightly. Danny instantly marked him out as the leader of the two.

'In my jacket,' he said.

Silence.

'Come closer,' said the Pole. 'Keep your hands in the air.'

Danny walked towards them. Rain coursed down his face. The gap closed to ten metres.

Five. He was under the bridge.

'Stop,' said the Pole.

Danny stopped.

His hands, still high above his head, were close together.

He saw now that the leader of the two Poles had tattoos on his neck. He also had a blade, which he held low. He looked like he knew how to use it. The second Pole had his arms by his side and was clenching, then releasing, his big hands. But not feeling for a weapon. There were no firearms here, Danny decided. But that didn't mean it wasn't dangerous, especially for Clara. If things went to shit, they'd go for her first.

The Pole looked him up and down, his face wary, yet still strangely arrogant.

'Any bullshit,' he said, 'I cut your fucking throat.'

Danny didn't reply. He just stood there, and waited for the Pole to get closer.

Because before he made his move, he needed less than a metre's distance between them.

Clara was making noises from her throat. He zoned them out. He needed to focus. On the Poles.

And on the violence that was going to happen in just a few seconds.

The tattooed Pole raised his knife.

'I'm going to look,' he said.

Danny nodded.

'Which side of your jacket?'

He looked down to the left.

Then back at the Pole.

Eye to eye.

The Pole took a step forwards through the driving rain. Danny could see his thumb caressing the handle of his knife. Like a pet.

Another step.

He kept his hands still.

The Pole stopped. Distance, two metres.

He looked back over his shoulders to where Kyle was still cravenly shuffling. Then he turned back to Danny. His eyes were sharp.

'Why you bringing money for junkie?' the Pole said.

Danny sniffed. 'He's my brother.'

The Pole grinned. He seemed to relax. If they're brothers, his demeanour seemed to say, they must be equally fucked up.

'Bad luck,' he said.

Danny kept perfectly still. 'You've got to help family,' he said.

The Pole's shoulders relaxed. He clearly felt in complete control of the situation. 'Fucking idiot,' he said. 'You should have come tooled up.' He took another step forwards.

'Maybe I did,' Danny breathed.

Ripley's motorbike security chain was secreted inside the length of Danny's left sleeve. One end was just peeking out of the cuff. At the other end, just above Danny's armpit, was the padlock. With his right hand, he grabbed the end of the chain and pulled. It slid easily from the sleeve. In the same movement, and with all the force he could muster, he swung it round. The heavy metal padlock cracked hard against the side of the Pole's skull. He roared in pain and fell to his knees, his hands clutching his suddenly bleeding head.

Before he hit the ground, Danny was stepping towards the second one. He barely seemed to have registered what had just happened and was staring dumbly at his collapsed mate. The second swing of the chain brought the padlock smashing against his left cheek. There was a sound of breaking bone. Blood sprayed from his lips. He staggered, but didn't fall. Danny swung the chain for a third time, bringing the padlock crashing against the other cheek. The Pole's eyes rolled. He hit the ground.

'*Jesus!*' Kyle's cracked voice sounded distant. And as Danny turned back to the first guy, he was only remotely aware of Clara's wide, horrified eyes, and of the increased, slightly panicked, protests that came from her throat.

The first Pole was dazed, but still conscious and trying to push himself up off the ground. Danny went to work on him with the chain. He whacked the padlock against his face three times in quick succession. It was like bruising a piece of ripe fruit. With each contact, the skin on his face split and started to weep with fresh blood. The final blow hit him in the left eye – a dull, wet slap. The Pole grunted, but not loudly. He was on the verge of unconsciousness now.

Danny turned to the second guy. His eyes were rolling, his limbs twitching. It only took a single crack of the chain to force his body to lie still.

There seemed to be blood everywhere. Streaks on the padlock. Spots on Danny's hand. The beam of the headlamp illuminated the swollen, bloodied faces of the two Poles, but also Clara's horrified eyes. Kyle staggered towards them. His hands were shaking, and he was cursing under his breath: '*Fuck, fuck, fuck . . .*'

'Shut up,' Danny said. He looked down at the two figures lying five metres apart. They weren't dead. Their chests were softly rising and falling.

He looked over at Kyle. 'This is what you wanted, right?' he shouted.

Kyle stared at him. He looked horrified, not just at the violence but at the state his brother was in.

Danny grabbed the second Pole by his ankles and lay him back to back with his mate. He took the bike chain and bound their necks together, before clasping the bloodied padlock through its links to keep it firmly in place. He looked around the towpath. Just a couple of metres away, by the bank, he saw a boulder, a little smaller than a football, but solid and jagged. He picked it up, then brought it over to where the Poles were lying.

'What are you doing?' Kyle said. 'What ... what the *fuck* are you doing?'

Danny gave him a stony look. 'Two drug dealers,' he said. 'Police won't give them a second look if they turn up dead. But only if we make it look like a drug killing.'

Kyle swallowed. Clara made impotent noises behind the tape.

'What did you think it was going to be, Kyle? A few sharp words and rapped knuckles?' He suddenly grabbed his brother by the throat with one hand. 'You want to know what I *do* for a living, Kyle? You want to watch me at work?'

He released Kyle, then put the boulder on the ground just next to the two Poles. He grabbed an arm, laid it out on the boulder, then smashed his foot down on the wrist. There was a splintering, cracking sound as the elbow broke. The Pole's body went into spasm. The eyes opened briefly and a gurgling sound escaped his throat.

'What the fuck ...' Kyle whispered.

'They're going in the river,' Danny said. 'And I don't want them swimming to the surface.'

It took less than a minute to break the remaining three arms. Danny was only vaguely aware of Kyle dry-heaving just behind him, or of Clara's whimpering. When he was done, Danny squeezed the rock into the pocket of one of the Poles. A bit of extra weight to help them down to the bottom of the river. They'd float back up, of course, after a couple of days. But by then, their bodies would be bloated and starting to decompose, and any trace of foreign DNA would be long gone.

The two Poles were a dead weight, but there was no point asking Kyle for help. So it was with difficulty that Danny dragged their chained-together bodies across the muddy towpath towards the water and rolled them into the river.

The water was deep. The bodies sank immediately. A flurry of bubbles confirmed that the Poles were still alive as they sank, but they had no chance of saving themselves. Danny stood quietly at the bank waiting for the bubbles to subside as the rain hammered against his body.

Then he turned.

Kyle was on his knees, ashen-faced. Danny looked down at him.

'Get out of my sight,' he said.

Kyle stood up, then staggered back, slipping in the mud. For the first time ever, he seemed lost for an insult. He wasn't looking at Danny with contempt. He was looking at him with fear.

'Go!' Danny shouted.

Kyle turned, and sprinted down the towpath into the night.

Danny didn't watch him go. All his attention was on Clara.

She was kneeling too, only half protected from the rain by the edge of the bridge. Her eyes were clenched shut and she was shuddering. Danny walked up to her, stopping only to pick up the tattooed Pole's knife that was lying on the towpath. The blade was gritty and splashed with blood. Danny wiped it on his trousers before kneeling down in front of Clara.

He placed one hand gently on her hair. 'I'm sorry,' he breathed. He paused. 'I shouldn't have walked away.'

She opened her eyes. They bore a strange expression. Danny had never seen it before. He couldn't read it.

He examined the tape wrapped round her head. 'I have to cut your hair,' he said.

She didn't respond. Shock, Danny told himself. He took the

knife, and gently sliced at the hair just above the tape. The tape fell loose from the back of her head. Now it was only stuck around her cheeks and lips. It would be very painful to remove.

Danny decided to free her wrists first. He walked behind her and carefully sliced the tape that bound her hands. It was clear that her arms were stiff, because once they were free it took a few seconds for Clara to move them round to her front and bend them at her elbows.

Danny crouched down in front of her again. 'I'm sorry,' he said. 'It's going to hurt.' He raised his hands to start pulling the tape from her mouth.

But suddenly she stood up. She staggered back into the rain. And when Danny stepped towards her, she pushed him away. Her hands felt for the tape. She yanked it away from her mouth, then gasped with the pain of it. She doubled over – involuntarily, it seemed – but then straightened up almost immediately. The area around her mouth, her lips especially, was raw and bleeding, but the rain washed the blood away. When she spoke, her voice was dry, painful. Almost inaudible.

'Don't touch me,' she said.

Danny blinked.

'Don't even come *near* me.'

'Clara, what the hell?'

She was shaking. Pointing at him, threateningly.

'I know you're angry,' Danny said. 'I shouldn't have walked away. I've been regretting it ever . . .

'*What* . . .' – she interrupted him – 'what did you *do* to those men?'

Danny looked towards the river, then back at Clara. 'They would have killed you,' he said.

'But what you *did*,' she whispered. 'How could you *do* that?' She brought one hand to her mouth, then snapped it away when the fingers touched the painfully exposed flesh. She stared at him in undisguised horror. 'What sort of a monster *are* you, Danny?'

'Clara ...' He felt his brow creasing in confusion as he stepped towards her again. 'The bombings,' he heard himself saying. 'I found out who ...'

'*Don't ... come ... near ... me!*' She stumbled backwards. '*Don't ever come near me again!*' Her eyes flickered towards the bridge, towards the beam from the headlamp, then back in the direction Kyle had run.

That was the way she chose.

She didn't run quickly. She wasn't able. She staggered through the rain and the mud. But she didn't look back, as she disappeared along the towpath into the night.

Danny didn't chase her. He barely even moved. His shadow, cast by the light of the motorbike, extended along the towpath, long, thin and stretched. The sound of Clara's footsteps disappeared as he stood there.

He was alone, as he always was. And as always, he was surrounded by darkness and by death.

He heard the words he had whispered to his brother.

You want to know what I do for a living, Kyle? You want to watch me at work?

He stared at the black river. Then he turned, bowed his head, and walked back towards Ripley's motorbike, his eyes blinded by the light.

EPILOGUE

'The mastermind behind the recent bombings in Paddington and Piccadilly has been killed, according to Downing Street. The radical cleric Amar Al-Zain, also known as Abu Ra'id, is thought to have died along with at least 50 other militants when a drone strike "completely destroyed" a terrorist base in northern Yemen. Abu Ra'id's wife, dubbed the White Witch, is thought to have taken her own life on hearing the news.

'In a statement outside Number Ten, the Prime Minister has praised the work of the security services: "Our intelligence professionals have shown, yet again, that there is no hiding place for anyone who threatens our peaceful way of life. Every man, woman and child in the country owes them our thanks."

'Responding to rumours that personnel from 22SAS were in Yemen at the time of the strike, an MoD spokesman said, "We do not comment on the activities of UK special forces."

'While Abu Ra'id's death will be welcomed by the families of the victims of the two bombings, questions are still being asked about his ability to remain in Britain for so . . .'

A knock on the door. Buckingham looked up from his copy of *The Times*.

'Come,' he called.

The door opened. Harrison Maddox stepped inside. He stared at Buckingham for a moment. 'I won't lie, Hugo,' he said. 'You look like shit. What the hell happened to you?'

Buckingham lowered the newspaper on to his desk and touched his bruised face lightly. 'It's nothing,' he said. 'A couple of kids went for my wallet. I saw the little buggers off.'

If Maddox disbelieved him, he didn't let it show on his face.

'You fly this afternoon?' Buckingham was happy to change the subject.

'Out of Heathrow,' Maddox said. 'It'll be good to get back to Langley. Not that this isn't . . .' He vaguely indicated Buckingham's rather small office. 'Of course, it wouldn't surprise me if next time we meet you'll be running the place. Or the one across the river.' And to back up his statement he held up a beige foolscap file. 'Hard copy,' he said. 'Safest way these days. Can't trust those geeks at the NSA and GCHQ.' He laid the file on Buckingham's desk and pushed it lightly towards him.

Buckingham took the file. Only when he had it in his hands did he say, 'You're sure about this?'

Maddox inclined his head. 'All Langley ever wanted to do was get to the truth about her. You should think of that file as your golden ticket, Hugo. It's all there, everything about Victoria's past. Pass it on to whoever you need. Rest assured that nobody will find her body. They'll put it down to suicide. It'll get hushed up, of course – I can't imagine your PM will want it to be known that a member of the security services was involved in all this, but there'll be plenty of slaps on the back for you for bringing it to their attention.' He smiled a broad, sincere smile. 'And when you're the *grand fromage*, Hugo, perhaps you'll be able to do us in Langley a favour some time. That's the way the world works, no?'

Buckingham nodded slowly. 'Of course,' he said. 'Of course.'

Maddox stood up. 'Well, if you'll excuse me, I have a plane to catch.' He stood up and headed towards the door. But before he got there, he stopped and turned. 'You know,' he said. 'Something bugs me.'

'What's that, old sport?'

'Danny Black. He did a good job, all things considered. But he knows the truth about all this. And as you and I understand, we can't entrust something as dangerous as the truth to just anyone.'

'Quite,' Buckingham said.

'I'm just saying, perhaps I made a small error of judgement letting him go.'

'Perhaps.'

There was a moment's silence.

'Where is he now?' Maddox said.

'Last I heard, on a plane to Eritrea.'

'How heartwarming.'

'Quite.'

'Have your people found his friend? Alive? Dead?'

'We don't know yet. But we have it in hand.'

Another silence.

'Danny Black is a situation the agency could take care of, if you understand my meaning,' Maddox said.

Buckingham inhaled slowly. He spun round in his chair and looked through the window, out across London. It looked just as it always had done. Grey, dirty, busy. The river running lazily into the distance. He found himself glancing up towards Marble Arch, then north: the area where Black had pummelled him. Black's eyes had been wild. Out of control. Unhinged. And Buckingham himself felt his temperature rising at the memory.

'Thank you for the offer, old sport,' he said. 'But I can deal with Danny Black.'

He spun his chair round again, and smiled placidly at the American.

Maddox shrugged. 'Well,' he said. 'If you ever change your mind . . .'

He gave Buckingham a meaningful smile. Then he left.